THE APPROACH

To G. Griffin Vine &
Spirits,
Enjoy the journey,
et buvez chaque jour!

A MARCUS HUGO ADVENTURE

THE
APPROACH

PARKER
LEE

Line editing, book design provided by
Indigo: Editing, Design, and More:

Line editor: Cooper Lee Bombardier

Cover design and interior layout:
Olivia M. Hammerman

For Katie, Henry, Hector, and Enzo.

"The only way to do it is to do it."
—Anonymous source

"Buvez chaque jour, vous ne mourrez jamais!"
—François Rabelais

"That is excellently observed....
But let us dig in our garden."
—Voltaire, *Candide*

FOREWORD

The Approach is a work of fiction. Any and all resemblances to real things, places, or people are purely coincidental. Of particular importance to note is that no client confidences have been betrayed in the writing of this book. Practicing lawyers are bound by an ethical duty to serve their clients' best interests, including maintaining the attorney-client privilege and confidentiality. It is this ethical duty that makes the practice of law a profession and not just a job. One of the great points of pride I've discovered in practicing law is how universally sacred this duty is amongst my fellow practitioners. Regardless of practice area or firm size, just about every lawyer I've come across believes in our ethical duties to represent our clients, just as knights, the historical forebearers of today's lawyers, believed that they were duty bound to their lords. While the companies and transactions described in *The Approach* may resemble real-world deals, they are completely made up, and no confidential client information was used in crafting them.

—Parker Lee

PREFACE

Paris, France.
August 2005.

THIS WAS THE PART OF THE TOUR THAT EVERYBODY loved: the nighttime ride across the Pont des Arts, dodging the picnicking, wine-drinking, and music-playing groups of people making the most of the surprisingly late Paris dusk, then through the east entrance of the Louvre into the illuminated Cour Carrée for a few laps around the beautiful circular fountain adorning the center of the square, underneath the three arched, open corridors and out into the wide-open west-facing façade and courtyard that housed the infamous, striking glass pyramid. Elation and wonder still coursed through Marcus's veins every time he made this ride, as the freeing sensation of riding a bicycle uninhibited through one of Western Europe's cultural treasures blended with the grandeur, beauty, and historical significance of the backdrop of the Louvre. This sensation was amplified exponentially as he realized the faces of nearly every single person participating in his tour showed that they were experiencing the exact same feeling. Paris truly had a magic to it that words alone could not aptly describe.

As he gathered his group together near the iconic glass pyramid and finished briefing them on the history of the Louvre, the highlights of the current art exhibit, and some helpful tips about when and how to visit the museum, Marcus couldn't help but think about what lay before him the next morning. He was scheduled to fly back to Texas to spend two days packing up his belongings, then jump in his beat-up, forest-green Chevy Blazer and make the long trek up to Charlottesville, Virginia, where he was due for first-year law student orientation in less than a week.

Marcus Hugo, the twenty-three-year-old young man leading his final tour on this cool Paris evening, had spent the past year working as a tour guide at Big Tire Bike Tours. The job had pretty much fallen into his lap. The founder of the company was a native Texan who, about five years ago, had started recruiting part-time employees from the University of Texas, from where Marcus had graduated the previous May. Two of Marcus's fraternity brothers had taken the job three years ago, and they had suggested that Marcus do the same. He had agreed, and before he knew it, he was living in a tiny, one-bedroom/one-bathroom apartment with five other tour guides in the lively 6th arrondissement bordering Paris's Latin Quarter.

Working on his feet leading two to three tours each day, he made just enough money to pay rent, sneak out to a café or pub every once in a while, and even book a few cheap flights to some neighboring European cities to explore more of the continent. The flight over from Texas to France the previous August was the first time he had even been to Europe, and now this place felt more like home than where he had spent his first twenty-two years. He had completely imbibed Paris; its history, its architecture, its pace of life, its cuisine, its personality. *Free* and *inspired* were the two words that most appropriately captured how Marcus felt. There were fleeting moments of empowered thinking where he planned to embrace spontaneity and throw his plans of going to law school and pursuing a career as a corporate lawyer out the window, to simply stay on as a tour guide for one more year and see where the Gaulish wind might blow him. But inevitably, his practical thinking always won out over those heartfelt illusions, and tomorrow morning's flight would be the physical embodiment of those triumphs.

He led the tour out of the Louvre and continued west in the bike lane on the right side of the road underneath the beautiful pillars and corridors of the Rue de Rivoli, past the in-bloom Jardin des Tuileries, through the maze of cars circling the Place de la Concorde and then over the Seine via the majestically adorned Pont Alexandre III. From there they raced along the Avenue du Maréchal Gallieni toward Les Invalides, its evening lights transforming the church and old hospital into a palatial landmark, and then deeper into the 7th arrondissement to Big Tire's office on the ground floor of a Haussmannian apartment building bordering the Champ de Mars. As was his custom, Marcus perfectly timed their arrival with the hourly twinkling of the evening lights on the Eiffel Tower to display one last serving of Parisian charm under his watch as their guide.

After thanking the group for taking the tour and making one final promotional pitch for the other tours that his company offered—day tours to Versailles, Claude Monet's private gardens in Giverny, and the chateaux and wineries of the Loire Valley—Marcus exited the stage and let his coworkers in the office handle the logistical pieces of wrapping up. Much to his chagrin, Marcus's career as a tour guide had officially ended.

IN KEEPING WITH company tradition, the staff had organized an evening gathering at the Highlander, a jolly ex-pat Scottish bar just on the left bank side of the Pont Neuf, as a send-off for Marcus and his fellow tour guide Graham Curry. Graham was also calling the tour guide life quits, but for him it was to pursue a career as a petroleum engineer. Graham had managed to convince his future employer, a large, global, integrated oil and gas company, to let him have a year off after college before joining the ranks of the energy industry behemoth. The fact that Graham had graduated as valedictorian of the petroleum engineering school at the University of Texas, had managed to squeeze in a minor in Arabic, and had job offers from every other major global energy company explained why he was able to exert such leverage.

GRAHAM WAS CLEAN-CUT, with short brown hair and a round, unassuming face that contained no truly notable features. He was neat in his appearance, stood just a bit under six feet and was a svelte one hundred and seventy pounds. While he was certainly a nice-looking young man and was amiable enough when engaged in a one-on-one conversation, Graham just kind of blended into the background, and Marcus got the sense that this was by design.

In stark contrast, Marcus, standing at six feet, three inches tall with shaggy blond hair, was conspicuous in almost any scenario. This was exacerbated here in Paris, where his light complexion and Anglo-Saxon facial structure, combined with his height, made it quite clear that he was not a native Frenchman. But the two made for a good pair and had become close friends while working and traveling together over the past year.

They had been good additions to Big Tire too. Graham technically had been a master tour guide: he had memorized every bit of history he could get his hands on for every single monument, or bridge, or museum, or church. He had test-ridden the different routes of the tours over and over again, at both day and night, to further familiarize himself with the traffic patterns and the views from a bike at different times of day. Marcus played up the entertainer and host aspects of being a tour guide. He inserted jokes, historical vignettes, and interesting bloopers and tales from previous tours. Without fail, he would memorize the names of every person on his tour and make it a point to have at least one conversation with each of them. Customers appreciated both approaches, and they let the Big Tire owners know it every time they returned from a Graham- or Marcus-led tour.

The turnout for the leaving drinks was good, and the vibe at the bar was enhanced that evening by a jovial group of Australian university students who chose the Highlander as their evening destination of choice for their one night in Paris. The night was filled with merriment, funny stories from the past year, and half-hearted descriptions of what was to come next. One by one, the rest of Graham and Marcus's coworkers stopped by to wish the two departing tour guides well before calling it an evening and turning in for the night. As the bartender announced last call, Marcus and Graham bellied up to the bar for one last ice-cold Kronenbourg 1664, the Alsatian beer that they had become accustomed to drinking.

Graham and Marcus clinked glasses. "*Santé*," they uttered to each other before taking a sip.

Graham put his cold glass down on the wooden bar, exhaled thoughtfully, then looked directly at Marcus. "You're really going to leave all this and trade it in for the next three years in the library as a law student?"

Marcus chuckled a bit and, imitating Graham's theatrical tone, retorted: "*You're* really going to leave all this and trade it in for a lifetime of doing whatever you petroleum engineers do at some office building in Houston?"

Graham gave Marcus a sarcastic look and then responded, "Come on, man, you damn well know that you love this place more than I do. Hell, you love it more than any other tour guide or any person I've met while we've been here. It's like this place has almost become a part of you. I just can't imagine you ever being as happy as you seem to have been over the past few months. I really don't think you should leave, dude."

Marcus took a long sip of the cold, pale lager. He stared blankly at the taps of beer in front of him, seemingly deep in thought as to whether he should or should not say something. Then, almost as if bolstered by some realization, he looked at Graham and proclaimed, "This isn't the end for me; you know that, right? I'm not done exploring and going on adventures, learning languages, and experiencing new cultures. That's what I'm going to do, just as an international corporate lawyer."

Shrugging off the respondent look of skepticism from Graham, Marcus continued, "Look, there are a lot worse things than three years in Charlottesville, all right? Then, as long as I work hard and do well in law school, I can get a job at one of these big international law firms in New York or maybe even London. Put my time in for a couple years there, maybe transfer to one of their foreign offices, like here in Paris, or in Milan or São Paolo, or maybe even in Singapore or Hong Kong. Then get on board with some client that does some cool international business, then I'm set!"

Marcus continued, almost as if to convince himself instead of his companion, "I'll be traveling all over the world, meeting all types of interesting, influential people, and getting paid a boatload of cash to do it all. That doesn't sound too bad, does it? No, tomorrow is not the end for me…"

Graham, no longer able to control his laughter, interrupted his interlocutor's diatribe.

"Marcus, you are delusional, my friend. You may land a job at one of those big New York firms, but they're going to lock you up in your office for the next ten years before you see the light of day. My dad's a lawyer and he's always told me to stay as far away from the world of law as possible."

Seeing the impassioned look of confidence fade from Marcus's face, replaced by one of shock and disappointment, offense almost, Graham raised his hands as if to admit he had gone too far with his last comment, then continued, "But hey, man, you already know all that. I'm sorry, I should be more supportive. You've got big dreams, and who am I to say you won't make 'em happen?"

Then, in an effort to both add support to the previous statement and signal that it was time to call it a night, Graham lightly pounded his fist on the wooden bar and proclaimed, "Cheers, brother, to both of us, to the next chapter and to fulfilling our dreams!"

While still taken aback by Graham's initial retort, Marcus thought better than to make an issue of it and just grinned and nodded and focused on the end of what his friend had said. He *did* have big dreams, and now that he finally knew what he wanted, there was nothing and no one that was going to stop him. And that was worth drinking to.

"Amen to that, and best of luck to you, too, man!"

And with that, the two young ex-tour guides emptied their glasses, warmly embraced their bartender, tossed a few two-Euro coins into the tip jar, and disappeared into the Paris night, both US bound the next morning.

PART I

The Grind

CHAPTER 1

Houston, Texas.
Fall 2013.

H E HAD ALWAYS LIKED THE VIEW FROM THIS office, and it felt good to be experiencing it again. Looking out, he could see the newly renovated Buffalo Bayou Park and further beyond toward the energy corridor, right down into the futuristic circular walkway over the busy downtown artery, which was at a near standstill with a horde of SUVs and pickup trucks headed home after another day of their drivers punching the clock. This building represented all that modern Houston stood for: first, it had been the cap-stone headquarters specifically built for Enron during the peak of its rise to domination of the US energy economy, and now it was the headquarters for one of the world's oil and gas supermajors. The circular walkway below seemingly proclaimed, "That's right, Houston; you all must drive underneath me."

It was surprising that they had let him keep this office during this current posting abroad. He had been living in Port Moresby, the capital of Papua New Guinea, for a year now, and he would be there again for at least another year once he returned after his mandatory four months back at headquarters. Not that Graham Curry was complaining; Houston was home, and it felt good to be back. Life in Port Moresby was slow, dull, and repetitive, but quite productive...for both assignments he was handling. He peeked down at the clock in the bottom right-hand corner of the computer screen and confirmed it was time to head over to the stadium. He closed out all of his open computer programs, locked his computer with both his fingerprint scan and his voice confirmation, placed his ergonomically friendly purple balance ball in the same seemingly random spot behind his office chair with the manufacturer's label pointed in the same direction as always, grabbed his blazer off the hanger behind his office door, and headed to the elevator bank.

The Toyota Center was about eight long blocks from his office. The oppressive Houston heat had finally abated so the evening was just warm, not hot and humid enough that he would sweat through his plain white oxford dress shirt before he arrived, so he decided to walk. Downtown Houston was certainly revitalizing, but this part of town was still uncomfortable at night, at least for most people. Graham had seen and been through much worse, and so was able to enjoy the stroll over. It allowed him to think back on the numerous interactions he and his contact had had over the years. Graham was looking forward to this meet, as he had grown to like this man and the work he was doing for him.

The first quarter was already halfway through when Graham got to his seat. This was only the second game of the year, and there was a lot of enthusiasm behind the Rockets for this season. They had acquired one of the NBA's premier centers to go along with their star shooting guard and the expectations were high. This was a Friday night game on national television against the hated in-state rival, the Dallas Mavericks, so the house was packed and there was already a high level of energy in the building. The seats he had been treated to were just a few rows off the floor and it made for great entertainment. Graham enjoyed the rest of the first quarter and most of the second before heading up to the bar in the club level at the agreed-upon time.

Graham didn't see his contact him when he arrived at the bar, so he went ahead and ordered a beer. After receiving his beer and closing his tab, Graham turned to go find a high-top table to wait and found himself face-to-face with his expected host. Slightly taken aback, but not rattled, Graham coolly switched his beer to his left hand, grabbed the memory stick out of his pants pocket, and deftly passed it over to the man in conjunction with their handshake greeting. Graham's host, already with his own beer in hand, responded with a steady and strong handshake, accompanied by the slightest glimmer of appreciation in his eyes.

"Welcome back. Feel good to be stateside?" the man asked, as he contemporaneously made the transmitted memory stick vanish into some unknown pocket of his one of his articles of clothing.

"Thank you," Graham responded. "It does, actually. I should ask you the same. Just in town for our meeting or something else?" They drifted over to a high-top table after the man had indicated as much with a tilting of his head.

"I would have come just for our meeting, but this time I have a legitimate business reason to be here— two, in fact. We are starting the process of opening an office here, so I was looking at office space. And then I was meeting with one of your competitors about doing a joint venture with them for a pipeline project." The man took a sip of his beer and scanned the bar with his eyes. There were few patrons; most people were engrossed in the final minutes of the first half.

"Interesting...domestic or international?" Graham ventured to ask.

The man chuckled and raised his eyebrows. "Confidential, sorry."

Graham laughed and shook his head. "That's quite ironic coming from you."

"Indeed," the man replied, then, shifting to business, continued, "So how is it over there?"

Anticipating this question, and sensing that their time was running short, Graham responded directly. "They're everywhere. Already fully invested. Telecom, mining, naval activity, and of course, oil and gas."

"Not surprising. We already got some of that from the State Department," the man replied, then quickly asked, "How are they doing telecom, and to what end?"

"Huawei contracts. Huawei has a big store in the mall in Port Moresby and they're signing up deals left and right. Our facilities are all signed up with Huawei, so they're crawling all over our project's information. They're laying the groundwork to be the preferred party for the undersea cable and internet infrastructure system they know is coming." Graham tried to summarize all he had seen in Papua New Guinea over the last twelve months in as useful a way as he could, but he knew his synopsis was vastly insufficient, so he added, "It's all in there. As detailed as I could get, with as much hard data as possible."

The man nodded lightly, then flashed a quick smile and asked, "How'd you get it out?"

Graham made a show of grimacing. "The method you recommended."

"It hurt?"

"Some, a bit of bleeding."

"And your project?" the man asked.

"Everywhere, knee-deep. They've got people all over Kumul, Papua New Guinea's national oil company. Our concession and development agreement required us to allow secondees, engineers, accountants, business development people, even welders, from Kumul so they could learn about oil and gas extraction and LNG development and 'participate in the industry growth,'" Graham added his own air quotes. "Those Kumul secondees just happen to be cultural Chinese that live in PNG, or so they claim. I can't decide if the audacity is insulting, laughable, or ingenious."

"All three," the man rapidly responded. "Good. Well, not *good*, but you know what I mean."

Graham shook his head knowingly and also realized that their conversation was ending. Before heading back to his seat, he added, "Good to see you, and thanks for the tickets. Good game. Safe travels."

The man quietly shook Graham's hand, then suddenly said, "Hey, we've recently lost someone in my division of our firm. Trying to find someone to replace them. Private equity, banker or lawyer type. Needs to be a good fit, someone who can operate internationally but seems normal. Not the typical recruit that the Shareholder usually employs. You know anyone?"

Graham was taken off guard by the question but quickly focused on scanning his brain for someone who might meet the description.

"You know," Graham responded, "I think I just might…"

CHAPTER 2

New York, New York. Thursday, June 26, 2014.

T HE CORNER OF MANHATTAN'S TWENTY-FOURTH
Street and Sixth Avenue never ceased to amaze
Marcus; even at 6:30 a.m. it was busy, loud, and fraught
with honking horns. Some adjacent construction site,
replete with a jackhammer, was busy at work, and it
was a jolting contrast to the dark, peaceful environment of his apartment a mere twenty-six floors above,
from where he had just emerged. This area of the city,
now often referred to as Flatiron/Chelsea had become
a magnet for development. What was once called the
Flower District, full of low-rise, dark brick buildings,
had been transformed into a corridor of luxury high-
rise apartment complexes that allowed for residents to
enjoy views of the Hudson River to the west, Madison
Square Park to the east, and the downtown Financial
District looking south. Marcus had picked this area
because of the combination of being close to Midtown,
where he worked, and proximity to the West Side

Highway and Lower Manhattan, where he liked to spend what little time he had when he wasn't working.

Today was a big day for Marcus, and he wanted to get it started off productively by going for a morning run before heading into his office. After becoming aware of the irregular hours and unpredictable schedule that comprised life as an associate at a big corporate law firm, Marcus had reached an agreement with himself that any weekday evening that he was out of the office before 9:00 p.m. meant that he had to get up early and work out the next morning before reporting back for duty. He'd made this deal with himself after so many of his evening departure times and early morning workout plans were railroaded by late nights at the office, early morning conference calls, and all sorts of other workflow unpredictability, all of which had helped Marcus to truly understand the professional service industry. So when the opportunity presented itself for an unmolested hour or two of exercise, Marcus had learned to take advantage.

He crossed over to the west side of Sixth Avenue, and then headed one block south to the wider, more exposed Twenty-Third Street. At this hour of the morning, Twenty-Third was not yet packed with masses of people making their coffee runs, stopping for a to-go lunch or sneaking out to run an errand. As he headed west, the sun, peeking up above the Flatiron Building and the perimeter offices of Madison

Square Park behind him, illuminated the way ahead and brought the gleam of the Hudson River and the wooded banks of New Jersey into view in front of him. The morning was warm. He enjoyed the mornings during this time of year in New York: June and early July presented the possibility of some early sunshine and warmth as he jogged along the West Side Highway, but without the heat and humidity that would follow over the back half of the summer. He would often divert his route to include running to the end and back of the three piers abutting the jogging trail between the start of the esplanade at about Fourteenth Street and the beginning of Battery Park City just so he could get out of the shadows of the morning and get a little extra sunshine before submitting to the will of the workday and a profession conducted indoors.

After completing the necessary five-block trek through the dense urban heart of Chelsea, Marcus's mind and body relaxed as he smelled the first hint of salt water and breathed in the fresh air coming off the Hudson. The open space and unobstructed view from this part of the West Side Highway was both therapeutic and energizing, and it allowed him to begin the real running portion of the morning's workout and to turn his thoughts on what lay ahead. As he picked up his pace and felt his leg muscles come to life, he thought to himself: *Yes, there are conference calls to direct, draft agreements to review and revise, and new Delaware case law to research and try to understand, but today there's going to be something else as well—today I find out if I'm going be spending the next three years in my favorite city in the world: Paris.*

As he came upon the first pier, he pivoted right and headed out toward the open water. He felt the sun warm his back and remembered the conversation he had six months ago, on a crisp, cold January day, when he last discussed the possibility of working in the Paris office. It felt like another lifetime, like an eternity had passed since then. John Dillard, colloquially referred to as just *Dillard* by his team of associates, was a very difficult man to get a hold of. He was the head of the law firm's energy and infrastructure industry group, or EIG. Marcus had come by Dillard's office three times already that day to no avail: once he was not in, once his door was closed and his secretary said he was in a meeting, and the third time Marcus had knocked on his open door to find him on the phone. Marcus took a step into the open office and knocked again, politely announcing his presence. Dillard, whose desk faced the open door, was holding the receiver of the phone up by his ear with his left hand and was tracing a sentence line by line on his computer screen with his right index finger. He didn't even lift his gaze from his computer screen to acknowledge Marcus's presence as he uttered, "Right...right...keep reading...provided, comma, however, notwithstanding anything to the foregoing…"

After thirty seconds of being completely ignored, Marcus returned to his desk and began plotting a fourth visit. Fortunately, Marcus was issued a deadline for that afternoon to turn a draft of a legal opinion for a private bond offering that required Dillard's signature. The executed opinion letter had to be emailed to opposing counsel that evening, so Dillard had to sign, on behalf of the law firm, that afternoon before heading home. Marcus stopped by Dillard's office at 4:45 p.m. He knocked on the open door once again.

Dillard leaned back in his chair, lifted his eyes above the top ledge of his computer screen and peered at Marcus through his circular, rimless glasses.

"Yes?" he barked, seeming to attach a two-second time limit for a response.

"This is the opinion letter for Phaethon, on Project Elixir. I've incorporated your changes and have the execution version ready for you to sign." Marcus quickly extended the execution copy of the response letter, opened to the signature page with a small yellow *sign here* tab next to the law firm's signature block.

"Do you have a redline showing my changes?" Dillard responded, refusing to extend his hand to accept the execution version.

"I do, sir. Here it is." Marcus reached into the middle of his stack of binder-clipped papers and found the redline, a comparison document that showed the changes between one draft to the next by marking deletions in red text and additions in blue text. He handed it to Dillard.

Dillard flipped quickly through the redline document, pausing periodically to read a sentence or two. Near the end of his review, he began shaking his head.

"I can't sign this! We can't give this opinion. I asked you to carve out the opinion about their foreign subsidiaries—that's not what this says."

Marcus was prepared for this objection.

"Yes sir, you did, he responded, "but I took another look at how the secretary's certificate for Phaethon is drafted, and because of the wording of that document, and the exceptions that we've built into this opinion, we can include the subsidiaries, and it effectively makes no difference in our liability. We didn't have that disclaimer in the previous deals, and I was able to get that into the secretary's certificate this time around with minimal fuss from the client. If we try to carve that out now, I'm afraid the client will be upset with us for trying to make that change this late in the process, and perhaps more importantly, they may give a more thorough review of their secretary's certificate and then try and revise the whole wording of the construct we inserted in the initial draft."

Dillard looked at Marcus quizzically, then flipped to another page of the opinion letter and read quickly.

"Hmm," he snorted. "And the secretary's certificate?"

Marcus reached back into his stack of papers and retrieved two documents. As he handed them to Dillard he added, "Here it is, along with a redline to the March 2013 secretary's certificate. The changed language is in 3A."

Dillard held the redline of the secretary's certificate in his left hand, and the opinion letter opened to the middle of the document in his right hand. He shifted his head back and forth, reading each page a number of times quickly. Then, after narrowing his eyes and rotating left and right slowly one final time, he handed the secretary's certificate back to Marcus, flipped the opinion letter to the signature page, removed the *sign here* tab, and put pen to paper, executing the signature of the law firm's full name: Macon, Smith, Franklin & Boyd LLP. He closed the letter and handed it back to Marcus without a word, then refocused on his computer screen.

Placing that memory on hold and returning his thoughts to the run, Marcus lifted his eyes toward the bay as he reached the Battery Park City esplanade. He continued along the railing, heading directly towards New Jersey, and breathed in the fresh, slightly salty air coming off the open water. As he reached the westernmost point, his gaze rotated south, succumbing to the gravitational pull of the Statue of Liberty. Pausing briefly to catch a few breaths, he lifted his right hand

and gave a stiff salute in Lady Liberty's direction, then executed an about face and began retracing his path back toward his apartment. His mind pressed play on the memory he had paused.

"Thank you, sir." Marcus uttered quietly, then cleared his throat and continued, "Sir, there was one more thing I wanted to ask you about."

Dillard continued reading something on his computer screen, then looked up.

"Yes, Martin, what is it?"

"It's Marcus, sir, not Martin."

"Ah yes, sorry. Of course. What is it, Marcus?"

"I submitted my paperwork for the foreign associate program in the Paris office six months ago. I spoke with Cecilia, the head of HR, and she said the paperwork looked good and that the only thing left was for the EIG partners to approve it. I've spoken with both Phyllis and Jason, and they thought it was a great idea and were excited for us to have someone in Paris to help build the links between the offices."

The foreign associate program was something that Macon Smith, as the law firm was popularly known, instituted roughly ten years ago where some mid-level associates, usually somewhere between their fourth and eighth years at the firm, would relocate to another of the firm's offices in a foreign country for a few years. The idea was to provide the associate a chance to develop their practice in another country, to build their networks within the firm and with clients abroad, and to make the firm a more cohesive unit as a whole. Law school students and experienced associates considering joining Macon Smith often asked about the program and noted it was one of the things that had attracted them to the firm. Indeed, it was one of the most important characteristics that had attracted Marcus to Macon Smith.

Marcus was a sixth-year associate now, at the prime experience level for the foreign associate program. He spoke French fluently, had familiarity with Paris from his days as a bike tour guide there, and had a very good record within the firm. He had built good relations with many clients active in the international arena, had spent six months on a client secondment that no one else was willing to take, and he felt that this was his chance to finally embark on the type of career he had been dreaming about.

"Yes…yes, Marcus. About that, umm…glad you mentioned that." Dillard entered a few words on his keyboard and watched his email inbox run a search function. He double-clicked his mouse, said to himself, "No, not that!" and then double-clicked again. "Yes, here it is."

Dillard narrowed his eyes again, read a few lines on the screen, and nodded his head a few times. Then he lifted his head, made brief eye contact with Marcus, leaned back in his chair, and lifted his gaze to the ceiling as he spoke.

"We've reviewed your application, and we think it is a very promising situation. But, given your experience level and the amount of work we anticipate over the first half of this year, we've decided to put the decision on hold for six months because EIG only has a few other associates at your level, and we'll need all of you fully dialed in. We feel like the Europe thing can wait for six months. I'm sure you'll agree."

Dillard stared at Marcus intently for a few seconds and glanced down at the automated clock on his telephone.

"Listen, I've got to run out to catch the 5:20 p.m. train to New Canaan. Make sure that Elixir matter is handled appropriately."

The jog back east along Twenty-Third Street required Marcus to dodge pedestrians and pop out into the road frequently. This part of the city was alive now and sidewalk space, even on a wide street like Twenty-Third, was at a premium. He nodded to Tony, the weekday morning doorman, as he hopped out of the revolving door into the lobby of his building. Marcus and Tony had a good rapport; Tony looked up at Marcus, and, seeing him in his running gear, held up four fingers on his right hand and raised his eyebrows and shrugged his shoulders. Marcus smiled, shook his head quickly, and held up all five fingers of his right hand and one finger on his left head. Tony pursed his lips and nodded slightly. "Not bad, Mr. Hugo, not bad."

Opening the door to his apartment, Marcus flipped on the light and shot a glance at his cell phone, which now doubled as his work email device, too, since the Blackberry had gone by the wayside. As usual, a small letter looking icon appeared at the top, indicating his email inbox had refilled during the hour he was gone. He keyed in his password, reviewed the emails, responded very quickly to one of them with a simple *Yes, will do*, placed the device back on the kitchen counter, and hurried over to the shower.

He showered, shaved, dressed, packed his bag for the day, and made his way for the door. As he did so, he cast a glance at the French grammar workbook sitting forlornly on the far end of the little dinner table that doubled as his desk. He felt a certain kinship with that book, the one Berlitz in Paris had given him when he took lessons there nearly a decade ago. It was a good resource and coupled with the French conversation sessions with the Berlitz teachers, had given him the base and practice he needed to develop his ability to speak French. At the start of the year, he had penned out a goal of reworking the exercises and reading passages during the first half of the year so that when this day came, the day he would finally get the approval to relocate to Paris, he would be on top of his game. That had not happened. The first half of the year had been extremely busy, and the late nights and long weekends at the office had been numerous.

"Damn," Marcus said to himself quietly. His phone buzzed in his hand as he shoved himself out the front door.

CHAPTER 3

Chelsea, New York City. Thursday, June 26, 2014.

"**D**IS TONY." THE DOORMAN HAD STEPPED INTO the back room where they stored the residents' packages to take this call.

"He out there this morning?"

The voice on the phone had become familiar to Tony by this point. It was strong, direct, confident, but still a bit sensual. It was obvious that she was very organized and professional, and he imagined she was attractive too.

"He was, apparently banged out six miles this morning. He just left the building about fifteen minutes ago. Looked sharp. Must have a big meeting or something." *It was true*, Tony thought to himself. *Mr. Hugo always looked sharp, but he had looked sharper this morning, a little zip in his step and some extra positive energy. Was wearing one of his nicer ties too.*

"Good," she said, "Any visitors lately?"

He knew what she was asking, and he realized that this entire conversation was a complete violation of

Mr. Hugo's privacy. Tony really liked Mr. Hugo, so he felt a little bit bad about it. But he didn't get the sense that this woman was trying to inflict any damage onto Mr. Hugo, and the thousand dollars in cash per conversation she was paying was not something he could turn down.

"No actually, none that I've seen. He had a buddy stay with him over the weekend a month or so back, but no one like you are thinking of lately. It seems like the guy has been working his ass off. Coming in late at night still in his suit, carrying a bunch of files with him a lot of the time." *Also true.* Tony had not seen Mr. Hugo with any girls recently and frankly, it didn't seem like the guy had the time for a social life given how much it seemed like he was working.

"Got it. Thanks Tony. Bike messenger should be arriving within the hour with your package. And, Tony?" the woman added before hanging up.

"Hmm?" *What was this going to be?* Tony thought to himself, then waited.

"This will be it," she said curtly, then added, "Thank you. You like him, don't you?"

The finality of this odd arrangement caught him off guard, but the follow-up question even more so. *But what the hell? Why not be honest with her?*

"He's a good guy, Mr. Hugo. Not just some prick in a suit. Treats us like people, not hired help. Works hard too. I respect that." Tony made himself stop. No reason to say anything else. Just get paid and be done with this whole thing.

Tony could almost hear the lady nodding her head at the other end of the phone line. "Take care Tony." She said, then the line went dead.

CHAPTER 4

Midtown Manhattan.
Thursday, June 26, 2014.

T HE BANK OF AMERICA TOWER SITS ON THE northwest corner of Forty-Second Street and Sixth Avenue in the lower portion of Midtown Manhattan at the address of One Bryant Park. The tower is an impressive, modern structure that sticks out amongst the hoard of brick and metal buildings due to its unique glass exterior and smooth, angular shape. Adjacent to Bryant Park and the New York Public Library, and one block east of Times Square, it is an iconic location that leaves no doubt in the mind of anyone entering the tower that they are smack dab in the middle of one of the world's financial capitals and busiest cities.

In addition to being iconic, the location was also rather convenient for Marcus. Each weekday morning, he spent approximately seven minutes on the B/D/F/M train, boarding outside of his apartment at the Twenty-Third and Sixth stop, and getting off two stops later at the Forty-Second/Bryant Park stop. This usually allowed him to read about three to four pages of whatever novel or non-fiction book he was reading, and to also take in the incredible cross-section of people that rode the subway each morning. Sure, there were plenty of other suit and tie-wearing lawyers, bankers, consultants, and accountants, but there were also day laborers and construction workers, wearing their distinctive outfits that were usually completed by a hard hat and a reflective vest. There were schoolteachers and professors making the trek to Midtown West, the Upper West Side, Harlem, and the Bronx. There were baristas in black skinny jeans wearing headphones to block out the world before having to caffeinate it. There were Brooklynites and Staten Islanders, ready to put an end to their long commute that involved a train change, a ferry ride, or a short bus trek. There were Chinese and Koreans reading newspapers in their native languages, and there were Dominicans and Puerto Ricans speaking an accented Spanish that was native only to the northern part of Manhattan Island. In short, there was everybody, and Marcus made it a point not to miss any of them.

On this particular morning, after amusedly taking in a few pages of detective Philip Marlowe's exploits in *The Big Sleep*, Marcus surfaced at the Bryant Park stop and refocused his mind on the business of the day. A creature of habit, he stood in line for five minutes in the ground floor level coffee shop to obtain his small cup of black coffee, then presented his ID badge to the computerized scanning device, passed through the hip-level, two-sided glass gate doors as they retreated away from one another with a beep, and keyed in the number forty-five on the elevator console. After thinking for a millisecond, the console displayed the letter *B*, and instantaneously the thin white light above the elevator marked *B* was illuminated, the door opened, and Marcus and two other young professionals stepped in.

Marcus's office was actually on the forty-seventh floor, but he made it a habit to always get off on forty-five, where the firm's reception area was. He liked walking into the office each morning and seeing it as a first-time visitor would. It helped him to remember how much of an accomplishment it truly was to be working at a firm like Macon Smith. The reception area had made a lasting impression on him when he first walked in for second round interviews as a second-year law student. Reliving that feeling a little bit each morning when he came to the office gave him some added inspiration and perspective, which was vital at times to keep a corporate law associate going.

Macon Smith was founded in New York in 1902, right at the turn of the century. The firm had focused on two areas of law initially: banking and shipping. As the New York banking industry grew along with the rise of the House of Morgan, Macon Smith grew right alongside. The complementary practice of maritime law brought an international bent to the firm's clients and transactions from the beginning. The initial location of the office reflected this dual focus too; occupying an office in Downtown Manhattan just off Wall Street, and not too far from the Battery, allowed the firm to be close to their banking clients and a stone's throw away from the shipping houses.

After the Second World War, enterprising American banks were busying themselves loaning money to Western Europe, and they needed lawyers to facilitate the process. Macon Smith was able to leverage its international shipping relationships alongside its domestic banking prowess to become one of the few American law firms doing finance deals in Europe in the middle of the twentieth century. By the time Marcus interviewed in the fall of his second year of law school, Macon Smith was marketing itself as one of the premier international New York-based law firms in the world, which was true, to a point. While the firm did maintain offices in London, Paris, Dubai, Hong Kong, Singapore, and Beijing, the focus was still decidedly New York-centric.

The move from the Financial District to Midtown had been contentious; there were many partners that wanted to stay true to the historic tie of the firm to being close to Wall Street. But the reality was that most of the firm's clients had moved to Midtown themselves. It made more sense to be near them, and to be near both Penn Station and Grand Central Station for those commuting in from New Jersey, Long Island, Westchester County, and Connecticut. In early 2007, just before the financial crisis, Macon Smith relocated to One Bryant Park and staked their claim to ten floors of space above Sixth Avenue.

When Marcus joined the firm, they had immediately slotted him into the EIG group due to his Texan roots. While he had not particularly appreciated this bland association, it had worked out to his favor. He was able to translate, both culturally and linguistically, between New York investment bankers and private equity guys and Texas oil and gas wildcatters and landmen. But Macon Smith's representation went beyond New York bankers and Texas wildcatters. The firm's clients represented the modern, sophisticated providers of capital: large investment funds engaged in infrastructure investing to provide a steady, tax-free alternative to their riskier equity bets, sovereign wealth funds wishing to get involved in the US shale revolution, pension funds seeking diversification, and family offices trying to maximize the practice of asset management.

Marcus was happy to be involved in all of it. Each transaction seemed to him the beginning of a client relationship that would eventually draw him into multiple cross-border deals, jet-setting client development, and the intrigue and prestige that seemed to come with being a global dealmaker.

After two and a half years of being a junior associate, Marcus realized that many of his conceptions were ill-conceived. It seemed that clients were content to let their private practice lawyers, billed out at an ungodly amount of money per hour, stay in their nice New York offices at all hours of the day and night to process requests as they came in, and to turn those requests around quickly. It was not his intellect that was valued, it was his willingness to be available that provided his assured path to success. But as he became more senior, that started to change. Being available remained important, but his intellectual and technical legal skills began to matter more and more as he moved to the front lines of reviewing and drafting commercial agreements. His ability to navigate relationships with other lawyers within the firm and with clients at many different levels of seniority within their own organizations mattered too.

There was still a lot about being a big firm corporate lawyer that was difficult, but now as a sixth-year associate, there were aspects of the job that he found fulfilling too. He enjoyed learning about different businesses and seeing the various strategies they were putting into play. He enjoyed getting to know his clients personally, even if only over email and the phone most of the time and learning about their backgrounds and experience. And he enjoyed thinking through difficult legal and business questions with his colleagues, although he mainly just listened in most of those discussions.

It was for this reason that he was so excited about the prospect of being selected to relocate to the Paris office through the firm's foreign associate program. He loved Paris, and he was beginning to almost like work, so he could envision a future in which he would be happy living and working as a corporate lawyer at Macon Smith Paris. *Macon Smith Paris*, he repeated to himself, *I'm an associate at Macon Smith Paris... no, wait: I'm a* partner *at Macon Smith Paris*! It just sounded right to him.

But before getting the news on that front, he had a few other matters to work through. He hoofed it up the two floors of stairs to the forty-seventh floor and made his way down the hallway, freshly vacuumed the night before, to his office. As a junior associate, he had been required to share an office with another junior associate. But now Marcus had his own office. It wasn't nearly as large and plush as the partners' offices, but it was on the perimeter of the building, so it offered him a beautiful view to the west, looking onto the Hudson River and across to Hamilton Park in Weehawken. The incessant blinking red light on his phone yanked his attention away from the view and back to his desk.

Marcus spent the majority of the morning reviewing a draft purchase and sale agreement for a pipeline
system in Pennsylvania and preparing an issues list to
send to his client, the prospective buyer, for discussion
before revising the agreement to send back across to
the seller. He kept his eye on his email, but instead of
receiving his congratulatory email regarding selection
to the foreign associate program his inbox piled up
with work request after work request. After wolfing
down a sandwich at his desk while on mute during a
conference call, Marcus turned his attention to a proposed corporate restructuring matter for their client
Helios Ltd. As this was outside of Marcus's primary
practice area, he spent much of the afternoon tracking
down advice from different restructuring and tax lawyers within the firm. This had distracted him enough
that, as he was in mid-conversation with Richard
Gallagher, a senior tax lawyer who was walking Marcus
through various observations from his review of the
Helios proposal, Marcus almost overlooked an email
that appeared in his inbox. He glanced at it, turned his
eyes back to the proposal in question, and then did a
double take back to his computer screen.

Dillard, John
Re: Foreign Associate Program

CHAPTER 5

Midtown Manhattan. Thursday, June 26, 2014.

CHARLES ARMSTRONG LEWIS IV SCREENED NEARLY all of his calls through his two secretaries. If someone wanted to speak with Macon Smith's august managing partner, or if they wanted access to Lewis's plush office, which was the size of a two-bedroom apartment replete with its own printing room and its own bathroom, they had to get through one or both of those secretaries. But this number was one of the few that Lewis answered directly. Lewis frowned slightly as his hand hovered over the receiver before picking it up. This was not a call to have on speaker.

"Charles Lewis," he declared as he picked up the phone.

"Lewis, it's me." The woman stated what she knew was already apparent to the man on the other end of the call.

"Oh, *you*. I was, umm…expecting your boss—or associate, I guess I should say." Lewis replied. He had mainly spoken with the man, but sometimes with this woman as well. For this particular conversation, he was expecting her boss, as Lewis assumed that the man was the one who made these types of final decisions.

"Sorry to disappoint. Dean & DeLuca at Rock Center in thirty minutes?" She wanted to be direct here, not to waste time with Charles Lewis on pleasantries.

"Ooh…can we make it an hour? I've got a few things to handle over here first."

She had been expecting this, but no matter. "Sure. See you then."

She hung up the phone, leaned back into her office chair, placed her hands over her head, and peered out onto Park Avenue looking north up toward Central Park. She pondered the upcoming meeting. She had never met Charles Lewis. She was intrigued by how he would handle her trying to take something away from him.

LEWIS WAS RECOGNIZABLE from far down Forty-Eighth Street as he walked toward their meeting point. The woman was already seated at a two-person table with a good window view of those coming into the coffee shop. He was an imposing figure, even from afar. His suit was clearly very high quality, as were his neatly shined shoes, his shimmering red silk tie, and his well-tailored white dress shirt. She met his eyes as he walked in and stood up to greet him. He looked important. *He was important.* He had been at Macon Smith his whole career since he was fresh out of NYU Law and had led the corporate tax department for a decade before being elevated to managing partner. As the leader of one of Wall Street's larger law firms, Lewis was prominent and clearly prepared himself accordingly. He had gray hair that held on to hints of brown at the roots, worn long enough to break and curl a bit at the ends. His face was healthy, not too thin and certainly not plump, and framed smartly by a pair of tortoise-shell glasses. She was surprised and pleased by the level of positive energy he seemed to bring to this meeting. *Well,* she thought, *I guess you don't make it to managing partner of Macon Smith without good reason.*

"Mr. Lewis, good morning." She extended a hand. He politely took it, gave her a firm handshake, looked her in the eyes, and nodded.

"Good morning," he said gently, without adding her name. He knew not to.

They sat.

"I got you a small black coffee, not sure if that's what you like. Milk and sugar are over there." She glanced to her right at a station containing an assortment of napkins, sugar packets and varieties of milk. She had taken the seat facing the door with the coffee bar behind her and the door and windows in front and wrapping around to the left.

"Thank you, this is great," he replied genuinely, and took hold of the small paper cup, moving it over to his side of the table, then added, "So, how may I help you?"

"We've made our decision on Mr. Hugo," she said directly. She didn't want to waste his time or hers. "The six extra months have been very helpful, so we appreciate you accommodating that request. What are your thoughts on him?" She already knew how Marcus Hugo was received within Macon Smith, but she wanted to hear it again—from Charles Lewis.

"You're not going to tell me your decision first?" he asked, then answered his own question, "Although, if you are asking, then my sense is that I already know your decision. But we're here so I will tell you. I like Hugo. We, as a firm, like Hugo. He represents a little bit of a different background than most of our lawyers. He's a state-school kid. He's from Texas. But he fits in and has done very well here. We threw him to the wolves with the assignment in Cairo and he survived. Came back stronger, more focused. A little bitter at first, but he fought through it. I haven't worked with him directly very much, but he has been a much-needed boost to the energy group within the firm. If he keeps going as he is, he should be a partner in a few years."

She knew what that meant at Macon Smith. It affirmed that Hugo was hardworking, organized, responsive, and intelligent enough. But it also meant that he could take orders, operate within the framework of an organization, and improvise when necessary, without breaking rank. She also knew what that meant financially. Rumor had it that upon ascension to the partnership, Lewis himself walked around to the offices of the newly elected partners, gave them a handshake, told them "Welcome to the partnership," and handed them an envelope with a check for a million dollars in it. That was something they would have to work against.

"What about Paris? You guys were going to send him before we intervened. You still plan on doing it?" She was curious to see how Lewis handled this question.

Lewis took his glasses off and put them on the table. He put his hands together with fingers intertwined and moved them to the middle of his chest as he leaned back in the cheap metal chair. He let a breath out of his nose, then responded, "We are—well, I should say—we are going to give him the option. If we don't, we'll probably lose him to someone else...besides you guys." Lewis tilted his head and raised his eyebrows as he added that last bit in a quieter tone. "But before we let him go, I'm going to speak to him personally, along with a few other members of our executive council, to try to convince him to push that plan off until he becomes a partner. I won't delve into it too deeply, but it's for his own good and ours if that is the plan."

She controlled the impulse to snort at this, and instead gave a knowing, conspiratorial smile. Give him what he wants but browbeat him into sticking around and dangle the million bucks at him. Put Paris in a drawer and hope that it never gets reopened. She got it.

"If Hugo insists on going, we'll let him go. There's some crossover in his industry group with what's going on in Europe and we could have him straddle London and Paris, cover clients from both offices, and hope for the best. His partnership prospects would take a serious hit, but you never know."

She didn't believe that, but she had heard enough. She shook her head subtly, then replied, "Thank you for that, Mr. Lewis. We're going to move on Hugo; we'd like to bring him in. The approach will take place next week while he is at a friend's wedding in Italy. To facilitate our recruitment, we request that you deny his Paris application."

She could have said more. Could have explained why they wanted Macon Smith to deny Hugo's application. She wasn't in the business of doing favors for their targets, but this kid deserved to know the reality of the choice that was about to be presented to him. If he turned them down, then so be it. But not because of a misconception about what his future at Macon Smith was going to look like. This was a power play though, so no need to explain. *Just make the request and expect it to be dealt with.*

Lewis started to say something, then stopped himself. He took a sip of coffee, grimaced, then nodded his head once. "Very well then, that's what we will do." He responded, deadpan. Then he produced his own knowing smile. "As we accommodate this request, we do hope that you and the Shareholder will keep that in mind going forward." He, also, did not need to explain.

WALKING BACK TO her office, she dialed a number on the other side of the Atlantic. His voice was crisp and alert, "What's the verdict?"

"They'll do it," She replied. "Same positive reviews from before. They've got him on the short track to partner, so Lewis wasn't thrilled. But he said he would do it."

"Good," he responded. "Guess that means Peppercorn will have to throw Macon Smith some business to keep Lewis happy. That's okay, should make the whole thing easier and more natural looking."

They both allowed a few seconds of quiet between them. Then breaking the silence he asked, "So, you make brief contact in Frankfurt, give me the green light, and I'll take the stage in Tuscany?"

"Let's do it." She concluded. "Speak to you tomorrow."

CHAPTER 6

Midtown Manhattan. Thursday, June 26, 2014.

U PON READING THE SUBJECT LINE OF THE EMAIL that just landed in his inbox, Marcus's heart immediately began thumping at twice its normal rate. The increase was so strong that he could feel the blood pulsating through the veins in both of his temples. In the place of what should have been excitement, a palpable wave of nervousness engulfed his insides. He stared blankly at the still highlighted letters of the email subject line, oddly hesitant to hover his mouse arrow over it and click.

Attempting to maintain his professionalism while continuing the conversation with Tom Gallagher, Marcus returned his attention to the rambling, lengthy explanation of the complex tax implications of converting Helios Corp into an LLC. He raised his open right hand and placed the space between his thumb and forefinger along his eyebrows, blocking his eyes from wandering back to the computer screen. He shifted the receiver of the phone from his left hand to his shrugged-up left shoulder, grabbed a pen laying on his desk, and furiously transcribed as much as he could onto his yellow legal pad. Realizing he was far too nervous about and preoccupied with the recent arrival to his inbox, he decided to copy as much down as possible, and just try to piece it all together after the call. Five minutes and a page and half of notes later, Gallagher stopped talking.

"Does that make sense?" Gallagher added after a few moments of silence.

"Yes, absolutely," Marcus responded while bobbing his head up and down.

Then Gallagher, seemingly washing his hands of the whole matter and bringing the discussion to a close simultaneously, exclaimed, "I mean, ultimately, it's a business decision for the client, but they should know what the possible effects are."

"Right, right." Marcus intoned, then added "well, that was extremely helpful Richard, thank you very much. I'll send you the client/matter number for this and will let you know if we need anything else."

Marcus quickly composed a short email sending along the promised information to Gallagher, all the while purposely ignoring the unopened item in his inbox. He made a very brief review of his scribbles on the legal pad, placed a few stars next to particularly important lines, then pushed it to the side.

He slid his chair away from his desk with his heels, placed his elbows on the chair's armrests, leaned back, and took in a deep breath. He exhaled quickly and said, "Here we go."

He double-clicked on the unopened email, which automatically maximized it on his second computer screen on the right side of his desk. His eyes focused in on the body of the email:

Marcus,

Please see attached.

Best,
John

That is odd, Marcus thought. *Why wouldn't Dillard just put his acceptance note in the body of the email?* This was probably a good sign, as a formal acceptance would look much better on Macon Smith's official stationery, he reassured himself. Marcus's heartbeat calmed slightly, and the beginnings of a feeling of relief started to take over his nervousness. He opened the attached PDF. There, under the professional looking Macon Smith letterhead, was the following message:

Dear Marcus,

We thank you again for your interest and application to Macon Smith's Foreign Associate Program. Your credentials and qualifications, coupled with your performance here at the firm, are quite impressive and of the highest quality.

Unfortunately, we are not able to accommodate your request and regret to inform you that we have chosen two other associates to participate in this year's program.

This by no means reflects how valuable we believe your services are to the firm. You are an important member of the Macon Smith team, and we look forward to your continued contribution.

Regards,
John M. Dillard

Just as the utter desolation of rejection took hold of Marcus, his phone screamed at him, jolting him to attention in his seat. He checked the caller ID; of course—John Dillard. He picked up the receiver.

"This is Marcus."

"Hugo, you can handle that, right?" John Dillard stated.

"Uh…yes, sure. I'm a bit disappointed but—"

Dillard cut him off. "Disappointed? What do you mean, *disappointed*?" His voice rose an octave on the final two syllables.

"I thought I was a shoo-in for the Paris office sir, but—"

"Oh, that. Didn't know that went out today," Dillard interjected again. "Look, view it as a complement," he commanded. "Too valuable not to have you around, or something like that."

This did not have a consoling effect on Marcus.

"My other email. You can handle *that, right*?" The last word Dillard pronounced in a manner that was forceful and crisp.

Marcus looked at his inbox and saw that roughly ten seconds before Dillard's call, he had forwarded an email along to Marcus. There were a number of documents attached and a long chain of emails below it, half of which contained multiple paragraph-long descriptions and instructions. The top email in the chain simply said: *pls hdl*.

Marcus never could quite understand the pervasive belief amongst senior partners that, immediately upon sending an email to an associate, that associate could review the entire message, attachments included, and speak intelligibly about it within fifteen seconds. He also hadn't figured out why they still used text message-style wording on emails they clearly sent from the computers at their desks.

After rapidly scanning some of the keywords from the email chain and giving two of the attachments a lightning-quick once-over, Marcus stuttered,

"So…Global Merchants…$400 million private notes offering…closing…*when?*" Marcus uttered this last word with a foreboding vision of his evening plans—after-work drinks with some law school friends then off to JFK to catch a late flight to Europe—being demolished like a condemned apartment building.

"Monday! Look at the Term Sheet," Dillard ordered.

"Sir, I'm supposed to be out all next week for my vacation. It's a wedding that I am in. I've had that one the books for ten months now…"

"Damn it, Hugo, just handle it." Dillard thundered, then continued in a calmer, yet pedantic tone, "They want it done Monday, so it needs to be done by Monday. I don't need to know how you make that happen, as long as it happens."

Marcus shook his head, then inhaled deeply and replied, "Understood."

"Good, it's settled then," Dillard concluded, "Look, I'm in the Hamptons tomorrow and then I am going to client meetings in Jackson Hole next week, so ask around if you need help, and shoot me a quick email when the deal is done."

Marcus heard the line go dead. Feeling his body temperature rise, Marcus clenched both of his fists as tightly as possible and writhed his midsection in his chair, all while applying every ounce of restraint he possessed to hold back a long, loud exhortation of "*Fuck!*"

Remembering that he was in the workplace, he gained control of himself and took a few deep breaths while staring at the granite-colored carpet underneath his desk. He returned his attention to his computer, closed out of the Global Merchants attachments he had opened, and fixated his eyes on one line of the last PDF he still had open on his screen:

Unfortunately, we are not able to accommodate your request and regret to inform you that we have chosen two other associates to participate in this year's program.

CHAPTER 7

Frankfurt am Main, Germany. Friday, June 27, 2014.

M ARCUS'S FLIGHT LANDED AT FRANKFURT Airport at roughly 11:00 a.m. local time. He had to will his eyes to remain open as he glanced at the departures screen to confirm the gate for his connection. Marcus wasn't a great sleeper on long flights and this time had been no different, so it still felt like five a.m. local Manhattan time to him. There were ninety minutes to kill before boarding his flight for Florence, so he decided to seek out a café near the connecting gate for a cup of coffee to power through. Immediately adapting to the local time zone on the first day of a west-to-east transatlantic trip was the only effective way that Marcus had found to combat the jetlag.

As he strode through the squeaky clean, well-organized terminal in Frankfurt it only took him a few steps to be absorbed by that familiar feeling of sly contentment that overcame him when he was out on the road traveling. Nothing seemed to heighten his senses and interest in observation quite like getting out and seeing other parts of the world. Even the most mundane seeming things, like the shapes of the gate markers or the selection of which three languages important airport signs appeared in, fascinated him. These basic differences of life in other countries made him feel like he was moving forward or evolving somehow by being exposed to something outside of his normal routine. For Marcus, it was not so much "traveling," as it was an attempt at sampling life in another place.

The nearest café to Marcus's connecting gate was a modern yet inviting looking one located in the center of the terminal corridor, affording its patrons the benefit of seeing the foot traffic from all directions. Marcus claimed an open spot at the bar. A few seats over to his left, a pair of older German-looking ladies were enjoying breakfast pastries and dutifully taking sips of their beers. The seats to his right remained open, save for a businessman skimming the morning papers and sipping a coffee at the end of the bar.

The open space provided Marcus the opportunity to take out one of his work files and read through an agreement he was tasked with marking up. After his maddening call with Dillard, he had briefly considered scrapping the whole trip, but he couldn't do that. He couldn't miss this wedding and let his friend down like that. For the most part, he had managed to hand off the Global Merchants offering assignments, Project Vulcan, as the transaction had been dubbed by the Global Merchants team, to other partners and associates to do the yeoman's work over the next few days to meet the Monday deadline, but this particular agreement was one that Marcus wanted to review and transmit the comments on himself. Much of the work he'd done during the flight from New York, but there were a few sections remaining that he wanted to get through before landing in Florence. At that point he wanted to shut the work part of his brain off for the next three days so he could fully immerse himself in Tuscany and the wedding that had brought him there. He'd carve off some time each day to check in on the project and make sure it was moving along as needed to meet the Monday deadline, but he wasn't going to spend his entire trip holed up in the hotel room.

Just as he flipped the agreement open to his earmarked section, the café's bartender stopped in front of him and made eye contact.

"*Bitte*?" she shot out.

Anticipating that he would be asked to order in German, Marcus had prepared the scant words he learned during his sojourn through Germany after taking the bar exam. This array of terms principally consisted of *please*, *thank you*, the numbers *one* through *three, water, coffee, red wine, beer* and, thanks to a random cheat sheet of important translated phrases he skimmed in a hostel, *apologies, my friend is drunk.*

"*Ein kaffe, bitte. Danke,*" Marcus responded, effectively exhausting his German linguistic capabilities. *One coffee please, thank you.*

Quickly realizing that Marcus was not fluent in German, but seemingly appreciating his attempt to order in German, the bartender responded: "*Ya, danke.*" Then she added, in nearly unaccented English, "Yes, okay. Thank you very much." She whisked the menu away and moved toward the German ladies to provide them with their bill.

Returning to the earmarked page of his agreement, Marcus tried to engross himself back into the world of indemnification and arbitration provisions. Just about then, a tallish blond lady claimed the bar stool two spots over from him. She was well put together, athletic looking, and had on a very nice full-length black coat, mid-calf black boots, and wore jewelry and an accompanying watch that spoke to both a sufficiency of resources and attention to detail. She had no luggage with her, only a very nice leather handbag that matched up with ones that some women used as the equivalent of a briefcase. The opening at the top of the bag allowed Marcus a glimpse of a few collections of papers clipped together, indicating that her presence was more likely business-oriented than for pleasure.

She was not beautiful nor striking, but she was pretty, and Marcus's gaze lingered on her face. Something about her was attractive. *Definitely attractive*, Marcus thought to himself. Marcus could not help but to look over at her again. He was unable to immediately surmise her nationality, but he guessed she was either German or American. The similarity in appearance between many Germans and his fellow native Texans had surprised him when he first visited the country, but then he reminded himself that many of the first Texas settlers had been German, so it made sense. This woman looked as if she could just as likely be from Fredericksburg, Texas as Hamburg, Germany.

The new arrival paid Marcus no heed as she glanced at the menu, then raised her eyebrows at the bartender, who obediently shuffled over. The woman ordered something in rapid, fluent German, asked a follow up question, and then responded to the bartender with something that caused the bartender to break into uproarious laughter. *German it is then*, thought Marcus.

Drifting back to his agreement, Marcus worked his way through the last few paragraphs and jotted down some notes in the margins of that page. He slipped the agreement back into a Redweld folder, which he placed into a compartment in his gray canvas workbag.

"Project Vulcan, huh? Must be pretty important with that name," the woman beside him exclaimed.

Trying to figure out how on earth this woman knew the project name of the transaction he was working on, Marcus glanced into his bag to notice that his Redweld had a white label on the top that read: PROJECT VULCAN—CONFIDENTIAL. Further perplexing though, was the fact that this lady's declaration had come in native-sounding English, without the slightest hint of a foreign accent, German or otherwise.

Seeking to recover from this minor shock, Marcus replied, "Oh yes, anytime a project is named after a Greek or Roman deity it must be of utmost importance. And obviously very confidential, too."

She gave a courteous chuckle, then added, "And even more so if it brought you over here from the US."

Interesting and bold, thought Marcus. Asserting he was American was closer to a clever observation than a wild guess, but bold, nonetheless. Intrigued, Marcus decided to play along, but in a more toned-down manner.

"Thankfully, pleasure is what brought me over this time, but the work needs to get done before I really enjoy the trip. And yourself? Is this home, or are you just stopping through?"

A benign question, especially compared to her previous statements.

"Stopping through," she replied. Then added, "but I stop through quite often."

"Very nice," replied Marcus. "Seems like a nice place to stop through."

Ignoring this nicety, she pressed on. "So what type of law do you practice?"

Very bold. But then again, Marcus realized that lawyers were probably the only professionals left who still carried Redwelds, and, given how classy and dynamic she appeared, she looked like the type who had employed a lawyer or two and could readily identify them.

"Corporate," he acquiesced. "Mainly in the energy and infrastructure industries." Then he added, "That isn't a takes-one-to-know-one observation, is it?"

"No," she responded, "God, no. Never."

She was not exactly polite, but Marcus was still intrigued. He attempted to change the subject. By this point he was fairly comfortable that this lady was American, so tried to dig into that topic a bit.

"You speak German very well. If you don't mind me asking, how did you learn?"

"As I mentioned, my work brings me to Germany quite often." Then, almost deliberately making a show of stopping herself, thinking about adding something, then allowing herself to go on, she continued, "I'm in fashion, and Germany is Europe's largest economy, so it helps business to come here often and speak the language. And I oversee some of our boutiques here, so I get to use it often."

Fashion boutique manager, huh? This lady is an interesting character, but I'm not sure I believe her, Marcus thought to himself. She was a professional for sure, but something about her directness and lack of veneer made him certain she was not in the fashion world, at least not a boutique manager. Something more confrontational, like consulting or human resources, would have been his guess.

As if divining Marcus's doubts, the lady interrupted his thoughts. "But I live in Paris, where our fashion house is based."

The mention of Paris lifted Marcus's spirits, reminding him that he was, after all, in Europe on vacation. Discarding his doubts about the validity of this lady's story and suppressing the sharp pain he felt recalling Macon Smith's rejection of his assignment to the Paris office, Marcus opted for the diplomatic route and ventured to take advantage of an opportunity to converse in French.

"*Ah, oui?*" he continued in French to declare that he loved Paris, and asked her where she lived, how long she had been there, did she enjoy living there, and other basic, surface-level questions about her time in Paris.

She spoke French exceptionally well. Marcus's French-speaking ability did not even garner an acknowledgement from her, as if it was to be expected. She reciprocated with questions of her own, asking

Marcus about his time in Paris, his thoughts on the city, and about France in general. She required a level of specificity from Marcus in his answers that was a curious, if not enjoyable, challenge.

Their conversation was momentarily interrupted by the bartender carefully laying down a traditional breakfast strudel, accompanied by a shot of espresso. The two women at the other end of the bar traded a series of barbs between them in German and a laugh or two. As the bartender vanished, the lady abruptly turned to Marcus, and switching back to English, she asked, "Do you plan on living in Paris again?"

The two German-looking women's exchange had afforded Marcus the opportunity to glance at his phone to check the time; boarding for his flight was about to begin. This question truly caught him off guard. Not just the substance of it, but the pointed nature of it, along with the focused switch to English.

Once again, opting for the diplomatic high road, he responded, "My job is in New York and it's a very good job, one I'm lucky to have. But if my work required me to live in Paris, then I guess I would have to oblige." He flashed a wry yet endearing—he hoped—smile as he uttered this last bit.

Instead of responding in kind, this woman's eyes narrowed slightly, burrowing into Marcus's own eyes, seeming to assess the conviction with which he had answered her question.

Glancing up at the line forming in front of the gate for the Florence departure, Marcus decided it was time to exit this stage.

"Well, I hope you have a nice time here in Frankfurt. It's been nice speaking with you. Enjoy Paris." He respectfully nodded his head in her direction.

She did not respond immediately. Then, as Marcus was walking away, she called after him, "Thank you. Enjoy Florence."

This last reference to Florence was too much for Marcus. *This encounter had been odd enough, but how did she know he was going to Florence?* He was certain he did not mention that in their conversation.

He turned on his heels and gave the woman a quizzical look. Her expression was nonchalant, then, as if to provide an explanation, she nodded her head toward the crowded gate with the words *Florenz, Firenze, Florence* displayed on the screen. Marcus sheepishly looked her way once again, making a show of embarrassment.

Marcus hustled over to the gate. As he walked down the jet way he wondered, *What in the world—?* And then, *That was a very strange interaction.*

CHAPTER 8

Montefollonico, Italy.
Sunday, June 29, 2014.

H IGH ATOP THE TUSCAN HILLS, NEAR THE BORDER
of Tuscany and Umbria, sits the small, pictur-
esque Italian village of Montefollonico. The winding
roads creeping up and down the surrounding hillsides
leading in and out of town are lined with tall cypress
trees and speckled with vineyards and olive orchards
on either side of the road. The juxtaposition of the
natural beauty of the land and the man-made order
of the vegetation creates a backdrop that practically
urges one to pick up a brush and an easel to try their
hand at landscape painting in an effort to capture the
beauty and emotion that it creates.

The village is small, so there is not much of the
surrounding area that announces its presence before
the road changes to cobblestones beneath the stone
wall with a red brick archway opening up into the
Centro Storico. The main cobblestone street, barely
wide enough for a full-size sedan, continues up the

hill past stone buildings on either side, with ornate green- and chestnut-painted wooden doors, windows accompanied by mahogany shutters and red Tuscan clay-tiled rooftops throughout, until it opens up into the central *piazza*. Around the corner, down one of the small capillaries to the main thoroughfare, sits the Relais La Costa, a hotel, restaurant, sometimes event center, and haven of Tuscan culture to which local Italians and tourists in the know flock for the combination of incredible views from its magnificent *terrazzo*, delicious Tuscan crostini and local Sangiovese wine, all replete with the companionship of Paolo and Paola, the native Tuscan restorers and proprietors of the establishment. Few things can make one appreciate the beauty and character of Italy better than enjoying a glass of Brunello di Montalcino and looking out from the La Costa terrace onto the Tuscan valley below as it rolls east into Umbria and the beautiful Lago Trasimeno and its surrounding mountains just across the border.

It was on this terrace that Marcus found himself on the morning after the wedding that had brought him to this lovely place, but with a glass of water in place of wine. He huffed and puffed, still sweating from the morning run that he had even surprised himself in making. But the slight pain reverberating from the previous night's festivities were no match for a bright, beautiful morning cruising through the Tuscan countryside and taking in all of its surroundings.

Breathing deeply, Marcus paused to linger over this incredible view. His eyes traced the movement of the silver and red *Frecciarossa* high-speed train, snaking its way through the valley, Florence-bound. Had it not been for the allure of fresh *cornetti* pastries filled with cream and marmalade, strong Italian espresso, and the joyful prospect of trading pleasantries with Paolo in the bar-turned-breakfast room behind him, he would have stayed on the terrace all morning to take in the views and soak in the Tuscan sun.

His cornetto and espresso were well worth it though, and the conversation with Paolo even more so. Paolo spoke almost no English, his strong, guttural Tuscan accent even made his Italian difficult to understand, and beyond a few basic introductory words, Marcus spoke no Italian. Yet the laughs and smiles being traded between the two indicated they were somehow able to converse; Marcus opting to speak in Spanish and Paolo gesticulating wildly and dropping in an English word here or there. The topics of conversation were the dance moves that Marcus had broken out late in the evening before as the wedding festivities reached their energetic peak, and the female guest who had accompanied Marcus to his room at the end of the evening. Paolo informed Marcus that his reservation had been a room for one, not two, so he would have to charge him double for the evening, followed by Paolo's jovial laughter at his own joke. Dropping his head, face reddened with embarrassment, Marcus moved toward the stairs leading to his room, but before departing turned to Paolo and gave his best impression of the French shrug of the shoulders and pursed lower lip, then spontaneously added in an exaggerated hand motion to accompany in an effort to Italianize his gesture. The attempt had its desired effect as the two laughed, then traded a chorus of: *"Ciao, Paolo, ciao." "Ciao, Marco, ciao, ciao."*

After a quick shower and change of clothes, Marcus departed La Costa to walk down into the town for a change of scenery and the hope of finding a morning newspaper to peruse. The wedding party was set to take a bus at 11:00 a.m. to Poggio Antico, a local Tuscan winery well known for its Brunellos, for a vineyard visit and wine tasting, followed up by a group lunch near Montalcino at a restaurant in the central piazza of the town. Marcus had to admit that this was his type of wedding celebration and a good way to get his mind off his work-related frustrations and disappointments back in New York. Unfortunately he did not have much time to linger in Italy after the wedding, as he had to get back to his desk and the opinion letters and the bond prospectuses…*but enough of that line of thinking*. He was going to try to at least take in some authentic Italian culture while he was here, and so he worked his way down to a bar that he had eyed on his way into town that lay just outside the *Centro Storico*.

Marcus had once heard someone describe the allure of Italian culture and life as "unrefined," but meaning it as a compliment. That is exactly what came to his mind as he turned the corner and ambled up to the Bar Sport in Montefollonico. The structure itself was fairly nondescript: a light-brown stucco building with a wide opening at the front door, a tile floor, and a set of small TVs in each corner of the bar. Outside was a dirt courtyard with one half replete with white plastic chairs and tables like the ones you might find at an old community pool in the US, and the other half dedicated to a makeshift *campo di bocce* that already had an active, if not very lively, game in progress. The men playing bocce were old, small, tan, and—almost to a man—smoking a cigar or cigarette. Half of them had a small espresso on a little table at one end of the *campo*, the other half drank small glasses of *limoncello*. And even in the heat of summer, all of them wore pants, well-worn dress shoes, some combination of button up shirts, sweaters, or polos, and most with an old sport coat on top. Marcus took a deep breath and let out a sigh of appreciation and contentment. What a spectacular way to spend a Sunday morning.

He made his way inside and located a small newsstand below that bar and selected a copy of *La Gazzetta dello Sport*. The numerous pictures and generally familiar subject of sports would make for a more meaningful cursory review of the paper than trying to piece together what Marcus could of *La Repubblica*. Marcus placed the newspaper on the counter.

"*E un espresso doppio, per favore,*" he said. *Thank you, Starbucks, for teaching me Italian*, he thought. After placing a five Euro note on the counter and waving his hand in a gesture to signal that he didn't need any change, he received a disinterested "*grazie*" from the old lady behind the bar who felt no need to feign interest in this tourist and what he was doing in this town. Marcus sidled up to one of the high-top tables, took a cursory look at the F1 racing highlights on one TV, then the reading of lottery winners on the other TV, and began flipping through the newspaper to see what transfers the big Italian football clubs of Juventus, A.C. Milan, and Inter Milan had made over the summer and how the integrations of those new signings were being marketed and portrayed. Marcus was the only patron sitting inside. He relaxed against the back of his metal chair in an effort to enjoy a few minutes of relative solitude and appreciate his unique surroundings.

A voice at the counter startled Marcus, as he had not heard anyone else enter the Bar Sport. He lowered the large pages of *La Gazzetta* to get a glimpse of a man standing at the bar, conversing with the old lady in quiet, fluid Italian and lightly waving his arms toward the man on TV reading off the latest winning lotto numbers. The old lady behind the bar began to laugh, and then gave the man a broad smile and handed him one of the *cornetti* that had been displayed in the glass shelves below the bar, followed by an espresso. Marcus squinted a bit to study this man, trying to figure out who this stranger might be. He was tall, thin, and fit. He had short, neatly cut white hair, and big dark eyebrows. He wore slim, navy-blue chinos, a white open-collared button up shirt, also slim cut, and a charcoal-colored sports coat on top that was somewhere between the look of an English tweed jacket and a Midtown Manhattan casual Friday blazer. He had on a pair of modest, yet tasteful Italian driving loafers and wasn't wearing any socks.

Marcus wasn't sure what to make of this man. Was he a guest of the wedding? Marcus hadn't seen him the night before, but this guy did look more American than he would expect a patron of the Bar Sport to look. But what about the Italian the guy had comfortably been speaking? Maybe he learned it in his neighborhood in New Jersey, but it sounded pretty authentic, and the lady behind the bar sure seemed to follow what he was saying. *Oh well*, thought Marcus, *Interesting for sure, but no need to try to figure this guy out.* If the guy was a part of the wedding group, Marcus was sure he'd see him on the bus to the wine tasting. If not, he was just another interesting aspect of this delightful trip to Tuscany.

Marcus glanced down at his phone to check the time; a few minutes before ten. Enough time to try to work his way through a few more simple articles in the paper before heading back up the hill and through the stone archway to meet the rest of the wedding group. He was looking forward to the banter and jokes that he was sure would come with the bus ride, as everyone recalled the events of last night's celebration and shared the gossip of what different groups of people managed to get into during the wee hours of the morning. But he was also glad he still had another half hour to himself to experience Montefollonico on his own.

Marcus felt a presence near him. Somewhat startled, he slowly lowered his newspaper to observe. The man was staring directly at him with full, light-blue eyes. Taken aback and confused, Marcus returned his gaze, then lifted his eyebrows and tilted his head as if to say, *yes?*

"Hello, Marcus," the man stated in clear, American English. "Mind if I join you?"

CHAPTER 9

Montefollonico, Italy. Sunday, June 29, 2014.

"I'M SORRY, DO WE KNOW EACH OTHER?" THE SILENT approach of this man caught Marcus off guard, but the man uttering his name and asking to join him completely waylaid him. *Who in the hell was this guy?*

"I saw you at the wedding last night. May I?" The man glanced down at the open chair across the high-top from Marcus. *Interesting,* thought Marcus. He hadn't recalled seeing this man at the wedding, and it wasn't that big of a group of people attending. But clearly this man was going to sit down, so Marcus obliged him by lightly indicating the open chair with his right hand, palm up.

The mention of the wedding put Marcus slightly at ease, but he was still confused. *Okay, so this guy is part of the wedding group. But why didn't I see him last night?*

"Beautiful ceremony last night. How do you know Matt and Heather?" Marcus asked. *Reasonable question,* he thought.

Marcus studied the man more in-depth now that he was at close range. He had sharp facial features and a distinguished disposition. He was lithe, smooth. His outfit, while not ostentatious or over the top, matched, and was of good quality and well-tailored. This man reminded Marcus of someone who could host a serious talk show, with long interviews and probing, intellectual questions.

"I'm here on business." The retort was emotionless, calculated. *That was an evasive response,* Marcus noted. When the man didn't offer any additional information, Marcus decided to take the social approach and probe further, "Not a bad place to be working. Are you doing photography or video for the wedding?"

Again, a reasonable question. What other work would this guy be doing here with the wedding?

"Not quite. More like talent acquisition."

Talent acquisition. Not exactly a profession that one typically associated with weddings. It sounded more like an eloquent way of describing recruitment for a hedge fund or organized crime. This was getting very weird. Marcus was uncomfortable. Time to get himself out of this conversation and away from this bizarre interaction.

"Okay...well, sounds interesting, sir." Marcus took a peek down at his phone, "well, looks like we are due for the bus ride pretty soon. Guess I'll see you up there. Nice meeting..."

"Poggio Antico." The man interrupted. This wasn't a question. "They typically make very good Brunellos, and the Lemartine is a good Tuscan blend. Not easy to find, actually, a good Tuscan blend."

What in God's name? This discussion was so far off the path of normalcy that Marcus almost felt like he was having an out of body experience. *Time for this to end. Now.*

"Looking forward to trying them out. Thanks for the recommendation. See you up there." Marcus abandoned his paper and empty espresso cup and made for the door. *Whew! Wow that was awkward. Who the hell was..."*

"You're still mad about Paris, aren't you?" The man's tone had suddenly changed, assuming a stance of authority. "That's why you were acting like an idiot on the dance floor last night, right? Why you thought it was a good idea to invite the bride's sister up to your room?"

These questions, really more like accusations, cut into Marcus's core like a sharpened butcher's knife. *What in the world was going on here?* Marcus decided that this had gone too far and the time for pleasantries was over.

"First off, it's called *having fun*. That's what you're supposed to do at a wedding."

"It was irresponsible, Marcus, and you know it. Always keep your wits about you and be under control. Especially in a foreign country. That's a lesson you've learned before."

This rebuke was more professorial, and frankly, correct. *But how did this guy know that? "…a lesson you've learned before…" What else did he know about Marcus?*

"Thank you, sensei." Marcus quipped. The gloves were officially off. "Listen sir, I don't know what you think you know about me, but I'm beyond uncomfortable here. You need to either tell me who you are, and what you want from me, or this conversation ends right now."

The man slightly chuckled to himself, then raised his gaze to meet Marcus's eyes and gave him a few tiny nods.

"All right, fair enough." He athletically bounded to his feet and gave Marcus a few forceful taps on the back in one fluid motion. "Let's get some fresh air."

CHAPTER 10

Montefollonico, Italy.
Sunday, June 29, 2014.

MARCUS RELUCTANTLY FOLLOWED THE MAN out of the Bar Sport to the left, away from the *Centro Storico*, along the winding road which led down the hilltop into the valley separating Montefollonico from its larger neighbor, Montepulciano. Marcus had run down this road earlier, and even now, in this odd circumstance, he couldn't help but appreciate the tall, thin cypress trees lining the street, the low stone wall on the uphill side of the street, the cicadas filling the morning with background noise, and the birds fluttering about up and down the hill.

The man in front of Marcus kept a steady but easy pace and walked with his hands in his jacket pockets, providing the effect of just a simple man on a Sunday stroll. *Why am I following this man?* And what was about to transpire during the upcoming conversation? But even though Marcus felt uncomfortable, there was nothing inside of him screaming *Danger, Danger,*

Danger! He was curious to see who this guy was, and in any event, he had a built-in exit route from the conversation because of the need to be back at the bus in half an hour for the wine tasting.

Once they were about fifty meters down the road, away from earshot of the Bar Sport, the man began speaking. "My name is Arthur Franz. I'm a partner at Peppercorn Capital Partners." This Arthur Franz produced a business card from his right hand and nonchalantly handed it over to Marcus. Marcus looked down at the card: white, quality paper, slightly thicker than the average card, and with plain black lettering: *Arthur M. Franz, Partner, Peppercorn Capital Partners.* There were two addresses on the card, in the bottom left corner, an address in New York: *245 Park Avenue.* Marcus knew the building, right by Grand Central between Park and Lexington. Nice part of town. In the bottom right corner, an address in Berlin: Behrenstrasse 68.

"The Behrenstrasse in Berlin...that's by the Brandenburg Gate, right? Near the US Embassy and the Hotel Adlon?" Marcus was a bit surprised, and a little embarrassed, that he remembered the name of that street. He had been to Berlin once with a good friend from law school after they took their bar exams and went on a "bar trip" to Central and Eastern Europe. It was really nothing more than a three-week pub crawl, but he thoroughly enjoyed the trip and, surprisingly, learned a lot. Berlin in particular had been a very pleasant surprise. But one night, after allowing themselves to be severely overserved, Marcus, unable to find a bathroom nearby, had made the poor, and desperate, decision to urinate on the side of a building. Sure enough, a police officer quickly shined his flashlight on Marcus's back and shouted something in German. Marcus spoke no German but clearly understood the instruction. He quickly finished his business and raised his hand to apologize. In short order, the officer realized that Marcus was an American and began chuckling from his gut, then relaxed and lit himself a cigarette.

"You are pissing on your own embassy, my friend," the officer explained. "You are lucky I'm not an embassy guard; that would be bad."

Marcus had looked up at the building. *This must be the back of the embassy*, he thought, noticing no identifying signs or plaques. Then he looked at the street corner to make a mental note. He was on the corner of Ebertstrasse and Behrenstrasse, across the way from the Memorial to the Murdered Jews of Europe. He would never forget that corner…a good example of Marcus not keeping his wits about him. It was one of those lessons he was supposed to have learned before that this Arthur Franz referenced.

"That's right, Marcus. Good memory." Arthur Franz neglected to add anything further, allowing some dead air to enter the space between them.

Marcus sought to continue the discussion. "So that's where you are based? Seeing as how you are here in Italy, not too far way I guess."

"Right again," responded Franz. "You've heard of Peppercorn, right?"

Marcus had heard of Peppercorn and was racking his brain to remember how. Definitely from a transaction he worked on. Then it came to him.

"You guys bought a terminal at the Port of Savannah, right? Storage for fuels, liquids, and the like. Pretty sure our client was the seller on that deal—"

"Global Storage Partners," Franz interjected, "That's right; we picked up those assets on the cheap back in 2012. Those have been very good for us."

Marcus remembered now. He had been a junior associate on the deal. One of his first big merger and acquisition deals to work on. He had really enjoyed it. Lots of late nights and weekend work, but he'd learned a ton. He hadn't had much direct contact with the Peppercorn business team but had been very impressed based on the little interaction he did have. They were sharp, very well informed, cordial, yet very tough negotiators.

"We also hold some senior debt of one of your clients, a big agricultural business that sells a bunch of soybeans, cotton, corn, and pork barrels to China," Franz continued.

"Markham Farms" Marcus replied. "Deceiving name for a company owned by one the largest private equity funds in the world. I remember talking to one of my colleagues about that, but I didn't work on it. You guys had some very interesting terms on that credit, didn't you?"

"Full information rights." Franz seemed proud to make that statement. "All the data on *who* is buying *what* internationally. Good information to have, for a number of reasons."

Marcus could see how that would be the case. Clear insight into demand across the globe could help someone know which business to go buy next...and which ones to dump. Extremely unusual to see in loan terms, though.

Marcus looked down at his phone to check the time again; he had fifteen minutes to be at the bus. It was time to bring things to a head. Their walk had led them to a fork in the road. One path turned left toward a larger road heading down the valley to the Strada Provinciale 146, the highway that circled around the Val d'Orcia. The other path, to the right, was a smaller dirt road looping back around to Montefollonico through a less trodden entrance. Marcus stopped walking and turned to face Arthur Franz.

"Listen, Mr...." Marcus made a show of looking down at the business card he still held in his left hand. He wasn't ready to buddy up to this guy yet, so he wanted to maintain a resistant tone, "...Franz,"

"*Arthur*, please" Franz interrupted.

"Arthur, then. Listen, what's this all about? How do you know so much about me, and why are you here at this wedding?"

Franz nodded his head a few times as if to acknowledge that the time had come to get to the point of the discussion. Franz glanced quickly back over his shoulder up the road, then tilted his head to the right and began walking down the smaller road in the direction of Montefollonico.

"You already know this, but this will lead us to the back entrance of town, and you'll be in time for your bus," Franz offered up, acknowledging the time limitation on this discussion. "I want you to come work with us, Marcus—come work for Peppercorn," Franz stated directly. "Start in New York, eventually move to an international office. You know the industry, you are a very good lawyer, and you work well with your clients. They like you. That's important."

This was not what Marcus was expecting to hear. *An inperson meeting that amounted to a cold call in the middle of Tuscany while he was on vacation?* It was a lot to take in, given the setting. But...it did pique his interest. He had thought about going in-house before, but the idea of being just a part of "legal" within a business where the stars—the people actually generating revenue—were in other departments didn't appeal to him. Plus, this seemed like such an odd way for a private equity firm to approach a candidate.

Before Marcus could say anything, Franz added, "We have a very unique culture, and we work very hard to find the right people that we think will fit into that culture. We need people who are smart, or course, but also business-oriented, adventurous, interested in doing things…maybe a bit outside of their normal course of operations. And, with respect to certain groups within the firm, we need people who can exercise a high level of discretion."

Adventurous. Discretion. Interesting, Marcus thought. *Very interesting*. All lawyers are bound to be discrete, bound to maintain client confidentiality. But he had certainly never heard "adventurous" and "ability to exercise discretion" as desired traits for an in-house legal candidate.

Marcus felt like it was his turn to say something. "Okay, interesting…but why are you contacting me *here*? Why not just use a headhunter like everybody else? Or just call me directly, but do it at my office?" *Seemed like the right question to ask*, Marcus affirmed to himself.

Franz nodded lightly again and gave a slight shrug as if to say they were reasonable questions. "We are very selective, and we generally do some things differently than other private equity firms. We do extensive research and due diligence on potential candidates— extensive. And when we find someone we like, we approach them personally."

This makes some sense, Marcus thought. But, while he may be a good candidate for this kind of job, it wasn't like he was some superstar banker that all of the premier private equity firms wanted. This seemed a bit excessive, and very aggressive. Unsure what to say, Marcus said nothing.

"But..." Franz said, returning to his pitch, "in this instance, there is something else..."

CHAPTER 11

Sant'Angelo in Colle, Italy. Sunday, June 29, 2014.

T HE GROUP OF FORTY OR SO WEDDING ATTEND-
EES worked their way down the hill from the
center square of the village toward the large charter
bus that would take them back to Montefollonico.
Nearly every single one of them was a little wobbly
making the advance, as they had just eaten and drunk
exceptionally well at Trattoria Il Leccio. The bride
and groom had arranged for an openair, three-course
buffet outside of the small trattoria that fronted the
village square, with three long tables accompanied
by understated yellow tablecloths, small metal chairs
and four large white umbrellas to fend off the early
afternoon Tuscan sun. The initial course, or *antipasti*,
consisted of a spread of various typical Tuscan dishes:
golf ball-sized mozzarella paired with fresh tomatoes
cut in quarter-moons, *prosciutto di cinta senese* with

a light base of olive oil, large golden potato and pancetta *tortas*, and crostini with friggitelli, tomatoes, and aged balsamic vinegar. The *primi* was a pasta dish of circular spinach ravioli cooked to a slight crisp and covered with flakes of freshly grated parmesan in a base of light cream on the plate. To finish, they were served *dolci* in the form of small squares of rich and creamy tiramisu followed by espresso upon request. To drink with the *antipasti*, guests were offered a choice between a *rosata di casa* the color of the inside of a grapefruit and a *bianchi Toscana pinot grigio.* Copious amounts of *rosso di Montalcino* in unlabeled bottles were brought out for the *primi* and *dolci.* The lunch was, in a word, superb.

Some of the group opted for a short stroll around the small village to work off some of the meal, peek into surrounding stores selling sundresses and Tuscan pottery, and take in the views of some of the other small hilltop towns. Others opted to continue the attack on Il Leccio's supply of *rosso di Montalcino* and, once enough had been consumed, pass around a rogue pack of cigarettes that someone brought along. All recounted stories of the evening before and other joyous times. When the sun began its downward tilt, signifying time for the inevitable return to Montefollonico, and then back to everyone's respective homes the next day, they gathered for a group photo on the stone steps of the Pieve di San Michele Arcangelo across the square from Il Leccio. A beautiful juxtaposition; travelers in the midst of a day of celebratory debauchery in front of the old church.

As everyone loaded onto the bus, Marcus made some laughing noises and showed a half smile as he walked down the aisle. He found a vacant set of seats near the back, away from most everyone else, and plumped himself down. The world—his world—of truths, appearances, and opportunities had been shaken to its core and he had not yet found his footing. He kept replaying the conclusion of his conversation with Franz.

"Your call, Marcus: stay the course, which admittedly is a good one, or jump," Franz had said. "You have my email. If you are interested, send me a note by nine Tuesday morning, New York time, with the subject line 'Teaser,' and in the body of the email, 'Please send when available.' If not, good luck. No second chances here, so if I don't hear from you by the deadline, the offer expires." They'd shaken hands. Marcus looked as deeply into Franz's eyes as he could.

"Enjoy the wine tour," Franz said, turning on his heel. He walked back down the road from where they had come.

Could this be real? Could any of that be true?

There had been no time to think those thoughts right when his discussion with Franz ended, as Marcus was cutting it very close to the deadline to be on the bus to the wine tour at Poggio Antico. He'd half-jogged over the old cobblestone streets of the tiny village, past the forest-green wooden doors of the small buildings with tiny front courtyards with old benches overgrown with vines on their edges. He ran past full clotheslines hanging in front of the little apartment buildings and down the small hill into the central piazza. The bus had already started up, and Eliza from Relais La Costa, who was serving as a makeshift wedding weekend assistant, stood outside the bus holding a clipboard, with her right hand raised over her eyes scanning the village like an actor pretending to search the open ocean from the decks of a boat for a glimpse of something important out at sea.

Marcus waved a hand to catch Eliza's attention and made a show of scurrying up to the bus, adding a slight grimace on his face to communicate an apology.

"*Scusa*, Marcus Hugo," Marcus said as he hopped up the stairs onto the bus.

"Ah…okay…*allora*…Hugo, *si, grazie*." Eliza nodded to the driver and exclaimed, "*Tutto completo*, Enzo. *Andiamo!*" The bus door shut, and the driver, named Enzo apparently, proceeded with the beginning of the approximately fifteen-point turn to head back out of the Centro Storico and on the road to Brunello country.

There was light chatter among the guests on the bus, and lots of sunglasses were worn despite the relative cloud cover. Some whispering, some laughing as Marcus worked his way down the aisle. A very red-faced sister of the bride pretended to be in deep conversation with the bride herself as Marcus passed by and shot them both a cheeky smile and a slight raise of the eyebrows. He was invited to sit next to an old friend and was immediately enveloped into discussion of the shenanigans that occurred after he had left the night before.

As the bus made its way up and down the Tuscan hills, some green faces began appearing within the group. Just in time, the bus slowed down, turned onto a long, red-gravel driveway with tall cypress trees evenly lined up along each side, and after tunneling through came to a stop, as Enzo emphatically stated, "*Signore e signori, Poggio Antico! Grazie.*"

The tour was lovely, as they were treated to a short explanation of the history of the vineyard, an explanation of the Sangiovese grape and the Brunello di Montalcino DOCG distinction, a walk through the fermentation and packing facilities, and finally a stroll through the vines themselves. The red grapes were plump and plentiful, as due to it being late summer, the *vendemmia* was just around the corner. They were even invited to pick a grape off the vine and have a taste.

But the real fun began as the guests were ushered into the tasting room, a red brick outcropping with a terracotta roof and vines covering its sides. The distribution of samples of the vineyard's various types of wines, blends of Sangiovese, cabernet sauvignon and Petit Verdot, Rosso di Montalcino and, of course, the trademark bottles of Brunello di Montalcino had the same effect on the wedding party as tossing old, dry newspapers onto the embers of a long-burning fire: the slow accumulation of smoke and then the bursting forth of vibrant flames. Laughter, joking, and enthusiastic requests for more samples sprang forth as the celebratory and slightly inebriated tone from the night before set in.

Marcus requested a hefty pour of the Lemartine blend, the same one that the mysterious Mr. Arthur Franz had recommended and moved away from the group to a vantage point on the deck of the main building of the winery. Earlier on their visit, the tour guide had noted that on a clear day from this spot one could catch a glimpse of the Tyrrhenian Sea and the Arcipelago Toscano out to the west. Marcus couldn't see it, but the view over the perfectly lined vineyards and through the rolling green hills slanting down toward the coast was breathtaking, nonetheless.

Marcus twirled the crimson liquid around his glass, as the man who dispensed the wine had instructed. Further following instruction, he then took a few quick, dog-like sniffs to see if he could smell any noticeable flavors in the wine. Then he took a small sip, breathed in and out slightly, coughed as he nearly choked himself, and then swallowed. The taste was... *damn good*. He wasn't sure where that flavor description fit in the oenologist's catalog, but that's what it was. Franz had been right about the wine...*but what about all the rest of that?*

"I represent one of Peppercorn's largest shareholders and serve as their proxy on the investment management committee," Franz had continued. "There are a number of investments that the firm makes at the behest of this shareholder. These investments, sometimes, have ends that are not strictly financial in nature. I oversee these investments along with a team of other professionals that, not exclusively but principally, work together on these projects."

So, Marcus thought, *this must some type of sustainability focused "green fund" with a touchy-feely "good for the globe, good for us" mantra behind it*. He offered up a filtered version of this observation: "Okay, so, like an environment, social, governance-focused platform then?"

Franz chuckled slightly. "No, not an ESG platform. These investments are focused on other ends: the gathering of information, the development of relationships, the exertion of influence in favor of the shareholder's interests."

They were approaching the end of the gravel road that led back to Montefollonico's main street. Franz stopped and turned to face Marcus directly. A sudden sense of intensity and formality enveloped the discussion. "Marcus, what I'm about to say is confidential in nature beyond anything you have ever even conceived of. Should you tell anyone about this conversation, we will know. And rest assured, that won't be good for you. No matter what you end up deciding, as long as you keep this between us, there won't be any problems. I want to make that clear now, before I say anything further. If that's problematic for you, please go ahead and leave now." Franz opened his stance and extended his right arm up toward the main road.

Marcus was struck by the sudden gravity of the conversation and felt his heart beating intensely through his chest. This all seemed a bit ridiculous, but he was taken in by the seriousness of Franz's ultimatum. "Understood, Arthur. Please continue."

A slow nod of Franz's head, then, "I work, both directly and indirectly, for the Central Intelligence Agency of the United States of America. Through a series of blocker entities and holdings companies, a real portion of the CIA's investments are, in fact, managed by Peppercorn. From a financial perspective, the returns on the investments have been great. But from an intelligence-gathering perspective, the Peppercorn relationship has allowed us to do things that we've never been able to do before. And those returns have been unquantifiable in their benefits."

Thump. Thump. Thump. Marcus could hear his heart beating up through the temples of his head. His legs had turned to cement. *The CIA? The CIA is a shareholder in a major private equity firm?*

Franz glanced down at his watch. "Listen, you have ten minutes before you need to be on the bus. I'm going to speak, and I'd like for you to just listen."

CHAPTER 12

Montefollonico, Italy.
Sunday, June 29, 2014.

M OST OF THE GUESTS HAD FALLEN ASLEEP ON the way back to Montefollonico and were only temporarily roused when the bus stopped in the town's main square, and everyone shuttled back to their hotel rooms to resume their afternoon naps. Marcus was one of the last to get off the bus, and after thanking the newlyweds and offering them more congratulations, strolled back up the cobblestone street to the intersection with the gravel road. It was quiet there. The butterscotch sun dipped down behind the opposing hill towns to the west, the afternoon heat giving way to a slight evening breeze. Some dark purple and gray clouds rolling in over Lago Trasimeno from Umbria. It was just the setting Marcus needed to replay as much of Franz's narration from this afternoon at this very spot as he could recall.

"You know how the private equity world works, Marcus, so I'm sure you can see how our involvement with Peppercorn would be beneficial. It allows us to operate in a clandestine manner, to rub elbows with banks, large multinational companies and their executives, other investment funds, both well-known and off-the-radar, and access to meetings and discussions that no government agency would ever voluntarily be invited to. And it works to an astonishing level. Our Peppercorn companies have not only made us money, but they've allowed us to make inroads with organizations we've never been able to penetrate, and to gather information and accumulate leverage in a way that traditional CIA operations haven't been successful in doing."

Marcus had decided to give this man the benefit of the doubt, just for the sake of hearing him out, and, if nothing else, for Marcus's own entertainment value. This part made some sense; he could see how a private investor, especially a well-known and seemingly legitimate one like Peppercorn Capital, could open some doors that a diplomat or some rogue, Jason Bourne-like agent probably couldn't.

"Depending on the nature of the investment, we take different strategies to find a way to bring a benefit to our shareholder." Franz spoke in a more professional tone now, almost as if he was giving a management presentation to some potential investors into the fund. Apparently that also meant that Franz was not going to refer to the CIA by name anymore, using just *the Shareholder*. "That may mean the acquisition of a business that handles certain physical materials, often in more emerging markets-types of scenarios. It may mean doing a joint venture with a wealthy individual to build that relationship and gain access to some of his or her books and records. It may mean squeezing a competitor's business dry to make that competitor's ultimate owners lose large amounts of money. All things we've done before. We've found that certain industries —infrastructure, logistics, oil and gas, other natural resources—lend themselves quite nicely to these types of things."

Marcus could see the light coming through the door that Franz was slowly opening. His face apparently displayed that thought, because Franz stated, "Yes, so that's where you come in. Now, please don't take offense to this, but you are not the typical recruit for the Shareholder."

Marcus did take some offense, as he could imagine that his state school undergraduate and law background was one of the many things that made him not the typical recruit for this shareholder.

"But that's good, that's what we want. People won't expect you to be working for the Shareholder," Franz added.

"Gee, thanks," Marcus responded in a sarcastic tone.

"Should you express interest, there will be a plethora of granular details to follow," Franz responded with a wry smile, "but suffice it to say for now that you would initially serve in the capacity of an in-house counsel and, assuming you progress as we would expect, eventually you'd transition over to a business role as an investment professional. You'll still be doing legal work, and much of it will be very similar to what you are doing now at Macon Smith. Much of it will also be mind-numbingly boring. But your, umm, training, will involve the development of several other skills as well. Things you'll need to perform properly on the front lines of these investments."

Marcus immediately pictured himself in a white *karategi* executing a roundhouse leg kick, then again in a black suit with earmuffs at a shooting range as he fired off rounds from a pistol. *No, nothing like that…right?*

Franz interrupted Marcus's thoughts. "You will also need to further develop your cross-border experience, so there will be international travel involved and almost certainly international placement. Those may sound glamorous, but as I believe you well know, they usually aren't. They're lonely, challenging, and dull most of the time."

Marcus did know this, as he had spent six months working at a client's office in Cairo as a second-year associate. Lonely, challenging, and dull was an apt description.

"Additionally, there will be times where your safety will be in jeopardy. We've had some close calls on assignments before, and so you are fully aware of the risks involved, there was a fatality. That person was ill-prepared for this type of work and made some critical mistakes. But the threat is real."

This didn't bother Marcus, but he appreciated Franz's candor. Assuming all of this was even real, it made sense to him that risk and danger would be involved in this type of work. There had to be some tradeoff for the intrigue and excitement.

"One more thing, Marcus," Franz paused, glanced down the main road toward the center of Montefollonico, then returned to Marcus's gaze. "As much as I think this is the right line of work for you, and that you are the right fit to help us, you should hear it from someone else that you have a good, solid gig where you are now. The reason they turned you down for Paris was because they like you so much, and they view you as an integral part of their business going forward. They weren't trying to punish you; they're trying to hold on to you. You are very much on the partner-track. A few more years and you're there. Find a nice girl to settle down with, start a family, buy a house in Westchester with a yard for the kids to run around in. That's a good life, Marcus; it would make a lot of people happy."

Maybe this was Franz's best recruiting tool, Marcus thought, as that scene was anathema to him at this point in his life. *But…he wasn't wrong*. With the right person, the right job, there could be more good than bad in that type of life. He struggled to see that when he thought of some of his bosses who had the appearances of that type of life, as there was so much about them that he didn't want to imitate. *It would be different for him though, right?* He'd figure out a way to balance it all, to do it his way. That's what he would have to keep telling himself.

"Well, Marcus, you need to go. I've told you how to proceed from here." Franz jolted Marcus's mind back to reality. He had two minutes to catch the bus for the wine tasting.

Franz extended his hand and gave Marcus a solid handshake, accompanied by a penetrating look into Marcus's eyes. "It's your call Mr. Hugo. Nine a.m., Tuesday morning."

PART II

The Rise

CHAPTER 13

Paris, France.
Musée d'Orsay.
Friday, June 28, 2019.

MARCUS HUGO STEPPED OUT ONTO THE TERRACE of the Musée d'Orsay to take in the view of the River Seine. Ever since his Paris tour guide days when he had heard rumors about private events taking place on this terrace, he had dreamed of attending one. And here he was, in a crisply pressed and neatly tailored tuxedo, holding a glass of champagne, looking out across the Seine at some of the world's most renowned landmarks. *Ah!* He thought as he took a sniff of the sweet sparkling wine, then a long, fulfilling drink of the cold liquid. He felt the tiny bubbles break on his upper lip. He worked his gaze from left to right. It was half past nine at night and the Paris sky was still full of light, embossing each of the venues across the way with a golden outline. The Tuileries Gardens stretched out behind the Quai des Tuileries toward the pewter-colored rounded archways of the Rue de Rivoli in the distance. The courtyard of the Louvre, with its glass pyramid still glinting in the middle, was surrounded by balustrades adorned with statues of celebrated figures from French history such as Suger, Jean Racine, and Voltaire. They looked out, both welcoming and inspiring the masses that were still flocking in their direction. The Pont des Arts, the pedestrian bridge connecting the Left Bank to the east end of the Louvre, was adorned with people sitting atop blankets next to picnic baskets and holding small plastic cups filled with wine, chatting, laughing, and listening to the occasional acoustic guitar. The pointed end of the Île de la Cité sat below the equestrian statue of the great King Henry IV, *Henri Navarre*, ender of the religious wars and unifier of France, in the middle of the Pont Neuf, which was dotted with couples and groups of people letting their bare feet dangle over the wine-dark surface of the Seine. The Bateaux Mouches, the white, open-topped tourist boats, plowed their way through the river in both directions, emitting a faint noise of a programmed tour guide describing the sights in a host of widely spoken languages.

"*Marrkoooz, chin-chin!*" Capucine Devereux exclaimed as she extended a full flute of champagne while making her way out of the interior of the top floor onto the balcony to join her date. Capucine looked beautiful. She wore a black silk slip-dress with a scoop neckline, and slim straps under a trim white three-quarters sleeve black blazer. She clipped across the balcony in black stilettoes. She had a lean figure, naturally tan complexion, long black hair with razor-straight bangs, and sports-car-red lipstick. She had a Gaulish nose which looked as if it had been broken on more than one occasion and owllike greenish-brown eyes. Those eyes, typically covered by thick, black-rimmed glasses were laid bare for the evening's event, sparkled. Capucine was French to her core and even though she spoke impeccable English from a grammar and vocabulary perspective, her accent was alluringly thick.

"*Santé*," Marcus cooed back, as they clinked their glasses and took big sips of the refreshing bubbles.

"Beautiful, isn't it?" Capucine suggested as she glided out toward the railing and admired the view.

"Indeed," Marcus responded, then, unable to help himself and only because no one else was within earshot, he switched to English added in a faux-British accent, "The view is not bad either…"

He knew this was corny, but she seemed to enjoy these little quips. Capucine rolled her eyes and then flashed a small, open-mouthed smile at him. In a sincere tone, Marcus, switching back to French as was their custom, added, "You do look absolutely gorgeous, Capucine."

She blushed slightly and twitched her face a little, then looked back out over the river.

She exhaled deeply, then uttered, "I will miss it, you know—Paris. And I'm going to miss you too, Marcus."

This was Capucine's last weekend in Paris before moving to the US to study comparative literature at Columbia University in New York. She had studied French and English literature at university in Paris, then done some associate professorship teaching. She was now heading off to continue her work abroad to study American literature and teach French literature. She was an extended member of the esteemed Devereux family, which had achieved great wealth through the establishment of a French telecom empire, and she could have easily opted for a life of leisure and largesse. But she hadn't. She was a very hard worker and was passionate about discovering original thought and original ideas about literature. How had it been influenced? What were the motivations of the authors? What does this novel or short story tell us about the period in which it was written?

They had met about six months ago at a house party of one of Marcus's Peppercorn colleagues. Capucine had known Marcus's colleague since *le lyceé*. She and Marcus hit it off initially over small talk, and then further as she talked about her plans to move to New York and study American literature, and Marcus described his favorite selections from Mark Twain's *The Adventures of Huckleberry Finn*, and Robert Frost's

"Stopping by Woods on a Snowy Evening." A few weeks later, Marcus, after getting clearance from the necessary authorities within the Shareholder, tagged along with Capucine and a small group from that evening's party for a ski weekend in Bansko, Bulgaria of all places. They had been casually dating ever since. There was a certain comfort in their relationship, as they both knew it had a natural end date, which was now almost upon them.

Marcus felt a group of people coming up behind them, and turned to find his colleague, Alexandra Mouer, along with a clustering of lawyers from Dunworths, the English law firm hosting the evening's event. One of those lawyers was Bamba Diop, managing partner of the firm's Paris office and head of the natural resources group. Bamba was the reason that Alexandra and Marcus had made the prestigious list of clients invited to this select event. Marcus was currently working on a project with Bamba and his team, which had allowed the men to get to know each other a little better. Bamba, born and raised on the outskirts of Paris by parents from Senegal, was a brilliant lawyer, a hard worker, and a great listener. He had joined Dunworths as a trainee and stayed at the firm ever since. He'd consistently delivered excellent work product and a high volume of hours billed year after year and methodically moved up the ranks from associate to partner to senior management. He spoke selectively and poignantly. Marcus was also under the impression that there was something going on between Bamba and Alexandra.

Alexandra had turned awkward over the last few months when Marcus referred to Bamba or Dunworths. Tonight Alexandra's eyes had been on Bamba often, as had Bamba's been on her when he wasn't engaged in client conversation.

Marcus met Alexandra's eyes and slightly dipped his head to acknowledge her heading his way. His colleague, really one of his bosses, looked radiant in a satin emerald-colored halter gown that showcased her athletic figure and toned arms. Her blond hair fell stylishly below her shoulders with a slight curl at the bottom. Her face, somehow both angular and full, was tan and healthy. She seemed to be floating with confidence. The same mystique and magnetic pull that she exerted almost five years before when he first saw her at the Frankfurt airport had only increased over time. Marcus pressed his hand to the small of Capucine's back just at the top of the low dip in her dress as he turned her to join the group. The touch was not lost on Alexandra.

"Bamba, what an event!" remarked Marcus. "The finest law firm event I've attended, that's for sure. *Santé* to Dunworths! You certainly know how to take care of your clients."

This was not said in exaggeration. The event was indeed a real treat for those lucky enough to be invited.

Dunworths had provided car services to and from the d'Orsay for those not walking or taking the Metro. Upon arrival, the guests were treated to a glass of Veuve Cliquot and a welcome reception in the central sculpture gallery on the ground floor. The effect was magic. The stone and marble sculptures, surrounded by attendees buzzing with restrained excitement and wearing their best colorful summer gowns and black-tie ensembles, was a scene worthy of its own repro-duction on a canvas. The gold crown molding along the sidewalls and giant gold clock above the entryway, mixed with the windows that allowed the early eve-ning light through, created a beautiful open, nega-tive space. This reminded the visitor that the d'Orsay was the old Gare d'Orsay, housing the Paris-Orléans Railway. And, like Grand Central Station and Milano Centrale, the Gare d'Orsay had been a functional work of art.

The welcome reception was followed by an efficient but enjoyable guided tour of the Impressionists Gallery, where Marcus and Capucine lingered over Monet's *Rue Montorgueil* and *Les Coquelicots*, and Renoir's *Bal du Moulin de la Galette*. From there, some escargot in garlicherb butter, Provençale stuffed squid, and duck *pâté en croute* paired with a choice of Bandol rosé, Côtes de Jura or…more champagne. It was just the type of menu arrangement for allowing yourself to get over-served in front of just the crowd you'd never want to do that with. *But well worth it*, thought Marcus, as he drained his glass of Jura pinot noir before absconding to the terrace with another flute of champagne.

"*Merci beaucoup, Monsieur Hugo, Mademoiselle Devereux*," gently replied Diop, zapping Marcus's attention back to the present as they all clinked their glasses together and imbibed their champagne. *Diop looks rather handsome in his tuxedo*, Marcus thought, *and the man plays quite the host*. He had been working his way from client to client all evening long. And doing so not in a glad-handed *welcome to my party* kind of way, but rather like a priest genuinely greeting his flock on their way out of a Sunday service and eagerly listening to what they had to say.

So it was to Marcus's surprise when Diop interjected, "Mr. Hugo, may I have a word with you please?" He ushered Marcus back over toward the railing of the terrace, out of hearing distance of the rest of the group or anyone else.

"Bamba, please, call me Marcus," he said, to regain some footing.

"Of course, Marcus," Diop replied, continuing to move the two of them away from the crowd. He looked over each shoulder carefully, then quietly advised, "Mauro Broccatelli just arrived. He and his date, Signorina Antonia Ravello, are enjoying a private tour of the Impressionists gallery now and should be out on the terrace in about twenty minutes. I'll make sure to casually introduce you, if you could just pass by when I'm talking to them." Diop bluntly added, "You'll know it's him."

"Yes, thank you, Bamba. I'm sure I will," Marcus responded while raising his eyebrows. He didn't need to tell Bamba that he knew exactly what Mauro Broccatelli and Antonia Ravello looked like—and a whole lot more about them.

"And Marcus, we finished the report you requested for Project Chopin," Diop continued, "A member of our team sent it over to you earlier this evening."

"Yes, I saw that. Thank you, Bamba." Marcus grimaced a bit before adding, "I appreciate your team getting that done in a timely fashion. It allows me the pleasure of spending all day with it tomorrow. I'll give you and our financial modelers my comments and follow up questions so we can submit our initial bid on Tuesday." The grimace was authentic, as the prospect of spending an entire Saturday in June in the Peppercorn office reviewing a due diligence report was not appealing. One of the many reminders that the unique nature of this job did not exempt Marcus from grunt work or other mundane day-to-day duties.

A HALF HOUR later Diop was listening intently as Mauro Broccatelli was giving a description accentuated by numerous hand gestures, some short and firm, others wild gesticulations. Alexandra looked across the small conversational circle to make quick eye contact with Marcus and provide a near-imperceptible nod. Marcus excused himself from the group, whispered something in Capucine's ear that caused her to suppress a smile, and casually worked his way toward Diop and Broccatelli. He stopped short to catch some of their conversation. Broccatelli spoke in French, with assistance from Diop on a few technical terms and compound past and future tenses. He was explaining to Diop what "really happened" in the breakdown of the Broccatelli family's recent failed attempt to purchase a northern Italian football team. Listening to Broccatelli speak made Marcus recall the pithy quote attributed to Jorge Luis Borges: "an Argentine is an Italian that speaks Spanish, thinks they are French but wants to be English." When Broccatelli's explanation concluded with, *"c'est pour ça que nous n'avons pas passé un accord!"* Marcus took his cue to step in. Diop looked truly relieved to see him.

"AH! MARCUS HUGO! I want to introduce you to Mr. Mauro Broccatelli. Mauro's family is involved in the energy industry." *That is an understatement*, Marcus thought to himself. Diop continued, "Marcus's firm is fairly active in that field as well."

Broccatelli immediately glanced down to the white nametag on Marcus's left lapel with large black block letters—*Marcus Hugo, Managing Director, Peppercorn Capital.*

What a wonderful tool these nametags are, Marcus thought, *effectively signaling whether this is someone I should get to know or not waste one more second on...*

Diop had been speaking in English, the common language of many of the event's attendees, and Broccatelli replied in the same language. "Ah yes, Peppercorn Cap-i-tal," he spoke the last three syllables slowly and drawn out, as if referring to the team from the lower division that somehow upset his club's perfect season. Broccatelli was clearly comfortable speaking English, but like many Argentines, he did so with a very thick accent. "You are the guys that sold your Argentine pipelines business to Greyshore instead of us."

Marcus, intimately familiar with the transaction, assessed that statement as having some degree of accuracy but substantially lacking in detail. *No matter, it sounded good.* Marcus shrugged his shoulders and replied with a smile, "They were the higher bidder. Better for you in the long run though, that one didn't end well for Greyshore." Peppercorn had sold the business to Greyshore Partners, a behemoth American private equity firm, at what turned out to be the top of the market for Argentine oil and gas. Greyshore had ended up selling the same business a few years later at a quarter of the price they had paid Peppercorn. Greyshore's buyer was none other than the Broccatellis.

"Yes, I guess you're right," Broccatelli responded as he extended his hand toward Marcus. "Mauro Broccatelli," he established, as if noting that the earth was round. No company name to be added to further identify himself. "Nice to meet you, Marcus."

At that moment, Broccatelli's date appeared by his side. "And this is Antonia Ravello." Ravello leaned forward as she and Marcus traded air kisses by their cheeks. She eyeballed Marcus's nametag as she pulled away and confusion overtook her face. She glanced over questioningly at Broccatelli as he explained rapidly in Italian something about working in private equity.

To describe Broccatelli and Ravello as a power couple would not do them justice. Antonia Ravello was the heiress to one of Milan's most well-known fashion houses. She was a model herself and had begun taking over certain aspects of the family's fashion business, most notably their social media accounts. She was, for sure, very pretty, but not jaw-droppingly so. She had naturally dark hair flecked with blond highlights, worn completely flipped over the top of her head from one side to the other, and dark eyes and eyebrows, along with an olive complexion and the requisite slim model's figure. She wore a pinkish-violet gown that displayed her family's recognizable knit patterns.

Broccatelli was well-placed by her side. He was impeccably coiffed, overwhelmingly so, like a professional athlete trying to shake their informal disposition and pivot into the business world. He had short, black hair perfectly parted and neatly sitting atop a chiseled visage of high cheekbones, an angular nose, and a marble jaw. His natural state was expressionless, and the formation of his wolfish smile seemed to require focused effort. He had deep, dark-brown, almost-black eyes. He wore a tightly cut, midnight-blue dinner jacket with black peak lapels and detailing over a white tuxedo shirt and satin black bow tie. His chocolate-colored pebbled calfskin loafers were clearly custom-made.

Capucine honored Marcus's whispered request and arrived next to him right on cue. She clearly caught Broccatelli's eye, who himself in turn caught a different type of eye from Ravello. Marcus made introductions all around and, upon discovering that she was a Devereux, Broccatelli and Ravello engaged Capucine in the type of excited small talk and name game that was commonplace for members of elite clans like *los Broccatelli*, *les Devereux*, and *i Ravelli*. Capucine abhorred these conversations, but she had experienced enough of them and had enough tact to politely participate. Recognizing that Diop had also been forgotten about, Marcus deftly mouthed *merci* around the outside of the circle, to which Diop lightly dipped his head and replied with an inaudible "*je vous en prie.*"

Marcus's eyes were drawn to a passing woman's firm back laid bare by the cut of her dress below shoulder-length blond hair, then interpreted the message conveyed by Alexandra's glimpse as she turned to enter the top floor: *Contact has been made. Don't linger. Leave him wanting to know more.*

CHAPTER 14

South Texas.
February 2015.

IT HAD BEEN A LONG, DESOLATE DRIVE, BUT HE was nearly there. The greenery and cedar trees outside of San Antonio were giving way to the low brush and cacti of South Texas, and he'd be arriving at the Hampton Inn in Carrizo Springs within the hour. He didn't mind the drive; it gave him time to think about the past year and think about the task ahead of him over the next few days. Plus, he was used to it. Growing up in Texas, those long road trips were rites of passage. It became a part of who you were: surveying the state through the front windshield.

He had sworn off smokeless tobacco after law school, but when he stopped to fill up the rental car a few hours back, he bought a can. It was a nasty habit, and he was glad he had given it up, but something about cruising along those roads with country music on the radio and a pouch of mint Skoal under his lip just felt right. It didn't feel so right in the overpriced suit, dress shirt, tie, and dark-brown loafers though. *Should've changed before I left Houston*, Marcus thought.

He popped in one last pouch for the final part of the drive and promised to throw the can out when he got to the hotel. Last summer, he had gone to Italy to forget about work and celebrate his friend's wedding. Now here he was, attending a private equity oil and gas conference in Houston one day, driving down to try to buy into an exploration and production company in the Eagle Ford Shale the next. All so that he could obtain the data the Shareholder wanted on oil and gas purchases and the cash flow of the Northern Mexican drug cartels. He shifted uncomfortably in his seat, thinking about the handgun he had found waiting for him in the glove compartment of this rental SUV. Then he put both hands on the wheel, pushed the accelerator down and turned the volume of his radio up a few ticks, narrowed his eyes on the road ahead, and thought back on the wild, unexpected ride that had brought him here.

MARCUS WASTED LITTLE time in getting back to Arthur Franz regarding his proposal after returning to New York from the wedding in Italy. The deadline for Marcus to respond had been nine a.m. on that following Tuesday, and Marcus had sent his simple response in the manner Franz had instructed ('Teaser,' and in the body of the email, 'Please send when available') well before the clock struck nine o'clock. What followed was a very formal recruiting process over the next few months, which required multiple phone interviews and in-person office visits to Peppercorn Capital's listed offices in both Manhattan and Washington, D.C. There was even back-and-forth negotiation over Marcus's salary, although this was more perfunctory than authentic, as Marcus was very pleased with the sizeable increase in salary that he was being offered. At Franz's suggestion, Marcus even went so far as to do the right thing and approach the partners on his team within Macon Smith and talk to them about the opportunity with Peppercorn and the pros and cons of leaving law firm life for an in-house counsel role at a large private equity firm. Because Marcus was considering leaving the firm for a current client, he would have the ability to influence which outside counsel Peppercorn selected for their legal services—as evidenced by the widening eyes and salivating mouths of the Macon Smith partners—and so the partners were receptive and understanding, as opposed to giving the immediate cold shoulder that historically characterized any similar discussions when a Macon Smith associate was thinking about lateraling to a different law firm.

The final Peppercorn interview took place in D.C. Initially it was scheduled at the listed Peppercorn office in Foggy Bottom, but it quickly was moved out to Langley, Virginia. Franz had met Marcus in the Peppercorn office himself, then ushered him out a back door into a black Mercedes waiting with a running engine in the alley behind the building.

When they passed the fringes of Arlington, Franz explained, "I want you to see the headquarters and the training facility before you formally accept. You'll be coming out here for about a week each month during the first year, so it's only fair that you get a taste for it all before you sign on the dotted line."

Langley was pretty much what Marcus had expected. Lots of white walls and glass, multiple computer screens on each of the hundreds of desks spread across the main floor, and a generally sterile smell permeated the entire place. It looked like one of the giant trading floors that he had seen at some of his clients' offices. He had taken the time to read some CIA exposé books in the months since his recruitment had begun, so he had an idea what he was in for. The personnel at Langley did some additional background checks and conducted another fingerprint test and retina scan... all very official-feeling. Marcus half expected them to walk him into a room and force him to shoot some unknown prisoner who was an alleged terrorist, but instead Franz invited him on a walk outdoors in one of the parks surrounding the main building.

It was mid-September, and the infamous D.C. humidity was pervasive. Franz removed his suit coat for the walk and Marcus did the same. There was a faint murmur of traffic from the nearby George Washington Memorial Parkway coupled with late-morning bird-song from the trees above. There was no one else out walking these paths, so Franz's and Marcus's own foot-steps were audible as well. The smell of freshly cut grass was a welcome change.

Franz broke the relative silence suddenly and di-rectly. "The intelligence world has changed greatly in recent years, Marcus. Our agents have become pre-dictable and largely ineffective. You have a chance to help us change that."

Marcus nodded understandingly. Then he thought to himself, *This is probably the time I'm supposed to ask any final questions I have…What is my career trajectory here? What are the characteristics of a successful agent? What do most people do after the CIA (Gulp) Is there an after the CIA?* These were the questions all of the inter-view books and the business school career counselors told you to ask in any interview, but Marcus knew those were pointless questions. Franz didn't know the answers because there were no answers. This was a new project and where it would go from here was completely undefined and unlimited. The hairs on the back of Marcus's neck stood up with excitement just thinking about it.

Franz paused, studied Marcus's face, then some-how managed to convey that he understood and appreciated that Marcus had no further questions. He looked Marcus up and down and nodded his head in satisfaction.

"Well, shall we make it official?" Franz asked, formally extending his hand out to Marcus. Marcus studied the hand, looked up into Franz's eyes, which betrayed no emotion. Then, fighting as hard as he could to keep the corners of his mouth from rising up into a giddy smile, Marcus replied, "Yes, sir." He extended his own hand to Franz's for a hearty shake.

Marcus led the way back to the main office building to begin the return trip to downtown D.C. On a haphazard look back to locate Franz, he saw that Franz was looking out into the forest toward the Potomac, and for the first time that Marcus could remember, he had the makings of a guarded smile on his face.

LIFE AS IN-HOUSE counsel for Peppercorn Capital was initially very much like life as inhouse counsel at any other private equity firm. Marcus showed up to work every day, now in the slightly more casual attire of the Manhattan Private Equity Uniform: chinos or slacks, a button-down, collared shirt without a tie, and some form of fuzzy fleece vest, jacket, or both. He was able to move the suits and ties to the back of his closet for more formal meetings and special occasions. Marcus's day-to-day work consisted of reviewing and revising the legal documents for Peppercorn's various transactions. He discussed legal structures with the various deal teams he was working with. He managed outside counsel for the live transactions Peppercorn had going. And he dutifully reported up to Peppercorn's general counsel and head of compliance. As he had been instructed by Franz, Marcus also spent portions of the day working closely on the business side of Peppercorn's investments. He took a basic financial modeling class each week to get a better grip on the ways that Peppercorn's investments actually made money and participated in calls and discussions regarding the advantages of debt or equity in the capital structure of a particular investment. As Franz had explained during recruitment, Marcus ultimately needed to be one of the faces of Peppercorn Capital so he could be a main point of contact with prospective business partners, but also to further develop his cover. To bring that migration from back office to the forefront to bear, Marcus had to slowly learn the business side of private equity, all the while maintaining his legal skills' sharpness and satisfying those duties.

Marcus put the long hours in and lost himself in the work. He didn't try to learn it all in one day, but instead focused on being a solid contributor each day and letting that momentum build. He knew that people often overestimated what can be accomplished in one day but underestimated what can be accomplished over months of sustained hard work. And this included his monthly visits down to Langley for a handful of days at a time. He received basic training in handling weapons, in hand-to-hand combat, in tailing someone or losing a tail, and in reading the behavioral patterns of others while masking his own. To maintain the façade of working from Peppercorn's D.C. office, he made the same daily clandestine trek to Langley that he had taken with Franz during his final recruiting visit. He stayed at the Ritz-Carlton Georgetown and made a point to visit the lobby bar, to be seen at the hotel restaurant, and to network with some of his law school friends who had made their careers in D.C. over drinks or dinners at D.C. hotspots. Each morning he got up and went for runs along the Georgetown Waterfront Park by the Potomac, past the new high-end restaurants and modern apartment buildings springing up in the background, onto the relative peace and quiet of the Capital Crescent Trail or the Chesapeake and Ohio Canal Towpath. Surrounded by greenery, he felt the dew on the grass underfoot and breathed in the fresh air, interrupted only by birds chirping and the occasional cadence of a coxswain calling a crew of rowers into rhythm through the mist slowly rising off the river. During these runs Marcus would reflect on all he had learned so far and try to ready himself for whatever new challenges his training held for him that day. From an outsider's perspective, he was "doing" D.C. as any other young, hungry private equity professional would.

In early January, the first opportunity to lead a Peppercorn investment landed on Marcus's desk. Presidente Petroleum, an up-and-coming exploration and production company based in Houston with large swathes of leasehold interests in South Texas along the Mexican border, in the famed Eagle Ford Shale play, was rumored to be looking for a partner to invest capital into their business and help them double the amount of oil and gas wells that they planned to drill. Marcus was familiar with Presidente from growing up in Texas, as it was owned by the Ramirez family, a very well-connected Texas-Mexican family that had bought up chunks of land in South Texas for their ranching operations years ago and turned to oil and gas with the discovery of the Eagle Ford Shale. The Ramirez family had become extremely wealthy but had also done a lot for the immigrant community in South Texas. One member of the family even made a surprising run as a candidate for Governor of Texas, only being narrowly defeated at the ballot box. A number of Ramirez family members had moved back to Mexico and settled in Monterrey, where they ran a successful real estate development company.

During the first wave of development in the Eagle Ford Shale, from about 2005–2010, Presidente had become the poster child for success in the region. But since then, many Eagle Ford producers had struggled mightily, as the center of the oil and gas world had shifted west to the Permian Basin in far West Texas and southern New Mexico. The Permian offered oil and gas wells with higher concentrations of oil, as opposed to natural gas, which was more plentiful in the Eagle Ford. Oil had proved much more profitable, as natural gas had ironically fallen prey to the success of those drilling for it due to the resulting massive oversupply in the market. Certain parts of the Eagle Ford Shale had also been subject to attacks by members of Mexican drug cartels, creating explosions, capturing and murdering workers, and tapping into the pipelines transporting natural gas and stealing it for themselves to use or sell on the black market back across the border. While Presidente had been subject to the sting of natural gas price declines, they had somehow avoided the Mexican drug cartel problems of their competitors.

The current market chatter was that Presidente had learned their lesson and were now focused on drilling more profitable wells with higher concentrations of oil. But to do that, they needed to drill lots of wells over the next few years in order to maintain their vast mineral interest holdings. And to drill those wells, they needed an investment partner to help share the cost and the risk.

Marcus was told to review the initial information received by Peppercorn from Presidente's investment bankers, and then dig deeper. He was to work with some of the Peppercorn associates to come up with an investment model that could justify a partnership with Presidente. He had until mid-February, when a handful of Peppercorn professionals, Marcus included, would travel to Houston for an annual oil and gas investment conference. If Marcus was able to put forth a convincing argument to invest with Presidente prior to the conference, he would extend his Texas trip by a few days to go meet with the Ramirez family directly and visit their South Texas operations.

A few weeks later, while Marcus was on his January visit to D.C., Arthur Franz appeared next to him in the cafeteria in Langley during lunch. Franz showed up unannounced, and as quietly as a cat. Marcus was sitting alone, taking a bite of his sandwich and glancing at the newspaper one moment, and suddenly hearing Franz's voice the next.

"We think they are quietly selling oil and gas to the cartels. They may also be laundering money for them and looking the other way while the cartels transport drugs across their lands into San Antonio and Corpus Christi," Franz said, as if he had been sitting there the whole time, nonchalantly looking down at Marcus's newspaper, then up to the translucent roof of the atrium that housed the cafeteria. Franz added, "For now, we want to focus on the oil and gas, not the drugs."

Recovering from the astonishment of finding Franz, or anyone for that matter, silently seated next to him, Marcus eased his way into the discussion.

"You mean Presidente, I take it. Or, the Ramirez family, I guess I should say." Marcus placed his sandwich on his plate and dabbed the corners of his mouth with a napkin.

Franz didn't respond immediately, as he was following the flight of a bird that had snuck into the building and was now trapped, flying from one end of the atrium to the other in search of an exit. "Poor guy," Franz stated distractedly, then breathed in deeply and audibly exhaled out of his nose. "We need proof Marcus. It shouldn't be hard to find the holes in their financial statements, likely some cute accounting metric. Presidente should be bankrupt by now from losses stemming from low natural gas prices, but they continue to somehow show a profit and pay out huge dividends to the family and other members of management. But we need to see physical proof, not just identify accounting tricks. If they are getting paid by the cartels, there has to be a record of it somewhere. And that is what we need you to find."

Marcus nodded, the full understanding of why Peppercorn Capital would want to take a risk on South Texas oil and gas fields washing over him like a crashing wave. "I see," he replied. Franz gave him a quizzical look, as if to say, *do you?*

Marcus finished his thought, "If Presidente is doing business with the cartels, and we buy into Presidente, we can have access to the amount of fuel the cartels are buying, the intermediaries they are using, their bank accounts, personnel movement, the works."

Marcus saw this clearly now; it wasn't about trying to punish the Ramirez family; they were just the minnows. This was about having an open book to the movements of the whales, the deadly, violent, and internationally powerful Northern Mexican drug cartels. It was genius, really—if one was willing to overlook the fact that they would be indirectly funding those cartels through this operation. *But perhaps that's how this whole thing works…*Marcus thought to himself, beginning to realize that he had much to learn if he was to become an effective member of the Shareholder's cadre within Peppercorn Capital.

Satisfied that the mission had been conveyed to Marcus, Franz gave him a light pat on the back and rose from his seat. As a parting shot, he stated, "You make the financial model work. I'll get the investment committee to agree to grant you negotiating authority, which will give you two days in South Texas after the Houston visit. You find the information. And *when* you do, we'll do the deal with Presidente." Franz paused before turning to leave, then added, "And you, Mr. Hugo, may find yourself on your first board of directors."

***

BY THE TIME Marcus and a select few of his Peppercorn colleagues landed in Houston in late February for the annual oil and gas conference, Marcus had two meetings on his agenda that he was particularly looking forward to. One meeting was purely business: Marcus's scheduled visit with the Ramirez family in South Texas to view some of Presidente's properties and potentially negotiate an investment by Peppercorn into a new joint venture with them. Marcus and his team had created a structure and financial model that was convincing to Peppercorn's investment committee, and the committee had extended Marcus negotiating authority and instructed him to meet with the Ramirez family. The other meeting was more social: a catch-up over drinks with his good friend and former fellow Big Tire Bike Tours guide, Graham Curry.

Marcus and Graham had arranged to meet the day before Marcus was to make his long drive southwest to Carrizo Springs for the Presidente meeting. Graham had sounded surprised that Marcus was coming to town for the conference; he didn't realize Marcus had such an interest in the US oil and gas business. They planned to meet in the lobby bar of one of downtown Houston's newer hotels. Marcus walked the ten blocks from the convention center where the conference was being held to the hotel, and even though it was late February, he was damp with sweat. He crossed over the modern light-rail tracks that the hotel faced, with near-empty passenger cars shuttling by and shook his head slightly as he thought about this light-rail and the hundreds of other projects like it in cities across the US that had become popular over the past decade. It was as if the real utility of these projects were meaningless; only the sentiment that they were features of a "modern city" seemed to matter. He discarded this thought as he nodded at the smartly dressed hotel doorman and breezed into the lobby.

This hotel was a good choice. There was a buzzy atmosphere inside, as the lobby bar seemed like a makeshift breakout room for the conference. Marcus recognized a number of individuals he had seen earlier in the day. They were seated at the bar, at high-top tables, and around plush couches and lounge chairs, all networking, catching up with old friends, and trying to put deals together. He took one of the two seats he had reserved at the bar and waited for Graham to arrive. Marcus scanned the room again: there was a guy Marcus went to high school with, chatting away in one corner; there was one of his college fraternity brothers just walking into the lobby with another of Marcus's college acquaintances; and finally, there was one of Marcus's law school classmates, who had made a beeline for Houston after leaving Charlottesville, entertaining a group of clients around a large table at the front. Marcus couldn't help but chuckle; all of these guys that he had grown up with and known from other parts of his life now made up part of the fabric of the US oil and gas business. *Incredible,* Marcus thought to himself, comically, *and somewhat terrifying, to be honest.*

Just then, Marcus saw the round, unassuming face of Graham Curry pass through the front door of the lobby. Graham was dressed in slate-gray chinos and a royal-blue and white gingham shirt covered by a black fleece pullover, which had a nearly unnoticeable emblem of Graham's company stitched onto the front left side. His attire was a stark contrast to Marcus's tailored charcoal business suit, light-blue dress shirt, and dark navy designer tie. Meetings and conferences, presenting the prospect of seeing "other people" outside of his private equity firm, were some of the few events that Marcus broke out his expensive suits for. Graham systematically surveyed the room, and, imperceptibly identifying Marcus's location, quietly made his way to the open chair next to Marcus. Graham didn't show the need to make eye contact, or nod, or wave to the numerous people in the room he probably knew, he just kept his head down and moved from point A to point B. But when he reached Marcus, Graham showed a warm smile and gave him a firm handshake and thorough bear hug.

The two old friends ordered beers and caught up on each other's personal lives. They had kept in touch over email and text messages but had rarely seen one another over the past ten years from the time they were nearly inseparable roaming the streets of Paris and its environs. They laughed heartily as they shared memories of their year together as guides: tours gone awry, interesting side trips to other European cities, nights that turned wilder than either one of them had planned. As they ordered up a second round, their conversation turned to their professional careers.

"I was curious as to why you were attending the conference; didn't think Macon Smith did too much work with oil and gas companies," Graham noted, "but then I saw your email address and signature block... Peppercorn Capital, huh? You hadn't even told me you changed jobs."

I didn't really tell much to anyone, Marcus thought before responding.

"Yeah, man, it all happened very quickly. I thought I'd be at Macon Smith at least long enough to go for partner, but there was some stuff going on there that I wasn't thrilled about, and coincidentally, right at that time, a recruiter from Peppercorn approached me. The more I thought about it, the more I felt it was a better fit for what I want to do."

"Hmm, interesting," Graham replied, then shot Marcus a look that made it clear he wasn't getting off that easily. "What was going on at Macon Smith that you didn't like?"

Marcus smiled and shook his head lightly. "I should have known that the stock explanation wasn't going to work for you...well, to be honest, I was slated to move to Macon Smith's Paris office last year, and sort of develop my practice there. They turned that down and said it would be better for my partnership prospects to stay in New York."

"Really?" Graham replied, feigning shock. "You would have been perfect for that role. Just liked we used to talk about...man, that's crazy." Graham shook his head with a slight exaggeration, took a sip of his beer, and looked down at the top of the bar to avoid eye contact with him.

Marcus bristled slightly, seeing Graham's reaction, and having a flash of recognition from one of his training sessions in Langley. He quickly shook the thought away and continued the conversation.

"Yeah, I was pretty bummed. But just then, the Peppercorn opportunity came my way. They were looking for someone to do all the legal work, but eventually transition to the business side. They've got offices all over the world—a big one in Paris actually—and they really value global mobility. And so far, it's been great. Really challenging, but great. I'm learning so much."

Graham offered a closed-mouth smile, then replied, "Wow, sounds like it was perfect timing."

Perfect indeed...Marcus observed internally, never really having made that connection.

Graham continued, "Well, that's great man. Really happy for you. But what are you doing down here, in the oil and gas world?"

Marcus tilted his head slightly, replying, "Good question."

There was no fooling Graham when it came to the energy business. As a petroleum engineer and now a project manager at one of the super-major oil and gas companies, Graham actually knew what he was talking about, which Marcus had quickly come to realize was often not the case with other energy professionals.

"Peppercorn has a number of other energy and in-frastructure investments, renewables, toll roads, some port projects, but, between us, and as evidenced by our team's presence here, we are looking at some more traditional oil and gas opportunities. My job is to come down here, use my background and network, and try to uncover some leads..." Marcus went to take a sip of his beer, then paused, looked back at Graham, and with a smile added, "Got anything for us?"

Graham couldn't contain an authentic belly laugh. "My, how quickly you've assumed the role of typical private equity guy. Just out here sourcing deals!"

It was true, and they both had a good laugh about it. Marcus turned the conversation to Graham's career.

"And what about you, Graham? I'm surprised I was able to catch you stateside. You sticking around for a while, or is it back to Papua New Guinea?"

Graham chuckled and shook his head gently. "No, no more of good ole' Port Moresby for me. I'll be here in Houston for a while…"

"And then…?" Marcus interjected. Since Graham had started working with his current employer after their time in Paris, Marcus had known Graham to have worked on a drill ship in the Persian Gulf, managed existing production in the Niger Delta region of Nigeria, and, most recently, led an exploration and production project in Papua New Guinea. He doubted Graham would stay in Houston very long.

"And then…," Graham acknowledged, "probably Colombia. We've got some refineries in Cartagena and a terminal near Barranquilla that are underperforming. Someone needs to go straighten them out. But that won't be for a few years. We are required to put in eighteen months in our home country between expat assignments. Plus, it would be good for me to put some face time in around our top brass here in Houston. I'll probably manage the project remotely from here for a while, make a trip down there every few months."

Marcus smiled, shook his head, then leaned back in his barstool and looked up to the sky, before uttering, "Ah, Colombia! You're killing me, man!" Then he chuckled, and added, "And I thought I was the one who was going to be living the expat lifestyle…"

Graham finished his beer, then calmly and assuredly looked at Marcus. "Don't worry, Marcus, you will."

THE WALK BACK to the Hampton Inn from Miguelito's Mexican Grill and Cantina was a short one, so Marcus was able to turn down the offer for a ride from Omar Ramirez in good faith. They shook hands heartily, and Marcus promised to be back in touch with Omar early the following week. *The visit with Presidente was a good one*, Marcus concluded as he neared the hotel. Guillermo "Willy" Ramirez, the current patriarch of the Ramirez family, and Omar, Willy's eldest son, had spent the last two days giving Marcus their full attention. They walked Marcus through Presidente's business and growth plans in impressive detail. Both Willy and Omar were incredibly sharp, down-to-earth yet sophisticated, and very plugged in to their business. Willy had a background as a landman, the person in charge of securing legal title to oil and gas properties, and he knew the history of ownership of just about every acre of mineral interests in South Texas. Omar had studied finance at the University of Texas, and he had overlapped with Marcus for a few years. They actually recognized each other from long hours in the business school's reading room but had never formally met before two days ago. Omar's financial acumen was a perfect complement to Willy's land background, and Marcus frankly assessed them as ideal partners for Peppercorn to go into business with.

Omar drove Marcus all over Presidente's properties in a big, white F-250 pickup truck with *Presidente Petroleum* emblazoned on the sides, and Willy served as master of ceremonies. They showed him their oil and gas wells, ranching operations, raw land they owned, and the central field office. It was this field office that Marcus was now planning to return to. If Presidente had records of its transactions with the Northern Mexican drug cartels, that's where they would be.

As any savvy and discerning potential investor might do, Marcus had bluntly asked Willy and Omar how it was that Presidente had been spared the attacks and security issues that plagued other Eagle Ford producers. Omar became quiet, and in a practiced manner deferred to Willy. Willy paused a moment, looking out over the vast horizon of flat brown land, spotted with greenery here and there, before responding. His response was letter-perfect, and clearly well-rehearsed. He touted the top-notch security equipment and practices of Presidente's employees, the integrity and quality of both the products they used and the Presidente people that used them, and most importantly, the Ramirez family's long-standing commitment to the people of South Texas.

"It is not lost on us how lucky we have been when it comes to evading issues with the cartels, but we believe that part of that comes from the goodwill and respect we've generated with the people of Mexican descent here in South Texas."

Had this been a gubernatorial campaign speech, this is where Willy would have paused for a rousing applause.

It was the look on Omar's face during Willy's soliloquy that told Marcus all he needed to know: Omar had looked down at his boots and the floorboard of the pickup truck, then briefly back at the road ahead of him, and finally sideways out of the driver's side window. Willy's response was articulate and probably accurate, but undoubtedly incomplete. Marcus was sure that the Ramirez family had a side deal with the cartels, now he just needed to find proof.

Marcus's room at the Hampton Inn was on the ground floor, in the corner farthest away from both the front desk and the parking lot on the side of the building. He wasn't overly concerned with being watched, but he figured the front desk attendant had been paid a little extra to report on Marcus's comings and goings, and that the Ramirez family would have easy access to the Hampton Inn's surveillance cameras. So earlier in the day, Marcus had moved his car to a neighboring parking lot a few buildings down. Upon returning to his room after dinner, he gathered a few belongings and slipped out the window of his bathroom and made for his car. Before turning the ignition, he checked the glove compartment to make sure that the handgun that had been hidden beneath the vehicle manuals was still there. Assured that it was, he started the car and began his route to the Presidente field office he had visited earlier that day.

The field office was about a half hour away, and Marcus killed his car's headlights as he turned off the state highway onto the dirt side road that marked the final hundred yards to reach the office. While Presidente may have taken security seriously with respect to their actual oil and gas infrastructure, they clearly did not have the same approach for the field office. Marcus had noticed this on his earlier visit and was relieved. *But after all*, he thought, *there wasn't that much in the field office worth locking up, so there probably wasn't a need for heavy security.*

There was one small surveillance camera though, so Marcus had parked the car a ways off in the distance, and made the last part of his arrival on foot around the back end. The field office was akin to two trailer homes bolted together, with an air conditioning unit and a large dumpster along one side of the building. These provided Marcus cover from the camera, and he huddled behind them as he tucked his gun into the waistband of his jeans and eyeballed the window he planned to enter through. He extracted a small flashlight and took a second to catch his breath. Here he was, his first "mission," and probably the easiest one he would ever have, and his heart was beating through his chest. He took a few deep breaths, then took in the silence of the pitch-black plains around him. He smelled the dust kicking up off the ground from the wind. He crouched and readied himself to open the window and make his entrance, when he thought he heard a movement off in the bushes. He recoiled and pressed his back quietly against the dumpster.

What the hell was that? Marcus thought. He took two more deep breaths and listened again...nothing. Marcus looked around one more time and saw nothing. He didn't know whether to be embarrassed or paranoid, but he finally decided to get on with the search. He quietly walked up to the window, slid it open wide enough to squeeze through, and hopped up to pull himself inside. He left the window half-open to better hear any noises outside.

It took Marcus all of twenty minutes to locate the files detailing the various Presidente transactions with what could only be the cartels. Someone had printed out Excel spreadsheets, and then entered the transaction details by hand. There were three codenamed counterparties: Pumas, Tigres, and Cruz Azul. *Someone is obviously a big Mexican football fan*, Marcus observed. There were dates, dollar amounts, bank accounts, and intermediary names. The transaction descriptions were not as forthcoming as he had hoped: "access," "product-heavy," "product-light," and similarly vague descriptions, but he figured the Shareholder could pair those up with the dollar amounts and make sense of it. He took out his phone and snapped a few pictures of the populated worksheets, saved the photos in a secret folder on his phone, then carefully put the folder back in its file.

As he turned off his mini-flashlight and readied himself to leave, he heard movement outside, then a loud bang on the side of the dumpster. He dropped to the floor instantly and pulled out his gun, flipping the safety off and holding the weapon closely to his chest with both hands. His heart began to race, and he remembered the breathing training from Langley and tried to calm himself. He listened carefully as he heard more commotion, and what sounded like aluminum cans hitting the ground. Then, after a few seconds, more movement. Marcus counted to ten slowly, then inched himself over to the open window, careful not to make a sound. He slowly raised his head up to look out and saw that the top of the dumpster had been flipped open. He waited a few more seconds and, hearing nothing, slipped outside and landed softly on the packed dirt. He crept to the back of the dumpster and slid his head around one side to observe what might be on the other side. Nothing.

Marcus decided to quietly make a break for his car through the surrounding darkness. As he began to transfer his gait from a quick walk to a jog, he heard movement again back off to his rear and dove forward to execute a barrel roll, landing crouched on one knee with his weapon drawn. He looked out over the flat landscape, and as a cloud shifted to reveal a sliver of moonlight over the land, two yellow eyes were fixed upon him from thirty yards away. Marcus cocked his weapon and aimed directly between the eyes. Marcus and the eyes locked gazes, and the ripped trash bag fell from the wolf's jaws. The wolf's long, red tongue showed at the bottom of its panting mouth. Marcus looked around him to see if any other wolves were visible. They weren't. Just this one. Marcus looked down the barrel of his gun again and found the yellow eyes peering back at him. The wolf growled and arched its back into a defensive posture. Marcus held the wolf's gaze a second longer and took a few deep breaths. He felt his trigger finger pulse and smelled his own sweat rolling down his neck.

"Ain't you I'm after, buddy," Marcus said out loud, as he calmed himself and lowered his gun. The tension in the wolf's body eased, and it tilted its head, as if surprised. Then it let out a long, loud, and bone-chilling howl before disappearing into the brush.

CHAPTER 15

Paris, France.
Left Bank.
Saturday, June 29, 2019.

MARCUS WOKE UP EARLY THE MORNING AFTER the Dunworths event at the Musée d'Orsay. Well, early for a Saturday in Paris. At the end of the previous evening, he had had to fight hard not to give in to his strong physical desire to invite Capucine back to his place for the rest of the night. He pictured walking up behind her slowly, running his fingertips gently along the tops of her arms and shoulders, then smoothly slipping off the straps of her dress and letting it fall to the floor as he…but it wasn't to be. They had made a pact to phase out their relationship before she left, and they had agreed to only one more night together, which would be tonight. Plus, Marcus had a full day of work ahead of him, and he needed to be fresh and focused.

There were several requirements that Marcus had to get used to when he joined Peppercorn as a member of the team working for the Shareholder. One was that he had to *appear* to be living lavishly. To portray the image of a highly successful, wealthy, and up-and-coming star in the world of private equity. *Not the worst thing a job can make you do*, he thought initially. But this requirement proved harder to satisfy and more inconvenient than he had expected, as it was contradictory to many of the ways in which he typically did things.

His Paris apartment, for example. When planning for his relocation to Paris from Buenos Aires two years earlier, Marcus had originally wanted a small, simple studio in a good area, close to a park or two, but in a tucked-away location. Mid-block on the Rue Madame near the Luxembourg Gardens, or near Convention in the 15th arrondissement. But Peppercorn had instead sent him three options, from which he was to pick one: a penthouse in the Marais district, a three-bedroom full-floor apartment in the 16th near the Trocadero, and a large two-bedroom with a huge terrace at the Place Vauban. All of these were locations that said something very clear about one's net worth. He'd need not concern himself with the rent as that would be handled by the firm. The choice was easy: Place Vauban. Marcus preferred the Left Bank, the apartment was within walking distance of the Peppercorn office and was well placed for runs or walks in the Champ de Mars, along the Seine, or in the Luxembourg Gardens. But small, simple, and tucked away it was not. The apartment was on the sixth floor of a seven-story apartment building facing onto Place Vauban and looking directly at the dome church of Les Invalides. The interior was a flash of blacks, reds, and whites, with inconveniently placed modern art. The neighborhood was a bit stuffy and trended toward older couples and families with children. The noise from the traffic below and the near constant flow of tourists visiting Les Invalides rendered the location far from quaint.

But the terrace was immaculate. It was a wraparound stone balcony, with a waistlevel balustrade held up by Roman columns and furnished with a metal table, folding chairs, a wooden bench and footstool, and two dark orange retractable awnings. And the views of the golden top and manicured courtyard of Napoleon's tomb, the nearby Musée Rodin, and the Beaux-Arts conservatory-style glass ceiling of the Grand Palais across the river were breathtaking.

Not my first choice…but sure as hell not bad, Marcus thought.

If he was going to spend most of his Saturday in the office, then Marcus had to get a good, long early morning run in for some fresh air and outdoor exposure. The summer had already been unbearably hot as the *canicule* swept across France and most of continental Europe, and Marcus knew that even at 7:30 a.m. he would get a good sweat in. He warmed up by jogging the length of the central esplanade from outside his building to the Louis Pasteur monument, then paused for a few minutes to stretch and shake himself loose. He jogged back down to the Rue d'Estrées. He turned right and broke into a comfortable pace along the Rue de Babylone, going against the grain of the non-existent one-way traffic en route to the Luxembourg Gardens, the large, much beloved public park in between Saint-Germain-des-Prés and the Latin Quarter.

The sun was rising in front of him and shined rays of light onto a waitress pulling out chairs and small circular tables from her café, a baker sliding a tray of freshly baked croissants and *brioches suisses* into the front window case at a corner *boulangerie*. The smell of the toasty crusts and melted chocolate escaping out onto the sidewalk whetted Marcus's appetite as he passed by. *I will see you boys later*, he thought, as he planned to grab a few pastries on the jog back home. He weaved his way past the church of Saint-Sulpice and up the Rue Bonaparte through the ornamental black gates which encircled the Luxembourg Gardens, punctuated by gold spikes at the top. The park's gates were casually unlocked each morning between 7:30 and 8:15 a.m., with no reliable order as to which entrances around the park were opened first, last, or anywhere in between. By the time Marcus arrived, he had lucked out in that the gate at the top of the Rue Bonaparte had just been unlocked.

He stuck to the gravel path that hugged the perimeter of the park, cruising past the empty tennis courts and the massive, modernized children's playground. Some toddlers already filled the air with the pure joy of uninhibited screams and laughter. *What a godsend that playground must be for parents that live nearby*, Marcus thought. There were a handful of other relatively early risers out *faire le jogging*. The occasional pounding of their feet on the gravel coupling with pigeons' coos formed a peaceful soundtrack to gradually awaken Marcus's mind. As he turned onto the path abutting the Avenue de l'Observatoire, he forced himself to think about the day's work ahead. The Shareholder had expressed a strong interest in helping Poland become a legitimate alternative option to Russia for supplying natural gas to Poland itself and to the rest of Europe. There was also the belief that direct involvement in that development would provide access to, and influence on, numerous industry and political players involved. It could be a treasure trove of data with respect to what Russia was doing to compete with Poland, who they were using, and how they were going about doing it.

Much had been made of the interest in exploration and production of shale gas in Poland at the beginning of the decade, but that petered out quickly because of poor drilling results and onerous environmental red tape. The Poles had proved resilient, however, and were now trying to secure their own supplies of natural gas through offshore production in the North Sea, to be connected to Polish ports by an offshore pipeline running through the Baltic Sea, and by importing liquefied natural gas, or LNG as it was colloquially known, from the United States. But to accomplish all that, Gas Polskie, the Polish national oil and gas company, needed expertise, industry connections, and money. Lots of money. Dangling the sword of Damocles over Poland's head was the Russian boogeyman in the form of NovaGaz, whose current supply contract with Poland was set to expire in the coming years and who was not enthusiastic about Poland's newfound desire to become natural gas self-sufficient. Negotiations for a new contract between Gas Polskie and NovaGaz had famously broken down, as Poland felt that Russia was using the natural gas supply agreement as a political weapon, and Russia was adamant in substantially raising their prices from the previous contract. *Who said the Cold War was over?* Marcus had observed at the time.

Boldly, Gas Polskie decided to reach out to the market to try to find a partner, a lender, or both. The project was risky, and in the early stages, as hundreds of miles of pipeline needed to be laid both onshore and offshore in Denmark and Poland, right-of-way had to be secured to allow for the legal right to lay that pipeline, and substantial development of port and storage facilities needed to be undertaken at Świnoujście, the Polish port on the Baltic Sea next to the German border. Further complicating the matter was Russia's own attempt to develop the Nord Stream 2 Pipeline to import Russian natural gas into Germany (and then into homes across Europe) through the Baltic Sea port of Greifswald, roughly one hour's drive from Świnoujście on the German side of the border. The sum of these complications was that many of the common financing sources, such as large multi-lateral lending institutions like the World Bank or the European Bank for Reconstruction and Development, were hesitant to fund the oil and gas business directly because of the environmental reputational taint that association with oil and gas carried, and thus were not willing to lend to the Poles. Potential political ramifications with the Russians put a chilling effect on the interest of the large oil and gas companies to step in as a partner and part-owner. So that left the most likely interested parties to be the large commodities trading houses, notoriously agnostic in terms of political niceties but also well known for extracting more than a pound of flesh for taking such risk, and private equity firms like Peppercorn, who were unlikely to possess the technical industry experience that Gas Polskie needed. And then, of course, there were the Russians. One of the best ways to get rid of a threatening competitor? Take them off the board by buying them out.

Marcus's task for the day was to conduct an in-depth review of a due diligence report that Bamba Diop's team from Dunworths had prepared, which summarized the hundreds of records, corporate documents, and commercial agreements that Gas Polskie had made available to potential bidders through an electronic data room. The report was also supposed to point out some of the perceived risks and issues related to the investment based on what was found, and more often, what was not found, in the data room. This was going to be tedious work, as Marcus was certain it would require not only reading the entire report but also checking many of the underlying documents themselves. Marcus had learned early on in his Macon Smith days that reading a company's commercial agreements was critical to properly understanding how that business worked and what the effect of a particular transaction would be. They showed you who the company's counterparties were, how those counterparties could slip out of those agreements, and, when reading several agreements together, how organized and coordinated the company really was. What was more, a shocking number of people in the business world never read their company's agreements, and simply took it on faith that what a salesperson—or worse, the counterparty—said was in the agreement was what was *actually* there. Peppercorn planned to submit a bid to Gas Polskie the following week, and Marcus's work today was critical in determining how much financial value the Gas Polskie relationship was worth. There was, of course, additional value of a nonfinancial nature for a select few of the Peppercorn team to consider.

CHAPTER 16

Paris, France.
Luxembourg Gardens.
Saturday, June 29, 2019.

"*UN MUSÉE À CIEL OUVERT.*" MARCUS HAD heard someone describe the Luxembourg Gardens that way once, and it seemed about right. Originally created by Marie de' Medici in the early 17th century to help her get over her grief from the assassination of her late husband, the great King Henri IV, the gardens were styled after the Boboli Gardens of the Pitti Palace in Florence, where Marie had grown up. It was difficult to trace those similarities, except for the part of the gardens that Marcus was jogging toward now. The *Grand Bassin* and the surrounding sculptures in front of the Luxembourg Palace was probably the most recognizable visual of the Luxembourg Gardens for most people. The scene, with little kids in maritime striped sweaters and Tshirts launching their *petits bateaux* into the fountain, did bear a striking resemblance to the Boboli Gardens. But the Luxembourg Gardens had grown into so much more over the course of its four-hundred-year history, and Marcus felt like he discovered something new every time he visited. There were the twenty white marble statutes of famed French queens, female saints, and celebrities flanking the *Grand Bassin*, featuring figures such as Sainte Geneviève, the patron Saint of Paris, Mary, Queen of Scots, who was briefly queen of France from 1559 to 1560, and Anne of Austria, wife of King Louis XIII, mother of the Sun King, Louis XIV, and forever immortalized by Alexandre Dumas as a central character in his novel, *The Three Musketeers*.

The gardens themselves were a mix of ordered, geometrical French-style shrubbery on one side, and wild, natural English-style flora on the other. There was the original bronze model of Bartholdi's *Statue of Liberty* tastefully placed in front of an American Oak hidden on the western side of the park. A wonderful integration of French, English, and Italian influences, with a respectful tip of the cap to the Americans. But what appealed to Marcus most about the gardens were the French people themselves, hundreds of them every time he came (save for his early morning jogs) just sitting on benches or in the little green metal chairs, reading, talking, drinking, thinking, smoking, and sun-bathing. Some doing all at once.

As Marcus looped around to the right of the *Grand Bassin*, he slowed his pace to a cooldown walk behind the Medici Fountain. This marked just about three full laps, not a bad run when paired with the jog over from Place Vauban. The fountain, usually one of the more popular sitting spots in the park due to its beauty and the shade the surrounding trees provided, was vacant except for a fellow jogger stretching her foot on a chair and queuing up a playlist on her phone. Marcus relished the shade from the trees above and walked the length of the basin below the fountain, passing the large stone pots filled with colorful flowers and their matching pairs directly across the pool. He reached into the fountain's basin to rub some water on his hands and then toss a few splashes onto his face. He paused momentarily to allow himself to catch his breath, and as he stared up at the rusted statue of Polyphemus surprising Acis and Galatea in the act at the head of the fountain, he recalled the last time he had been at this spot roughly six weeks before.

ARTHUR FRANZ SHOWED up unannounced at the Peppercorn Paris office that Tuesday morning in the middle of May. Marcus was sifting through the morning's financial press when he heard a knock on his glass door, and looked up to see the bushy eyebrows, neatly cut white hair, and ever-inquisitive countenance of Franz. *How does he do that?* Marcus pondered, as with the combination of all-glass office windows and Marcus being in the middle of the hallway, he was always able to spot someone coming his way before they arrived…but apparently not Franz. He smiled, nodded, and waved Franz into his office.

"In from Berlin?" Marcus asked.

"Lunch in the Luxembourg?" Franz responded, ignoring Marcus's question.

Yes was the only possible answer to this question, so Marcus acquiesced, "Yes, sounds great!"

Franz pursed his lips and gave a slight, curt nod, as if now accepting a request. "I'll stop by at noon." He added, then vanished.

Marcus spent the rest of the morning brushing up on the status of his current projects, as he figured those would be the subjects of discussion during lunch. Franz appeared promptly at noon. Marcus grabbed his blazer off the hanger in the small closet in his office and they headed out. Most of the large investment banks, law firms, and private equity firms had their Paris offices on the other side of the Seine, the Right Bank, somewhere within the large triangle between the Arc de Triomphe, the Place Vendôme, and the Gare du Nord. And several large companies had their Paris offices out in La Défense, on the western edge of Paris outside of the Boulevard Périphérique. Peppercorn was unique in that its offices were on the Left Bank on the Rue de l'Université, between the Boulevard Saint-Germain and the Quai Voltaire. They had chosen this location mainly because it was convenient to where many of the managing partners lived within the city, but also to separate themselves physically from many of their competitors and counterparts, bolstering the firm's image as both refined and independent. The upshot, for Franz and Marcus's purposes on this particular day, was that it was within manageable walking distance of the Luxembourg Gardens.

Marcus followed Franz as they dipped into a small bakery off the Rue de Rennes and grabbed takeaway sandwiches, then continued into the Luxembourg Gardens. The mid-May weather was cool, the winter chill having disappeared and the summer heat yet to arrive, so they were able to make the twenty-minute walk comfortably. Along the way Franz alternated between providing pointed historical details on places they passed by and succinct updates on various firm projects and initiatives. They entered the gardens off the Rue des Fleurus and passed by a game of *pétanque*, the tweed jackets of the old men playing the game hanging on a portable metal coat rack on the side of the court. On their way to the Medici Fountain, Franz noticed two boys, one older, one younger, looking pensive in shabby clothing. Without speaking a word, he broke off half of his sandwich and handed it to the older boy, then shooed off some approaching swans who had misinterpreted Franz's generosity. He then continued to the base of the Medici Fountain, found two seats in the shade out of earshot of anyone else, and sat down in one of them.

Marcus joined him and they began to eat. After one bite, he marveled at how a basic baguette with ham, hardboiled egg, tomatoes, and goat cheese could taste so good. He could smell the freshness of the bread and taste the juicy ripeness of the tomatoes. That sensation never got old, and never ceased to amaze.

"So, how are your Miller Family investments going?" Franz asked, breaking the cadence of light background noise behind them. "The Miller Family" was how they referred to the Shareholder when speaking to others within the firm, and how the Shareholder was characterized when a counterparty was interested enough in the Peppercorn corporate structure to demand details. The necessary blocker corporations and shell companies had been created to establish the façade of careful tax planning, and as far as most people at Peppercorn were concerned, to protect individual members of the Miller Family from any potential personal liability.

Marcus provided an update on some of the initial research on the Gas Polskie possibilities, and also explained the continued difficulties with an investment they had made in a telecommunications holding company in Central Africa called TeleCAR. Franz listened quietly, intermittently nodding his head very slightly as if confirming something that he already knew. Franz allowed a few seconds of silence to hold the space between them when Marcus finished his explanations.

Then he glanced up at Marcus. "Well?"

Marcus looked at him in silence, then blinked.

"Your recommendations?" Franz continued.

Thinking that this question might be coming, Marcus had prepared his positions.

"TeleCAR is a lost cause. Financially, it's a disaster. Revenue growth in a telecommunications business is dependent upon functioning telecommunications infrastructure. Without a reliable federal government to work with, that infrastructure is never going to get built, or existing infrastructure won't be maintained. And strategically, for the Miller Family, it's worthless. There is nothing we are getting from the company that we can't get from State. Efforts to develop business relationships with tribal groups and terrorist cells through payments to build cell towers on their lands have failed because we can't get government approval and licenses to legitimize those efforts. Let's tap our investment bankers to get the sale process going and just cut our losses now."

"Agreed," Franz replied, "And Poland?"

"Poland is a green light. We know the natural gas space as well as anyone, and Europe is ripe for development there. There is real scale on that business if we can add an inland transport hub down near Krakow at the end of the Vistula River. We could help them turn that into a legitimate hub for commodities trading and transport in the center of Europe. It is going to be a competitive process though, as there are lots of deep pockets also looking at that project. If we can get the Miller Family rate of return approval, then I think we can win the auction."

Marcus's reference to the "Miller Family rate of return" was how they characterized the strategy of offering incredibly favorable financial terms to a counterparty for assets or projects that the Shareholder wanted, even if it meant losing money. Peppercorn Capital could not independently justify those types of financial terms. So in order to get approval for these kinds of transactions from Peppercorn's investment committee, the Miller Family had to step in and agree to invest alongside Peppercorn. In industry terms, this was called a "coinvest."

"Mmm," Franz replied. An unhelpfully non-committal response.

"Strategically…" Marcus drew this word out in response to Franz's grunt, "in addition to the geopolitical benefits of weakening Russia's stranglehold on European natural gas supply, which of course I don't need to tell you about, there are numerous contacts in the Eastern European energy world we can tap into. And if we structure the investment properly, we can get access to all of Gas Polskie's historical contracts and financial records. We will create an open line of communication with the Polish government. And we will be in the room for any future negotiations with the Russians and the Ukrainians."

Franz nodded along with Marcus's explanation, and then looked up, awaiting the final point he knew that Marcus had to address.

"But all of that…the financial, operational, and strategic upside of the Gas Polskie project will be completely undermined if the Russians are flowing cheap natural gas into mainland Europe through Germany. The success of Gas Polskie is contingent upon the Nord Stream 2 Pipeline failing."

The implications of this statement were clear. As Peppercorn's senior professional in the Berlin office, and one of the Shareholder's principal strategists on German and Russian affairs, the task of convincing the Germans to shut down construction of the Russian gas pipeline into Germany fell very squarely within Arthur Franz's ken. If Nord Stream 2 was going to die, then Franz had to kill it.

"Very well," Franz responded thoughtfully. "You are green for the initial bid in the first round of the auction. Get us to the final round with Gas Polskie, and then I can tell you if we get the Miller Family rate of return on the project."

Marcus bowed slightly, simultaneously conveying gratitude and subservience. Assuming the discussion was concluded, Marcus looked around from his chair to locate one of the green metal mesh trashcans to swing by on their way back to the office. As Marcus was getting up to leave, Franz surprised him.

"Mauro Broccatelli."

Marcus froze in his tracks, then slowly turned to look at Franz.

"You never met him during your time in Argentina, nor any of the Broccatellis for that matter?"

So the discussion is not over, Marcus thought as he planted himself firmly back into his chair. The gardens had filled up during the time Marcus and Franz had been there, and a nearby couple carrying their own boulangerie sack with a baguette sticking out had excitedly walked in Marcus's direction when he briefly vacated his seat. His entrenchment back into the chair disappointed their search for open seats.

"Not personally, no," Marcus replied, as he crossed one leg over the other, leaned back in his chair, and interlocked his fingers. He made himself comfortable; he might be there for a while. "But of course," Marcus continued, "I know who they are. They almost bought our midstream business down there, but wisely were not willing to pay anything near what Greyshore paid for it. They own it now, though…"

Franz was of course familiar with the huge financial windfall that Marcus had helped engineer with Peppercorn's development and sale of the Argentine midstream business, and equally familiar with the precipitous crash in value of that business after Peppercorn sold it. *Perfect market timing*, that was how it had been described in the financial press. And within Peppercorn it had been that deal that cemented Marcus Hugo as a rising star. But Franz and Marcus both knew they had been lucky. The Argentine investment, and Marcus's two years living there to manage that investment, had been part of developing his cover further as a global private equity pro and jet-setting playboy. In the long run, though, the real windfall may have been that the Broccatelli family ended up buying the pipeline business for pennies on the dollar and as a result held Peppercorn in high esteem as a savvy counterparty for fleecing Greyshore.

"Yes, the Broccatellis do own it now," Franz acknowledged. "How much do you know about the family?"

"Oh, just the stuff you read in the papers, really. Biggest oil and gas family in Argentina, owners of *un holding* as they call it in Argentina, with diversified businesses all over the world. The two brothers in the line of succession…and then of course the rumors…"

Marcus knew more than that about the Broccatellis, but he could tell Franz was about to provide extensive background and there was no need to delay the inevitable any further.

"I'll pretend that's all you know," Franz said as he raised his eyebrows in skepticism, then added, "if nothing else for the sake of providing a full briefing."

As was customary, Franz would start at the beginning. No papers, no files, no pictures. Ever. Just a description that laid the predicate for a logical sequence of events as to what should happen next. He would lead Marcus to the door, and then suggest just where the crack in that door might be. Then, in Marcus's own way, he would find a way to open the door and walk through with reckless abandon.

CHAPTER 17

Paris, France.
The Left Bank.
Mid-May 2019.

"ALFREDO BROCCATELLI ARRIVED AT PORT LA BOCA in Buenos Aires on a ship from Genoa in the mid-1950s. He was originally from the outskirts of Milan but had read about job opportunities building railroads in Argentina and took off for the new world. After landing in Buenos Aires, he quickly made his way west to the farm country in La Pampa. He started a farm equipment business, then realized there was a greater need to sell equipment to oil and gas producers, so he adapted. Before long, he moved from the equipment sales side of the business to the production side of the business and created Broccagas."

Franz had suggested they walk and talk for the briefing. He believed that remaining in one place too long was poor tradecraft, as it made one more conspicuous. As Marcus had first learned five years ago in Tuscany,

Franz liked to do his briefings on the move. They had exited out of the Luxembourg Gardens behind the Medici Fountain and started walking down the busy Boulevard Saint-Michel toward the Seine. The bustling boulevard was a good place for discussing Miller Family business matters. Franz walked close to Marcus and spoke into his shoulder, mouth toward the ground, in a tone just loud enough for him to hear over the busy traffic.

"Alfredo had two sons, Diego and Fernando, with Diego being the eldest by two years. Broccagas grew into a large local producer, and by the time Diego and Fernando joined the business after university, it was the largest oil and gas company in Argentina. This was the military junta period in Argentina, the Dirty War."

"A nasty period of time," Marcus interjected. The military junta in Argentina had been the result of a coup d'état in 1976 that overthrew Isabel Perón as president and installed a right-wing military governing body. The *Guerra Sucia* or Dirty War that followed consisted of the killing or disappearance of roughly 30,000 Argentines that were viewed as opponents of the state by the military. It was a time where fear gripped the daily lives of Argentines, and the mere mistake of not having your *documento,* or identification card, handy could mean that you were arrested and never seen by your friends or family again. Marcus had never heard of the Dirty War before moving to Buenos Aires but had learned much about it while there.

"Nasty indeed, including for the Broccatellis," Franz responded. "Diego, the older son, had gone to the University of Buenos Aires before returning to the family business in La Pampa. When the military junta took over, they approached Broccagas to get a consistent supply of fuel, which Broccagas was willing to do, but the military also wanted names of Broccagas employees, counterparties, and general business contacts that were 'a threat to the state.' This, Broccagas, and Diego in particular, was not willing to do. The military then looked into Diego's activities and friends from his time at "*la UBA*" and started to make threats. Things escalated…"

"And that's when Diego died in a motorcycle accident," Marcus chimed in.

"Correct," Franz responded, "And slowly, albeit reluctantly, Alfredo and the young Fernando Broccatelli gave the government enough information to appease them. But they never forgave the Argentine right and have done everything they can to ally themselves with the Peronist successors since. Also, like many Argentines to this day, the Broccatellis firmly believed that the United States was behind the whole military junta movement and harbored a fierce grudge against all things US from then on."

Marcus knew better than to ask the logical question of, Well, *did* we support the junta? Those matters were best left unknown. So instead, he asked, "So what makes you bring up Mauro Broccatelli, as opposed to Fernando?"

Franz bristled a bit, then placed both hands out in front of him, palms down, and made a gesture toward the ground, as if to calm Marcus down, then responded, "All things in time."

They ceased speaking as they passed through the busy Place Saint-Michel and reached the Quai des Grands Augustins. Franz paused and looked out over the river toward the cathedral of Notre Dame. Roughly one month earlier, the entire roof of the world's most famous church had been ablaze for hours. While the structure of the building still stood, the famous steeple was gone after crashing to the ground during the fire. They both took a deep breath. This time, Marcus couldn't help but asking one of those questions that he knew he shouldn't.

"Is retribution appropriate for all of that?" Marcus nodded his head in the direction of Notre Dame, even though it was obvious what he was referring to. This was Marcus's roundabout way of asking if the burning of Notre Dame had been an act of terrorism.

Franz sighed again. It was clear he was physically affected by looking upon the church for the first time in its newly dilapidated state.

"I don't think so. At least not something *we* would participate in. I keep hoping it was just a mistake made by one of the workers."

They both steadied their gaze on the scaffolding and rubble still surrounding the façade. Then, quite out of character, Franz added, "But if I'm wrong, then God help them. Because I'll sign up for that mission myself." Without hesitation, he wheeled around and began walking the other direction along the *quai*. Marcus stared admiringly at Franz, then followed.

"After the Falklands War and the disintegration of the military junta, Broccagas took off as a company. Alfredo stepped aside and Fernando took over, like a man possessed. He grew the business beyond Argentina, first in Ecuador, Colombia and even Venezuela, then in Central Asia. By the early 2000s, Broccagas was one of Argentina's five largest companies, and Fernando Broccatelli was in Forbes 500, easily worth a billion dollars. Fernando had moved the family to Buenos Aires in the late 80s. Gigantic penthouse apartment in Recoleta. An estate in one of the country club communities of San Isidro. Golf, sailing, and of course, polo. They created their family holding company and started diversifying their asset base. They invested in real estate, tech venture capital, fashion, and wine. Lots of wine. All the while, the oil and gas business expanded too, into refining, mining, and shipping."

"Fernando married Claudia Müller, an Argentine actress of German descent. They had two boys, Roberto Cesare Martín Broccatelli-Müller, and his younger brother Mauro Augustus Walter Broccatelli-Müller. Roberto and Mauro grew up as elite, wealthy children. Top education, travel all over the world, and each spoke Spanish, German, and English fluently by the time they were ten. But they became very different people despite their common upbringing, and their paths diverged around high school. Roberto was the golden child, boarding school in the US at Deerfield, undergrad at Yale, and a JD/MBA from Harvard. Mauro, on the other hand, went to high school locally in San Isidro, where he was a great athlete, and not just in elite sports like polo, sailing, and rugby, but also in soccer and boxing. He excelled in rugby though and played at University of St. Andrews in Scotland. He tried to play professionally for a few years, but then hung his cleats up to go to INSEAD for business school."

Marcus was more familiar with the recent history of the Broccatellis.

"And they have essentially split the businesses up, right?" he contributed, "Pappa Fernando still technically owns and runs everything, but Roberto and Mauro have pretty much divided up the empire."

Franz grimaced. *This man just hates absolutes*, Marcus reminded himself.

"Kind of," Franz acknowledged, "From what we can tell, Roberto runs more of the high-minded or white-collar enterprises: the luxury real estate company, their venture capital and tech fund, and their merchant bank. He is also the political mouthpiece for the family and likely has aspirations on that front. He lives in Buenos Aires but has a home in D.C. and spends a lot of time there. Politically, he carries the torch for the family's continued support of populism through the Peronist party. He's friends with the ex-president and spoke up on her behalf often. This is one way in which the grudge from Diego's memory lives on."

"And the other?" Marcus insightfully ventured.

This drew a slight nod of appreciation from Franz, who continued, "Mauro is more on the…physical side of things, I'd say. He has taken over their wine holdings and sits on the board of their fashion business. It is also rumored that he's trying to buy a European football club. But he is also heavily involved in their oil and gas businesses, particularly shipping and transport. The father, Fernando, still seems to control the domestic Argentine oil and gas activities, but Mauro appears to be running the international side."

A connection was starting to take shape in Marcus's mind. And now he understood why this briefing had started with Mauro Broccatelli.

"And Mauro lives in London, right?" Marcus added.

Franz lightly tilted his head from side to side, then responded, "He does, but spends most of his time in Italy at their family home in Menaggio on Lake Como, or at an apartment in Milan near the Porta Nuova. This allows him to be close to their vineyards in France and Italy, which he visits frequently."

They had reached the turning point to go back to the Peppercorn office, with the Pont Royal on the right side, and the Rue du Bac on the left. The conversation had reached a threshold point as well, and Marcus allowed silence to mark that arrival. Franz was unperturbed, standing coolly in silence and not making for one direction or the other. Giving in, Marcus motioned his hand toward a nearby red awning with gold lettering indicating a café, then led them to the bar. Marcus ordered shots of espresso, then took in a waft of fresh French fries on a plate with a glistening *croque monsieur* on the edge as it passed by him.

Interpreting this interlude as Marcus's equivalent of *go on...*, Franz continued.

"There are pieces of information that suggest the party in question, principally through their shipping business, but also through refining and international oil trading, is transacting with participants that are otherwise cut off from the market. And potentially doing so at the behest of their own government."

Marcus noted Franz's use of non-specific terms and vague references now that they were within earshot of others. Translating what Franz had just said, Marcus was floored by their implications. Broccagas was potentially serving as a broker for oil, gas, and who knew what else to countries subject to sanctions. Venezuela. Iran. North Korea. That likely meant Chinese involvement here too. And potentially doing so as a front for the Argentine government. Marcus blinked at the bar a few times, then took down his espresso. He laid a few two Euro coins next to his empty cup and they made for the street.

Back outside, Franz added, "It's also quite possible they carried out the Nisman affair."

Stunned, Marcus simultaneously stopped dead in his tracks and caught his jaw from dropping for too long. "I'm sorry, what did you just say?" Marcus needed to be sure he heard Franz's last statement correctly.

Nonchalantly, and in a matter-of-fact manner, Franz responded, "Well, not them personally of course, but we believe they were in charge of arranging it."

The Nisman affair, or "*el Caso Nisman*" as it was colloquially referred to in Argentina, was the name given to the alleged suicide of Alberto Nisman, an Argentine federal prosecutor. He was found dead in his home in Buenos Aires on January 18, 2015, one day before he was scheduled to publicly present his findings from an investigation into the AMIA bombing, which was a suicide car bombing at the Argentine Israelite Mutual Association building in Buenos Aires in 1994. Eighty-five people were killed, and hundreds were injured in the attack. The AMIA bombing was the deadliest terrorist attack in Argentina's history. It was widely believed that Nisman was going to present incriminating evidence against the then-current Argentine president and other high-ranking Argentine officials related to potential collusion with the Iranian government into the AMIA bombing and its cover up. *El Caso Nisman* had received global media attention, but this resonated with Marcus in particular because he moved to Argentina in late 2015, and it was still very much in all of the local Argentine headlines at that time.

Baffled, Marcus moved his mouth without saying words for a few seconds, skipping over the first four or five questions that came to his mind. They had come to a full stop in the middle of the block catercornered to Peppercorn's office. Marcus stood with his back to the Seine a few blocks behind them, a small Proxi convenience store just behind him and big, forest-green double doors with an arched stone colonnade above them marked the entrance to an internal courtyard of a building just to his right. Franz, with his back to the windows of the office, was looking directly at Marcus. The sun shone over the pewter tops and upper-floor greenery of the cream-colored stone Haussmann buildings pervasive in that neighborhood, illuminating the rectangular floor-to-ceiling glass windows and dark gray Juliette balconies on the west side of the street. Marcus knew the time allotted for this briefing was coming to an end, and progress needed to be made here. His countenance morphed from one of confusion to one of resolve.

Marcus rotated his chin down, and placed his right hand over his mouth, feigning a pondering stance, then through covered lips concluded, "Iran. Broccatellis. The president. Nisman was going to expose the Broccatelli's involvement."

A flash of light coursed through Franz's eyes, confirming Marcus was on the right track. The dizzying array of puzzle pieces that had been dancing around in Marcus's brain suddenly arranged themselves in a straight line and fastened themselves together, like the tracks of a child's train set. Marcus began nodding his head with potent energy, then through a knowing smile he added, "We're going into business with Broccagas."

Franz turned toward the Peppercorn office and, with a nod of his head, indicated for Marcus to do the same. As they crossed the intersection and strode toward the office entrance, Franz responded, "Let's start with an introduction first. And I know just the right event for it."

CHAPTER 18

Paris, France.
Luxembourg Gardens.
Saturday, June 29, 2019.

MARCUS RETURNED HIS ATTENTION TO THE present as he thought about the prior evening's event at the Musée d'Orsay, the very event that Arthur Franz has referred to at the conclusion of their meeting back in May. The process had begun. Marcus had met Broccatelli, they had carried on a cursory discussion of business matters, and, with the incidental help of Capucine, Marcus felt confident that he had become a blip on Mauro Broccatelli's general radar. *But where to go from here? Unclear*, Marcus thought to himself, then satisfied himself by concluding that he wasn't going to solve that problem today. He reached back down into the base of the Medici Fountain and spooned another handful of cool, fresh water onto his face. *On to today's problem...Gas Polskie!* Marcus thought as he shifted his focus to the day ahead of him.

He walked down one of the main gravel paths toward the entrance of the park near the Place de l'Odéon and crossed over the street where the Rue de Vaugirard turns into the Rue de Médicis. It was still early by Paris standards for a Saturday, and a green street sweeper plowed across the Rue de Vaugirard ridden casually by a green-uniformed worker wearing the obligatory yellow reflective vest hanging off the back and taking a drag on a morning cigarette. The noise of the vehicle gearing up to take on the Montagne Sainte-Geneviève, the small hill atop which the Panthéon sits, and the scent of burnt tobacco greeted Marcus as he reengaged with the city. As he customarily did after Saturday runs in the Luxembourg, he stopped at a small newspaper kiosk at the Place Pierre-Dux before jogging back to his apartment. He picked up weekend editions of *Le Figaro* and *The Financial Times*, grabbed a small bottle of water, and traded pleasantries with the endearing lady who ran the kiosk.

Marcus walked a few blocks as he downed the water and glanced at the newspaper headlines, which focused heavily on the heat wave and its expected effect on the upcoming summer vacation season. He was making his way past the senate building and the Petit Luxembourg as he noticed a man up ahead of him stretching in front of the Hotel Luxembourg Parc. The man was well-built, obviously very fit, had short dark hair, and was decked out head to toe in the latest fashion of popular Swiss running shoes and gear. Marcus looked again, narrowing his gaze to confirm, then smiled inwardly and looked up to the heavens and mouthed *thank you*. He had always believed that good luck followed from getting an early start to the day, but somehow the "early bird gets the worm" cliché did not quite do this one justice.

Marcus took one more sip of his water and tossed the bottle into a nearby garbage can, then jogged casually toward the athletic figure in front of the hotel ahead. The dark-haired young man performed one last set of arm circles, looked down to fiddle with his watch, then raised his head alertly at the sound of a person nearing him. His dark-brown eyes settled on the passerby, then he blinked and inched his head forward, squinted, and declared, "Marcus Hugo!"

Marcus, feigning aloofness, slowed his jog and looked confusedly at the young man who had just called out his name. Then he raised his eyebrows and offered a quizzical smile, as if trying to place the young man.

"You are Marcus Hugo, from Peppercorn Capital. We met last night at the Dunworths event." Again, declarations, not questions, from the young man.

"Yes…Bamba Diop's friend, right?" Marcus responded, beginning to drop the charade. "Mauro, isn't it? Mauro Broccatelli?"

Broccatelli nodded softly, appraising Marcus's figure and running shoes, the sweat-soaked shirt, the glint of his brow that followed from nearly an hour of running at a vigorous pace, and the newspapers he held in his left hand. Broccatelli seemed appreciative, and at least somewhat intrigued. As if remembering a portion of their discussion from the night before, Broccatelli shifted into his native Spanish, flavored with a noticeable *Porteño* accent, and in a near-challenging tone said to Marcus, "Looks like you got an early one in today. Do you live around here?" Broccatelli remained tense, awaiting Marcus's response.

Marcus had been expecting this, but it still caught him slightly off guard. Fortunately, Marcus was quite familiar with the Buenos Aires accent from his time living there, and when he was around other Argentines he could easily drift back into that same accent, intonating his words more dramatically, substituting the *sh* sound for the *ys* and *lls*; *me shamo…sha veo….*Pausing perhaps one second longer than was comfortable, and seeing the thought of *does this idiot even speak Spanish* creep into Broccatelli's mind, Marcus responded slowly at first, "Well, yes, not too far from here…" then shifted gears into full throttle, "about two kilometers and change. A nice, easy warmup and cooldown jog before a good run in the Luxembourg. You going for a run yourself?"

Broccatelli's eyes widened as Marcus vaulted into his rapid response, then Broccatelli almost staggered back, and ultimately completely altered his disposition into one of comfort and enthusiasm. Marcus had seen this type of response before and was pleased by it. Argentines are generally not used to hearing non-natives speak with an Argentine accent, especially Americans.

"Yes, I love running in the Luxembourg and always try to do it when I'm here in Paris," Broccatelli smiled, "It's one of my favorite parks in the world."

Marcus nodded along, genuinely in agreement. He then pointed up at the Hotel Luxembourg Parc behind Broccatelli, "You staying here?" *Not the Hôtel de Crillon or the Ritz?* Marcus thought to himself.

Broccatelli smiled slyly, indicating the affirmative, then responded with pride, "The only place I stay in Paris. Excellent service, perfect location, and no unwanted attention. The top floor suite with the terrace is exquisite. I think of it as my Paris office."

Marcus was floored. For starters, he also loved this hotel. He agreed that it was the perfect Paris location and a much more enjoyable place to be than some of the more exclusive hotels. But in his experience, it was not one that many foreigners knew about. And more surprising was Broccatelli himself, suddenly loose and alive, charismatic.

They continued trading some running notes and comparing good routes within Paris. Broccatelli all the while was interested and engaged, clearly an avid runner and someone who knew Paris well. Sensing the end of the conversation nearing, Marcus ventured a joke, "and *la signorina* Ravello isn't joining you on this morning's run?"

Broccatelli laughed audibly, then pointed up to the room and made the sign of someone sleeping. "She had a bit more fun than I did last night. But she prefers yoga, and has a class scheduled later this morning."

They politely wished each other a good day and made for their respective separate ways. As Marcus was just about to break into a jog, he heard Broccatelli call out from behind, "Hey, Marcus—do you like cycling?"

The correct answer to these types of questions is always *yes*, but in this case, it was also true. "*Claro*." Marcus replied. *Of course.*

Broccatelli smiled, then responded, "I thought you might. Why don't you clear your calendar for the last week of July? I take a group of friends and business contacts on a cycling trip and winery visit every year. This year we are going down the Rhône River, all the way to the Mediterranean. I'll count you in. My secretary will send you the details."

And with that, Mauro Broccatelli turned the other way, pressed a button on his watch, and disappeared into the Luxembourg Gardens at a gallop.

CHAPTER 19

Buenos Aires, Argentina. June 2017.

LO DE BEBE WAS THE RIGHT PLACE TO HAVE THIS conversation. Marcus had considered one of their favorite coffee shops nearby in Recoleta for a quick and direct talk over an Americano. But he had learned from previous breakups that "short and sweet" was not the right approach, as to the person being broken up with it translated as selfish, hurtful, and inconsiderate. Then he had considered something more formal, like a visit to the beautiful and decadent Museo Nacional de Arte Decorativo, followed by a meal at the fabulously authentic French bistro connected to the museum, Croque Madame. But given that the reason for ending things with Luchi was Marcus's impending move to Paris, Croque Madame seemed in poor taste. So a nice, comfortable dinner at this casual *parilla* where they had enjoyed many great meals together seemed appropriate. He wanted to honor the time they had together, express his sincere affection for Luchi and appreciation for all that they had shared, and then wish her the best of luck going forward. His job had offered him an incredible opportunity to move to Paris, and he had accepted. It was something he couldn't turn down, and he would be leaving Buenos Aires for good within two weeks.

Marcus reminded himself of all of this on his walk over to Lo de Bebe. He arrived a little after ten p.m. that Wednesday night. It was still on the early side for dinner in Buenos Aires, where the locals, called *Porteños*, were also often referred to as *noctámbulos*, or night owls. Even on a night like tonight, in the middle of the week, it would be at least ten thirty or eleven p.m. before a place like Lo de Bebe would fill up. The familiar red awning with *Parrilla* printed on the side marked his arrival. The handful of red metal tables and chairs were covered with a local beer's and placed along the wide sidewalk in front of the restaurant. He strolled inside and was greeted with the rich, familiar smells of the smoke from sizzling red meat, musty red wine, and intense, black espresso. He breathed in the powerful cocktail of those mixed smells and felt a warm sensation come over him. *God, I'm going to miss this city*, Marcus noted to himself.

Lo de Bebe was a no-frills, low-key restaurant located in the Barrio Norte neighborhood of Buenos Aires, close to the popular Palermo neighborhood with its famed nightlife. And while the restaurant's appearance was humble, the food off the *parilla*, or the barbecue grill, was spectacular. The inside was small and colorful. Square wooden tables painted in various solid-colored hues stretched to the back toward the kitchen in a long, thin space by the bar. Two of the familiar bartenders, Juan and Facundo, who doubled as hosts for the restaurant and waited the tables, were consumed by a rare mid-week, late season Argentine premier league football match on TV between River Plate, the local Buenos Aires-based club that both Juan and Facundo supported, and Aldosivi, a smaller, less successful club from Mar del Plata. They traded pleasantries with Marcus as he ordered up a pint of Quilmes, the ubiquitous local Argentine beer. Marcus took a few playful jabs at Juan and Facundo about the success of Boca Juniors, River Plate's hated crosstown rival, who was at the top of the table that season and would soon be crowned league champions. Facundo feigned disgust, then shared a few laughs with Marcus. Marcus motioned toward the open dining spots outside, and Facundo quickly nodded his assent before returning his attention to the TV.

Marcus plopped himself down at one of the outdoor tables and felt the light chill of the beginnings of winter in the Southern Hemisphere. He zipped up the front of his charcoal-colored cashmere hooded sweatshirt. He knew Luchi would be close to a half hour or so late—on purpose—so he took a long drink of his cold beer, then stuck his hands into the pockets on the front of his sweatshirt and got comfortable in his seat. He considered reading a few pages from the paperback of short stories by Roberto Fontanarrosa he was carrying in his back pocket but decided instead to sit quietly and reflect on his time here in Argentina, seeing as how it was coming to an end very soon. *What a wild and unexpected time this has been*, Marcus thought incredulously.

The opportunity had come up suddenly, and certainly was not part of Arthur Franz's original plans for Marcus. Two years ago, one of the major European oil and gas companies had decided to sell off their struggling midstream, or hydrocarbon transportation and storage, business in Argentina. Marcus's team from Peppercorn had conducted due diligence on the company and discovered that it was actually an incredible opportunity, as the midstream company had near-guaranteed revenue from fees for transportation and storage of the oil and gas production from the selling company, who would enter into long-term commercial agreements with the new buyer at the closing of the transaction. The midstream business was only for sale because the seller didn't really know how to develop and operate a midstream company, and they wanted to stick to what they were good at: finding and producing oil and gas. Peppercorn made a lowball offer as an opening salvo, and to the Peppercorn team's surprise, it was accepted—on the condition that the transaction was completed within thirty days and construction of new pipelines begin shortly thereafter. It became clear that someone from Peppercorn needed to get down to Argentina quickly to take charge of final negotiations and then to lead the business after the deal closed. Franz encouraged Marcus to volunteer.

When Marcus expressed hesitation and concern that he would not be fulfilling his role at Peppercorn as a representative of the Shareholder, Franz had summarily dismissed those thoughts.

"The Shareholder is an investor in the Peppercorn fund making this investment, and it really is a great business opportunity. We could make a lot of money here, and it would look great on your legitimate business résumé. Your Langley training is just about concluded anyway. You already speak Spanish, but you can further develop those language skills. And we will work in some side trips for you around the region to build contacts down there. The way I see it, this is a perfect way to further develop your cover," Franz had assured him.

Within a week Marcus had cleared out his New York apartment in Chelsea and moved into a beautiful two-bedroom apartment with a balcony in the heart of Recoleta, within walking distance of the new office he was opening for Peppercorn in Microcentro, Buenos Aires's busy downtown. What followed was a whirlwind of recruiting a management team of midstream experts from both the US and Argentina to help run the new company, numerous trips out to Neuquén in the western part of Argentina to finalize the transaction and begin construction of new pipelines, getting a crash course in the intricacies of the Argentine government's red tape and figuring out how to navigate around it, and establishing a notable presence of Peppercorn in Buenos Aires. It was hard work, and Marcus and his team put in long hours and weekends, but within six months they had built a reliable and promising midstream business for Argentina's oil and gas industry. The combination of experienced midstream professionals from the developed oil and gas industry in the US, savvy and connected Argentines who knew how to work through the bureaucracy of Argentine regulations, and Marcus working tirelessly in the background to keep everyone organized and motivated had allowed them to succeed where so many others had failed. From that point forward, Marcus's whole team knew they had built the equivalent of a gold mine. They worked toward continuing to grow the business and polish it up for a lucrative exit opportunity down the road.

And my, how lucrative it was...Marcus thought to himself. In the past week, the culmination of Marcus's team's hard work and skilled execution had come to pass; Peppercorn Capital had sold the Argentine midstream business for over ten times what they had bought it for only two years before. They had been lucky, as oil and gas production in Neuquén had grown at an unexpected rate during those two years. But they had also been smart, as Marcus's team had not only proven capable of building the pipelines needed to transport production for their anchor customer, the company who previously sold them the midstream business, but they had also signed up favorable transportation agreements with other prospective companies who had been successful in finding and producing oil and gas. Marcus's team had provided a viable and reliable product transportation option and, as if buoyed by the ability to get their product to market, the oil and gas producers had drilled successful wells.

Marcus's and his team's compensation structures had granted them sizeable amounts of equity participation in the company, so their payouts were massive when the company was sold. Marcus made more money in one day than he had ever imagined making as a lawyer at Macon Smith. He figured out a tax-efficient way to share much of it with his parents and other family members, set aside another chunk of the money for the luxuries and trappings of the life he was supposed to be living as a high-flying private equity guy, and was still able to put eight figures' worth of money away as a nest egg for saving and investing. He knew that this position at Peppercorn Capital could vanish just as quickly as it had materialized. He also knew that the day might come when he would need to walk away on his own. In either case, he needed financial security to fall back on. One of the old-school senior partners from Macon Smith once called it "Fuck You Money."

As if things couldn't have gotten any better, within forty-eight hours of closing the sale of the company, Arthur Franz informed Marcus that, after shutting down the Peppercorn Buenos Aires office, Marcus was to report to duty at the Peppercorn Paris office, where he would help lead the firm's European, Middle Eastern, and African energy investments. Franz also assured Marcus that there were "other matters" for Marcus's attention that would be better managed out of Paris.

It was a dream come true, without a doubt. Marcus would be returning to Paris, and this time in his professional capacity with a private equity firm...*and whatever else it is I'm doing here at Peppercorn*, Marcus added to himself. He was beside himself with excitement for what lay ahead.

But it was also bittersweet. Leaving Buenos Aires, leaving Argentina, was going to be painful. The city, the country, and the people had crept into Marcus's entire being and left an indelible impact on who he was. *How to properly describe this place?* Marcus wondered. Paradoxical, and in so many ways. The beautiful grand Beaux-Arts style buildings lining Buenos

Aires's major avenues; and then the scores of run-down, shockingly poor *villas* that permeated the roads leading out to Ezeiza International Airport. The intense metropolitan feel of Buenos Aires, with its *Subte*, vibrant street life and horrendous traffic jams, and then the vast open plains of La Pampa, the pristine mountains and lakes of Bariloche, and the monumental glacier of Perito Moreno. The European-feeling high culture of Buenos Aires's restaurants, the polo fields of its suburbs, and the thriving wine industry around Mendoza, then the down-home, almost blue-collar intonations and hand-gestures of Argentine Spanish, or *castellano*. The vast number of natural resources, the large size of the country, and the very intelligent populace which should make Argentina a global powerhouse comfortably in the G-8, and then the continued stumbling of the country's economy and consistent defaulting on its international debt obligations.

And then most special of all, and paradoxical beyond all belief, were the Argentine people. Marcus chuckled just thinking about them. On the one hand, the people were the most highly selfeducated and interested he had come across: nearly all multilingual, avid readers of everything from the classics to British poetry, and capable of describing more about US politics than Marcus even knew existed. On the other hand, Buenos Aires was full of petty criminals and thieves, leaving no bag or wallet safe unless under careful guard, creating a bitter undertone to the relaxed and vibrant feel of the city. The *Porteños* were made up of numerous different national backgrounds, most of them European: Italian, Spanish, German, Polish, Irish, and many others. This was often evident in learning a *Porteño*'s full name: Lucas Gonzalo O'Farrell Heiner, or Sylvia Scholz Ramos Fontivario. Yet all of them came together, and shared the same day-to-day language, with its unique, animated accent.

Marcus downed another gulp of his beer. In the distance he saw Luchi walking down the sidewalk toward Lo de Bebe. He pulled out his phone to check the time: 10:29 p.m. She was walking with pace and pomp, bobbing up and down as she tried very hard to look like she didn't care. She had on slim-fit, whitewashed jeans, a form-fitting white T-shirt under a black leather jacket, and a pair of black Chuck Taylors on her feet. The ensemble looked like something Mick Jagger might have worn in the early '80s, but somehow she still looked beautiful as ever. Marcus rose to greet her with a quick kiss on the lips as she arrived. She was unapologetic for her late arrival. She sat down and immediately extracted her rectangular metal tin of tobacco, rolled a cigarette, lit it, and took a deep drag before exhaling smoke out to the side, then laid her big brown eyes on Marcus. This look of hers always seemed to say, *What are you going to do about it?* Sometimes challenging, sometimes playful, oftentimes both.

She had a naturally olive complexion from her Italian and Spanish roots, but she was pale this time of year. Her face was fleshy and her nose a bit too large. She had black hair that was long and straight, flipped back over her forehead and with a natural part in the middle. She was of short- to average-height, and was skinny throughout except for her bust, which was surprisingly large compared to the rest of her. Her disposition was guarded, which she accentuated on purpose. But her sweet, awkward smile and the twinkle in her eyes when she laughed made her irresistible. *I am really going to miss this girl*, Marcus thought as he worked up ideas for small talk to get through the meal.

Facundo appeared with a plate of four empanadas, two of ham, cheese, and onion, and two of shredded beef. These were Luchi's favorite, and she shot Marcus a sly look of gratitude. Luchi and Marcus ordered entrées from memory without consulting the menu, and then went to work on the empanadas. Marcus asked how her day had been, how the internship was going, and how her classes were. She was studying for a master's degree in architecture and was also doing an internship at a local design studio. Marcus had met Luchi, ironically enough, in the Plaza Francia at an artisans' market, which took place pretty much every Saturday in the walkways around the Centro Cultural Recoleta. The market was Marcus's favorite in Buenos Aires. In an open-air setting with all types of unique Argentine arts and crafts for sale, it was set above the large hill and rolling green grass of the park below. Luchi was helping one of her friends sell handmade jewelry at a booth in the market. Marcus had stopped at the booth next door to look at some kits for drinking *maté*, the traditional South American tea, and noticed Luchi. Although he had no interest in the wares Luchi and her friend were selling, he wandered into their booth and chatted with Luchi briefly. He invited her to join him after the market closed. Marcus and his friends were playing some football in the park and after they finished playing, they were going to lay down some blankets on the grass for a picnic dinner.

Marcus was relaxing, reading *Final del Juego*, a collection of short stories by famed Argentine author Julio Cortázar, when Luchi snuck up next to his blanket. Luchi, who had rightly guessed that Marcus was American during their brief chat in her friend's booth, playfully scoffed at him for being *"un típico ejemplo del yanqui"* for reading a book *"tan conocido en Argentina."* But the truth was that she was impressed that Marcus cared enough to delve into Argentine literature, and she started quizzing Marcus about the book. They engaged in a lively conversation about how much each of them loved Cortázar's writing and before they knew it, they were cracking jokes and getting on very well. That had been the spark for a relationship going on for nine months now.

Luchi gave Marcus an apathetic account of her day at work, and then an enthusiastic description of her architecture class at the University of Buenos Aires. *It's clear where her interests lie*, Marcus thought, as he chuckled to himself. Facundo returned with a plate of mixed grilled meats and seasoned French fries. The meats were some of Marcus's favorites: *morcilla*, the cooked, black blood sausage, *entraña*, a grilled skirt steak, and *bondiola*, a braised pork shoulder. They were all clearly fresh off the grill, as smoke was still rising from their exteriors, small drops of juice dripped onto the plate underneath, and the smell of the slight searing of the meats reached Marcus's nose. Accompanying the plate of meats and fries were two small side dishes of sauces, one of forest-green chimichurri and another of soft-orange *salsa golf*. Then Facundo placed a liter-sized blue ceramic jar on the table which contained the house red wine, an affordable and spectacular Argentine Malbec. He poured the wine into two run-of-the-mill glasses, which could easily have been used for water or soda. Upon arriving in Argentina, Marcus had quickly concluded that the Argentines kept all the good Malbec for themselves, as the ones he tasted here were much better than what he remembered of Malbec stateside.

Luchi skillfully and intentionally carved through the meats and consumed well over half the plate. She seemed to be particularly forceful with the knife this evening, clanging the metal against the plate on various occasions. Marcus shuddered internally. Luchi began to ask Marcus about what his company was planning on next in Argentina, since they had sold off "that other businesses of yours," as she put it. The two of them rarely discussed anything substantive related to Marcus's work, so there was clearly an ulterior motive to Luchi's questions. Marcus mumbled his way through the meal by talking about closing Peppercorn's sale transaction and helping some of his colleagues find new jobs, both in Argentina and back in the US. Facundo rescued him by coming to remove their completely cleaned plates, and ask if they wanted dessert, some *alfajores* or *dulce de leche*, perhaps? The looming conversation had clearly wiped away any appetite for something sweet, as they both declined the dessert offer and opted for espresso instead. They both took large gulps of the Malbec to ward off the silence, and when Facundo returned with the espresso and two little glasses of sparkling water to accompany them, Luchi rolled another cigarette and lit it.

Marcus took hold of the handle of the little coffee cup and downed his double espresso, as if to bolster his strength for his next utterance. The liquid and foam warmed the insides of his chest against the chill of the evening, and he embarked on swallowing the proverbial frog. He spoke in a manner that was lucid and linear, as if working through a logical theorem. He tried to make eye contact at least half the time, and as best he could, stick to the script he had rehearsed in his mind so many times already that day. He even remembered to come full circle at the end, thanking her for their time together and intentionally avoiding saying *"no sos vos, soy yo…"*

Luchi looked him up and down when he was done, then blew out a long breath of smoke from her cigarette. She dropped her coffee cup loudly onto the little plate it came on. After that, silence dominated until a man chatting away on his cell phone walked by with somewhere between eight to twelve dogs on leashes all around him. Marcus could see the anger and frustration building inside of her. She shook her head deliberately from left to right, almost like she was performing a stretch. Then she spoke, "And I always thought that you would leave me to go back to the US. But Paris…" Another long exhale of cigarette smoke. "…who can blame you for that."

She packed up her tin of tobacco and slid it into her little handbag. Then she fiercely slapped Marcus square across the face, making a loud clap that turned Marcus's head to the side. Lo de Bebe had just about filled up by this time, and the other patrons stopped everything to stare in Luchi and Marcus's direction. Silence overtook the restaurant.

Marcus had been half-expecting something like this. He calmly rotated his head back in Luchi's direction and made an effort to remain expressionless. She stood up, zipped up her leather jacket, then walked over to Marcus and gave him a long, flat kiss on the lips. He cherished the taste of the freshly burned tobacco and the smell of her faint perfume, knowing this was the last time he would experience them. Without a word, she turned and emphatically walked away into the darkness. Subtle chatter at the tables nearby started up again slowly. Marcus took out his wallet and prepared to ask for the check. Facundo appeared by Marcus's side and placed a shot glass of dark greenish-brown liquid on the table. Marcus instantly recognized the drink as Fernet-Branca from the strong smell of licorice and earth. Then Facundo made firm eye contact with Marcus and stated, "*Esta noche, la casa invita.*" Then Facundo waved away Marcus's outstretched hand holding a credit card.

Marcus knew it made no sense to protest, so he raised the shot glass in Facundo's direction and then to the other patrons sitting at the outdoor tables. They greeted his toast with laughter and raised glasses of their own. He swallowed hard to down the thick, sweet liquor. Then he briefly shook his head, knowing he would never see Luchi again.

CHAPTER 20

Paris, France.
Place Vauban.
Monday, July 1, 2019.

M ARCUS FELT VERY MUCH A SINGLE MAN AS HE walked to work that morning. Capucine was likely standing in line to board her flight to New York, and today marked the effective end of their semi-serious dating relationship. They had dined with a group of good friends the previous Saturday night at Capucine's favorite restaurant, Chez Gladine, a delightful Basque restaurant at the top of the hill on the Rue des Cinq Diamants near the Place d'Italie, as a send-off. Saturday dinners at Chez Gladine tended to be social, loud, tons of fun, and fantastically delicious. They had joined the like-minded crowd spilling out onto the cobblestone street and surrounding sidewalk in front of the restaurant as they waited for a table, enjoying beers on draft or glasses of wine from one of the neighboring bars and restaurants. Once inside, they took their place at one of the long wooden tables covered in informal red-and-white checkered tablecloths, packed in tightly next to other full, loud tables. They immediately ordered up multiple bottles of the house wine special for the evening, written up on a chalkboard behind the bar, an Irouléguy from the Basque country. It was a fruity red wine best for volume consumption and arrived at the table in stock clear glass bottles with metal hinges and rubber stoppers at the top. Just about everyone ordered Chez Gladine's famous *confit de canard*, a crispy duck leg accompanied by wild mushrooms and a plateful of crisp circle-cut French fries, all accented by a white Roquefort cheese sauce. It was a succulent delight and a joyful farewell to Capucine from the group.

The private farewell between Marcus and Capucine was of a similar character. They took the number six Metro line from Corvisart to La Motte-Picquet-Grenelle, then walked down the Avenue de la Motte-Picquet by the Champ de Mars, just in time to catch the Eiffel Tower performing its sparkling lights routine on the hour. They had both seen this hundreds of times before, thousands of times in Capucine's case, but each still unconsciously stopped and stared wonderingly. They held hands and tilted their necks as they stared in a way that only a person well-lubricated with alcoholic beverages can. Capucine pulled Marcus toward her body, closed her eyes, and gave him a long, wet kiss. He could feel her thin, firm body pulsating against his.

They made love with a primal instinct in Marcus's apartment, sweatily falling asleep afterwards. Marcus awoke in the middle of the night, gently roused Capucine, extracted a bottle of champagne from the refrigerator, and escorted her to the white-cushioned chaise lounge on the balcony. They took turns sipping out of the bottle as Capucine found a slow, easy rhythm in Marcus's lap, his free hand on her bony hip as her small, taut breasts rocked in front of the Paris skyline.

They laughed at the previous night's behavior over coffee and croissants the next morning, then said goodbye like grown-ups, not prolonging the inevitable. Marcus made it a point to be busy the rest of the day. Realizing he had now committed himself to cycle across a quarter of the country in a month, he went for a long bike ride. He rode over to the Boulevard Raspail, then took it all the way to the end at the Parc Montsouris, then out the Boulevards des Maréchaux across the Seine, past the Stade Roland-Garros and into the Bois de Boulogne. He wandered aimlessly until hitting the Hippodrome de Longchamp, made a loop around it and then headed home. He spent a few hours reviewing the updated draft of the Gas Polskie due diligence report that Bamba's team at Dunworths had returned after getting Marcus's comments the day before. In the early afternoon, he wandered over to a grassy spot near Les Invalides and lay down on a blanket to get some sun and make progress on Maupassant's *Bel-Ami*.

The description of Duroy's winding railroad trip up the Seine to Rouen lulled Marcus to sleep. He consoled himself that night with a gyro sandwich, some French fries, half a bottle of slightly chilled Chinon red wine, and some further research into the Broccatelli family and their vast holdings.

There was a light drizzle outside on Marcus's walk to work that Monday morning, making the quiet Monday-morning Paris streets even quieter. Beneath his large black umbrella, he reflected on his relationship with Capucine. He would miss her, for sure. And he would likely see her again when she was back in Paris, or perhaps when he was in New York, but it would be different then. Part of what allowed them to have such an enjoyable relationship was the freeing knowledge that it would end, and now it had. This brought some comfort, but deeper down it stoked anxiety about his future. *Will it always be like this? Just like it was with Luchi in Argentina? Am I destined to gravitate toward relationships that have a natural end? Is that what I committed to when I signed up for this job, this life?* These types of questions bubbled up to the surface of his consciousness on rare occasions. He didn't have definitive answers to these questions yet, but deep down he hoped that the answers were *no*. That it wouldn't always be like this. That one day, he would very clearly and fervently commit to someone unconditionally—the consequences be damned. And they would commit to him too. And while that inner voice was buried deep down, beneath the bravado of his cover, it had yet to be completely silenced. This gave him hope and allowed him to move those thoughts and questions to the side and keep barreling along with the task at hand.

THE FIRST MONDAY of the month at Peppercorn meant a meeting of the investment committee. This was the group within the firm that granted the authority to transact on the firm's behalf: invest in new projects or get out of current ones. Any investment the firm made or was considering making was typically managed by one particular mid- to senior-level person, and that individual would make their case to the investment committee at these meetings. On this Monday, Marcus was one of those individuals. He had dressed the part as well, that is, the part he was playing as a typical private equity professional. His personal preference would have been something subtle and solid, but instead he wore a trim, deep-sea-blue Italian suit with slim lapels and a faint sheen, a crisp, slim-fitting white dress shirt with a forward point collar, and a light-red silk tie that left little doubt as to which designer made it and how much it cost. The fact that he and everyone else participating in the investment committee meeting were dressing up at all to meet with each other, the same people they worked with every day in more casual clothing, was somewhat baffling. *Well, guess this is just one more thing to make us all feel even more important than we already think we are...* Marcus thought to himself, then scolded himself for being cynical and discarded the thought.

INVESTMENT COMMITTEE MEETINGS took place in the European afternoon, so that New York could join during its morning. This allowed Marcus much of the day to prepare for the meeting and attend to other work matters. A message from the personal assistant to Mr. Mauro Broccatelli had arrived promptly in Marcus's email inbox at nine a.m. He reviewed it quickly to see that it was the official invitation and information packet for the cycling trip down the Rhône River at the end of the month. He replied straightaway, confirming his plans to attend and noting that he would send along the particulars of his travel plans once available. Then he put the message aside for a detailed review once he could devote his full attention to it. Marcus spent the rest of the day reviewing and tightening up the PowerPoint slides he had prepared for the committee, seeking input and assistance from Alexandra Mouer on some finer points to the presentation and the Gas Polskie project's financial model. He was going to cover two topics: selling TeleCAR and submitting a bid for

Gas Polskie. Making the case to sell TeleCAR should be easy; the investment had not done well as an operating business and, shockingly, there were several strategic telecommunications companies clamoring to increase their foothold in Africa. So they might be able to sell the company at a high enough price to save face on what had admittedly become a challenging investment. The case for investing into Gas Polskie, on the other hand, was going to require some serious convincing.

Marcus knew that, ultimately, Franz could use his influence within the firm and leverage his relationship with the Miller Family to push through an investment that was truly strategic for the Shareholder. But that could only happen so many times, and more importantly, it was antithetical to the whole reason for causing the Shareholder to work through Peppercorn. The investments not only had to *look* real; they had to *be* real. A counterparty doing a deal with Peppercorn had to be certain they were working with an independent financial investor who had one master, and one master only: money. If Peppercorn invested with someone doing something nefarious, that party had to know that if Peppercorn found out about the nefarious activity, it would be in Peppercorn's financial interest to look the other way. Franz's team within Peppercorn had intentionally cultivated a reputation within the financial world as an investor that was willing to take risks, and to do business in geographies and with parties that many other investors were not comfortable with. For that reason, Marcus had to make the Gas Polskie investment one that made sense for Peppercorn as a firm, and ultimately, was likely to make money for the limited partners that entrusted Peppercorn with their money. It also needed to provide strategic benefits to the Shareholder.

At four p.m., they gathered in Peppercorn's central glass-enclosed modern conference room for the meeting. Members from other offices such as New York or Berlin appeared on four large video screens, grouped together to form a large rectangle mounted on one end of the conference room. Stretching away from the video screens was a twenty-foot-long, live-edge wood table, freshly polished on top, replete with printed wire-bound copies of all of the day's relevant presentations stacked on top of each other at each seat. The remote attendees on the video screens were distributed electronic copies of the presentations, and each presentation would also be shown as presented on an additional large rectangular screen at the front of the room. Once all were present, Laurent Béjot, the head of the Paris office, sitting at the lone seat on the far end of the table from the screens, nodded at Alexandra Mouer, seated to Bèjot's left. The remaining places at the table were filled by senior professionals that had observation rights, but not voting rights, for investment committee meetings, and finally, Marcus and his two other fellow presenters. The three presenters were seated in the middle of the table, so that they could readily address the rest of the table and the remote attendees. As head of investor relations, Alexandra also attended all investment committee meetings. She was smartly dressed as well, wearing a snug, khaki-colored pencil skirt, a silk navy-blue blouse with small, white polka dots, elbow-length sleeves, and an open neck. Her blond hair, beginning to show highlights from the summer sun, was pulled back neatly. *This woman exudes preparedness and professionalism*, Marcus thought as Alexandra pressed a button on the table. The floor-to-ceiling glass walls around the conference room immediately turned from translucent to opaque, as if frozen solid in an instant. Now the meeting could begin.

Peppercorn had three different types of industries, referred to as verticals, that it invested in: complex financial securities, consumer goods, and what they called "real assets," which encompassed real estate, infrastructure, and energy. And while different professionals focused on different verticals, there was one investment committee that oversaw them all. The current members of the investment committee were Béjot, Mike DiNardino, a New York-based managing partner that was in charge of real assets in all of North America, Morgane Fournier, another Parisbased partner in charge of the real assets portfolio outside of North

America, and Arthur Franz. Fournier was seated opposite Alexandra, just to Bèjot's right, and DiNardino and Franz were two of the four faces present on the screens at the front of the room. All of Peppercorn's investments needed to make sense on paper, and each member of the investment committee would zero in on the math and the financial model of any proposal. A good internal rate of return, or IRR, was necessary for any Peppercorn project, but it typically wasn't sufficient. There needed to be additional compelling reasons to make an investment. And each member of the investment committee had their own idiosyncrasies to appeal to, or to watch out for, to get their approval for a project.

By paying close attention to the questions each member asked, or points they drilled down on, in prior meetings, and from general conversation with them in the halls of the office or at some of the office social events, Marcus had come to know what got each member of the investment committee excited about a project, and what made them uncomfortable. Béjot loved the idea of "new energy" and "clean energy," progressive investments toward a greener platform for the firm, propelling the industry into a more environmentally friendly future. Accordingly, he was terrified to invest in companies that did not have a pristine ESG record. DiNardino, Marcus's former boss from his first year at Peppercorn in New York, was a real stickler for the numbers and would hammer away at financial models and figures. He didn't accept the seemingly universal assumption that all businesses grow in real life like they do on a spreadsheet or on a PowerPoint slide with an image showing a hockey stick graph. He wanted details on exactly how and why a particular business would grow, and to understand the math behind those projections.

Fournier wanted Peppercorn to be a household name globally, and she loved projects with big growth opportunities, or in industry-speak, *lots of scale*. But she was also very focused on "synergizing the portfolio" as she called it, using the other Peppercorn businesses to help each other grow and avoid redundancy at all costs. And Arthur Franz cared deeply about the macroeconomic investing trends and being in front of everyone else in that respect, but he hated losing money for the Miller Family. That was the image Franz portrayed at least. Marcus knew that inwardly Franz cared deeply about the strategic goals of the Shareholder.

At Marcus's allotted time, he directed the committee to the PowerPoint slide deck that each attendee had a printed copy of. An electronic version of the deck appeared on the large rectangular screen at the head of the table. Marcus made quick work of the TeleCAR divestiture proposal; a few concise, direct slides bared the poor financial position of the company and the surprisingly hot market for comparable businesses. The committee readily agreed that a sale was wise and that they should move forward with that process. Marcus acknowledged the committee's approval. *Easy enough... now, on to the fun part...*

Now it was Marcus's turn to nod at Alexandra. As he did so, she pressed another button on the table, and the lights in the room slowly dimmed until they were off. A completely black slide appeared on the screen. Marcus remained silent for a count of three uncomfortable seconds. Then an image of continental Europe at night appeared on the screen. Thick yellow clusters and spider webs of light covered the easily recognizable dark outline of the Old World. This slide had conveniently been omitted from the deck sent around to the committee prior to the meeting. While technically a violation of protocol, the theatrics made their intended effect. Marcus could feel the curiosity brimming within the room.

"Peppercorn Capital is committed to powering Europe into the future," Marcus paused for effect, then continued, "and to do so in a profitable, yet responsible manner. Coal and nuclear power are politically toxic. Renewable energy has promising aspects, but still looks to be a long way from being able to support the power grid on an around-the-clock basis. Natural gas is the bridge fuel: a cleaner-burning fuel source that is likely to power the cities, factories, homes, and vehicles of Europe and much of the world during the lion's share of our lifetimes." He looked back in Alexandra's direction, nodding gently again. She held his gaze a split second longer than necessary and he caught the corners of her mouth lift ever so slightly before she reversed the dimming effect and slowly brought the light in the room back. *Was she flirting with me...no, stay focused*, Marcus thought.

"That's the position that this firm has taken, and so far, we have benefited greatly from it," Marcus stated. The next slide showed the substantial IRR Peppercorn had recouped on five previous natural gas-related businesses that it had sponsored, including Marcus's Argentine transportation business and the Texas exploration and production properties he'd helped develop.

He continued, "Now, we may differ individually as to when or if we think renewable energy sources will come online in full force. But you've seen the data our research team has prepared, and the case for European natural gasfired power demand is strong. As things stand today, that demand will principally be satisfied by Russian natural gas with very little outside competition." The implications of this last sentence were not lost on a room full of private equity professionals; the Russians would get filthy rich selling gas to Europe. Marcus paused for an uncomfortably long moment again and looked around the room. The faces looking back at him showed a mixed range of emotions: curiosity, enthusiasm, skepticism...but not boredom. *Good*, Marcus thought, *they're paying attention*. Then, with an emboldened look in his eye, Marcus continued, "But we can change that. We have a unique opportunity to help satisfy that demand, to create a competitive alternative to Russian natural gas for the European market, to help develop a more environmentally friendly alternative to coal and a safer alternative to nuclear...and to make lots of money for our LPs and the firm along the way." And with that, Marcus vaulted into the background information and financial case for the Gas Polskie project.

PEPPERCORN WOULD PLACE a bid to purchase a portion of the ownership interests, or equity, of the existing Gas Polskie company. They would then work with the current Gas Polskie team to continue developing the core business: building an import terminal that could receive LNG and convert it back from a liquid into a gas, and then sell that gas to power producers who would use it to create electricity. As a quasi-Polish governmental entity, Gas Polskie had priority rights to sell gas to the Polish government and municipalities for power production, and also to acquire additional land next to their import terminal on the Baltic Sea in Świnoujście. They would need to either buy gas from other companies that produced it, or Gas Polskie could simply serve as a middleman and, for a hefty fee, convert the LNG back to gas and transport it for someone else. The financial model that the Peppercorn team prepared showed that, if all went according to plan based on Gas Polskie's existing projections, the revenues from the sales contracts were significantly greater than the expected costs to buy gas and to build the terminal.

"Well, what if it doesn't go according to plan?" DiNardino had immediately asked, his hard New York accent booming into the conference room, amplified by the surround speakers connected to the audio feed from his screen.

"Good question," Marcus responded calmly, point-ing to DiNardino's screen, then looking around the room and nodding slowly. Marcus had anticipated this objection and had prepared a response. He directed the committee to the next slide where an additional iteration of the financial model was prepared to show the anticipated profits if only two thirds of the reve-nues came in—still a decent return.

Alexandra, interjecting unexpectedly, added an important point in a reasoned and dispassionate tone. "Even if revenues were only as depicted in this revised model, a sale opportunity down the road would still likely fetch a high price. Development of the termi-nals and gas sales for power would make owning this project much more appealing because almost all of the development cost and risk would be gone." Her point seemed to hit home with everyone around the table and on the screen, as their enlightened faces nodded along involuntarily. Marcus shot Alexandra a quick glance and light tip of the head. *Touché…and thank you*, he seemed to convey.

"That's right," Marcus noted to the group, then added intently, "And remember, those projections are *before* we get our people in there to optimize these assets and make use of our contacts and other businesses on the continent." His gaze settled on Fournier as he emphasized this last point. Her excited countenance portrayed that it clearly resonated with her.

"And, the additional attractiveness of this project," Marcus piled on, "is its growth opportunities and resulting potential for a huge cash out sale down the line." He then explained that, through the priority right on additional land at the port from the Polish government, Gas Polskie could very cheaply build out more terminals to allow it to handle products beyond gas, such as other petrochemicals or agricultural products. There was also the potential to significantly expand the number of customers by beginning to sell natural gas to other European countries. And Marcus's personal favorite, the opportunity to acquire additional cheap land from the Polish government outside of Krakow, in the south of Poland near the Czech and Slovak borders, bordering on the Vistula River. This would allow for construction of an inland terminal and transport center there, creating connectivity to the center of Eastern Europe with Gas Polskie's terminals on the Baltic Sea by using the Bydgoszcz Canal, linking the Vistula to the Oder River, which flows into the Baltic near Świnoujście.

The various growth options hit home with the committee, as Marcus could see them nodding their heads in approval. But questions remained.

"What about the Russians? Can this project really compete with their stranglehold on European gas supply?" Fournier asked, in her perfectly British accent that she had picked up from graduate studies at Cambridge, a finance degree from the London School of Economics and then three years as an investment banker at Barclays in London.

"Thank you, Morgane," Marcus acknowledged her concern, "This needs to be considered carefully to move forward with this investment." Marcus outlined two points that would mitigate against Russia's ability to squash the Gas Polskie project. First, through contract due diligence, Bamba's team at Dunworths had found an obscure provision in some of the Polish government's gas and power purchase agreements with the Russians that allowed for termination of the agreement if a Polish company was able to "locally produce or source" similar products. The upshot was that once Gas Polskie was up and running, the Polish government could terminate its agreements with the Russians and enter into new ones with Gas Polskie. A look of pleasant surprise permeated the room, followed by subtle nods as if to acknowledge the depth of diligence that had clearly been undertaken by Marcus and his team of internal and external advisors in researching this opportunity.

"And for the second point…" Again, Marcus paused, looked around the room, then added, "I'll let Arthur Franz explain," as he gestured toward Franz's face on the screen at the front of the room. This caught everyone by surprise. Arthur Franz was laconic as it was, but to have a member of the investment committee speak on behalf of any particular project was almost unheard of. Their lack of comfort was quickly replaced by fascination as Franz opened his monologue by expressing the extremely confidential nature of what he was about to say. The room leaned forward with bated breath. In a meeting like this, already highly confidential by its nature, for someone to add a layer of confidentiality was tantalizing. Franz then tactically described the Russians' reliance on construction of the new Nord Stream 2 pipeline to remain competitive, and the various diplomatic, political, and economic factors he was secretly aware of that might prevent that construction from ever happening.

"Again, the information just shared is not known by the market, and it would behoove all of us to keep it that way," Franz reiterated, alluding to the fact that if the Nord Stream 2 issues were widely known, the price to buy into Gas Polskie would skyrocket due to it being a much more viable option. *He really has a gift of saying things without actually saying them*, Marcus observed internally, as he saw the reactions Franz's statement brought forth.

Once this bit of information settled into the room, and the resulting dollar signs were blinked away from the eyes of the meeting attendees, Béjot ushered the presentation to its final act, "*D'accord,* Markooz," he said in a heavy accent, "what iz your, uh, investment proposal? Or?"

A polite way of getting to the dollars and cents. Marcus nodded understandingly.

"They want $400 million for half of the company. That's too expensive and too great of a risk for us to take at the outset. Our proposal," Marcus looked to Franz's face on the screen, then over at Alexandra, and back to the rest of the group, "is to offer $200 million for 25 percent, but to also extend Gas Polskie financing in the form of a bridge loan at a favorable rate until the project is further developed and ready for more traditional financing, at which point the bridge loan would be paid out and replaced by the new lenders. In exchange, we would require an option to purchase another 25 percent of the company in the future, but at today's price."

He watched Béjot and Fournier squirm at the table, and DiNardino's brow furrow on the screen. Only on rare occasions did Peppercorn go into an investment as a lender, and that was typically reserved for something with developed, steady cash flow. Not a speculative bet on Polish gas development.

"And the Miller Family has agreed to participate as well, in the form of a coinvestment," Marcus added, just before their objections could be aired, "We would set up two new investment vehicles, one jointly owned to hold the equity, and a second one principally owned by the Miller Family, with Peppercorn maintaining a nominal ownership stake, for the debt. This will allow the Miller Family to take on the financing risk and offer Peppercorn a preferred return on cash flow during the life of the investment, in exchange for an agreed payout bonus if the project is sold."

The look of a hitchhiker being shown an open car door came across the faces of Béjot, Fournier, and DiNardino.

"Arthur, given your, umm, involvement in ziss project, we will assume you ahr in favoohr?" Béjot replied, regaining his composure.

A curt nod from the white hair and dark eyebrows on the screen.

"*Un moment, s'il vous plait*," Béjot replied, then wheeled his chair over to Fournier and conferred briefly with her before typing something into a private connection with DiNardino on the other end. There were a few more messages exchanged before Béjot looked at Fournier resolutely.

She looked at Marcus, then stated "*Bon*. You are authorized to make the initial bid and, should we be invited for the second-round site visit and meeting with Gas Polskie, to negotiate on the terms discussed today. But the investment committee will be required to make final approval, and—" Fournier emphasized, dipping her head at the same time as if pulling Marcus's leash back toward her, "*she* must go with you." Fournier pointed at Alexandra. Taken aback for the shortest of instances, Alexandra centered herself quickly and did her best to look stern. The committee's intent was clear: by having Alexandra go along, an unbiased, practical thinker would be in the room to help Marcus adhere to the authority extended to him.

"Understood. And thank you for your time and consideration," Marcus replied, looking each committee member in the eye, and then finally, into Alexandra's vibrant chestnut-colored eyes, which looked directly back at him. *Hmm…*Marcus pondered, *maybe there is something between us here.* Then recalling how he had just officially ended things with Capucine, he further reflected, *am I already walking into another untenable relationship?*

CHAPTER 21

Paris, France.
1er Arrondissement.
Saturday, July 6, 2019.

MARCUS HAD TO AVOID A NEAR-STAMPEDE OF jolly, red-faced patrons exiting the front doors of Ô Maison with their arms full of bags and boxes of wine bottles as he arrived late that Saturday afternoon. He held the door for the group and flashed a conspiratorial smile as he let them file out onto the Rue Jean-Jacques Rousseau. *My, those people looked like they had fun. Olivier just never fails...*Marcus thought, as he entered the wine bar's front bar room. He paused and took a deep, long sniff of the air inside Ô Maison. *Aaahhh! I feel more relaxed already*, he thought. As he allowed the faint scents of must and charred oak to enter his nostrils, the slight sensation of humidity gently enveloped him. *Olivier even makes this place feel like a wine cave.* He quickly spotted his good friend, Olivier Lafont, enthusiastically pointing to the magnum-sized bottle in a patron's hands, handing the man a receipt, and then delivering the punch line of some joke in English before Olivier, the patron, and a woman standing with the patron erupted into laughter. Marcus chuckled internally as he caught Olivier sneak a wink at the woman when the male patron looked down to drop the receipt in wine bag that came with the purchase. The woman was still blushing as she and the man with her shuffled past Marcus toward the exit.

Olivier was of medium height, trim but not overly-so, in the way of someone that works on their feet all day. He had short, shaggy brown hair, a round face, a pointed nose, cloudy blue eyes, and an eternal five-o-clock shadow. He was wearing dark, snug, blue jeans, black leather sneakers, and a white linen button-up shirt. If one had to guess his nationality on looks alone, Eastern European would be more likely than French. He was a pleasant-looking guy, for sure, but it was when Olivier began to speak that people became enamored. The combination of his incredible subject matter knowledge, his engaging and personable approach, and the timely placed use of his French accent reeled people in.

The bar room had emptied out except for Marcus, Olivier, and a young lady with long blond hair and milky white skin who presumably worked at Ô Maison, given her white dress shirt, black apron, and black pants. Olivier wrote down a few notes near the cash register, typed something into the computer, then gave some instructions in rapid French to the young lady, who nodded and laughed. Olivier then added, "Luisette, *bravo! Un travail bien fait.*"

She smiled genuinely, then replied "*Merci,*" before disappearing to Ô Maison's kitchen and back office.

"Looked like another group of satisfied customers," Marcus offered up, as he greeted his friend with a warm hand clasp and American-style hug and back slap.

"Not bad, actually. Our new trainee, Luisette, had them in a trance," Olivier replied, clearly pleased. Then he added, "It never gets old, you know? Seeing that mix of fascination and the beginnings of intoxication when people really show interest in learning about wine."

Olivier spoke English perfectly, with the slightest hint of a French accent. He had one American parent and one French parent and had spent some of his junior high and high school years in South Florida. This made him one of those rare people that spoke both French and English as native languages. He came from a food industry family, and he had gravitated toward wine at an early age. Ô Maison was his Paris foothold; technically it was a wine bar, but they also served small plates of food, hosted events, and most notably, offered classes on French wine and its different regions. The *Tour du Vin de France*! These classes, typically given in English, had become wildly successful with tourists, such as the class that Olivier and Luisette had just wrapped up. And, as apparently had been the case today, these classes often ended in lots of wine sales for Ô Maison.

Marcus had first met Olivier and learned about these classes during his Paris tour guide days roughly fifteen years before. In those days Olivier was giving his wine classes in his apartment near the Place de la République. And while the setting wasn't quite as nice as Ô Maison, the quality of the classes was equally high. Marcus remembered how Olivier had brought out a giant contoured map of France, with different colored blobs in all of the wine-producing regions. Then Olivier poured out a bevy of healthy sipping pours from wines from Bordeaux, the Rhône, Bourgogne, Champagne, Alsace, the Jura, Provence, and Languedoc-Roussillon. They tried reds, whites, and rosés. Tasting all of the different wines together and learning just a thimbleful of information about the different areas had a real lasting impact. For Marcus, who at that time considered a jug of cheap sangria to be the apex of viticulture, Olivier's class opened the doors to the world of wine drinking and appreciation. Since then, Olivier had received a business degree from ESSEC Business School in Paris, had spent a year working in the wine industry in California, then returned to Paris to open Ô Maison as a base from which to build several different wine businesses. Ô Maison itself had become a resounding success and remained Paris's largest wine bar. Throughout the years, Marcus and Olivier had remained friends and stayed in touch. Marcus had made it a point to visit Ô Maison every time he was in Paris, and Olivier had met up with Marcus in New York a few times during his visits there. When Marcus returned to Paris with Peppercorn Capital, the two had rekindled their friendship.

The previous work week weighed heavily on Marcus. After getting investment committee approval for the Gas Polskie project, he had worked deep into the night on both Monday and Tuesday to get Peppercorn's initial bid package submitted by the noon deadline on that Wednesday. Then that Thursday was July 4, Independence Day in the United States. While it was fun to celebrate abroad with expats, this was Marcus's fourth year running, and he missed celebrating the Fourth of July in the US with friends. It wasn't until that Friday that Marcus had time to dig into the itinerary for his cycling trip with Mauro Broccatelli and the other select attendees. Two principal themes of the trip displayed themselves immediately: cycling, and lots of it, and wine, and likely lots of that too. *Hopefully not simultaneously*, Marcus thought, then somewhat reconsidered, *but…"*

Marcus immediately forwarded the itinerary to the Shareholder's secure email inbox for travel clearance. Marcus took his lunch break that day to drop his road bike off at the shop for a tune-up, and then scheduled a follow-up appointment for the Monday before the trip. Finally, he sent Olivier an email with the subject line "À l'aide!" describing the trip, the venerable host, and asking if he could stop by Ô Maison the next day to chat about Broccatelli Wines, the Broccatelli family's vast wine empire, the Rhône Valley, and to brush up on his wine terminology.

"You get paid to ride bikes and drink wine with Mauro Broccatelli in the Rhône Valley?" Olivier's initial response had been followed up by an invitation to stop by Ô Maison at five p.m. the next day, between the last wine class and the opening of the evening bar service.

That Saturday, Marcus set off on foot from Place Vauban at about four and walked by Les Invalides, which, in spite of the heat, was packed with shirtless football players, rosé sipping picnickers, and tons of children sprinting aimlessly around the large grassy squares. He took a right at the river and walked down the Qaui d'Orsay, past the outdoor shipping container-like bars that had popped up there over the past few years. The Seine was alive with various Bateaux Mouches, police cruisers, and small recreational boats humming up and down the river. Bikers and runners zipped along both banks, and packs of tourists teemed across each bridge along the way. Marcus scaled the stairs before the Pont des Arts, crossed over to the Right Bank, and then up the Rue du Louvre over to Ô Maison.

Olivier nodded his head toward one of the bar stools, and Marcus took a seat.

"I've just got to finish up one thing here," Olivier explained, then asked, "Drink while you wait?"

Marcus nodded back assuredly, then asked, "French craft beer?"

This drew a sideways look of scorn from Olivier, quickly followed by an excited look and a raised index finger that seemed to say, *aha!* He turned his back and then reappeared with two glasses of rosé. The cold liquid caused the glasses to sweat. The wine inside was a darker pink, with a faint tinge of orange, like the color of a flamingo's wing or neck. Marcus typically preferred the lighter-colored rosés, as he felt like they were not as sweet as the darker-colored ones. But that was a very unscientific generalization, and on top of that, he was damn thirsty from his walk over. They clinked glasses.

"*Chin chin,*" Olivier said. Marcus took a sip, then a good size drink. The cool liquid went down his parched throat smoothly, and he got that initial kick of a sensation, that warm internal feeling, that good times were ahead. Olivier swirled the glass, took a few sniffs, then sipped. He returned to his computer screen to type in a few more things. Marcus looked behind the bar at the various bottles behind an eye-height metal refrigerator that ran the length of the bar horizontally. This refrigerator contained a number of wine bottles attached to spigots, which allow them to be served on tap, as opposed to being poured. There were hundreds more bottles, black, dark green, light green, and clear, on display above the refrigerator. Behind him, in the open area of the front room, were a few high-top metal tables with black stool seats below them. The walls were painted a dark purple, adding to the feeling of displacement from the busy urban setting out front. There were various maps of wine regions, quotes about wine, and wine-themed photos tastefully hung on the walls.

Marcus reexamined the wine in front of him. He did his best imitation of a swirl, held the glass up to the light, took a few sniffs. The wine had a crisp, clean smell, but no particular fruit or vegetable smell jumped out at him. Then he sipped. He tried to breathe in heavily over the wine, which filled the bottom of his mouth, to make a vortex of sorts in the top half of his mouth. He ended up coughing loudly, with hints of rosé in his nostrils. Olivier looked over at him, then back to his computer screen. Marcus tried again, this time with a little less liquid in his mouth and was successful. This sip tasted more like a red wine and was bone dry.

"Tavel," Olivier said as he used his mouse to click out of one final window. He turned toward Marcus, then took another long sip of his own. "Historians believe Tavel was the first *rosé* (*wwhoahzzay*) ever produced in commercial volumes." Olivier's English was perfect, but he was not about to anglicize the names of French wines. "It is a very small *appellation* right across the Rhône from Châteauneuf-du-Pape. Only produces *rosé*. And you, my friend, in about three weeks will likely be biking right past the very vines from which this wine was made."

He handed Marcus the bottle. Marcus wasn't sure what to do with it, but he took the same tack he had read one should take when handed a business card by someone from Japan: hold it up, pretend to give it a good study, then try to look impressed.

"Pff!" Olivier exclaimed, not the least bit fooled. "Come on..." he said, shaking his head, "follow me."

"I've only got an hour, so I'll walk and talk," Olivier said as he led Marcus back to what was probably Marcus's favorite individual room in all of Paris; the Ô Maison *Bibliothèque du Vin*, or Wine Library. It was a private room behind the bar, separated by floor-to-ceiling glass windows and a giant glass door. Inside were the same dark purple walls as the front room but covered by rectangular wine shelves on the two sidewalls, and a giant oval-shaped shelving unit on the back wall. The shelves were broken up into mini-compartments, each of which was chock-full of wine bottles standing up, laid on their side, or still in boxes. Some bottles were clean and shiny, reflecting the lights from above. Others maintained a film of dust on the exterior. There was even a sliding ladder on one of the walls, and in the middle section of that wall were separate compartments that contained books and maps instead of wine bottles. In the center of the room was a long, rectangular old oak table, with big, plush, brown leather chairs surrounding it. Luisette scurried out as they entered, and Marcus saw that several bottles and wine glasses were already laid out at the far end of the table. He made brief eye contact with Luisette and mouthed *Merci*. She replied with a slight nod of the head and the makings of a smile.

Marcus looked around appreciatively, then inhaled through his nose as deeply as he could, taking in the smells of leather from the chairs, cleaned wood from the recently wiped-down table, and the embedded scent of fermented grapes from the thousands of bottles that had been opened and consumed in this room.

"Let's start with Broccatelli Wines," Olivier said, as he walked over to the sliding ladder. He positioned it in front of the books section and began to climb. "The Broccatellis are very serious players in the wine industry. I mean that; they are the real deal. It started with Mauro's dad, Fernando." Olivier extracted a tall, thin red leather-bound book from his left with *Wine Regions of the World* written on the spine. He then grabbed two framed maps from his right and worked his way down the ladder. "Fernando Broccatelli bought a few Argentine vineyards near Mendoza in the early

90s. These started to do pretty well, and he essentially rode the Malbec wave and ended up selling those to a California winemaker for an ungodly sum of money. Excellent timing."

Funny how that always seems to happen to them, Marcus thought.

Olivier placed the maps down on the table and opened the book to a page on Argentina and Uruguay. "Next, Fernando developed new wineries in Uruguay that turned out to make some pretty good wine. The Broccatellis still own them," Olivier pointed to a spot on the map. "It seems like after that, they pivoted in strategy and started picking up what I like to call 'vanity vineyards'; expensive plots of land in very well-known wine regions that produce wine that retails for a high price." He flipped to the California page and pointed to an area in Napa Valley and another in Sonoma. "They hired celebrity winemakers and excellent marketing teams and made stuff that I generally think tastes like a mix of a flat soft drink and melted licorice." Olivier stopped, then looked directly at Marcus, and said, almost obligatorily, "Just to be clear, there are some excellent California wines, I just don't like the ones the Broccatellis made."

Marcus put his palms up, as if to say, *Hey, no offense taken here.*

Olivier then flipped the page to Bordeaux and indicated a spot on the upper left bank of the Garonne

River. "They bought into a few of the famed Bordeaux wine houses. Now those wines are incredible, no doubt about that." He flipped the page to Italy and pointed in the general direction of Tuscany. "They also bought into some places that make the so-called 'Super Tuscans,' which are extremely commercial in nature."

That doesn't sound like a compliment, Marcus thought. He took another big sip of the Tavel he still had in his hand, and asked, "So, not Brunello di Montalcinos?" Marcus was drawing on his Italian wine knowledge from the wine tasting he attended in Tuscany after his friend's wedding.

Olivier laughed condescendingly, then shook his head. "No."

Olivier began opening the bottles on the table. Olivier opened the bottles with such skill and familiarity, it was like watching a concert pianist set his music sheet and stretch his arms before tickling the ivory. Marcus recognized a few: Châteauneuf-du-Pape, Côtes du Rhône, Crozes-Hermitage. Others he didn't recognize.

"The Broccatellis have basically created a high-end, commercially focused wine empire," Olivier continued, "They love the Chinese market, and it almost seems like they have historically catered specifically to it. But," he paused, made a *pop* as he uncorked another bottle, "the last few years they seem to be doing some more interesting stuff. They recently acquired a beautiful vineyard down in Cassis, near Marseille, that makes very good whites and *rosés*. This property is offpiste for them, as it is not commercial and is almost unknown outside of France."

They sat down and Olivier poured out a few glasses, then returned to his last thought. "Mauro seems to be pretty involved in the wine business, Marcus. And my sense is that he might be the one responsible for some of their more recent, creative winemaking activity. If that's true, I like his taste and he will be one to watch in the wine world. Try to learn as much as you can from him."

Very interesting, Marcus thought. All that stuff about commercial vineyards catering to Chinese demand sounded like the stiff board of a man that Marcus met at the d'Orsay, but this last bit sounded like the utterly transformed *castellano*-speaking running enthusiast and lover of the Luxembourg Gardens.

"*Et, voila!*" Olivier said as he poured more wine into the remaining empty glasses. "On to the actual wine portion of the visit."

Marcus moved to the front of his seat and inched his chair closer to the large block of oak.

"Now," Olivier said, stepping back from the table and rotating to face Marcus, "you told me that you wanted to learn more about Broccatelli Wines, which we just discussed, but also to…how did you say, *umm*, 'get smart' on wines in general and Rhône wines in particular."

Marcus winced upon hearing his cliché repeated back to him. He made it a point to avoid using those at all costs, but…*casualty of the profession. Still no excuse though*, he chided himself internally. Olivier then added, "So, basically, you want to impress Mauro Broccatelli, *non*?"

Marcus's reply was a sheepish grin, then he finished the last of his Tavel.

"The truth is, Marcus," Olivier continued, his level of excitement rising, "you already know a lot about wine!" A smile took over Olivier's face. "When you and I have had wine together before, it's obvious that you have some particular wines that you like. Like the Brunello di Montalcino you mentioned earlier. Languedoc-Roussillon wines, and a lot of the Rhône Valley wines. So, you are already off to a great start. What I want us to do today is help you recognize what you already know about wine, get you prepared to learn more in the next few weeks, and then allow you to be able to intelligently talk about wine and not be bowled over by a bunch of wine mumbo-jumbo.

"In looking at your itinerary, my guess is that you will pretty much cover the Northern Rhône on your first day, the Southern Rhône on the second day, and then, on the last day, a beautiful ride south from Avignon past Arles and into the wilds of the Camargue, tracing the brackish waters of the Rhône River Delta into the glistening Mediterranean at Port-Saint-Louis-du-Rhône."

Marcus was reminded that part of what made Olivier so good at talking about French wine was his ability to describe the land itself, the natural surroundings, the climate, the type of soil or rocks on the ground, the geological history, the slant of a hill and the time of the day at which sunlight shone on it, the elevation. All these things that Marcus had learned combine to make up the oh-so-French word *terroir*. Apparently Olivier's descriptive skills extended beyond just wineries.

Olivier picked up a glass and handed it to Marcus, encouraging him.

"Just take a sip?" Marcus asked.

"For now, yes, just enjoy. Remember, that is what wine is supposed to be all about, enjoyment. Pleasure. Let's not overcomplicate it. We want to try new wines, figure out what you like, and then make sure you know where to find it," Olivier replied, launching into his lesson.

"Now, let's begin with the general, although not always correct, premise that new-world wines, the US, Australia, South Africa, *etc.*, are identified by the grapes in the wine. And that old-world wines, France, Italy, Spain, *etc.*, are identified by the region, and then more particularly what we call in France the AOP, what used to be called the AOC. AOP stands for *L'appellation d'Origine Protégée*, which basically means the name for a particular quality of wine from the same place. The

AOP is, without a doubt, the wine characterization most likely to help you identify a certain type of wine. In Italy this is called the DOC or DOCG, and the DO in Spain. You are going to a French wine region, so let's stick with AOP."

Olivier picked up the bottle from which he had poured wine into Marcus's glass and rotated the label around to the front. "The wine you are drinking now is a Crozes-Hermitage." He handed Marcus the bottle, then asked, "So what does that mean?"

Marcus examined the bottle, and then responded, "That's the region?"

"Not quite," Olivier responded, gently laughing. "The Rhône Valley, and the Northern Rhône to be more specific, is the *region*. Crozes-Hermitage is the *AOP*. That means two things really: the first, d'*Origine*, is that all of the grapes that make up that wine were grown within a particular geographic region. So in that sense, as an American, think of a county within a state, with the county being d'*Origine* piece of the AOP, and the region being the state. This means that this wine reflects the particular elements of a specific corner of the world, its *terroir*." The last word sounding so smooth and natural coming from Olivier.

"The second word, *Protégée*, means that this wine has been produced according to particular, time-honored, and honed rules. That usually includes the mix of grapes allowed to be used, but it may also mean the alcohol content, or if sugar can be added. These rules are intended to reflect the best practices from generations and generations of wine makers, in order to most effectively express the character of that *Origine*. So there is a particular attention to quality and mix of grapes that must be used in order to obtain AOP status. You see," Olivier paused, swirled his glass, tilted it a bit to see the wine through the light above, took in a big whiff from within the glass, then tasted, before continuing, "an AOP designation is not a given. It must be earned."

Marcus did an impression of Olivier's swirling.

"Good, that's right," Olivier encouraged, then added, "Think about color, body, smell, and then taste. You swirl the glass to wake the wine up a bit, get its aromas to come to life. Hold it up to the light, or in front of a white background, if you can. Is it cloudy or clear? Is it the same deep, dark purple on the edges as it is in the middle? You don't need to memorize this stuff, just think about it and see what sticks with you."

They both swirled their glasses again, then they smelled.

"There are different approaches to smelling," Olivier explained, "I like two, really big sniffs, but many people prefer lots of smaller sniffs. Try to pick up familiar smells and add that to your description. For example," Olivier went on as he raised the glass and smelled again, "in this wine, I smell some black pepper and a little of what we call *garrigue*, which is like brush."

Then he tasted and added "Same thing on the taste, but maybe a hint of bacon there too. But the smells and flavors you identify are not a Jeopardy contest, they'll be different for most people. Just think a little bit about what it tastes like and try to start noticing which tastes you like." Olivier raised his eyebrows and his right index finger and added, "And just as important, what tastes you *don't* like."

Marcus smelled, then took a sip. The black pepper was definitely there, but maybe that was because Olivier just said it should be. The wine was good, but not his favorite.

"Not your favorite, huh?" Olivier, as if reading Marcus's mind, observed, "My guess, given some of the other stuff you like, is that you are going to like the Southern Rhône wines better. For me, personally, I love the Northern Rhônes, the AOPs Hermitage and Côte Rôtie are my favorite red wines in the world. These wines tend to be smooth, almost velvety, but also very complex. Now, the Southern Rhône wines, like the Chateauneuf-du-Pape or some of the Côtes-du-Rhône Villages wines, are big, bold wines that are almost grainy at the end, with a powerful aftertaste. Perfect with a nice *steak-frites*."

Olivier then explained that, in addition to the larger AOP of Côtes-du-Rhône, there was also a smaller, more select AOP called Côtes-du-Rhône Villages, which covers 17 small villages in the Southern Rhône region that tended to make wines of a little higher quality and consistency than the Côtes-du-Rhône AOP.

"Really try to take note of the differences that you taste between the two regions, and then think about the differences in *terroir* too as you are biking along, because you will get an incredible view of hundreds of wineries along the route," Olivier continued.

Olivier gestured back at the bottle in Marcus's hand, then continued, "Take a look at the label. Most labels are like this one; the property's name at the top, a nice little picture below, the AOP, the year it was made, or *vintage* in wine-speak, and then you also have the owners of the property. For French wines, on the back you often find the types of grapes used to make the wine. As you learn more about particular AOPs, you won't even need to look those up!"

A huge smile covered Olivier's face as he gave Marcus's shoulder a light tap with the back of his hand.

"In the Rhône Valley, as a rule the Northern Rhône wines are predominantly made from Syrah grapes, and the Southern Rhône wines are from Grenache grapes. Want to know a little trick I have for my English-speaking Rhône wine lovers?" Olivier asked Marcus, raising his eyebrows a few times, and looking from left to right a few times, as if he was about to betray a long-held state secret. "Syrah…is not South. You see? Syrah is mainly in the North. Just remember that and you'll never mix up the whole Syrah, Grenache divide!"

Marcus couldn't help but laugh at how into wine Olivier was. He said it to himself, *Syrah is not South... not bad*, he thought, *I can remember that*. They worked their way through a handful of Rhône wines, a Northern Rhône white wine called Condrieu, a glass of the more exclusive Hermitage, which Marcus found tasted similar to, but better than, the Crozes-Hermitage, and then down to the South for a Chateauneuf-du-Pape, a Côtes du Rhône, and then a very nice, albeit lighter, wine from the AOP Ventoux. The mention of Ventoux reminded Marcus of the famous Mont Ventoux of Tour de France cycling fame—and how much cycling he had ahead of him. This thought encouraged him to take it somewhat easy and have some water during the tasting.

As they came up on the hour, Olivier enthusiastically explained, "You see? Such a difference between each AOP. So learning about different AOPs, recognizing what makes those wines unique, and what you like about a particular AOP, is going to help you figure out the types of wines you like to drink. And think, there are almost five-hundred different AOPs in France! And that only covers a little over half of all the wine produced in France, because many don't obtain AOP status!" Olivier's passion for French wine was infectious, and it was clearly rubbing off on Marcus as he laughed and nodded his head joyfully.

"And don't just settle on a few AOPs you like either. Keep trying new things, even if you don't think you will like it. This will help broaden the boundaries of your wine-drinking mind. Drink lots of wine, think about what you like, maybe even write it down in a journal or notebook; these are all great ways to learn more about wine," Olivier summarized as he began cleaning up the bottles and glasses to conclude their visit. "But the absolute best way, the *best*, is to go visit a vineyard and taste their wines. Being there, seeing the grounds and vines and grapes and features of the land around the vineyard—this is how you learn. Meet the winemakers; that will tell you a lot about the wine too. So, by my calendar," Olivier said, as he looked down at this phone, "you have two full weekends between now and your trip. That means you need to ride your bike as much as possible between now and then, but also make a day trip out to a winery in the Loire, or one in *Bourgogne* and go taste some of the wines. Practice learning about wine."

Marcus considered the suggestion and thought it wouldn't be a bad way to kill some time during these quieter summer weekends. He told Olivier he would do that and thanked him immensely. He gave his friend a solid handshake, which then turned into a bear hug.

"One last thing," Olivier said, holding up a finger. He ran back into an office, then returned carrying something behind his back. "There are a lot of people who talk about the structure or balance of a wine, which is usually thought of as the components of acid, tannin, alcohol, and sugar. Don't worry too much about understanding those for now, but I think reading the first few chapters of this will help," he said, extending a small book over to Marcus.

Marcus looked down to see a copy of *Enjoy the Journey: A Trip into French Wine with Olivier Lafont*. He opened the front cover to see a smiling head shot of Olivier standing in front of a hill covered in vines behind him on the left side, and a note and autograph on the first blank page. Marcus read the note:

Cher Marcus,

What a wonderful beginning to your own wine voyage you have ahead of you. I hope this helps you accomplish your objectives. To many more tasting sessions together, *Santé*!

Cordialment,
Ô.

Olivier smiled and said, "I hope you are okay with the English version. We are all out of the French ones."

Marcus looked up at Olivier, flashed his own big, warm smile, then responded, *"C'est parfait. Merci!"* He looked earnestly at Olivier and asked, "What do I owe you for all of this? Those were some nice wines, and we opened quite a few bottles."

Olivier responded by frowning, then slightly shaking his head, and waving one of his hands from side to side. Marcus protested.

"I tell you what, if your new friend Mauro Broccatelli happens to need a business consultant for his wine empire, perhaps you can whisper my name into his ear," Olivier countered.

Marcus chuckled then acquiesced. He planted that piece of information into the recesses of his mind, like being dealt an auspicious card and then waiting for the right hand to play it.

CHAPTER 22

Cartagena de Indias, Colombia. July 2019.

G RAHAM CURRY ROLLED OVER ONTO HIS BACK peacefully and stretched his arms and legs out as far as they could go. The Caribbean sun was creeping into his third-floor bedroom through the partially open white wooden shutters separating his bedroom from the balcony. The light found its way onto Graham's king-sized, white bed, which sat atop a chocolate-colored wooden plank of a bed frame only six inches off the white stucco floor. He peeked at the alarm clock, then felt the cool breeze from the small electric fan plugged in on the far side of his white nightstand. He leaned his head over to the other side, and made out the inflated, round figures of the framed Botero print in the middle of the wall. After brushing his teeth and throwing on his bathrobe, he grasped a small ceramic turquoise cup holding the double espresso his little coffee machine had just prepared and stepped out onto his wide, open, third-story balcony near the center of the *ciudad amurallada*, or walled city, in the old, colonial quarter of Cartagena.

A panorama of colors stretched out before him, creating a delightful contrast to the background of his whitewashed apartment building. Over the tops of the red-tiled roofs of the neighboring buildings, Graham looked out onto the sunrise over the Caribbean, the sea smooth and light-blue at this time of the morning, stretching out endlessly. Lining the street below, old wooden balconies painted pink, yellow, lime-green, and paprika-red overflowed with green plants spotted with violet, red, and rose-colored flowers. A wooden cart pulled by a medium-sized grayish-white horse, with a dark-skinned driver wearing a buttoned-up white dress shirt and a flat, wide-brimmed black hat, clattered by. Graham nodded genially at the driver, who returned the gesture. Graham surveyed the simple, beautiful scene around him once more, then took a long, slow sip of the fresh espresso, smelling the powerful aroma and feeling the slightly sweet bite hit the insides of his jaw. "Ahh," he stated aloud.

This colonial corner of Cartagena had drawn him in when he first came for business trips, and more so now that he lived here. During Graham's days at Big Tire Bike Tours in Paris, he had taken a long weekend trip with Marcus Hugo and a few other tour guides to the port town of Cádiz, far in the south of Spain's Andalusia region. They had reveled in the beauty of

Cádiz's colorful architecture, green courtyards with tropical flora, old stone walkways, and the crystal-blue waters of the Mediterranean that surrounded the ramparts of the town. They learned that Cádiz was one of the Western world's oldest continually inhabited civilizations, originally settled by seafaring Phoenicians, and that it had served as the longtime home of the Spanish Navy. Many of the voyages to colonize the New World had left from, or passed through, Cádiz's port. When Graham first visited Cartagena in Colombia, he was amazed at the similarities it bore to Cádiz, from the similar skyline, the port, and the high walls around the city, all the way down to the Andalusian architecture of the town's buildings, showing the Moorish influence of repeating double colonnades under rounded arches and internal courtyards with idyllic fountains. It made sense, Graham had realized, as much of Cartagena was built by Spanish colonizers that had likely just come from Cádiz. But to see that connection between two places that old and separated by an ocean between them was fascinating. It was as if there was a living spirit of history all around him.

Graham peered out over the bay again, and the modern glass high-rises of Bocagrande loomed in the distance, doing their best impression of downtown Miami. Seeing them made Graham shake his head. He never understood why so many of his colleagues and other expats living in Cartagena opted for the modern beachfront peninsula, when they could instead be a part of the rich culture, history, and essence of Cartagena which was on display before him in the *ciudad amurallada*. *A discussion for another day*, Graham thought, as he retreated into his apartment to prepare himself for the day ahead.

THE DRIVE FROM his company's refinery in Cartagena to their port facility in Barranquilla had taken a little over two hours. He had taken the more scenic highway along the Caribbean coast to take in some nice sea views along the way and trace the clear-blue water until it ran into the mouth of the muddy Magdalena River, but it had been a long drive, nonetheless. Graham's work so far in Colombia had been an overwhelming success for his company. They had recruited excellent people from Colombia to take over the refinery operations, they had full capacity of product, and were benefitting greatly from the growth in Colombia's oil and gas industry. When he had stopped by the Cartagena refinery this morning to check in on a particular shipment of interest to him today, he was proud to conclude that they had just about turned that failing operation completely around.

But one day a month, he had to do this other job. There were people in next-door Venezuela working very hard to get the current Communist president/

dictator off the throne and help remake Venezuela's society and economy into something similar to what Colombia had; a progressive, modern state with legitimate opportunity for individual people to rise and succeed. But the Venezuelan government had a stranglehold on the country's massive oil and gas resources, and the government was not about to provide these so-called rebels access to fuel. Arthur Franz had asked Graham to see to it that these rebels got the fuel they needed. So once a month, Graham made sure a barge full of fuel barrels that his company had refined made its way here to Barranquilla, and then he personally oversaw the exchange of the barge to people working with these rebels, who then took it down the Magdalena and into the heart of Northern Colombia. From there, they could transport the fuel to their compound in Cúcuta, on the Colombian-side of the border, and clandestinely cross into Venezuela and deliver the fuel to the rebels.

This was an antiquated method of transporting fuel, but it was necessary for the rebels because they didn't have a sophisticated dock on the Magdalena to extract fuel from the barge. So old school barrels had to do.

The operation had been going on for close to a year, and so far, there had been no issues that Graham was aware of. He pulled up to the dock, parked his car and spotted the fully loaded barge moored to one of the boat slips. He checked his surroundings quickly, and seeing nothing out of the ordinary, made his way onto the dock.

There were usually two barges at the dock: one full of shipping containers storing barrels of fuel, which would go down river with the rebels' agent, and another full of empty shipping containers, which was being returned from the previous month's delivery and would make its way back to Cartagena. This time, oddly, there was only one barge. As Graham could tell by how weighted down its hull appeared, this barge was clearly full of fuel.

Graham looked up and down the dock curiously, then spotted the agent who would drive this full barge down the river. It was the same pilot who had always shown up to pick up the barge, but this time he looked flustered and sweatier than normal. Graham, who had become impressively fluent in Spanish after close to two years living in Colombia, addressed him.

"Antonio—what's going on? Where's Juan?" Graham asked, referring to the pilot who had sailed the barge over from Cartagena.

"Oh, he already left, you know? Said he was in a hurry and that you told him he could turn right back around to Cartagena," Antonio replied in an exaggerated manner.

This is strange, Graham thought. *Juan was a bit squirrely sometimes, but this seems a little much, even for him.* Then Antonio interrupted his thoughts.

"Hey—there's a problem with one of these containers. I think a barrel is leaking or something." Antonio pointed to one of the containers on the side of the boat opposite the dock.

What the hell? Graham thought, *What else can go wrong here?* Graham shook his head and exhaled deeply. He needed to keep this operation as quiet as possible, so best to go deal with whatever the hell this was himself. He begrudgingly hopped up onto the barge and walked toward where Antonio had pointed. One of the containers was open and sure enough, a dark, viscous liquid dripped out of one side.

"I think it's one of the barrels in the back," Antonio said.

Graham gave him a hard look. *Why hadn't Antonio fixed the leaky barrel himself?* He shook his head again and made his way into the open container. He walked toward the back in search of a punctured barrel, then froze in his tracks. Juan was lying face down at the end of the container, with a pool of blood seeping out around his head. Graham tensed his body up to make a move to hide behind some of the barrels when he heard a rush of footsteps outside the container, then a loud creak as the container door closed, followed by a heavy thud as the door was locked. Graham heard a number of voices outside, then felt the boat drift off its moorings, and found himself surrounded by utter darkness.

CHAPTER 23

Paris, France— Northern Border between Germany and Poland. Mid-July 2019.

THE FOLLOWING MONDAY AFTER MARCUS'S VISIT to Ô Maison, Peppercorn received notice from Gas Polskie that they had been selected for the final round of the bid process. There wasn't any additional information provided on how many other parties had made it that far, but there was an invitation to a site visit at the terminal in Świnoujście and a follow up meeting at Gas Polskie's office in Warsaw for Marcus and any other Peppercorn representatives that wished to join. The site visit was set for that Wednesday afternoon, with the follow up meeting in Warsaw the next morning. Alexandra and Marcus coordinated with Arthur Franz and, after confirming travel plans with the Shareholder, they booked early flights for Wednesday morning from Paris to Berlin. Franz would pick them up at the Berlin-Tegel Airport and drive them the three hours northeast just across the German-Polish border to the port at Świnoujście on the Baltic Sea. They would visit the existing Gas Polskie LNG facility there, and then fly from the local town of Szczecin to Warsaw that afternoon. They would meet with the entire Gas Polskie management team in their Warsaw offices the following morning.

That was to be the end of the scheduled visit, but Marcus had more in mind. If Peppercorn was going to invest in Poland, he wanted to see more of the country and more of its people. In particular, he wanted to see Krakow and a site along the Vistula River outside of the city that his team had identified during due diligence as government land that Gas Polskie might have a favorable option to purchase. So Marcus and Alexandra made plans to fly back from Krakow to Paris on Friday.

Marcus reached out to Lukasz Dembski, Gas Polskie's chief executive officer, to invite him along for the Krakow visit. He wanted to get Dembski away from the rest of the Gas Polskie team, and any other Polish government-related individuals that might be attending the site visit and Warsaw meeting, so that Marcus could both explain his vision for the growth and management of Gas Polskie, and also get a good feel for Dembski himself. To Marcus's satisfaction, Dembski readily agreed. Turns out he was from near Krakow and was going to take the opportunity to visit his mother as well.

Marcus and Alexandria arrived at Tegel on an early morning flight. It was cool for a mid-July day, and louds hung on the horizon out toward the Baltic. Marcus spent much of the near two-hour flight looking out the window at the manicured squares and rectangles of German farmland below, dotted with villages where the houses, churches, and markets were all clumped up together. He was reminded of how large Germany was, and how important its economy was to the rest of Europe. An organized, quietly churning force of over 80 million people, driving the future of the European Union. And they needed power to do that.

Make no mistake about it, Marcus thought as they made their descent into West Berlin, *without Germany on board, Gas Polskie has no future*.

Franz was waiting for them in the passenger pickup area in a non-descript, black Mercedes-Benz sedan. They wheeled their carry-on luggage in front of two yellow and white airport shuttle busses and joined him in the car. The three of them tried to avoid traveling together in an effort to preserve continuity of the Shareholder's project in case something were to happen. But Franz had insisted on taking advantage of Alexandra's required inclusion on this trip by the Peppercorn investment committee to get a few hours together, which they rarely had the chance to do. He had run additional security checks and monitored any potentially related background chatter. Everything had been clear.

They settled into the rhythm of the road as Franz drove north. He asked Alexandra and Marcus to walk him through the investment thesis for this project again, from Peppercorn's perspective. Alexandra took the lead and presented an ordered, balanced financial case for the underlying business. She highlighted the European power market's documented need of cheap power that didn't come from coal or nuclear, the lack of reliability on wind and solar to fully satisfy that need based on current technologies, the numerous sources of natural gas supply that Gas Polskie had secured, the clear show of support and enthusiasm that the Polish government had showed toward Gas Polskie, and the projected revenues to be generated by selling gas to generate electricity within Poland and surrounding countries, with or without Germany.

She neatly concluded her analysis by showing that the inclusion of Germany as a customer, or the removal of Russia as the prime competitor, and ideally both, were the factors that could justify a satisfactory return on investment for the firm.

"Those are the real-world facts that we have built our financial model on, and the way we would explain it to our investment partners," she stated. "And for the dream world, I'll hand it over to Marcus." She looked over her shoulder from the front passenger seat and shot a daring grin back at Marcus, who sat in the back seat, flipping through a bound presentation book they had prepared for the Warsaw meeting. He glanced up from the book to receive her grin and take the transition.

"Gladly, Alexandra, I appreciate the warm introduction," Marcus began. He then explained a number of compelling points for growth of the business. Putting in Peppercorn's own seasoned team of energy infrastructure professionals should kick-start development and significantly reduce costs. Taking advantage of Peppercorn's other oil and gas investments for good, long-term deals on natural gas supply, and the firm's relationships within Europe to sign up additional power producers, should lead to an uptick in profitability. And building out the commodities products' transportation network from the port at Świnoujście into the center of Europe could lead to Gas Polskie being the bedrock for a potential "virtual pipeline" from the Black Sea to the Baltic Sea, a combination of rail, barge, truck, and pipeline transportation. This last concept would lead to a massive increase in revenue for Gas Polskie through transportation fees but would also be a huge blow to Russia by providing increased energy independence for not only Poland, but a host of other former Eastern Bloc countries like Ukraine and Belarus.

"Which," Marcus transitioned, "coincides with the investment thesis of this project from the Shareholder's perspective."

They hadn't planned this discussion, but Alexandra seamlessly took Marcus's cue and began to list the vast network of current and historical communication that Gas Polskie had with individuals in the Russian energy market at NovaGaz but also at other Russian oil and gas companies. These companies often had a mask of purported directors and executives visible to the outside world, but figuring out who was actually on the ground, running operations, and negotiating deals for them was not easy. One had to be in the rooms where that happened, or at least have authorized access to the records of those conversations.

At no point during this entire discussion had Franz displayed any emotion or indication of a reaction to the proposal. He allowed for a few seconds of dead air after Alexandra finished her explanation, and then began, "So…your view is that…"

After waiting long enough to realize that Franz had no intention of continuing that sentence, Marcus jumped in.

"That a successful Gas Polskie will both severely harm the Russians' sway over energy supply in Europe *and*," Marcus made a tiny, slow motion karate chop with his right hand, as he continued, "provide us with access to the real people running the Russian oil and gas business. Because if Gas Polskie is successful, at some point the Russians will need to either do business with us or offer us a ridiculous amount of money to take us out of the market."

Franz waited a few more seconds, inhaled deeply, and then exhaled. Almost inaudibly, he stated, "A jab to the face, then an invitation into the tent. I like it."

Marcus settled back into his seat, then playfully gave a slight kick to the underside of the seat in front of him. Alexandra suppressed a smile as she thrust her attention back into their presentation booklet.

As they neared Anklam and could see the Szczecin Lagoon out their windows to the east, Franz gave a brief update on his own progress on the diplomatic front of convincing Germany to throw a wrench in Russia's plans to finalize the Nord Stream 2 Pipeline on German soil, and instead look to Gas Polskie as an alternative. He had gained the ear of influential members of the German chancellor's cabinet and had completely won over the US ambassador to Germany. But without an internationally respected investor propping up Gas Polskie and moving the project forward, it looked as if Germany would be non-committal. The message was clear: Peppercorn Capital would bear the risk, not the German government.

"I realize that is not the answer you were hoping for," Franz acknowledged to both Alexandra and Marcus. Then, somewhat surprisingly, he added, "But you have my commitment to continue pushing. Just being able to say that Peppercorn has conducted a site visit and is in serious negotiations to join up with Gas Polskie should go a long way with the right people. And this may be one thing that we can run all the way to the top of the flagpole back in Washington." Franz paused to allow the statement to have its effect. He then clarified, "But any support from that front will need to be made through back channels. And that's my job."

Marcus understood. In no event could Peppercorn look like a conduit for US political interests, as that would undermine the firm's reputation as not only opportunistic, but fiercely independent. Increased scrutiny of Peppercorn was also the last thing the Shareholder wanted.

They rode in silence for a while, each taking in the views of the flat horizon that announced the presence of the Baltic Sea.

Franz interrupted the quiet by asking, "How did things go at the d'Orsay a few weeks ago?"

Marcus chuckled internally. This was another way of Franz asking if he was making any progress with Mauro Broccatelli. He looked over to the front seat where Alexandra sat. He remembered how magnificent she had looked that night, how skillfully she had drifted around his conversation with Broccatelli and shot him that dart of a look, a command to wrap it up for the night.

"Quite promising, actually," Marcus responded. He then filled Franz in on the subsequent encounter with Broccatelli the next day in front of the Hotel Luxembourg Parc and the plans for the upcoming cycling trip from Lyon to the Mediterranean coast.

Marcus watched Franz process the information, turning it over in his head, looking for threats, doubling back on the sequence of events. *A follow-up invitation on a cycling trip down the Rhône Valley?* Marcus ultimately saw Franz let it go and nod his head gently a few times to signal *well done* to Marcus, but it was clear Franz wasn't done analyzing what Marcus had just explained.

Franz and Alexandra traded a glance.

"It's a great opportunity, Marcus. Take the advantage while you can, and get close to him on the trip," she instructed. After a pause, she stated, "We may need to press that relationship sooner than we thought."

AS THEY HEADED east toward the Polish border, out the left side of the car they could almost make out the German town of Greifswald, the supposed final link for Nord Stream 2 to connect to Germany. Less than an hour later, they crossed into Poland. As they did, Franz explained to them that he had been monitoring the situation and, as of now, there had been no indication of a threat during their visit.

***

"BUT DON'T THINK the Russians aren't aware of this," he warned. "They are going to figure out who is visiting from Peppercorn and try to learn as much about you as possible." He looked up ahead and identified their drop-off point, then continued, "Should the need arise, field pieces will be available as usual."

In Alexandra and Marcus's hotels in both Warsaw and Krakow, small, fully loaded handguns would be taped somewhere underneath the beds in their rooms. This reference caught Marcus slightly off guard. He hadn't sensed that sort of threat for this trip, as he had been blinded by the growth potential story for the project he had been crafting in his head.

Franz dropped them off at the ferry crossing on the west side of the Piast Canal, which they would have to cross over to reach Gas Polskie's LNG terminal on the other side. A team of professionals in business suits and yellow hard hats waited outside a white van with smiles painted on their faces and all waiving in unison.

"Polish hospitality," Franz observed, pulling the car to a stop. He popped the trunk, then looked seriously at Alexandra and Marcus. He offered them some parting guidance.

"Remember, this project, both for Peppercorn and the Shareholder, only works if the project will be a commercial and financial success. Otherwise, it's a disaster for everyone." He added, "Marcus, the project is your call. But if it's a go...at least try to extract the best terms possible."

Marcus nodded his assent, then opened his door to get out of the rear seat. Before Alexandra could do the same in the front seat, Franz gave them one final bit of advice.

"Don't forget to be careful." With that, he executed a U-turn and headed back toward Germany.

CHAPTER 24

Świnoujście, Poland— Krakow, Poland. Mid-July 2019.

T HE SITE VISIT WAS AS SUCCESSFUL AS IT COULD be. They walked the site, they turned some nobs, they visited the control room. It all looked like functioning equipment, and Marcus and Alexandra truly were impressed with the overall quality of the facility. It was clean, organized and up to date. Marcus's fears of seeing a bunch of old, repurposed Soviet steel were unfounded.

One promising aspect of the visit was the vast swath of undeveloped land to the east, which Gas Polskie had an option to acquire at a significant bargain. There was clearly the opportunity to expand the facility to assist with growth of the overall business. But the overwhelming upshot of the visit was Gas Polskie's CEO, Lukasz Dembski. It took Marcus all of about ten minutes to realize that Dembski was the engine driving the business aspect of Gas Polskie. The other members of the hosting party were highly technical engineers, recycled government bureaucrats, and one apparent specialist in "safety of operations." Each one clearly focused only on their own specialized area. Dembski knew each area just as well as the specialist, but he also talked about them as an integrated whole. And he was the only one that talked about the non-technical parts of the business, like marketing, building a brand, developing relationships, and having an overall strategy beyond moving molecules through their LNG terminal. After one of Dembski's particularly blunt observations, Marcus traded a look with Alexandra.

"No one wants to buy power from Poland. Most people think half our country doesn't even have power."

Promising...this guy, at least.

They all took the short flight from Szczecin to Warsaw together on a small regional discount airline. When Marcus and Alexandra finished checking in to their hotel, Marcus fought off his desire to invite Alexandra for a nightcap at the hotel bar. He could tell from her body language that the full day of travel and meetings had worn her out. He felt the same way. He settled instead for a half-bottle of Polish red wine, a pinot noir from the south of Poland, which was surprisingly not bad, alone in his hotel room. Marcus performed Olivier's recommended review of the label and tasting activities and wrote a few small notes about the wine in his daily journal.

He then flipped on the television and found a Polish sports show showing highlights from that day's stage of the Tour de France bike race. The course was a looping, hilly ride through the Vosges Mountains in the Alsace region of Eastern France. Multicolored jerseys of riders flashed along the road through lush, green hills beneath intermittent shadows from the pines above in one scene, then between lined vineyards on a sunny, flat road in the next. A helicopter shot of an angular, mountaintop castle, followed by a close-up of townspeople decked out in white shirts and blouses, red-and-black vests and skirts, topped off by wide-brimmed black hats, standing in front of thatched-roof houses with red and yellow flowers hanging from the windows, all reminded the viewer of the region's Germanic history and influence. The broadcast was in French, overlaid by commentary in Polish from the show's hosts, with English subtitles all along the way. The announcers were enthusiastically applauding the yeoman-like effort put forth by one of the two Poles competing in the race. When he had finished in forty-ninth place, one announcer declared, "his team had performed well and no doubt partly due to the Pole's skill and willingness to contribute..." Marcus felt like he was listening to one of the technical engineers from that morning's site visit. *Come on Poland, win! Don't just contribute...*Marcus thought as he zapped the TV off and called it a day.

Marcus typically tried to get up early and go for a run when he was on business trips. It was a good way to get the day going, but it also provided some walking-around knowledge of the local area, which usually made for good conversation starters with whomever he was meeting that day. But Franz's warning rung in Marcus's head, and while it was probably a ridiculous precaution to take, he opted instead to walk around the block and find a café for a pastry and some coffee. He employed some of the tradecraft he had been taught along the way: doubling-back, stopping suddenly, and walking in an indirect route. Nothing stood out to him.

He greeted Alexandra in their hotel lobby, and they walked over to the Gas Polskie office down the street together, rolling carry-on baggage in tow. The quintessential business travelers. They were subjected to endless rounds of handshaking, business-card trading, and general glad-handing for the next few hours. A fringe cabinet member of the Polish government attended to signal the president's support of the project, "and his desire to find the best result for the Polish people."

Marcus and Alexandra both played the part of the eager and interested investor, asking questions to which they already knew the answers, nodding when called for, and furrowing their brows at times to maintain some negotiating positions. Marcus could sense the boredom emanating from Dembski, who sat across the table from him, looking uncomfortable in a suit and tie. But he could also see that Dembski was making the effort to mask that boredom and make sure his guests were engaged. Dembski clearly wanted this venture to work, and to do that, he needed a good partner.

When the meeting concluded after a few hours, it was Dembski who walked Marcus and Alexandra down to the building's lobby. Dembski made polite conversation along the way, then thanked them for coming.

"I'll see you in Krakow this afternoon," he said. "I've got to take a later train, so I will have to meet you there. Now you'll have the first-class compartment all to yourselves!" he added with a laugh.

Not a bad consolation, Marcus thought, as he observed Alexandra gracefully shake Dembski's hand and share a smile with him. Dembski's eyes were wide-open with amusement, as he clearly enjoyed Alexandra's company. Marcus shook Dembski's hand as well, and then he and Alexandra climbed into the taxi that Dembski's had arranged to take them to Warsaw Central Station for the two-hour train ride south to Krakow.

As they crossed over the Vistula River in the center of the city, the same river they would be visiting later that afternoon outside of Krakow, Alexandra glanced over at Marcus. The playful energy in her eyes transformed into the alert gaze of a fox, and she asked, "Did you see them?"

Marcus cocked his head curiously. "Who?"

She responded with a slightly reproachful look, then explained, "Two tails, coming out of the office. They jumped in a cab not long after us, but I don't see them behind us. Keep your antenna up, Marcus."

We were outside for barely thirty seconds, Marcus thought to himself. But she was right, he had been preoccupied watching Alexandra joke with Dembski and hadn't been paying particularly close attention to his surroundings.

"Russians?" Marcus asked, acknowledging his mistake and Alexandra's superiority in surveillance detection as indirectly as possible.

She gave him a look down her nose and a half smile, then batted her eyes at him sympathetically.

"Right." Marcus responded. *Who the hell else?* "Well," he added with a smile, "I'm guessing they already know where we are going. So…" He let the sentence hang there between them.

Alexandra issued a genuine smile, not taking the bait. "Yes…" She said, prompting him to finish his thought.

"So…" Marcus put his hands behind his head and leaned back in his chair, then explained, "We carry on as usual. Don't let them know we're on to them." He closed his eyes and exhaled comfortably.

Alexandra was caught between incredulous and impressed. "Wow, that…yeah, uhm…profound, Marcus.

Top-notch tradecraft," she responded sarcastically, before turning her head towards the window and smiling. He was right, she'd at least give him that.

MARCUS LOADED HIS and Alexandra's luggage into the compartments above, and they settled in to their first-class compartment. It was clean, comfortable, and had sliding glass doors separating it from the aisle, complete with privacy shades that could be pulled down over the doors. There was a light gray Formica half-table by the window that folded down from the wall. They both unconsciously exhaled deeply and relaxed into their respective seats as the train pulled out of the station. A few stragglers shimmied their way down the aisle outside, excusing themselves as they twisted their luggage to be as narrow as possible.

THE MOVEMENT OF the train beneath him simultaneously comforted Marcus and piqued his interest. He peered out the window as the center of the city turned to suburbs, and the suburbs turned to farmland. His eyes fluttered as he eased into and out of a light slumber, awakening frequently to views of small villages surrounded by green meadows, golden yellow fields glistening in the sun, or by the *whoosh* of a train heading past in the other direction. *I thought Poland was supposed to be bleak and grim...I don't even see any horse-drawn buggies*, Marcus thought, admiring the lush surroundings. He leaned his head lazily up against the glass separating them from the aisle to watch a jolly couple and their two kids scurry by with a handful of snacks from the dining cart, then observe a smartly dressed older gentleman across the aisle consume a daily newspaper. The man snorted and laughed aloud, then shook his head a few times as he turned the page. Marcus smiled appreciatively, then yawned as he began to wake himself up.

His eyes came to rest on Alexandra across the booth, sleeping. Or at least with her eyes closed. She looked like she was trying to relax, like performing a calming yoga pose of some sort. Her head was tilted back, accentuating her high, broad cheekbones and pointy nose. She was wearing a professional, navy-blue women's suit, the pants form-fitting and the jacket tossed onto the chair beside her. Her light-blue, short-sleeve cable knit sweater hugged her firm torso and accentuated the rise of her breasts. Her taut, tan arms stretched down to her lap where her elegantly manicured hands laid one over the other.

Marcus thought back to the first time he saw her. A conspicuous stranger, saddled up next to him at the Frankfurt airport bar outside of the gate for his flight to Florence, banging away with the bartender in fluent German. She also spoke French fluently, and he wasn't sure what else. *Who is she? Why is she here?* Marcus thought, *Why is she with Peppercorn?* He had interacted briefly with her during his recruitment process, and then while he was in New York and going down to "meetings" at Langley during his first year. Her move to the Paris office had more or less coincided with his, and they had been working in the same office for two years now. But only recently had they really had the chance to interact. He enjoyed working with her. She was smart, organized, and had a confident and professional disposition. She showed up on time and never missed a day. She inspired him. But there was also a human side to her that he was just getting to know. She was funny, witty, unintimidated, but not intimidating. When she wanted you to see them, she had a soft smile and warm eyes that felt like a blanket around one's shoulders. Marcus also found her attractive, undeniably so at this point.

Marcus knew she had worked for the Shareholder in a more traditional capacity before coming to Peppercorn, but he did not know the specifics. It was clear she had been in the field, most likely abroad given her language skills and level of comfort around different cultures. *But why is she here?* Marcus kept coming back to that. *Did something happen? Did Franz drag her into this?* Marcus knew nothing about her family. And other than a suspicion that she and Bamba Diop were seeing each other, he knew nothing about her personal life. *Hell, I don't even know how old she is,* he thought, then walked that back a little bit, as he knew she was older than Marcus, but not by too much. She had the vivacity of someone in their late twenties, coupled with the maturity of someone in their late forties. But there were moments of silence, things unsaid, a cold memory seemed to move around a void inside of her, making Marcus think that her path had not been an easy one.

Alexandra opened her eyes slowly, comfortably meeting the royal-blue rings around Marcus's pupils. The corners of her mouth twitched up almost imperceptibly, and she looked toward the aisle at the rolling cart of first-class passenger food that was yet to arrive. They each ordered premade sandwiches, which were shockingly good, along with some chips and two bottles of water. Marcus had looked forlornly at the multiple bottles red wine on the rolling cart but knew that a liquid lunch was probably not the best idea, given all that was going on around them.

"What happened to Capucine?" Alexandra asked out of nowhere, interrupting their view of the rich Polish farmland outside.

This was quite the surprise of a question, but a pleasant one. Marcus smiled deeply, then replied, "She left me for New York." Then he shrugged his shoulders and put his palms out wide.

"I don't blame her." Alexandra responded, returning the smile, before adding, "She was very pretty, though. So French."

"You seem quite surprised."

"No, not surprised. Just intrigued." This last bit Alexandra uttered almost to herself as she looked down to the ground.

Marcus felt an uptick in his heartbeat, then remained silent as he controlled himself and allowed Alexandra's comment to linger.

"Well, I was lucky to be with her for the time that we had," Marcus responded, deflecting slightly.

Alexandra nodded her head gently, lightly rocking back and forth. "She was lucky, too, Marcus."

Marcus returned her smoldering look, then leaned forward close to her, putting his elbows on his knees. He flashed her an almost goofy smile.

"I feel like we're going to make out," he observed. When she responded by raising her eyebrows in mock surprise, he pulled her close by the arms and placed his lips on hers. She returned a closed-mouth kiss, then put her hands in his hair at the back of his head. She leaned over and put her lips next to his ear and whispered, "Marcus?"

He had an immediate vision of him pulling down the shades to their compartment, followed by a steamy, torrid affair of suppressed, coworker sexual tension unfolding. He waited for her to give him the cue.

"This is…exactly…what we are not supposed to be doing." She slowly backed away. "Don't get me wrong, I'm flattered." She explained, "But this needs to be all about business, and we have got to be professionals. Our heads need to be clear and focused."

Marcus sought to hide his disappointment, but he knew she was right. *What was I thinking?* he asked himself. Then he leaned back into his seat, nodded his head to acknowledge that he understood and agreed. He couldn't help but to shrug his shoulders and purse his lips. *Guess it was worth a shot.*

They were pulling into the Kraków Główny, the main railway station just on the perimeter of Old Town, the medieval walled city center. They packed their workbags up, and Marcus retrieved their luggage from the compartments above. As they formed a line to exit the booth, Alexandra looked at Marcus, raised her eyebrows and mockingly said, "I feel like we're going to make out…" then burst into laughter. Marcus, red-faced and clearly embarrassed, had to do the same. In his defense, he replied, "Hey, it almost worked."

CHAPTER 25

Krakow, Poland.
Mid-July 2019.

MARCUS SAT AT THE LOBBY BAR OF THEIR HOTEL and ordered a glass of the local Żywiec beer on draft as he waited for Alexandra to come down. This "luxury hotel," as its name unabashedly declared, was recommended by Lukasz Dembski as the best option for Krakow and it did not disappoint. It was located just outside of Krakow Old Town on a slight rise looking out onto the Vistula. It was a four-story boutique hotel, with a polished exterior and a well-kept front courtyard that led to a small park across the street and the river below. It looked like a cross between a townhome in Belgravia and an alpine villa. The interior was ornate, with a touch of dark modernity. A jazzed-up lobby from the Austro-Hungarian Empire. The barroom was small but well-appointed; a unique arched brick ceiling and an eye-catching chandelier filled the room with energy.

Marcus made pleasant small talk with the bartender, who was a young man of about twenty-five with short brown hair on top of a round face. His cheeks were pudgy, but he was not. He spoke English very well but offered to speak German or French "if that would be more convenient." When Marcus mentioned that he was in from Paris, the bartender enthusiastically reminded Marcus that Frédéric Chopin, the great composer, was in fact Polish, even though many mistook him for French because he lived in Paris for such a long time. The young man looked fit, so Marcus asked about some good running routes around the hotel. Delighted to respond, he asked Marcus for permission to go the lobby. He soon returned with a detailed map of central Krakow and quickly marked out a handful of five- to ten-kilometer trails.

"My personal favorites are the paths along the Vistula. Very peaceful, lots of people bike and run there. You can go as far as your feet can carry you and won't be interrupted by any cars or traffic. Plus, you get great views of the city!"

Marcus studied the map. He had seen the large pedestrian paths that surrounded the river abutted by wide, green lawns separating the paths from the roads and the city. They did look inviting. Unlikely that he would get to go explore them on a jog this trip…but maybe he would be coming back to this place more often.

The visit that afternoon to the potential expansion site along the Vistula outside of Krakow had gone very well. There was lots of space to add a terminal and storage facility, with great railroad connections. The river was wide, free-flowing, and deep enough to support barge traffic. Perhaps most promising was the information Dembski shared: to the right party, the Polish government was willing to lease the land out for ninety-nine years for next to nothing.

Dembski loved the expansion concept, both from a technical perspective and from a macroeconomic perspective. He felt like there was enough interest and product supply from the surrounding Central European countries of the Czech Republic, Slovakia, Hungary, and Romania to help support the project. And it was also one step further in advancing the long-stated goal of Ukraine, Belarus, and Poland to create a Black Sea-to-Baltic Sea pathway, circumventing Russia. They had all planned to talk business further that evening over dinner.

"And this is my favorite monument in all of Krakow!" the bartender enthusiastically interrupted Marcus's train of thought.

"Really?" Marcus played along as he finished his beer. The bartender pointed to the empty glass. Marcus glanced in the direction of the lobby, and not seeing Alexandra yet, shrugged his shoulders to the bartender and signaled for just a little bit more. The bartender found this quite amusing, and obliged Marcus by filling his glass about a third of the way full.

He gave an exaggerated wink as he passed the glass back across the bar and then, nearly in a whisper, explained, "On the house." He then returned his finger to the location of his favorite monument on the map. "Džok, the most faithful canine friend ever!" He brought his pen out again and marked it with a star. "You know the story, of course?"

Marcus did not.

"Well, one day Džok and his owner were out along this path for their normal walk, and all of a sudden the owner had a heart attack. Died on the spot! The ambulance came and took the owner away, but of course would not let Džok go to the hospital with his owner. Unperturbed, Džok stayed right there waiting for him to return. For one whole year, Džok waited at the spot. Through heat and cold, sun and rain, Džok waited. The good people of Krakow gave him food to help sustain him, but Džok refused to leave the spot because he was waiting faithfully for his owner to come back. Exactly one year to the day after his owner's death, Džok accepted his owner's death and was willing to go live with another family. In honor of his unmatched display of loyalty, the people of Krakow commissioned a monument right where Džok had waited. It's beautiful, you must see it!"

Alexandra gracefully strolled into the bar just then. She was striking in a black, textured, and noticeably well-made halter-top, accentuating her tan skin and blond hair hanging over her shoulders, sparkly, dangling earrings, and tight white jeans. They had planned to walk to the restaurant, so she had on stylish black flats and carried a light black jacket on her arm. Marcus had on dark jeans, a white button-down Oxford shirt with the sleeves rolled up, driving loafers and a navy-blue linen blazer in hand. A dark-brown Redweld with a stack of documents inside rested on the chair next to him. They weren't used to seeing each other in non-office attire, and openly appraised one another, each one's eyes lingering for a second on the other's jacket. Both came away satisfied; they made a nice pair.

"Thought I might find you here," she said, then glanced at his empty glass. "Shall we?"

Marcus nodded his assent and made to settle up with the bartender. "I didn't get your name. I'm Marcus." He said, extending a hand across the bar. Pleasantly surprised, the bartender recovered and firmly pumped Marcus's hand a few times.

"Jakub. Jakub Pawlak. Nice to meet you, Mr. Marcus."

Marcus laughed, then replied, "Nice to meet you, Jakub. And it's just Marcus, no *mister*."

Jakub glanced over at Alexandra, then back to Marcus.

Taking his cue, Marcus responded, "And this is Alexandra. Alexandra, this is Jakub. Best bartender in Krakow and part time tour guide."

Alexandra tilted her head slightly in curiosity, then smiled and greeted the blushing Jakub.

"Very nice to meet you, Jakub, and thank you for the tips," Marcus said, indicating the map he was folding up to place into the Redweld he gathered up under his arm.

"My pleasure, Marcus. Have an excellent dinner. Enjoy Krakow!" They all traded smiles as Marcus and Alexandra turned to leave for dinner.

"Friendly guy," Alexandra observed.

"So far, they all are. Very welcoming." Marcus replied, genuinely impressed.

They had decided to take a scenic route and walk through the main open square of the medieval Krakow Old Town. It was a beautiful, stone square with a town hall and tower in the middle and various fountains and churches around the edges. There were throngs of people enjoying outdoor seating at various cafés, and a small chamber music group playing on a makeshift stage at the end of the square that they walked by on their way out.

They passed through the greenbelt surrounding Krakow Old Town and headed in the direction of Kazimierz, Krakow's old Jewish district, where the restaurant Dembski had suggested for dinner was. They walked in silence for a bit, taking in the surroundings of colorful four- and five-story buildings lining both sides of the street, and the tramcars shuttling up and down the middle. A clump of collared, black-gown-clad priests in training passed by. When they reached another greenbelt on the edge of Kazimierz, they passed a handful of lively establishments with what looked like university students spilling out onto the plaza outside. Marcus looked up to take note of the name: Café Pub & Laundry. Intrigued, he reflected internally: *Not sure I've seen that one before…not a bad idea actually*.

The sun peeked beneath the horizon and night began to fall as they made their way into the heart of Kazimierz. The buildings around them transformed into old, bombed-out looking stores and apartments. The reds and yellows and blues of the façades turned into the complete scale of off-white to black. Dark courtyards, lit by gas lamps or candles, sat below low-hanging trees in between and in front of cafés and restaurants full of people seated at outdoor tables. The faint scent of tobacco migrated out onto the street. Marcus and Alexandra, in their fancy evening wear, began to stand out from the bohemian crowd around them.

The palpable history of the horror that had taken place here surrounded them. Krakow had once been a center of Jewish life in Europe, a part of the famed

Pale of Settlement, where Jews were explicitly allowed to live, though outside the confines of the rest of Europe's larger cities. On the eve of World War II, the Jewish population in Kazimierz alone was estimated to be around sixty-thousand people. But the Jews of Krakow were particularly decimated by the Nazi regime, and only about three- to five-thousand of them survived. Many of those survivors were saved by the famed Oskar Schindler, immortalized by the film *Schindler's List*, which had all taken place right around where Marcus and Alexandra strode over the old cobblestone streets. The night grew darker. They sank deeper into Kazimierz and neared the restaurant. Long, large shadows of pedestrians exploring the quarter flickered off the pockmarked walls.

Ahead in the road, waiting outside of the restaurant, was Lukasz Dembski. He wore a loose-fitting, black cotton button-down shirt, unbuttoned to mid chest, light-colored blue jeans, and a pair of dark leather sneakers. A big smile graced his face, which was angular in the nose, eyes, forehead, and chin, but almost rubbery in the lips and cheeks. He had thin, brown eyebrows, and a stylish European haircut, close-cropped sides and long on top, almost like a German cyclist or footballer. It looked very natural and surprisingly professional on Dembski. He was chatting amiably with the hostess outside the restaurant, and he gestured in Marcus and Alexandra's direction as they approached. The hostess laughed, nodded in agreement, and then gathered three leather-bound menus in anticipation of their arrival. She asked Dembski a question, and he gestured to the tables outside of the restaurant in the front courtyard.

The restaurant was a nicer Polish place, but still had a relaxed feel. There was a man playing an acoustic guitar and a young lady with a microphone on a small stage set up on the other end of the courtyard from where they sat, just beginning to play a set. A waitress arrived promptly and conversed in Polish with Dembski, who appeared to order a few things, then she greeted them in very good English and handed out menus. Marcus took note that Dembski seemed to be in a gregarious mood this evening and was enjoying playing the role of host. Tonight needed to be about business; he and Alexandra were going to convince Dembski that Peppercorn Capital was the right partner for Gas Polskie. And Dembski would then convince whoever he needed to on the Gas Polskie side. But Marcus had learned that there were different ways of convincing, and sometimes sitting back and listening was more effective than any high-pressure sales pitch. Alexandra would take Marcus's cue, and as the waitress returned to their table quickly with the three small glasses of housemade Polish vodka that Dembski had ordered, Marcus exhaled deeply and contentedly, allowing an honest smile to spread across his face.

Dembski enthusiastically explained that this vodka was made by the owner of this restaurant, then raised his glass and exclaimed, "*Na zdrowie!*"

Marcus and Alexandra laughed, then tried to repeat the phrase. As the cool, clean liquor burned down Marcus's throat, he placed his hands into his jacket pockets and relaxed back into his chair, prepared himself to keep his mouth shut and ears open, then asked Dembski, "So, Lukasz, how did you end up at Gas Polskie?"

AS THE WAITRESS cleared away the empty plates of beef cheek, duck breast, and pork knuckle, Dembski made one last request. She smiled and nodded knowingly and waved to her colleague who had apparently been waiting in the wings. A bottle of Hungarian Tokaji dessert wine was brought forward, along with three thin glasses. They made another round of cheers and tasted the sweet, honey-colored wine. Marcus typically stayed away from dessert wine, but Tokaji was not to be turned down, and it did not disappoint.

"THIS SWEET WINE was considered the wine of kings in the eighteenth century and preceded the popularity of French wines among continental nobility. These days, Tokaji wine is difficult to find," Dembski said.

But not here in Krakow, Marcus thought. Right in the heart of Central Eastern Europe, Krakow was a place where goods from the surrounding areas converged. During dinner, they had polished off two bottles of Moravian red wine from the neighboring Czech Republic.

Marcus and Alexandra had learned about Dembski's childhood in Krakow, a child in a Soviet satellite state in the late 70s and early 80s. He had learned Russian in school, then was forced to speak it when he was drafted into the Polish military. But the military had given him the chance to study engineering and find a career. He worked at a large Polish engineering company after his service, then went back to school for the Polish equivalent of an MBA. He began to work on government-backed infrastructure projects in the early 2000s, and when the initiative to develop Poland's own oil and gas fields was hatched around 2010, he was a natural fit to help push that forward. But when the big international oil and gas firms left the country after realizing drilling shale wells in Poland, or anywhere in Europe, was not going to pass political or regulatory muster, Dembski was forced to pivot along with Poland to the idea of importing and distributing gas... and continuing to buy it from Russia in the meantime.

Marcus asked about Dembski's family too. They learned he was married to a Polish girl from Warsaw who he had met at university where he got his MBA;

she studied art history, while he studied business. They had two boys and a little girl. Dembski was fanatical about Polish football, but also loved to cross-country ski with his family. And he playfully complained that he had become the de facto sports coach for nearly all of the teams that his kids played on.

During dinner, a large, bald man with a permanent-looking five-o'clock shadow had entered the restaurant and taken a table for one in a dark corner of the courtyard. Around that same time, a smaller, thinner man with short, dark hair, bushy dark eyebrows, and the eyes of a hawk, had made a similar maneuver at the café across the street. Without interrupting Dembski, Alexandra and Marcus had traded glances and slight nods as they spotted the men.

They returned their attention to Dembski, who had resumed the discussions around business. Dembski was clear about his desire for Poland to move forward as its own self-sustaining nation, and that was present throughout his narrative. He was clear, too, about his exasperation at the many times those desires had been thwarted. He threw up his hands in mock surrender, and punctuated the explanation by saying, "So, now here we are, forced to choose, on the one hand, between the status quo and the sure thing of Russian money, gas ,and control, or, on the other hand, to take a gamble, financially, and politically, with you… or someone like you, I guess I should say."

He was trying to at least maintain the appearance that several other bidders were still interested in the Gas Polskie investment. Dembski was not some idealistic academic or politician, nor some Polish technocrat, so he didn't try to couch the plausible eventuality of Gas Polskie letting the Russians win as a play for the greater good. He was a practical man. He wanted Poland to do well on its own, but they needed money. The Russians could buy the company, provide cheap gas to the Poles, and he and his other executives would probably do pretty well when they were bought out at some point down the road.

Marcus recognized that it was his turn to speak. He nodded his head gently, then took a long sip of water.

"Fair enough," Marcus acknowledged. He then began by walking through Peppercorn's proposal and making sure that Dembski clearly understood the basic economic terms and what Peppercorn's expectations were. The 25 percent equity purchase, the bridge loan at a favorable rate during the project's early-stage development, and the option to buy another 25 percent down the road. He admitted that on paper, that might not sound as enticing as a big chunk of cash right now from someone buying the full 50 percent of the company.

He then thought about all the things that Dembski hadn't said but clearly wanted to.

"So yes, if you go with the…umm, with *someone else*, you might make more money right now. But what we have in mind for the company is real development, the growth of a true Polish success story. And with our investment comes our expertise." Marcus pulled out a stack of papers clipped together from the Redweld under the table and flipped them across to Dembski. They landed with a thud and a rattle. Each document had a handful of colorful little flags hanging off the sides of various pages. Dembski, caught off guard, tried to make sense of what now stood before him.

"Those are all of your current gas supply contracts," Marcus explained. "Our team has gone through and highlighted all of the provisions where your suppliers can either get out of the agreement early or raise the costs of the product on you. And those different scenarios are definitely not considered in the financial models that you shared with the bidders." Marcus allowed this to sink in, then added, "But if you work with us, we'll go out to all those suppliers and get the contracts fixed. If they don't agree, we'll get our companies in the US Gulf Coast to sell you gas under long-term agreements."

Marcus paused to read Dembski's reaction. Instead of an embarrassed, guilty, or scared man backed into a corner, he saw a light beginning to go on inside of Dembski, a thesis forming in his mind.

Thud and rattle. A second stack of papers landed in front of Dembski. Highlighted portions stuck out on some cover pages; flags littered about like the other stack.

"Those are a large number of the Polish government's and Polish power companies' gas purchase contracts with NovaGaz."

Dembski looked up at him with curiosity, genuine surprise.

"I know, they weren't in the data room...but there they are," Marcus said, "This time, what's highlighted is the nearly universal provision that allows all of those agreements to be terminated by the Polish counterparty if, and only if, they are able to purchase gas from a 'Polish-sourced' gas supplier instead. That stack of papers alone is a map to doubling your revenue in the next five years."

Dembski glanced at a few of the agreements. He smiled and began to press the papers back across to Marcus, who stopped him.

"Those are a gift, Lukasz, a gesture of goodwill."

Dembski nodded appreciatively, then looked up at Marcus.

Marcus saw that he was striking the right chord, so he continued. "That is just a sample of the effort and skill we are going to bring to this project. We've got a pool of exceptional operating partners that have worked for us on projects like this one all over the world, and you'll have them at your fingertips. And you'll have me, too, because I'll be on the board as the Peppercorn representative." Marcus looked across the table into Dembski's eyes and gave him an assuring nod, then added, "You know, you were right earlier. If you go with your other option, it may be a comfortable and secure decision...for you. But what about your kids, Lukasz? What type of Poland do you want them to grow up in? Empowered, dynamic, maybe even a little brash? Or just that same old satellite state...working hard so that someone else benefits from it all?"

Marcus paused again. Under the table, he saw Alexandra's hand extend down, signaling to him to hit the brakes. He realized she was right; he shouldn't push this man too hard. Sensing that he had just about, but not quite given Dembski what he needed, Marcus changed tacks and brought in a different type of argument.

"What I'm going to tell you next is for your consideration only, and not the rest of your team."

Marcus looked at Alexandra, glanced over at the two suspicious characters still sitting alone at their tables, then back to her. She gave him a nod.

"We believe that your neighbors to the west are not entirely convinced that a new pipeline connection with your neighbors to the east is in their best interest," Marcus continued.

Dembski raised his eyebrows noticeably, catching on quickly and communicating that he understood the message so far.

"They want to see a big, international, non-biased, financial investor display confidence in the project, and that should tip the balance enough for them to take the leap," Marcus added, "They need to know it will work for them economically and that the project is reliable. We can help make that happen."

Dembski absorbed the force of this information by blowing air out of his cheeks and sinking back into his chair. He stared blankly at the table for a while. Then, returning to life, he grabbed his glass of Tokaji, looked at Alexandra and Marcus, and replied, "*Na zdrowie.*"

THEY BADE DEMBSKI farewell and began the walk back to the hotel. The night had turned black, and the streets of Kazimierz had grown darker along with it. The candlelit courtyards were empty, the previously locked doors down dark alleyways now teemed with people waiting in line to get in, the bass of house music oozing out from within. They made toward the river to take in a different vantage point back to the hotel.

ALEXANDRA BUMPED HER shoulder up against Marcus's, then added, "I think you got him. Nice work, Marcus."

"Thanks to you…I was about to quote Gandhi or the Bible to the poor man, but you made me realize I had pushed far enough. Seriously, thanks." He gave her a look of appreciation that she could tell was genuine.

"'Be the change you want to see in the world.' Something like that?" Alexandra asked. "Well, regardless, I think we convinced him."

Marcus thought for a second, then replied, "'Do not be arrogant, but tremble.'"

She looked at him, shook her head, and laughed, "You're full of surprises, you know that?"

Seeing her knowing response, he shot back, "So are you."

Then a noise from around them grabbed their attention. They both heard it at the same time—an unnatural cadence to a step, somewhere behind them. They didn't need to acknowledge it to each other, so they kept walking.

Alexandra looked down at Marcus's jacket pocket, then quickly up at him. He gestured in the affirmative. She did the same and rolled her eyes in the direction of her own jacket. Their followers could only be the two men that they had spotted earlier in the evening during their dinner with Dembski. And if those men were following them now, this late at night and after their meeting with Dembski, that meant things were likely to turn hostile.

Through an opening between buildings, they caught a glimpse of someone walking a parallel track on the next street over. The opening of the river appeared before them, and the relative comfort of the Kazimierz background chatter gave way to the calm, constant sound of black water flowing by.

Marcus spotted the wide, paved path down by the river in front of them and headed in that direction. The trailing footsteps had quieted now, and Alexandra took the lead in doubling their pace to put distance between them and their followers. There was a good-sized hill leading down to the river, so Alexandra and Marcus had momentary cover. Marcus spotted a raised monument over to his right, halfway down the hill, and made a break in that direction, pulling Alexandra along. They reached the monument and sat on the ground to hide behind its large concrete base.

Catching their breaths, they calmed themselves and shifted into full operational mode. They needed a plan.

"We need to get back to the hotel, preferably unnoticed. Last thing we need is a tangle with these guys while we are here on Peppercorn business," Alexandra stated, working her head around the side of the monument to make sure they weren't visible. Then, in a more commanding, strategic tone, she added, "But we should assume they know where we are going, so avoiding them might not be that easy."

"You're sure they are going to try to confront us?" Marcus asked.

"I'm not certain, but it's likely. If they were just gathering information, they would have left us alone after the meeting with Dembski. Their continued pursuit of us is a bad sign," Alexandra replied knowingly.

Marcus nodded in agreement. A few beads of sweat ran down the side of his face. He wiped them away with his hand and caught a glimpse of the metal tablet on the front of the base of the monument. The word *Džok* appeared at the top. He looked up to the monument itself to see a metal dog with its left paw extended forward, and a pair of large human hands surrounding it. He looked down to read more of the inscription at the base.

The most faithful canine friend ever…

Marcus chuckled slightly, then reach down into his pocket to retrieve the map that the bartender Jakub had given him. He studied it quickly. Alexandra looked at him in bewilderment. There they were, right at Jakub's favorite monument. Marcus looked intently at the map again, nodded slightly, then folded the map back up and put it in his jacket pocket.

Still looking on in disbelief, Alexandra whispered, "What the hell are you doing?"

"I've got an idea," Marcus responded, "Let me draw them out, and you get back to the hotel safely. If they try to close in on me, I'll make a break for it."

Alexandra looked sideways at Marcus, as if to say, *that's not much of a plan now, is it?* She thought for a moment, then changed her demeanor and replied, "Tell you what, follow your plan. Draw them out, and I'll take care of the rest."

While not too much different from Marcus's original plan, this sounded infinitely more promising, and

Marcus knew it immediately. Alexandra was, at least he thought, a trained field operative. He nodded his approval, then, retrieving the map again and pointing to a spot, informed her, "I'll cross this bridge here, and be visible about it, and lead them over to this bridge here." He indicated a second bridge near their hotel.

Alexandra tried very hard not to laugh but couldn't help it. She allowed a chuckle to escape, then nodded along to appease him.

"Okay, Maverick, you do that. Just remember the two rules: no gunfire or bloodshed unless it is a last resort, and don't get captured. That's probably what these guys want, unless they are just trying to scare us."

Marcus indicated he understood, then turned to head off. Alexandra grabbed his jacket, then when she had his attention, she motioned two fingers in front of her eyes.

"I got it," Marcus responded, "I'll look for you."

MARCUS STAYED LOW and hugged the hill at a jogging pace until he reached the first bridge, then popped onto the running path casually and began strolling across to the other side of the river. Halfway across the bridge and at its high point, he caught some movement on the street level above the Džok monument. He reached into his jacket pocket and fingered the loaded Glock, if for no other reason than to assure himself it was there. He had retrieved it from underneath the bed in his hotel room, taped to the underside of the box spring just as Franz had said it would be. Now, he tried to take his own advice and carry on as normally as possible.

HE REACHED THE south side of the river and turned onto the running path on that bank. He had a good vantage point, as his pursuers would have to cross over one of the two bridges that he could see clearly if they wanted to get to him. He glanced casually back toward the Džok monument, but Alexandra was nowhere in sight. Some low-level noise hummed from the terrace of a hotel bar on that side of the river, and Marcus felt himself relax slightly. He looked up ahead, where the river bowed back to the left, and he saw a figure, big and bulky with a shiny bald head, walking swiftly on the walking path on the other side, making his way toward the second bridge. A few barges tied up together on the side of the river creaked, and Marcus caught himself from jumping back. He looked around coolly and saw nothing near him, but he did catch a figure a hundred or so yards behind him. A slim, wiry physique with short dark hair, head down, and hands in pockets.

Pincer movement, huh? Marcus thought to himself, then was reminded of his genius strategy…*draw them out*. Not the most developed plan he had ever come up with, but that's what he told Alexandra he would do. So now he had to do it.

He pivoted onto the ramp leading up to the second bridge and began walking across. There was almost no traffic on the street portion of the bridge, and the old gothic style gas lamps made for long, bending, and re-peating shadows as he advanced back across toward the north side of the river. The hotel was a mere five-minute walk from the other side of the bridge, but a bulky body and bald head stood between Marcus and that end. Marcus made his way over to the ledge of the bridge, looking out onto the river. He advanced slowly, taking in the view. Back behind him, a shadow appeared on the other end of the bridge where Marcus had just come from.

As Marcus reached about three quarters of the way across the bridge, the bulky figure came within speaking distance. Marcus continued along calmly, moving closer to the rail over the river. Further along the bridge, past the approaching bulky figure, Marcus saw the slightest change in pattern. The bulky man had been watching Marcus, and seeming to notice Marcus staring at some-thing, started to turn his head back behind him.

Marcus reached into his jacket pocket quickly, then exclaimed, "Excuse me! Sir, do you speak English?" Marcus was holding his map out wide in front of him, moving it toward the light above the rail. The man was surprised and confused.

"English? Yes, you speak English, right?" Hearing no response, Marcus continued, "Oh good, that's wonderful. Can you help me please? I'm a bit lost. I'm trying to go here." Marcus pointed to a random spot on the map and pushed it further toward the rail. The man, a tough face beneath his bald head, had recovered himself and flashed a slight smile, catching on to Marcus's ploy.

"*Yhiss*, I *zpeak* English," he replied slowly, with a heavy accent, moving toward Marcus. Marcus could smell a mix of cologne, sweat, tobacco, and vodka coming off the man. Back behind him, Marcus could sense the pace of the footsteps coming from the other end quicken.

"Ah. Lovely! Well then, could you take a look at this for me?" Marcus leaned his arms out, holding the map above the dark water below, pressing it into the light emanating from the lamp above. The man approached the map slowly and got close enough to shake Marcus's hand. The man put one hand on the rail, then reached his other hand to the back waist band of his black jeans.

Marcus fought back his animal instinct to either run, grab his own weapon, or some combination of both. He continued blabbing about finding the Wawel Dragon sculpture as he prepared to make a move. As the man's hand came forward, Marcus heard two quick footsteps from behind the man and a whoosh of sound.

The man let out a guttural yell, as a force pushed him head-first over the other side of the railing. He yelled even louder as he fell toward the river and made a giant splash that pierced the quiet of the evening. From the barges tied up on the bank, a few voices called out in what sounded like Polish. Further back, where the other figure had been approaching, a loud scream emerged, and the other man looked down into the river over the rail. He yelled out a name, indecipherable, a handful of times. The figure turned to Marcus, staring for a second. Then he checked the street, and not seeing any traffic, bounded across to the other end of the bridge and down to the water.

Alexandra was rubbing her left shoulder in the shadows near Marcus, one knee bent down to the ground. Marcus grabbed her hand.

"Let's go!" He urged and led her across the last portion of the bridge toward their hotel. She grunted once, then hopped to her feet and followed along. The hotel lobby was empty, and the bar shut down when they arrived. They made quickly for the elevator and rode up to Marcus's room. Alexandra was clearly in pain, holding her left shoulder with her right arm. She leaned her head into Marcus's shoulder, and not knowing what else to do, he put his arm around her. They hurried down the hall into his room and shut the door. He quickly locked it behind them. It was unlikely anyone else was following them, but adrenaline was still coursing through their veins.

Marcus sat Alexandra down on the bed and layered a few pillows beneath her hurt shoulder.

"Is it dislocated? Do you need me to pop it back into place?" Marcus asked, then thought, *Not that I know how to do that...*

Alexandra winced, but shook her head from side to side. "No, I don't think so. Seems more like a pulled muscle or something."

Marcus looked around the room and located the elegant minibar housed in the dark oak-colored dresser. To his surprise, inside there was an ice bucket, a bottle of American bourbon, and a white card resting in front of the bottle. Marcus quickly dumped a few handfuls of ice into a plastic bag, tied it up, and rested it on Alexandra's shoulder. Then he opened the envelope and found a short note on hotel stationary inside:

Welcome to Krakow! Hope to see you again soon. On the house! —Jakub

God bless that man, Marcus thought as he poured a few fingers of bourbon into two glasses resting atop the dresser. The wooden, sweet smell of the bourbon put Marcus a bit more at ease, and he pulled a chair over next to Alexandra, handing her a glass.

The ice on her shoulder seemed to be helping, and she took a big sip of bourbon. Marcus refilled her glass and she quickly downed it, then melted comfortably back into the pillow behind her. Marcus took a sip too, felt the burn in his chest and fought back a wave of nausea. He wasn't much of a bourbon drinker, but the occasion called for something, and this was the first thing available. Exhausted, Alexandra leaned her head onto Marcus's shoulder once more. Her hair was damp, and he smelled her crisp, salty sweat and a waft of her elegant perfume as well.

He raised his bourbon glass. "*Na zdrowie?*"

She laughed and clinked her glass against his. "*Na zdrowie*, indeed."

They both took long, thoughtful sips.

"That was incredible work. You're quite the pro. Thank you." Marcus acknowledged earnestly, softening his tone as the endorphins from the chase slowly dissipated.

Alexandra nodded, then replied, "You, too. You hung in there until the end. Well done." She looked up at him, her eyes still pulsating with energy. Her face looked woozy, from the pain, the adrenaline, or the bourbon, he didn't know. She leaned in close and brought her lips up to Marcus's. He smelled the bourbon on her lips, recalling his brief encounter with those lips earlier. How badly he wanted to kiss her again. And, uncharacteristically, he stopped himself. He raised his chin up to the top of her forehead and pulled her in for a hug. She didn't seem bothered by it in the least. He held on tight for a few more seconds, then leaned back in his chair and polished off the rest of his drink.

They spent the night together, platonically, in Marcus's room. There was no real expectation that they were still in danger, but better to play it safe and stick together. Marcus rose early, called down to order breakfast and a new bucket of ice from room service, and went to shower while Alexandra continued to rest. *That shoulder is going to be sore as hell*, Marcus thought, and winced just thinking about the pain.

As he was getting dressed and packing up his suitcase, he heard a thud out on the balcony outside his room. It was loud enough to wake Alexandra, and Marcus signaled to her to remain quiet. He crept over to the window and grabbed the Glock out of his jacket pocket on the way. He lifted the curtains and was relieved not to see anyone standing on the balcony. He checked the surrounding balconies as best he could, then decided to step out. He flipped up the collar on his hotel-issued white cotton bathrobe and cinched the belt around his waist tightly. He opened the door and jumped back excitedly. There, laying on the floor of his balcony, was a large, dead bald eagle.

PART III

The Deal

CHAPTER 26

Washington, D.C.
Late July 2019.

ARTHUR FRANZ CHECKED HIS APPEARANCE IN the mirror once more and was almost satisfied. He straightened his royal-blue and white repp tie so that it was centered over his white dress shirt and navy-blue suit coat, then nodded his head assuredly. He didn't wear a full suit and tie often, but this occasion certainly called for one. He picked up his black canvas work bag and made his way out of the hotel room.

The Director was waiting for him in the lobby of their hotel, the Ritz-Carlton Georgetown. Despite the heat, the Director insisted that the two of them walk the thirty minutes over to Foggy Bottom. Franz observed the Director's attire: a worn, baggy, patterned dark-blue suit with pleated and cuffed pants, a once-white dress shirt with a buttoned-down collar frayed around the neck, and an imitation-silk, orange tie with what looked like blue images of the planet Jupiter on it. This ensemble was capped by a pair of square-toed, lace-up brown dress shoes with worn-out heels, and a backpack featuring the name of the law firm the Director worked at fifteen years ago before joining the agency. The Director and Franz made quite the contrast, with Franz in his high-quality, trim, European-cut suit and sleek Italian loafers. Franz wasn't a spendthrift or a vain person, but the combination of his position within Peppercorn Capital and living in Berlin had encouraged him to invest in presentable clothing. Then again, this was just another day for the Director, and it was clear he didn't feel the need to impress anyone…not even the lady he and Franz were on their way to see.

Exiting the hotel, they quickly found an already busy K Street and headed east toward Washington Circle. The morning traffic was loud enough background noise to allow the Director and Franz to speak frankly.

"So it sounds like things in Poland went…well," the Director stated nonchalantly.

"It looks that way, yes." Franz responded, then added, "We'll start negotiating the transaction agreements with Gas Polskie in a few weeks. There won't be anything official in the press until we actually sign those agreements. So probably another month."

The Director responded with a methodical nod. He took a breath in as if about to speak, paused, then a few seconds later asked, "But there was some…interesting activity along the way. Was there not?"

"That's right," Franz responded. "Two operatives, we believe Russians, made a semiaggressive movement toward the two Peppercorn investment professionals. They could have been from NovaGaz, from the Russian government, or both."

The Director took in this information that he already knew, then narrowed his eyes as he asked, "And one of them ended up...wet, shall I say?"

Franz knew the Director well enough to recognize that look, discerning and feigning confusion. It was as close as the Director ever got to a smile.

Franz inhaled and nodded gently a few times before responding, "Yes, apparently he fell into the river there in Krakow just as he was making a move toward one of the Peppercorn professionals."

"Mmm," The Director replied, then added, "Quite the coincidence."

They looped around Washington Circle and began walking down Twenty-Third Street.

"And that was Odysseus?" the Director asked, using one of the code names adopted to describe specific agents working in the field.

"Well, it was," Franz confirmed, but then clarified, "But Athena was the cause of the slip and fall. She nearly dislocated her shoulder, but that was the worst of it."

"Ah, yes...Athena. How is she...doing?"

Franz gave a contemplative look, then replied. "She's doing well. Seems to be almost all the way back."

The Director gave a single nod, then asked. "And Odysseus…seems to be doing quite…well. Isn't he?"

Franz chuckled internally at The Director's proclivity to end all his statements with a question, like he had often found British people doing.

"He is. No question. But give credit to Athena there as well. She watches over him and gives him necessary guidance at times."

The Director knowingly shook his head a few times in admiration. Then he looked at Franz expectantly as he asked, "Well? Are we risking these…Russians… being onto us?"

Franz dipped his head to acknowledge the predicament. Then he replied, "We need to create some friction between Peppercorn and the US government to get…whoever that was…off the scent. We have a contact at the SEC who has a trumped-up Peppercorn securities law violation on ice for times like these. I suggest we tell her to initiate the investigation. And to be a little noisy about it."

They were across the street from their destination. The Director paused, blinking a few times and looking blankly ahead. The streetlight changed. There were a few loud dinging noises and a white light indicating a pedestrian figure flashed in their direction. The Director's gaze focused in at the imposing building in front of them, and he replied, "Okay, do it."

WALKING IN THIS part of D.C. near all of the federal government buildings always reminded Arthur Franz of the intense efforts that architects and builders had undertaken to make this city look like Imperial Rome, or fifth century BC Athens. Imposing white or gray buildings that, while not tall, still felt massive and seemed to occupy so much space. The wide sidewalks and spacious lawns surrounding the buildings. The vertical columns, the ordered and uniform placement of windows. Squares, rectangles, and triangles all arranged in a manner to project power. Power over you, and power over everyone else.

The Harry S. Truman Building, home to the US Department of State, was no different. The Director and Franz made their way inside and checked in at the front reception desk. The attendant's eyes grew large when she keyed in their names and identified with whom they had an appointment.

"Right away, gentlemen," she offered directly, "Please, follow our security guard here." She gestured to a tall, well-built young man in a black suit, white shirt, black tie, and an earpiece. The Director clearly knew the drill and followed along out of habit. Franz unconsciously pulled tight the lapels of his suit jacket and clicked along dutifully. After the obligatory five-minute wait in basic chairs up against the wall in the hallway, looking like two naughty boys about to be summoned to the principal's office, they were admitted entry.

Christine Snyder, US Secretary of State, greeted them warmly and enthusiastically, as if this was the meeting she had been waiting for all day.

"Mark Taylor, so great to see you! Please, come on in and have a seat," she stated, as she gave the Director an energetic double-handed clasp and handshake.

"Madame Secretary," the Director responded.

"None of that now; call me Chris!" the Secretary corrected. Then, turning to Franz, she stated, "Mr. Arthur Franz, we have not met. Chris Snyder. Very nice to meet you."

Franz offered up a closed-mouth smile and shook the Secretary's hand. Her reputation as friendly and down-to-earth preceded her, and it was true to fact. All three of them sat.

Franz observed the Secretary, never having seen her up close. She was tall and in good shape for someone of her age, with short blond hair and an energetic face. She wore a healthy amount of makeup and was colorfully, yet tastefully dressed. Franz looked around the office to see numerous framed pictures. Some with what looked like kids and grandkids, some with notable foreign dignitaries, and some that were obviously from the days of her previous job, as they showed her in front of an oil derrick in a dry desert, or in a board-room with a geological map behind her. There were diplomas and framed letters and newspaper articles on the walls. Open-faced cabinets full of trinkets and paraphernalia of a successful career and a life lived on a grand scale.

Prior to becoming the Secretary, Christine Snyder had a long and successful career as an engineer and geologist at one of the major international oil companies. This had culminated in her reign as the CEO of that company for a decade and a half, making her one of the most powerful corporate leaders in the world. She had traveled the world and lived abroad as both a project manager and executive, showing positive results all over the globe and building a wealth of personal relationships along the way. Under her tenure, her company had at one point been the highest-valued company on the New York Stock Exchange. In a business that had typically been male-dominated, especially at the executive ranks, Chris Snyder had not only succeeded, but done so in spectacular fashion.

When the offer to become the Secretary was presented to her, she viewed it as an obligation and a privilege to serve her country and had taken to the job seamlessly. But this, what the Director and Franz were about to go over with her, was one of the difficult parts of her job. One of the less glamorous, but oh-so-necessary and important parts of her job.

She had thrust forward a tray with water and coffee for all three of them and took a long sip out of the coffee cup in front of her before opening the discussion.

"Well, gentlemen, how can I help you?"

Franz handled his own coffee cup, and looked down into it before taking a sip, leaving an opening for the Director to begin.

"Madam…umm…Chris, as you are likely aware, from time to time we enlist the assistance of certain… well-placed…civilians to assist us in activities that are…helpful to what we do at the agency. This practice has fared quite well over the years. And…oftentimes… we enlist that same civilian to help us on…different fronts." The Director's predisposition to speaking slowly and deliberately came in handy in situations like these, where the diction of the speaker allowed the recipient of the message to read into what is being said at the appropriate places.

The Secretary nodded slowly, then peered at the Director over her coffee cup. *I follow. Go on.*

"Yes…well, it seems that one of those…helpers…is currently…missing." The Director took a sip of water, before continuing. "Arthur Franz here," the Director gestured toward Franz in the next seat over, "who has been…friendly…with this helper can provide some more detail."

Franz had been looking downward, fixated on a particular pattern on the rug, with a serious look on his face during the Director's discourse. Now that it was his turn to speak, Franz's countenance morphed into one of concentrated energy, a light flowing into his eyes as he looked up at the Secretary. Not a playful light, or a hopeful light, but an infectious light that instantly grabbed the attention of the Secretary.

"Madame Secretary, Graham Curry is the downstream project manager for Colombian operations at..." Franz named Graham's employer, one of the biggest competitors of the Secretary's former company. A wave of recognition and understanding came over the Secretary's face. "Last week, he was performing a task that we ask him to do once a month. He oversees the transport of a fuel barge, refined at his company's Cartagena facility, to a dock in Barranquilla. In Barranquilla, he transfers custody of the barge to an agent acting on behalf of an organized group of rebels within Venezuela that are fighting to push the current president out and put in the man that our government has publicly stated is the rightfully elected president. The barge from the previous month's shipment is returned by the agent, and one of Curry's employees pilots the barge back to Cartagena. This operation has been going on successfully for close to a year."

Franz paused to allow the Secretary to ask any questions, or for the Director to add any color. The Secretary blinked, then continued staring at Franz without expression. The Director stared into his coffee cup.

"Last week, something happened. The barge never returned to Cartagena. Curry's truck was found in the parking lot next to the barge. No sign of Curry. No sign of the barge driver." Franz paused to allow the Secretary to absorb this development. Anticipating her likely questions, he continued. "No word has surfaced from the Venezuelan government yet, but our State Department officers in Colombia suspect that Curry is being held, and…" Franz exhaled audibly. "…the barge pilot is likely dead. Nothing in the press anywhere yet, and nothing from Curry's employer."

The Secretary sat back in her chair, then grimaced as if she was experiencing physical pain. She furrowed her brow, then looked up at the wall behind Franz. Her mind seemed to be working through various scenarios.

Then, breaking her silence, she asked Franz, "Why do we think the Venezuelans are holding off on announcing anything? That seems unlike them. With their current president, you would think Curry would have been marched through the streets of Caracas on live TV.… Who else wants Curry? What has he done for us before?"

Franz bobbed his head, impressed by the number of leaps that the Secretary was able to successfully make on such little information. He looked over at the Director, who tilted his head gently in Franz's direction. *She's brilliant. Go ahead, continue.*

"Good questions, Madame Secretary," Franz responded as he made eye contact with her again. "About six years ago, Curry was working as a project manager in Papua New Guinea. At that time, we had him keep records on the way in which the Chinese were infiltrating Papua New Guinean society, and critical businesses in particular, namely telecom and oil and gas. He was able to export a zip file of information, a treasure trove of leads for us. That information has proven incredibly valuable." Franz paused, then added, "We think it likely that the Chinese found out about Curry. And now they've put the word out that they want him."

"And the Venezuelans are holding him. Going to try and make a deal with the Chinese," the Secretary concluded.

Franz nodded his head in agreement. "That's right."

"We wanted to make you aware, as we wouldn't want you to be… in the dark…before the information goes public," the Director jumped in. "If it goes public."

The Secretary indicated that she understood, then added, "Thank you Mark, Arthur, for letting me know." She leaned back in her chair again and took another long sip of coffee. Then, in a matter-of-fact manner, she stated, "But that's not going to happen. Because you, Arthur," she looked directly into Franz's eyes, then released a faint smile, "are going to get Curry back. And you're going to figure out a way to do it so that neither the Venezuelans nor the Chinese could ever go public with it."

CHAPTER 27

Lyon, France.
Wednesday, July 24, 2019.

MARCUS TOOK THE TEN A.M. HIGH SPEED TGV train out of the Paris-Gare-de-Lyon and arrived at Lyon-Part-Dieu station a few minutes before noon. He hopped in a taxi for the short trip over to his hotel on a cobbled pedestrian street in the lively Presqu'île neighborhood. Presqu'île was smack-dab in the center of Lyon, on a peninsula, the word *presqu'île* literally meaning "almost island" in French, with the Rhône River running along the east side and the Saône River along the west side. The rivers combined at the southern tip of Presqu'île, called *la confluence*, with the Rhône being the sole river continuing south. Marcus peered at the river conspiratorially as his taxi crossed over the Pont Wilson into Presqu'île, knowing that over the next three days he and the Rhône would be spending a lot of time together.

The cycling voyage, business networking trip, boondoggle, and Shareholder-specific mission was set to begin the next day. The group would depart from Lyon on Thursday morning and, with a healthy boost from the infamous *Le Mistral* wind, arrive at the glistening Mediterranean Sea at Plage Napoléon, just past Port-Saint-Louis-du-Rhône, on Saturday afternoon. A trip of approximately three hundred and twenty kilometers...*damn near two-hundred miles*, Marcus noted.

They would principally trace the path of the southern part of the ViaRhôna, a bike path that led from Lake Geneva in Switzerland all the way down to the French Mediterranean coast. Much of the way would be through the vaunted Rhône wine country, and Broccatelli had arranged for their group to make a number of stops along the way for wine tastings and specially prepared meals at some of the finest vineyards in the Rhône Valley.

But this was indeed a business trip for Marcus; both for the Shareholder and for Peppercorn Capital. Marcus and a team of Peppercorn associates had been probing the Broccatelli energy business empire over the past few weeks for investment targets. Then, yesterday, Arthur Franz had reached out to Marcus.

"Consider any opportunities with Broccagas Trading & Shipping," Franz encouraged, "Looks like it could be a promising investment."

Cryptic as usual, but Marcus could see the reasoning behind it. Marcus's team had discovered some curious financial results from Broccagas Trading &

Shipping, unexpected gains when all other signs would have pointed to losses from the same general difficulties that the shipping industry was facing globally from increased environmental regulations and the realization that Chinese demand for everything was not going to increase eternally. But a trading and shipping business would also be a nice complement to Peppercorn's current portfolio of companies, as the firm successfully developed and sold a Rotterdam-based trading and shipping business earlier in the decade and had not yet invested back into that space.

Marcus reminded himself of all of this as he unpacked his suitcase in his hotel room and drew back the curtains to look down upon the massive, wide-open Place Bellecour, the largest pedestrian square in Europe. Its unique red surface spread out below, with the sizeable equestrian statue of King Louis XIV in the center, and the unique Basilica of Notre-Dame de Fourvière, which looked down on it all from the steep, forested hill above.

"Ahh," Marcus intoned as he took in the view. Yes, this was a business trip, but he had never been to Lyon before, and he decided he may as well take advantage. So he had come early to make a day of it and explore a bit before hopping on the bike the next morning.

Marcus changed into his running gear and set out from his hotel for a jog over to the Parc de la Tête d'Or, the giant urban park across the Rhône in Lyon's 6th arrondisement. He snaked through the windy streets of Presqu'île to cross the river on the Passerelle du Collège, a beautiful nineteenth century pedestrian-only stone suspension bridge.

As he rounded the corner of the bridge to head north toward the park, his eyes drifted to a storefront window with numerous bottles of rosé wine, almost crystal clear but with the slightest tinge of pink, on display. They lined the entirety of the window and ranged in sizes from *demi-bouteille*, standard, magnum, and even a gigantic jeroboam. Marcus unconsciously licked his lips and was reminded that he was, indeed, venturing into the heart of French wine country.

He ran along the *Berges du Rhône*, the wide, open running and biking paths next to the river. Moored to the banks of the river were a handful of boat-restaurant-bar establishments teeming with people enjoying the summer afternoon. Many of the patrons sat at long wooden picnic-style tables on the lawn next to the boats. And even though it was lunch hour on a Wednesday, a full glass of wine or a frothy pint of beer could be spotted at just about every table.

Marcus worked his way deep into the park along the manicured gravel paths separating large grassy areas full of picnickers on blankets and young children grouped together with teachers or camp counselors. Unexpectedly, he happened upon the Lyon Zoo, smack-dab in the middle of the park. Most stunning of all was the makeshift African plain contained within the zoo, where Marcus saw antelopes and giraffes moseying around in what seemed like an unenclosed space. He shook his head in amazement as he made an about-face to head back to his hotel.

That afternoon, Marcus paid a visit to Lyon's fascinating *Centre D'histoire De La Resistance et De La Deportation*, a museum commemorating Jewish deportation and French resistance during World War II. Marcus had read how Lyon was considered the center of the French Resistance, and so was interested to see what the museum housed.

The museum told the story not only of some of the more well-known French Resistance figures, such as Jean Moulin, but also of the numerous contributions made by everyday French citizens in the fight against the Nazis. It was particularly interesting to learn that the museum sat on the location of the old French military health school, which was taken over by the Nazis and became an office for the Gestapo in Lyon. Gestapo leader Klaus Barbie, the infamous "Butcher of Lyon," had used the building to torture French Resistance members, including Jean Moulin.

Marcus made his way across both the Rhône and Saône to the Vieux Lyon neighborhood for dinner. This part of town had very much of a village feel, with the old four- and five-story buildings huddling up next to one another along the banks of the Saône. A narrow cobblestone street wound up the hill of Fourvière, with a bevy of bars and restaurants on one side and the steep hill on the other. What looked like old gas lamps lit the path, and live music poured down from Les Nuits de Fourvière concert series taking place in the old Roman amphitheater above.

Dining alone, Marcus enjoyed a fantastic meal at Bouchons Les Lyonnais. The exterior of the restaurant was painted a hearty French blue, with red metal tables and chairs along the sidewalk. Inside, the energy of the restaurant was infectious. Marcus sat at a classic-looking wooden table by the window, and marveled at the numerous pictures of French heroes, celebrities, and historical figures that adorned the walls.

Within France, Lyon was known as the gastronomic capital of the country. Given all the wonderful food Marcus had on a daily basis in Paris, he found that hard to believe. But Bouchons Les Lyonnais did not disappoint.

He began his meal with a massive *salade Lyonnais*, served in a wide and deep bowl, the green salad generously infused with chunks of thick bacon, a soft poached egg, and crispy croutons. It was followed by a caramelized duck-leg confit cooked in garlic juice, served with a side of hot French fries. He skipped the cheese plate that the waitress recommended. But knowing he would be biking for a good five hours each day over the next three days, he allowed himself to indulge in the dessert special of the evening, *oeufs à la neige*, a dollop of merengue floating on a plate of crème anglaise. And to wash it all down, he had enjoyed a few spectacularly smooth, yet flavorful glasses of Crozes-Hermitage.

Marcus enjoyed the opportunity to meander back to his hotel on Presqu'île, walking off both the meal and the wine. He remembered reading once that at the end of the fifteenth century, King Louis XI of France had seriously considered moving the nation's capital from Paris to Lyon. The rationale then was more related to Lyon's physical proximity to the well-trodden trade routes of Italy and Savoy, and to be closer to the Pope. Reflecting on his own day here in Lyon, this former capital of the Gauls during the Roman Empire, known back then as Lugdunum, Marcus had to admit that it wouldn't have been a bad alternative to Paris for a capital city.

THE CYCLING GROUP gathered the next morning at seven at one of the boats-turned-restaurants on the *Berges du Rhône*. What had been a bar the night before was transformed into a café for the morning crowds. Mauro Broccatelli was meticulous in his attention to detail in planning the trip. He'd arranged for all the participants' bikes to be picked up from their hometowns and transported to Lyon. Two all-white Volkswagen EuroVans carrying bikes, food, water, spare parts, with a handful of mechanics doubling as drivers, waited on the road just above the grassy plain beside the river where the riders sat.

SOME RIDERS, MARCUS included, sat comfortably at picnic tables enjoying croissants and coffee, making small talk with one another. Others, Broccatelli included, were downing sports drinks, goos, gels, and meal bars, while engaging in active stretches to loosen up before beginning the ride. At 7:15 sharp, Broccatelli called the group together with a few active claps of his hands and a huge smile on his face. Broccatelli's dark-brown eyes, seemingly lifeless and frozen when Marcus first met him at the formal event at the Musée d'Orsay, were alive with energy and glinting from the morning sun reflecting off the Rhône.

Broccatelli gave a quick outline of the plan for the entire trip, and a more detailed description of the schedule for that day. Then he went around to each trip participant and gave their names, current city of residence, and of course, the all-important employer and job title. There was a total of twelve riders. The roster was a veritable list of European-based masters of the universe. A handful of bankers from London: English, Spanish, and German, judging by their names. Andrea Ravello, a scion of the Milanese Ravello family fortune and the brother of Broccatelli's beloved Antonia Ravello. Some London-based private equity managers. A private banker and a commodities trader, both from Switzerland. And two of Broccatelli's colleagues from Broccagas: one from the company's European headquarters in London, and the other from Turkmenistan, where Broccagas had substantial oil and gas operations.

Broccatelli asked everyone to break up into groups of four to make some quick personal introductions before they got on the road. Marcus found himself standing next to Broccatelli's two colleagues and the English banker. The native English speakers sheepishly gravitated toward one another.

Marcus took the lead and introduced himself. The English banker, whose name was Nicholas Sewell, cheerily shook Marcus's hand and commented, "Peppercorn Capital, eh? You're the chaps that stole the Gas Polskie deal from the Russians, aren't you?"

Marcus recoiled slightly, genuinely surprised that any information about that potential deal was known in the market. He chuckled and tried to ignore the question.

"Well," Sewell continued, "Our team could not believe that Gas Polskie would pick a firm of your size. But cheers, mate, we're rooting for you guys!"

So polite…yet so condescending, Marcus noted to himself.

The comments from Sewell had caused the duo from Broccagas to raise their eyebrows and exchange a subtle look showing that they were impressed...and interested. They introduced themselves around.

The Broccagas man from London was Simon Walker-Kelly. He was about six feet tall and looked like he kept in shape. He had short brown hair and a casually well-trimmed brown beard. He seemed naturally reserved and like a man of few yet select words. Broccatelli had introduced Walker-Kelly as the head of the Broccagas Trading and Shipping desk, a point of which Marcus took note.

And from Turkmenistan, although it turned out he was an Australian engineer, was Liam Sturgess. A bear of a man, Sturgess was a good four or five inches taller than the rest of them and looked like a rugby player. Which Marcus quickly learned he was, at least before becoming an engineer. Sturgess was gregarious and full of life, with a megawatt smile and curly blond hair that fell to just above his shoulders.

An air horn blew, and the mechanics began wheeling down the bikes from the vans above. Broccatelli stood at the front of the pack and clipped into his pedals. Nicholas Sewell, who, between his bike and his clothing had north of ten-thousand dollars' worth of gear, huddled up next to Broccatelli. The rest of the group fell in line, and one of the mechanics chuckled as he raised a white work cloth and counted out, "*Un, deux, trois, partez!*" The mechanic then snapped the cloth down to open the starting gates.

And with that, the voyage to the Mediterranean began.

CHAPTER 28

Tain-l'Hermitage, France. Thursday, July 25, 2019.

T O MARCUS'S SURPRISE, THE BIKE ROUTE SOUTH had started by diverting away from the Rhône and instead going for about an hour and a half on a non-descript and not particularly scenic regional French road. But once they reached Vienne, they rejoined the Rhône and cruised the rest of the way along the banks of the river on the ViaRhôna.

Sloping hillsides covered with vineyards rolled down into the blue-green river as the bike path snaked its way south. The vineyards appeared in neat green rows in one area, and then in clumps on manmade terraces in the next. They were predominantly found on the right side of the river, and so were soaking up the sun as the group cycled by. Many of the vineyards contained large white placards with the name of the producers in big, bold print. Some of these were well-known names in the wine world that Marcus had heard of before, names like Chapoutier,

Delas, and Guigal. But many of the names were complete unknowns to Marcus.

He breathed in the fresh, open air and felt the wind at his back as he took in the beautiful scenery around them. The group rode at a good pace and generally kept together. Simon Walker-Kelly had snuck up to the front of the group early on and had been in the lead ever since. Along the path, a few riders engaged in some coordinated sprints and faux-races to liven things up. Marcus hung in the back half of the group and engaged in some casual conversations with a few the riders, thoroughly enjoying the opportunity to get to know this interesting cast of characters.

As they neared the end of the day's ride in the early afternoon, the vineyards switched from the right side of the river to the left, and the massive hill of Hermitage appeared before them. It was covered in organized vineyards, with a small break in the middle of one of them for what looked like a small stone church. The town of Tain-l'Hermitage sat on the plain by the river at the bottom of the hill, peering up at the surrounding vineyards.

The cycling group slowed their pace to a crawl as they crossed over the Rhône on an impressive pedestrian-only suspension bridge into Tain-l'Hermitage. There they dismounted, congratulated one another on a good day's ride and passed their bikes along to the mechanics awaiting them with the white vans.

Broccatelli led them to the collection of apartments rented for the night and informed the riders who their roommates were. One of the mechanics handed out keys to the rooms, and Broccatelli reminded the group of the wine tasting to be followed by dinner that had been arranged at a very special tasting room: a cave and restaurant owned by one of the marquee local producers just a few blocks away from where they were staying.

Marcus was pleased to learn he was rooming with Liam Sturgess, the Australian engineer from Turkmenistan. They found one another and went to locate their apartment, before unpacking and preparing for the evening's festivities.

THE *BAR À VINS DU FAMILLE DUMONT* was an expertly decorated establishment facing onto the main town square of Tain-l'Hermitage. It had a paneled-wood and windows exterior, with a few large, decorative wine barrels on either side of the front door. The entry room was a neatly organized and modern-looking wine boutique selling the Dumont family wines. Boxes and buckets of wines lined the white walls. Aged and stained wooden planks ran the length of the ceiling. This room gave way to a tasting room behind it, where, on the right side of the room, a large bar ran perpendicular to the front door and extended for a good fifteen feet. There were several stools on one side of the metal bar, and plenty of space for three or four employees to conduct a wine tasting from the other side. On the left side of the tasting room were a handful of tables, with benches connected to the wall on one end and wooden chairs on the other. Finally, behind the tasting room was an inner courtyard with an open roof and two large tables covered with white tablecloths and full place settings.

Marcus and Liam arrived a little before six and found most of the group already there. Marcus noted the strong, musty smell that permeated the interior of the restaurant, and breathed it in deeply.

They were afforded ten minutes in the wine boutique to look around before being ushered into the tasting room. Waiting for them behind the bar, flanked by four assistants, was an early-middle-aged woman with dark-brown hair, a thin, pointed nose, a plain but pretty face, a puckered mouth, and piercing blue eyes. She wore a white button-up shirt with thin, faint pink vertical stripes and an open neck, highlighting a lean, fit figure underneath. She displayed a big smile on top of a serious and focused manner.

A hush fell over the group as Broccatelli made a few clinks on a glass. He proceeded to gushingly introduce the leader of the tasting as none other than Caroline Dumont, owner and head winemaker for the Dumont wineries and "one of the most respected professionals in the wine world." Broccatelli also noted that Caroline Dumont was previously a champion equestrian, and currently a very accomplished marathon runner—both things that Broccatelli clearly admired.

Dumont affected a practiced blush before thanking Broccatelli and noting to the group that Broccatelli was an extremely talented wine professional and considered a rising star in his own right. This caught Broccatelli off guard, but it clearly pleased him. A pinkish hue from pride and embarrassment covered his face.

Dumont began her presentation. She spoke English very well, but with a noticeable French accent and a British bent to her pronunciation.

"As Mauro said, my name is Caroline Dumont." *Wow, that sounds so much more pleasing on the ear than when Broccatelli said her name*, Marcus thought.

"Our family has owned Le Domaine Dumont for six generations, stretching back over a hundred and fifty years. And while we do own other vineyards in Bordeaux and Bourgogne, this—" Dumont stretched her arms out beside her and looked around the tasting room, making eye contact with her assistants, "will always be our home."

"Now I understand that you guys have just cycled a very long way, and through some of the most beautiful country in the Rhône Valley. This afternoon, we are going to be tasting wines made from those very same vineyards that you saw today on the slopes of those hills."

Dumont pulled out from behind the bar a colorful framed map of the Rhône Valley, with the cities of Vienne at the northern end and Arles at the southern end. She pointed to Vienne.

"Wine has been made here in the Rhône Valley for over two thousand years. It is even rumored that Julius Caesar, in the first century BC, was so adamant about conquering the territory of Gaul because he wanted Rome to have control over the vibrant Gaulish wine trade." Dumont raised her meticulously shaped eyebrows, and there was the storyteller's twinkle in her eye.

She allowed the faint murmur of laughter, interest, and surprise to linger before she began indicating certain colored sections of the map bordering on the Rhône, working her way from the area just below Vienne down to the village of Tain-l'Hermitage.

"Côte-Rôtie, Condrieu, Crozes-Hermitage, and, most important of all," she said with flair, again raising her arms in front of her, "Hermitage."

Dumont clapped her hands, as if an inspiration had just physically hit her, and exclaimed, "*Suivez-moi!*" She walked quickly through the boutique room and out the front door. The group hesitantly followed and finally arrived outside in the town square. The smell of the fresh summer air was a pleasant contrast to the musty scent of the tasting room.

"*Voila!*" Dumont declared. She pointed up at the large vineyard-covered hill above the town, a light green mass framed by a slowly fading blue sky. There was a large white placard, like those Marcus had seen earlier in the day, in the middle of the hill that read *Domaine Dumont*.

"Many of the grapes you saw on the vines today were Syrah. In fact, the Northern Rhône is well known for its mastery of Syrah." Marcus, recalling his wine lesson with Olivier at Ô Maison, thought to himself, *Syrah is* not *south…genius!*

"But here, on the hill of Hermitage, is the spiritual home of the Syrah grape." Dumont closed her eyes and breathed in and out deeply. Opening her eyes, she asked enthusiastically, "*Alors*, who is ready to taste some wine?"

The Dumont wine tasting was a glorious affair. Marcus found himself at a table with the Spanish banker whose name Marcus had forgotten, Andrea Ravello, who was Broccatelli's girlfriend's brother, and with Nicholas Sewell, the English investment banker. Sewell, as it turned out, was quite the colorful and enjoyable character. Marcus's initial impression of Sewell as chummy, hollow, and patronizing had proven premature.

MARCUS CAUGHT UP with Sewell during the day's ride and the two had ridden together and chatted for a good hour. In addition to sharing a number of common interests professionally and personally, Marcus had found real depth in Sewell's knowledge and character, even though it was enmeshed with the levity and nonchalance of his persona. Their discussion had flowed from talking shop on transactions they had worked on, to both of their preferences in literature, and back around to each of their respective experiences with cycling.

And much to the rest of the table's entertainment and something that wasn't discussed previously between Marcus and Sewell, one of Sewell's great passions was wine. French, Italian, and Spanish wine. And Sewell was not the least bit hesitant to share that passion and knowledge as they worked their way through the tasting.

The Côte-Rôtie, he said, was "Velvety and sumptuous. Like you are biting a bowl of chocolate mousse." The Condrieu, the wonderful white wine from the Viognier grape, was "Golden, with undertones of violet and apricot." And quite impressively, after each detailed description given in English, Sewell would then give a similar description in Italian to Ravello. When Marcus complemented Sewell's Italian, Sewell waved his hand dismissively and replied, "We had a little villa in Tuscany when I was growing up and my parents would banish me there from London each summer."

When the tasting advanced to the Crozes-Hermitage, Dumont once again got the attention of the crowd. She pointed out that, up to now, all of the wines the group had tasted grew predominantly on the *rive droite*, or the right bank of the Rhône, as the group was biking from north to south. But the Crozes-Hermitage and Hermitage grew on the *rive gauche*, or the left bank.

"You see, it's this left side of the river that makes for the perfect climate for Syrah growth," Sewell explained quietly to the table. Sewell was mesmerized by Dumont and the tasting as a whole. When the prestigious Hermitage wine was poured, Sewell tasted it and declared, "Superb, just superb. Aged for ten years, just the right amount of time, and beginning to show tastes of black pepper, venison, and undergrowth."

In what seemed to be the surprise finish, Dumont passed around a few bottles of the rare, rich, dry white wine from the Hermitage vineyards, the Hermitage Blanc. Broccatelli in particular seemed excited to taste this rare wine, enthusiastically swirling his glass and sniffing deeply.

Dumont's assistants collected all of the glasses, and some members of the tasting group began to move toward the dinner tables set up in the next room. Just then, Dumont called for the group's attention once again.

"Not dinner time yet, gentlemen," she spoke in a loud but tantalizing manner. "Because Mauro here is such a bright star in this wine world of ours, we wanted to give your group a very special treat."

The assistants returned with a fresh set of wide, bulbous wine glasses and set them along the bar. Then

Dumont placed two already-opened green wine bottles with clean, but old looking labels on the front of them in the center of the bar. Sewell's eyes bulged from his head, and then his body performed a convulsion that could only be described as orgasmic.

"Oh my," he uttered, involuntarily.

Curious, Marcus took a closer look at the label and read the words *Hermitage* across the top, *La Chapelle* near the bottom, and *Domaine Dumont* at the very bottom. Further up the bottle was a smaller, separate label with *1961* written on it.

Looking over at Broccatelli, Marcus could see the goosebumps forming on Broccatelli's arms as his mouth hung slightly open.

Dumont continued, "These are two bottles of what may be our finest vintage. Mauro," *Mowwoah,* she indicated through her French accent, "this is a way for us to say thank you for bringing your group here, and to express our gratitude for your shared enthusiasm about wine."

She raised her eyebrows again and chuckled genuinely as she declared, "I can count on just one hand the number of times we've opened this one for a tasting... anybody want to try?"

Dumont's assistants poured samples into the glasses, and everyone did their best to taste like a pro. Sewell was beside himself with excitement. After three rounds of viewing the color and smelling the glass, he took a full sip.

"Magic!" He replied after puckering his mouth, then considering thoughtfully. "None of us will ever taste a better wine. I've heard rumors about how good this was supposed to be, but my, my, it's so much better than I could have imagined."

Marcus's eyes snuck away from the group to study Broccatelli. The Argentine had stepped away from those surrounding him for a brief moment as he swirled his glass and sniffed. Then he raised the glass and took a sip. He gurgled the wine ever so slightly, then swallowed it down. His eyes closed as he breathed out slowly and deliberately. Then he looked up, as if looking through the roof of the tasting room and into the sky, opened his eyes, and gently nodded his head appreciatively.

CHAPTER 29

Châteauneuf-du-Pape, France.
Friday, July 26, 2019.

ACH MEMBER OF THE CYCLING GROUP WAS covered in a thick lather of sweat as they finally made it to *La Grande Fontaine* in the center of town in Châteauneuf-du-Pape. It had been a long, hot day of riding, but also a beautiful one. They had stopped briefly for repose and a snack after crossing the beautiful Himalayan footbridge over the Rhône outside of Montélimar. And for the final few hours of the ride, they were surrounded by vineyards as they passed the town of Orange and mercifully stopped a short while later in the quaint little town of Châteauneuf-du-Pape.

Marcus had noticed the short, almost wild-looking shrubs, with soil covered by hand-sized flat rocks that made up the vineyards around the town. And he was pleasantly surprised by how nice, simple, and beautiful the town of Châteauneuf-du-Pape itself was. It had been a hard day's ride, and he was looking forward to getting off of the bike.

Knowing that they had another long ride ahead the next day, Marcus had been judicious in his wine intake during the wonderful dinner following the Domain Dumont wine tasting. But he found himself unable to say no to Liam Sturgess's offer of a night cap at a local bar before heading to bed. The big Australian had the personality and vibe of someone that you wanted to like you, and Marcus was keen to hear about Sturgess's work life for Broccagas in Turkmenistan.

They found what appeared to be the only open bar in town and settled onto some barstools for a pint. Marcus began asking Sturgess about Turkmenistan, and then just sat back and listened as the floodgates opened on Sturgess's interesting work stories from oil fields in Turkmenistan and further beyond. But the conversation wasn't all one way, as Sturgess was interested in hearing about Marcus's experience in the oil and gas business in the US and Argentina as well.

Marcus had met several people that worked in Central Asia, East Africa, or the Middle East, but actually lived in Abu Dhabi or Dubai. This was typically motivated by the Emirates' luxury lifestyle and friendly tax regimes. When Marcus asked Sturgess if he also had official residence in the UAE, Sturgess recoiled and shook his head.

"Ah naw, mate, you got to live with the people. With your workers. You got to get out and get to know these places." A blaze of excitement emanated from his eyes. "My family and I live in Ashgabat, the capital. But our production facilities are due north in the middle of the Karakum Desert, so I shuttle back and forth between our corporate office in Ashgabat and our field office near our drilling rigs."

Fascinating, Marcus thought. He had never even heard of the Karakum Desert. He asked Sturgess what it was like.

Sturgess laughed before replying, "Desert. Sand everywhere, as far as the eye can see. But have you ever heard of the Darvaza gas crater?"

Marcus indicated that he hadn't.

"Ah mate, you got to see it. The Gates of Hell is what they call it. It's a giant hole in the middle of the desert that has been burning for almost fifty years. It's actually a collapsed natural gas field that the Soviets were trying to develop. When their rig sank into the crater, they decided to light the field on fire for the safety of any people that lived nearby. Damn thing has been burning ever since. It's beautiful if you see it at night, especially if you fly over it. Just incredible!"

They went on and on like that all the way back to their shared apartment before calling it a night. Sturgess had made a good impression on Marcus, as he seemed genuine and like an experienced professional.

In addition to Marcus's mission for this cycling trip of getting to know Mauro Broccatelli better, he also wanted to learn about the people that worked with Broccatelli. Who Broccatelli surrounded himself with would say a lot about the man himself. And if Peppercorn Capital was going to invest with Broccagas, Marcus needed to know the stripe of his future partners.

The cycling group was lodging in a large, rented house of beige-colored stones, red-tiled roof, and light-blue painted wooden door and window shutters, on a cobblestone street near the center of ChâteauneufduPape. The rented house had a large living room with a few long tables, and, after retiring to their rooms to shower and change clothes, many members of the group had claimed spaces on those tables with their workbags in tow. Marcus, instead, set out to walk around the town and do some exploring.

As Marcus left the house and stepped into the hot afternoon sun, he spotted Mauro Broccatelli walking alone at the far end of the street. As Broccatelli turned the corner, Marcus couldn't help but follow. Broccatelli strode past the town's main square and along one of the thoroughfares leading out toward the wineries.

Marcus employed some rudimentary tracking techniques and maintained an eye on Broccatelli from a distance. *Where is he going?* Marcus thought. Broccatelli was moving at a quick pace and took a right onto a wider street. Marcus hurried along so as not to lose him.

Halfway down the block, Broccatelli slowed his pace as he looked at a white sign outside of an enclosed domain. Seemingly satisfied with what was on the sign, Broccatelli entered the domain through the segmental arch out front.

Marcus moved close enough to make out the words on the sign, and read *Musée du Vin*

in large, black block letters. Marcus chuckled to himself as he felt the intrigue of the chase deflate and become supplanted by his own personal curiosity. Curiosity about the *Musée du Vin*, and even more curiosity about the patron that had just entered the museum.

Marcus calmly walked up to the entryway and read on the glass doors, *Musée du Vin Brotte—Dégustation et Vente*. He entered the building and felt refreshed by the air-conditioned front room, then that familiar musty, gamey smell of these wine tasting rooms that he was finding himself in so much these days.

Broccatelli was standing in front of him, talking to the museum employee at the ticket counter. Hearing another person enter, coupled with the singsong *"Bonjoouuurrrrr!"* from the employee, Broccatelli did an obligatory half-take behind him. Then, as he began to turn his attention back to the museum, his head rotated back quickly to make eye contact with Marcus. Broccatelli was clearly surprised to see Marcus, but also seemed pleased.

They exchanged quick pleasantries, then Marcus asked, "Mind if I join you for the museum visit?"

"Of course not!" Broccatelli responded, lightly patting Marcus on the shoulder before adding, "I'm just surprised that you also had it in mind to visit this museum. Not too many people know about it."

"Well, I just happened upon it, but was intrigued." Marcus responded. Then, changing the subject, he gestured toward the metallic stairway leading up to the second level of the museum and stated, "Let's take a look."

They worked their way slowly through the small museum. Marcus observed and listened as Broccatelli, who had clearly been here before, guided him through the different exhibits. There were old-fashioned wine making tools, such as plows, sickles and buckets. There was a feature on the winds of the Rhône Valley and how they affected the grapes. There were side-by-side comparisons of old wine bottles and barrels against their modern counterparts. There were detailed maps, replete with raised topographic features and precise coloring for the different AOPs in the region. There were large, close-up pictures of Grenache and Syrah grapes so one could compare their similarities and differences.

But the exhibits of the *Musée du Vin Brotte* paled in comparison to Mauro Broccatelli. He was alive, all-knowing, and fascinated by every aspect of the wine-making process. He explained to Marcus the importance of the weather each year, and the impact it had on the timing of the *vendange*, or picking, of the grapes. He talked at length about the ancient histories of the land of particular parts of the Rhône Valley and how it changed how those wines tasted. In a picture of some Châteauneuf-du-Pape vineyards, he pointed out the small, flat rocks surrounding the vines that Marcus had noticed on their bike ride into town earlier.

"You see," Broccatelli explained, narrowing his eyes and lowering his voice. He pointed toward the stones in the picture, "These stones are from the shoreline of an ancient island that used to be here. The stones retain heat from the sun during the day, and then release that heat at night. This can speed up the ripening of the grapes. The stones also help keep moisture in the soil during the summer, which keeps the vines from drying out."

The conviction and interest with which Broccatelli spoke about wine was palpable. Marcus felt like someone who unknowingly asked Julia Child about French cooking.

Broccatelli looked around the museum, appreciating it as if he was seeing it for the first time. Then he shook his head gently, as if in amazement. "That's the thing about wine. And most people don't appreciate it, but every bottle represents something unique. An old ocean that used to be on top of a vineyard two-hundred million years ago. The limestone rock a few feet beneath the soil. The heavy rains from a particular year that influenced how the grapes grew. The side of the valley that a vineyard sits on. The hundreds, even thousands, of years of repetition and perfection in winemaking that go into developing the specification of wine from a particular region. It's history, knowledge, and the fruit of the earth combined together in harmony. And if you know what to look for, you can taste it in every drop."

Marcus did the only thing you can do when someone says something like that; he stood back and admired. The beauty of the thought and exploration that had gone into Broccatelli's statement presented itself like a symphony playing in Marcus's head. After a few moments' reflection, one question immediately sprang to Marcus's mind: *How in the hell is this man what amounts to a world-class criminal?*

A VISIT TO the *Musée du Vin Brotte* ends with a piece of timeless marketing genius: a wine tasting of the Maison Brotte wines. Marcus and Broccatelli were happy to partake. A young man, clearly not much older than twenty, greeted them and introduced himself as their server for the tasting. He steered them to a tasting station, which consisted of an old wine barrel-turned-bar table, two nondescript empty wine glasses and a host of open bottles.

They tasted the Brotte Condrieu, a white wine, the Brotte Paradis, a rosé, and then the Brotte Côtes du Rhône, a red wine. Then their server made a show of pouring them the last wine of the tasting, the Brotte Châteauneuf-du-Pape, made from grapes grown just down the road from the museum. The last wine was by far the best to Marcus's taste, and he nodded his head in appreciation.

Broccatelli took a sip and held an expressionless look on his face as he quietly slurped the wine around his mouth. He swallowed, then peeked at the bottle again.

"Of course," he said to no one in particular. Then, in French, and as if speaking to one of his employees, he said to the server, "Bring us a bottle of the 2016 Châteauneuf-du-Pape. We are going to taste it alongside this 2017."

The young server looked confusedly at Broccatelli, then at Marcus, and then back at Broccatelli. Finding the granite gaze and cold, dark-brown eyes of Broccatelli a second time, the young man dipped his head dutifully and replied, "*Oui, monsieur, tout de suite.*"

Marcus hid a smile inside and waited quietly as the server went to retrieve the requested bottle. The server returned quickly, moving at a hurried pace. He carried a bottle seemingly identical to the open Châteauneuf-du-Pape in front of them, and two large, wide wine glasses. He skillfully cut off the aluminum over the top of the bottle, and rapidly extracted the cork, making a *pop* noise. He sniffed into the bottle quickly, then poured out a half-inch of wine into each of the new glasses.

Broccatelli lifted the glass, tilted it this way and that, then swirled the wine. He sniffed with his eyes closed, then finally took a sip. He sloshed the wine around his mouth a bit, then swallowed. As he opened his eyes slowly, Marcus was surprised to find Broccatelli's eyes fixated on Marcus. They were only half-open but contained a faint twinkle. The corners of Broccatelli's mouth were slightly elevated. Broccatelli looked down at Marcus's wine glass and inclined his head in that direction.

Marcus took his cue and made the obligatory tasting maneuvers. There was a mouth-watering warm, peppery, and earthy smell in the glass. As Marcus took a sip and tasted the wine, he was baffled. The 2017 they had tasted earlier was a very good wine, but this 2016 was on a completely different level. He couldn't believe that those two different vintages had come from the same vineyard, likely even the very same vines.

Broccatelli chuckled as he observed Marcus's reaction. Speaking in French, for the benefit of the server, he stated, "2016 was an incredible growing season. One of the all-time greats in the Southern Rhône Valley. Warm days and cool nights that summer." Broccatelli took the 2016 bottle, refilled Marcus's glass and his own, then grabbed an empty glass from one of the unused old wine barrel tops next to them. He poured an inch of wine into it and handed it to the server.

The server was caught off guard at first, then, with a look at Broccatelli, seemed to understand. He wound up his glass for tasting and gave it a few smells before taking a sip. He smacked his lips appreciatively, then gave them a fulsome explanation of the color, smell, and tasting notes that he was getting. It was a thoughtful and interesting description that enhanced the group's enjoyment of this spectacular wine.

There was something so lovely in the taste of the wine and the ambience of the moment that it made Marcus recall a quote framed on the wall of Olivier's front bar room at Ô Maison.

Seizing the moment, Marcus raised his glass before reciting the quote:

"Buvez chaque jour, vous ne mourrez jamais!"

Broccatelli and the server traded glances, then knowing smiles, before simultaneously stating, "Rabelais!"

They all chuckled and added a hearty *"Santé!"* as they clinked glasses and finished their wine.

CHAPTER 30

The Camargue, France.
Saturday, July 27, 2019.

THE FINAL LEG OF THE CYCLING PORTION OF THE
trip began just on the south side of Avignon and
would end at the Mediterranean. But in between, they
would pass through Arles before plunging into the
lowland wilds of the Camargue. Marcus had never been
to this part of France before, and he was very much
looking forward to seeing it from two wheels with
the rest of these fascinating people forming Mauro
Broccatelli's hand-picked group of cycling companions.

The afternoon before, in Châteauneuf-du-Pape,
they were treated to what is known in the wine world
as a "horizontal" tasting. This was Greek to Marcus,
but he quickly learned that it meant they were going
to taste wines from a number of different Châteauneuf-
du-Pape producers, all from the same vintage. And in
this case, because Mauro Broccatelli would have it no
other way, it was to be the famed 2016 vintage. Glass
after glass had been of remarkable consistency; superb

across the board. Marcus again noted that Broccatelli was in his element, and fully engrossed in every aspect of the tasting.

The weight of the wine and two hard days of cycling had made for a nice but quick dinner and early bedtimes for pretty much everyone, Marcus included. But the upshot had been that the group woke up early and refreshed and made it to the open road in high spirits. Sensing that they were nearing the end of this incredible three-day ride, the group's pace had picked up noticeably.

Marcus was feeling reasonably good about the relationships he was developing with Broccatelli and his friends and colleagues; that was the whole point of the trip after all. If Peppercorn Capital was going to find a way to work with Broccagas, then it was up to Marcus to create a dialogue and find an opportunity.

There was one important member of the group that Marcus had yet to foster any relationship with: Simon Walker-Kelly. Walker-Kelly, the laconic head of the Broccagas Trading and Shipping desk, had quietly and consistently taken on the difficult job of being the head of the peloton from the minute they left Lyon, riding at the front by himself and setting the pace for everyone else.

In the off-bike portions of the trip, Walker-Kelly was friendly but reserved. On a few occasions, Marcus sought to engage him in conversation but with no real success. Walker-Kelly was polite for sure but had simply not opted to open up. Marcus had the impression that there was a wealth of intelligence and insight locked behind the door of Walker-Kelly's guarded tongue.

As the cycling group accelerated out of the gate that morning, Marcus looked ahead to Walker-Kelly at the front of the bunch again. A thought popped into Marcus's mind, and then, recalling one of his favorite Mark Twain quotes, he said to himself, '*Why not go out on a limb? That's where the fruit is!'* ...*Oh, but going out on this limb is going to hurt...*

Marcus took a big drink from one of his water bottles, then clicked his bike up a few gears and accelerated. He felt his legs come alive with that unique mix of pain and energy that one feels when pushing themselves near their limits. He cruised by the other riders and soon found himself at the head of the pack, shoulder-to-shoulder with Walker-Kelly.

Walker-Kelly gave him a sideways glance, unemotionally acknowledging Marcus's presence. Marcus gave a quick nod, then smiled.

"We can't make you hold the pace the whole time, now can we!" Marcus dug deep to push slightly ahead, providing a small draft for Walker-Kelly to slip into just behind Marcus. He pushed through the pain in his legs to find the right rhythm to maintain leadership of the group, and locked in. Putting his head down and glancing back over his right shoulder, Marcus observed the slightest nod of appreciation from Walker-Kelly.

ROUGHLY THREE HOURS later, the group entered the final stretch of the ride. Marcus and Walker-Kelly led them deep into the Parc Naturel Régional de Carmargue, past reddish-pink salt flats, small, blue salt-water lakes and green marshlands peppered with pink flamingoes and herons. They smelled the fresh, salty air of the rapidly approaching Mediterranean as they made their way into the Rhône River Delta. Marcus was drenched in his own sweat but was able to maintain a respectable pace thanks to the flat road of the lowlands and the excitement he was feeling from viewing the beautiful scenery around him.

As they passed Port-Saint-Louis-du-Rhône, the last town on the route before the half-hour cruise to the beach of Plage Napoléon, Walker-Kelly pulled up alongside Marcus and gave him a firm pat on the back.

"Nice ride. And thanks for the company," Walker-Kelly said with an appreciative smile.

Marcus was exhausted, but managed to return the smile and reply, "Absolutely, it was my pleasure. It's a hell of a job you've been doing the last couple days, so I figured someone else should share the burden."

They emptied the last of their water bottles into their mouths, then rode in silence for a few minutes.

Walker-Kelly eventually cleared his throat, then asked, "So it is true what Nicholas Sewell was saying about Peppercorn Capital and Gas Polskie?"

Marcus recalled how Sewell, the British investment banker, had stated aloud just before the group left Lyon that Peppercorn had won the Gas Polskie auction. It was true, to some extent. Dembski had called Marcus and Alexandra the Monday after their visit to Poland to inform them that Gas Polskie was ready to enter into exclusivity with Peppercorn to negotiate a deal on the terms Marcus had proposed. So the parties had begun preparing the deal documents, but it would be a good month or so before everything was properly papered up and executed. And Marcus remained under a confidentiality obligation not to disclose those negotiations until the deal was official and announced.

Marcus exhaled and gently chuckled in response to Walker-Kelly's question. Walker-Kelly returned the gesture with a knowing chuckle of his own, and replied, "Right. You can't say anything. I'm sorry, that was not an appropriate question to ask."

Marcus thought for a second, then, realizing that Broccagas Trading and Shipping could be a potential supplier and maybe even a customer of Gas Polskie, and justifying to himself that he was beginning the practice of marketing the Gas Polskie brand, replied back, "I'll tell you what, something I can share is why a firm like ours would be interested in a company like

Gas Polskie." Marcus tilted his head slightly, as if to say *Is that good enough?*

Walker-Kelly's eyes widened, and he nodded his head slowly, signaling back the equivalent of *fair enough.*

Marcus launched into a tailored and somewhat redacted version of his Gas Polskie investment thesis. Walker-Kelly was fascinated, fully engaged, and posed questions and counterpoints throughout the discussion. Marcus was impressed and pleased to see some of Walker-Kelly's high level of intelligence on display. But the discussion also helped Marcus to see that Peppercorn was, in fact, ahead of the curve on the Gas Polskie investment, as there were aspects of the Peppercorn investment thesis that Walker-Kelly clearly had not considered or appreciated.

But what impressed, or at least interested, Walker-Kelly the most was Peppercorn Capital's appetite for risk and willingness to pursue what many people in the market viewed as something between a toxic asset and a foregone conclusion.

"So, you, er, someone like you," Walker-Kelly shared a conspiratorial smile before continuing, "were not concerned about NovaGaz and the Russians? I mean, won't they try to run Gas Polskie out of business now with cheap gas into Europe through the Nord Stream 2 Pipeline? Wouldn't NovaGaz shut Gas Polskie's new partner out of the Russian market entirely?"

Marcus thought back to the dead bald eagle chunked onto his balcony the morning after his and Alexandra's close call with the presumed-to-be-Russian agents that evening in Krakow. What had perhaps been naiveté at how hard the Russians would fight for the Gas Polskie project had now turned into a burning desire to bring the project to fruition and deal NovaGaz an economic blow.

"Well, those are good points," Marcus replied.

Something clicked in Marcus's brain as he pondered those particular thoughts from Walker-Kelly, and then recalled Franz's description of Broccagas as potentially being a clandestine arm of illegal trading of commodities and who knew what else. Surmising that he may very well be making an indirect pitch to Walker-Kelly for Peppercorn to go into business with Broccagas, Marcus added, "Whoever ends up partnering with Gas Polskie, assuming that partner is not NovaGaz, is going to have to be an apolitical entity. Someone who is focused on economic returns, and not afraid of some bad press or becoming a pariah for a period of time. They'll have to be willing to stand up to a country like Russia, and deal with the risks that implies."

"And…" Marcus thought of Arthur Franz's efforts to wreck the Nord Stream 2 project, then, with a wink in WalkerKelly's direction, concluded, "they'll have to be a little bit lucky."

Walker-Kelly nodded his head thoughtfully, then, clearly turning something over in his own mind, replied, "Touché."

Concluding their conversation, Walker-Kelly lifted his eyes in the direction of the road ahead. Following Walker-Kelly's cue, Marcus looked up. Spreading out before them was the wide, flat horizon of the sand of Plage Napoléon, the shining blue-gray waters of the Mediterranean, and a few scattered white clouds in the early afternoon sky. The smell of salt grew stronger, and little drops of water from the sea blew in their direction.

Marcus and Walker-Kelly slowed down to let the rest of the group catch up, and they all rode the final kilometer together as a tightly clumped group. The white EuroVans were already parked on the beach, ready to collect all of the riders' bikes. Two buckets of ice sat on the sand, each holding two bottles of champagne. And anchored in the bay in the distance was the largest yacht Marcus had ever seen.

CHAPTER 31

Cassis, France.
Saturday, July 27, 2019.

THE RIDERS HANDED THEIR BIKES OFF TO THE support team to be loaded into the EuroVans and were given their respective overnight bags in return. They hopped into two launch boats that had made their way to the beach from the massive yacht in the bay. As the launch boats arrived back at the yacht and everyone boarded it, Marcus noticed that Broccatelli had gathered with Simon Walker-Kelly and Liam Sturgess. The three of them were engaged in what looked like a semi-serious discussion, and Marcus pretended not to notice as they glanced furtively in his direction more than once.

Marcus surveyed the scene around the bay. To the east, the light-blue water turned dark as the sea deepened, then light again as it approached the dry, brownish-green coastline heading toward Marseille. There were a handful of sailboats and other yachts in the distance. But there were also a number of large tanker vessels. Some of them were sitting still, anchored in the bay and bobbing up and down lightly along with the waves. And others were slowly making their way toward the other end of the bay, across from Plage Napoléon, toward ship canal at the port of Lavéra.

The crew of Broccatelli's yacht provided the group with a quick tour around the boat, which, due to its size, took half an hour. Then Broccatelli gathered them all together and provided scant information regarding their destination.

"We are heading to a very special place, one near and dear to my heart. It is the perfect culmination of this week's voyage. We'll spend the night there, and tomorrow morning we will get all of you home in an expeditious manner."

With that, Broccatelli nodded at a member of the crew. The anchor was raised, the engine warmed up, and they were on their way.

Marcus followed the herd toward the full-service bar on the boat and ordered himself a beer. He peered out toward the front of the boat and saw Walker-Kelly standing by himself, looking intently at the various tankers scattered around them. Then he noticed Broccatelli, also on his own, along the portside rail of the boat and looking blankly toward the coast. Something seemed to weigh heavily on him.

Marcus ordered a glass of rosé, then sauntered over to Broccatelli.

"You look thirsty," Marcus observed, as he extended the glass in Broccatelli's direction.

Broccatelli looked surprised, and then appeared to shake off some distant, dark thought. Attempting to be cheery, Broccatelli warmly took the glass from Marcus.

"*Merci, santé!* Quite the ride you had out there today Marcus, it takes a lot to stay in front of Simon Walker-Kelly. You definitely earned this." They clinked glasses and took long sips, then both stared quietly out at the dry, rocky coast.

After a few moments, Marcus broke the silence.

"I bet that is quite the facility you guys have over there," Marcus indicated toward the coast in front of them.

Broccatelli looked just as surprised as before, then chuckled gently before responding, "You are well-informed Marcus, that's impressive. I would guess that only you, Simon over there," Broccatelli nodded toward the front of the boat where Walker-Kelly remained alone, observing the tankers, "and me have any idea that Broccagas has one of its largest port facilities just over those hills."

Broccatelli looked out at the coast and breathed deeply, before continuing, "But I'm learning that I probably shouldn't be surprised. You seem to know your stuff, Marcus, and both Simon and Liam feel the same way."

Before the trip, Marcus had done some leisurely traveler's research on the various stops along their itinerary. Plage Napoléon was novel to him, so he looked at the surrounding area to see what he could learn. He had no idea that the Port of Lavéra, a small oil and petrochemicals port and refinery site, lay tucked inland at Port-de-Bouc just across the bay. There, amongst the sun and glamor of the South of France and the Mediterranean coast, lay one of Southern Europe's refining sites.

Because Broccagas, like all of the Broccatelli family businesses, was privately owned, there was not a ton of publicly available information about the company. But Marcus distantly recalled a vague reference to Broccagas Lavéra or something similar from the small amount of information turned up during his initial study of Broccatelli and the tentacles of the Broccagas empire. He did more digging and had his investment team look into it as well and was fascinated to learn that Broccagas had a giant oil refinery, related port, and petrochemical storage facilities that constituted a large portion of the Port of Lavéra. It was a beast of a facility with numerous different operations conducted there, and it gave Broccagas substantial opportunities to trade all over Europe and across the Mediterranean. He wasn't sure the opportunity to share that knowledge would come up during the trip, but he was certainly glad that it had.

"I can only imagine how valuable that facility is for you guys. That place must give you more trading options and flexibility than you'd ever thought possible," Marcus replied to Broccatelli, ignoring the compliment and trying to stay focused on Broccagas.

Broccatelli nodded and made a closed-mouth smile that was bittersweet and betrayed fatigue.

"It is valuable, invaluable in fact. But it's also very expensive. It requires more attention and capital investment than we expected."

This was the first time that Marcus had discussed Broccagas business with Broccatelli, and the subject seemed to wear on him. Broccatelli exhaled deeply again, then continued, "Broccagas Trading and Shipping owns that facility. And Broccagas Trading and Shipping is just that: a trading house. The oil refinery and ports and storage facilities are a lot for us to manage."

Marcus refrained from responding, allowing the silence to echo the magnitude of that shockingly honest admission. Prompted by the silence, Broccatelli added, "We want to keep growing, but the truth is we don't really know how to manage that growth."

Marcus's mind was racing at top gear. There was so much information being shared by Broccatelli's simple statements, and there were any number of avenues for Marcus to pursue. *Broccatelli was opening himself up…but to what end?* Marcus thought. He intentionally slowed his mind down and forced himself to breathe easily. Then, calmly, he replied back to Broccatelli.

"Well, Mauro, there are a lot of people out there that can help you realize that growth, and also manage it."

Broccatelli chuckled again, then responded, "There are indeed. But there is a price for that assistance. And that price is giving up control. And you can only give up control to someone you trust." Broccatelli shook his head deliberately, then looked directly at Marcus, and asked, "Who can Broccagas trust?"

Marcus was both ecstatic and bewildered. He thought to himself, *Is this an invitation, or a threat? How much does Mauro Broccatelli know?*

Calming his mind and nerves again, Marcus replied coolly, "I can think of someone."

"Peppercorn Capital?" Broccatelli replied. Then he shrugged his shoulders in a way that seemed to say, *Maybe so.*

"I like you, Marcus," Broccatelli stated, then continued, "And I know that you are smart enough to see that Broccagas is not my first love."

Marcus smiled with his eyes and tilted his head toward Broccatelli's wine glass.

Broccatelli nodded gently, then paused, as if deciding whether or not to say anything else.

"We want to take it public," he added, "Broccagas Trading and Shipping, that is. Simon Walker-Kelly should be running the business, not me. And a public offering is a way for our family to respectably transition the business to the market with Simon leading it. But we need some time, and we need a partner. We need an internationally respected firm to come in, pump some money into the business, and help us legitimize it for a few years prior to a public offering. That partner will have to pay a lot to get in, but they should be in line for a very lucrative exit a few years down the road. But we could only allow in someone we trust beyond any doubts."

Marcus listened carefully and began to see that what Broccatelli was saying made perfect sense from a business perspective. And Marcus began to suspect that perhaps it had been Mauro Broccatelli seeking to evaluate him as much as he had been trying to evaluate Mauro Broccatelli.

"There's a reason I wanted you to come on this trip, Marcus." Broccatelli paused, took a sip of his wine, then continued, "What I said earlier is true; I do like you. But I also think that your firm could be a good fit for partnering with us. We need a partner who has the capital and the skill to manage an investment, of course, but we also need someone that is willing to take risks and, how should I say this…not worry too much about what the public might think."

"What you did in Argentina was brilliant. Lucky, for sure," Broccatelli shot Marcus a sideways look, then continued, "but brilliant nonetheless." Broccatelli tilted his wine glass toward Marcus's beer.

"And if what Walker-Kelly tells me about your Polish investment is true, then your firm may very well have just the right combination of boldness and indifference to public opinion we are looking for...along with the money and skill." Broccatelli flashed the same rehearsed, wolfish smile that Marcus had first seen on the balcony of the Musée d'Orsay.

Marcus couldn't tell if he was walking into a trap, or just the opportunity that the Shareholder was looking for. *Well, only one way to find out*, Marcus concluded.

Trying not to look too eager, Marcus opted for a professional response.

"I think you may be on to something, Mauro, Peppercorn would certainly be interested. But why don't we enjoy the rest of this incredible trip you've put together and leave business for next week when we're back in our offices. I'll send a follow-up note to your assistant to figure out how best to consider next steps."

Marcus looked confidently and sternly into Broccatelli's dark-brown eyes, until finally they relaxed and found the energetic glow they had possessed for most of the trip. Broccatelli smiled, genuinely this time, and nodded his head toward the rest of the cycling group huddled around the main bar.

Marcus followed, and, trying to make good on his suggestion to enjoy the trip, jokingly asked Broccatelli, "Now, are you really not going to tell us where we are heading?"

***

THE MASSIVE YACHT found deeper water and continued heading east. After a short while, they passed the sprawling city of Marseille on the now-distant coast. A half hour later they maneuvered back toward the hilly, rocky coast and into the azure-blue water. They headed directly for a small inlet dotted with villas crawling up the hills and a small town at its center.

As they sailed past the town, they observed several yellow, orange, and sandstone-colored buildings, accented with red terra-cotta roofs and vibrantly colored window shutters, sitting behind a small, rocky beach and an informal marina. They cruised past the town, which had now been revealed as the village of Cassis and passed a series of *calanques* rising above the water and came to anchor in a tiny bay of the Plage du Corton.

To their right, a small peninsula jutted out into the water. At its point was a thick gathering of pine trees bordering a small barn. Marcus could catch a faint whiff of the pines mixed with the salty smell of seawater. To the left of the barn, rows of perfectly tilled soil and terraced green vines sloped up the hill away from the surrounding sea below, creating a stark contrast with the soaring cliffs covered by wild greenery behind them. Keeping watch over the vines from one end and peering into the shallow bay from the other, a yellow, three-story chateau with bright, blue-painted window shutters perched atop the farthest point of the inlet.

Broccatelli stood behind the group, each of them to a man gawking at the scenery in front of them, and announced, "Gentlemen, welcome to the newest addition to the Broccatelli family of vineyards, Le Clos Sainte-Magdeleine."

He allowed them a few seconds of awe to take in the announcement, then nodded to the crew to begin lowering the launch boats and ushering the group to shore. Marcus soon found himself in one, gliding over the smooth, turquoise-tinted water by the shore and heading directly toward the chateau.

From a distance, he heard the chopping sound of propellers in the air. He looked up to locate a small helicopter approaching from the mainland. The helicopter continued in their direction and made for a landing on the estate of Le Clos Sainte-Magdeleine above.

When his launch boat group finished scaling the stone walkway from the beach, they saw the helicopter parked on the small, finely cut lawn in front of the chateau. The blades eventually stopped whirling and the crew exited from the cockpit. Mauro Broccatelli, leading the group from the other launch boat, which had landed before Marcus's, diverted from the pathway of crushed gravel and headed toward the helicopter.

The crew opened the helicopter's side door, and two men exited. The first was of average height and was thin, almost bony. He had dark-brown hair that was beginning to gray, and he wore it neatly parted and combed but somewhat long. He wore a fine, white linen suit and a dark-blue shirt with a band collar, opened at the neck. He was pale for that outfit, and he moved stiffly.

Marcus knew that this had to be Roberto Broccatelli, Mauro's older brother, the golden child. Mauro made his way toward Roberto but stopped a noticeable distance away from him. The two brothers exchanged hard glances, and for a moment seemed frozen. Then Roberto glanced quickly at the cycling group behind Mauro, then back into Mauro's stare. An awkward smile appeared, and Roberto uttered a few words, barely opening his mouth, as he closed the distance between himself and his younger brother. They shook hands firmly, the clasp lingering a touch longer than a normal handshake. Then, without any acknowledgement of Marcus or any of the other cyclists, Roberto made his way toward the entrance to the chateau.

The second man to exit the helicopter was of naturally dark skin, seemingly of Middle Eastern origin, with a thin, wispy tuft of black hair atop his head. He wore a pristinely tailored dark suit, a crisp, white, collared dress shirt with a solid, navy-blue necktie. His face was thin and clean-shaven, and he wore a pair of tortoise-shell horn-rimmed glasses. He moved gingerly, and greeted Mauro Broccatelli cordially with a nod, before following Roberto Broccatelli's path into the chateau.

Mauro Broccatelli remained standing still for a few moments, his back to the waiting group of cyclists. His muscular back rose and fell from a deep inhale and exhale. Then Broccatelli turned to rejoin his guests with a casual smile.

"My brother, and his business associate," Broccatelli explained. "They'll be joining us this afternoon and evening." Then he turned on his heel and led them toward the chateau's arched portico and massive oak door, which served as the front entrance.

Marcus fell in step with the rest of the group to follow Broccatelli inside, as he thought, *My word, that was a cold exchange.*

THAT AFTERNOON THE group was treated to one final event to cap off the trip: a spectacularly catered meal of Provençal delights from the neighboring Michelin-starred restaurant, La Villa Madie, and a tasting of the rare, but highly rated *Cassis blanc* from Le Clos Sainte-Magdeleine. Marcus had made sure to enjoy this last wine tasting experience of the trip beside the affable and loquacious Nicholas Sewell.

***

AFTER PROVIDING MARCUS with a short history of how the Albizzi family of Florence, "eternal rivals of the Medici and Alberti clans, of course," Sewell had noted as if it were elementary common knowledge, had brought the wines of Cassis to grand European notoriety during the Renaissance, he shared one final tasting note.

"Mmm, spectacular. Look at that color, pale yellow with sparkles of green. A bouquet of mineral and fruit and…wait…yes, that's it, white pepper! Quick, Marcus, we must enjoy this wine with some prawns."

As Sewell led Marcus over to the platter of hors d'oeuvres, Marcus noticed Mauro and Roberto Broccatelli, flanked by Roberto's unnamed business associate, in a hushed but somewhat heated discussion. Mauro was making short, decisive hand gestures as if walking through a sequence of logic. Roberto remained unmoved, except for a few short utterances to interrupt Mauro from time to time.

Mauro looked up to scan the crowd and, finding Marcus, returned his attention to Roberto and made a quick comment and tilted his head in Marcus's direction. He then began walking toward Marcus. Roberto and his business associate reluctantly followed.

"Marcus, there you are," Mauro announced as he joined Marcus and Sewell at the high-top table they had found to rest their plates and glasses, then added "Hello, Nicholas, hope you enjoyed the *blanc du Clos Magdeleine*."

"*C'est super!*" Sewell responded, then, recognizing that Mauro was intending to speak to Marcus on a matter of some level of importance, politely exited the conversation by asking, "Excuse me, Mauro, where was the loo again?"

Mauro gestured toward a small outer building, and then returned his attention to Marcus.

"Marcus, I'd like to introduce you to my brother, Roberto."

Marcus looked up to make eye contact with Roberto Broccatelli, and firmly extended his hand. Roberto made short eye contact with Marcus, then glanced to the side, down at Marcus's hand, then back at Marcus. He made a forced, closed-mouth smile and then offered a bony, limp handshake in return. Marcus did what he could to shake Roberto's fingers, then retrieved his hand.

"It's a pleasure to meet you, Roberto," Marcus noted politely.

"Yes. My little brother speaks highly of you and your firm. Pinpoint Partners, is it?"

Roberto Broccatelli spoke a clean version of American English with only the slightest hint of an Argentine accent.

"Peppercorn Capital," Marcus replied flatly.

"Huh," Roberto snorted, then added, "This is my friend and business associate, Samih Salem."

The man in the dark suit stepped forward graciously and offered a friendly handshake, "You can call me Sam. Pleased to meet you, Mr. Hugo. I've heard a lot about your firm, it's an…impressive outfit."

Salem spoke with a high-toned British accent, and came across as a genuine, skilled networker.

"Thank you. Nice to meet you as well, Sam."

"My little brother suggests this…Peppercorn…firm of yours might be a good partner for us. Is that right?" Roberto asked accusingly.

"Well, I think we have a ways to go before I'd definitively say that. But yes, Roberto, we would be interested in exploring that possibility. Cheers by the way; this white wine of yours is excellent." Marcus had noted that neither Roberto nor Salem had a drink in their hand, but he wanted to shake up the conversation.

"Of *his*," Roberto hissed as he directed his head toward Mauro, then added, "Not mine."

Mauro glanced at Marcus, then breathed deeply through his nose as he looked to the ground.

"Well," Roberto continued, "we may in fact need a partner. But let me assure you, Mr. Hugo, when we find a partner, we make sure to know everything," he paused for effect, then finished his sentence with raised volume, "absolutely everything, about them."

Marcus returned Roberto's gaze. This was an unexpected escalation in the tension of the conversation. But Marcus had dealt with this technique before in negotiations, both from his Macon Smith days and from his time at Peppercorn. *With a man like this, one must meet strength with strength*, Marcus reminded himself.

He took a sniff of his wine, then calmly took a sip and looked down at the glass admiringly. Seeing that Roberto Broccatelli was impatiently awaiting a response, Marcus looked back into Roberto's eyes.

"So do I, Roberto." Marcus drained what remained in his glass. He looked over at Salem, then at Roberto, and concluded the conversation by adding, "Good evening. Gentlemen. Pleasure to meet you both."

CHAPTER 32

Paris, France.
Mid-September 2019.

AUGUST HAD CRAWLED BY. PARIS WAS PRACTICALLY deserted by its natives taking summer holidays and filled up with tourists from farther afield doing the same. Attempting to play his role as jet-setting private equity professional, Marcus had taken the obligatory jaunt down to the French Riviera, spending a handful of nights at the Hotel de Paris Monte-Carlo. He took a suite on the hotel's top floor, with a view onto the port and Mediterranean Sea below. He sunned himself below the palm trees around the hotel's pool, ordering up a bottle of rosé to accompany him, and making small talk with the models and society women strutting around the pool in their bikinis and designer beachwear. He had drinks and played cards in the casino with business acquaintances he stumbled across during his stay.

But he was also quite busy at work for Peppercorn and used the slow month to grind away and make progress on those matters. There was TeleCAR, Peppercorn's telecommunications holding company in Central Africa, that needed to be sold. The Gas Polskie project needed to be transmuted from negotiated deal points and terms to legally binding transaction documents, and Marcus was the one to drive and oversee that process. And, after the surprising opening offered up from Mauro Broccatelli, there was a potential deal with Broccagas to analyze and negotiate.

So after his glamorous trip to Monaco, Marcus opted to dig in at the office in Paris instead of fleeing for other vacations spots. Many of his senior-level colleagues were on holiday, so Marcus often found himself at the office with only a handful of junior associates and analysts. He tried to set a good example by showing up each day and providing a senior presence, and also took the opportunity to get to know his junior colleagues better.

By the summer bank holiday at the end of the month, they had made great progress. They had run a sales process for TeleCAR and narrowed the potential buyers down to two deeppocketed suitors. The Gas Polskie deal had been finalized, and Marcus was putting together a select group of seasoned oil and gas industry professionals to add to the Gas Polskie management team. Marcus and his junior colleagues had prepared a detailed presentation regarding the

Broccagas Trading and Shipping investment opportunity to be shared with the investment committee at the September meeting.

When Marcus's friend, Olivier Lafont, reached out to invite Marcus to an Ô Maison special event in the middle of September, Marcus was clamoring for some leisurely social interaction.

"Throughout the fall, we are putting on a series of events called 'Ô, you didn't know?'" Olivier chuckled at his inventive play on words. "We are doing tastings of lesser known, but still excellent of course, wines. And we are doing those tastings in lesser-known venues throughout Paris. We have one this Saturday at the Musée Marmottan Monet in the 16th. Why don't you come join? Luisette and I could actually use an extra person to help set up."

Marcus would have joined anyway, but the mention of Luisette, Olivier's colleague that Marcus had met a few months earlier during his wine lesson at Ô Maison, was even more reason to accept. She had caught Marcus's eye that afternoon at Ô Maison, and he had meant to look for a way to see her again. This sounded like just the right setting.

Plus, Marcus had only visited the Musée Marmottan once before, and he was excited to peruse its excellent collection of Impressionist paintings and other artworks, as well as see the beautiful chateau where they were so tastefully displayed.

Marcus arrived at the Musée Marmottan early that Saturday and greeted Olivier and Luisette with a warm smile as they exited Olivier's white EuroVan that he used for Ô Maison business. It was a sunny, cool September day. Luisette's milky white skin retained the last vestiges of a summer tan, and her long blond hair was even brighter than Marcus had remembered it. She wore dark-colored jeans that hugged her legs, and a tight white Breton-striped sweater with the sleeves pulled up high on her forearms. Her build was naturally thicker than most women Marcus had seen in Paris, but firm and healthy. Her face was plain but pretty, and her somewhat pointy nose and ears gave her the look of a subdued fox. She had a few sightly light-brown moles on her lower neck that were accentuated by naturally pale skin. There was a sleepy, almost dreamlike quality about her greenish-brown eyes that made Marcus think she would have been right at home in the 1960s with a wreath of flowers around her hair.

Olivier and Marcus set up a few folding tables in the front lawn, then covered them with white tablecloths. Olivier went inside the museum to speak with the director and coordinate the afternoon's event, leaving Marcus and Luisette to unload the numerous bottles of wine for the tasting from the back of Olivier's van.

"Ah, Chinon!" Marcus stated as he examined one of the bottles, then added, "That's a great wine. Most people just think of the whites, the Sancerre and similar varietals from the Loire, but Chinon is excellent as well."

Marcus spoke in French, and Luisette smiled as she replied in the same language.

"Well, I guess you were paying attention in the little wine class Olivier gave you."

Marcus returned the smile and continued placing the bottles onto the table.

After a few moments of silence, Luisette added, "Chinon fits with the whole theme of these little events we are doing, you know? Lesser-known wines that we want to bring to people's attention."

They found a good rhythm of working for a bit, then continued their conversation. Marcus shared some of the highlights of his recent winery visits in the Rhône Valley and Provence. And while Luisette clearly found that interesting, she also wanted to learn about Marcus's background as a lawyer and what he currently did.

Marcus observed that Luisette was probably around thirty, so a little bit older than someone who typically would be doing apprentice-level work in the wine industry. He asked about her background and learned that she had grown up in Dijon, near the famed Burgundy wine region, before moving to Paris to get a master's degree in accounting.

"And so I was an accountant for five years at one of the big four accounting firms, right over there,"

Luisette explained, as she signaled in the direction of La Défense, Paris's business center located just outside of the *Périphérique* and not too far from the Musée Marmottan. "I had always loved wine and teaching people how to appreciate it, but being from *Bourgogne*, I felt like I needed to get away from it."

"And what more exciting diversion from the wine world than accounting!" Marcus put in with a smile and raised eyebrows.

"Exactly," Luisette responded with a chuckle, acknowledging the irony in Marcus's statement. She looked out in the direction of La Défense again, paused for a moment, then added, "I missed the wine, the people, the education, and the surprises that each bottle may hold. I got tired of being at the office all the time. So one day, I just decided it was time to give it a shot in the wine world."

Marcus nodded admiringly. "And I bet you don't regret it for one second."

They picked up the last box of wine from the back of the truck and walked it over to the tables.

Luisette shook her head from side to side with a smile, and replied, "Not one."

Olivier returned from his discussion inside the museum just then and observed the set up.

"Just in time, Olivier, all the hard work is done. You just have to open all this wine and drink it with people all afternoon," Marcus joked.

Ignoring this playful jab, Olivier declared, "I still cannot believe that you got to taste the 1961 Domaine Dumont Hermitage La Chapelle. And, to boot, got to visit Le Clos Sainte-Magdeleine. Damn, I'm jealous!"

"Yeah, it wasn't bad." Marcus replied, sharing a playful glance with Luisette.

"And you never even mentioned my name to Mauro Broccatelli or Caroline Dumont? Or at least Ô Maison?" Olivier continued prodding Marcus.

"In due time Olivier; I just need to pick my spot."

Olivier gave Marcus a sarcastic nod of the head, then noted, "Well, Luisette and I are going to finish setting up and doing some tasting preparation here before our first guests arrive."

Marcus took his cue and wished them luck before heading inside the museum to check out the collection. He made his way through the ornate chateau, perusing the tapestries, sculptures, and unique pieces of the Middle Ages and Renaissance collection before making his way toward the more renowned Impressionist and Claude Monet-focused wing of the museum.

He circled around the gallery displaying the various Monet paintings of water lilies, London's parliament building, and Rouen's cathedral. The light hardwood floor of the gallery contrasted perfectly with the flowing, colorful tapestries. The room had the noticeable clean, synthetic scent of a place that displayed priceless art.

He saved his favorite painting in the collection for the end of his visit: *Impression, soleil levant*, Monet's iconic depiction of the port of Le Havre, its grey, blue, and purple water highlighted by a bright reddish-tangerine disc of a sun rising into the morning sky and reflecting on the water below. It was this painting, rejected by the august *Salon* of the Louvre, France's institution of art patronage, that had given its name to the Impressionist movement.

As he made his way in that direction, he paused as he saw an athletic-looking blond woman, wearing light jeans and a fitted black sweater, standing before the painting. It was a figure Marcus recognized instantly. *What is she doing here?* Marcus thought as he resumed his walk in her direction.

"Fancy seeing you here," Marcus uttered, as he lightly nudged up against Alexandra's shoulder.

She nodded lightly without removing her gaze from the painting.

"It's hard not to smile when you see a painting like this, isn't it? The beauty of it just takes your emotions over."

Marcus tried to think of something cheeky to say, then he realized that Alexandra wasn't smiling at all. He had not seen much of her since their trip to Poland. She had stayed home for a week nursing her shoulder injury, then had disappeared for the month of August. She had been in and out of the office during September, but they had said little to each other beyond passing greetings.

Marcus started to ask how she was feeling, then stopped himself. He just stared at the painting instead. She was right, an involuntary closed-mouth smile overtook him as he lost himself in the swirl of colors.

Then Alexandra's firm voice broke his concentration. "Come on, let's go for a little walk."

CHAPTER 33

Paris, France.
16th Arrondissement.
Mid-September 2019.

MARCUS AND ALEXANDRA PASSED BY OLIVIER and Luisette's table on their way out of the museum grounds. The event was teeming with people, full glasses of wine in hand and smiles on their faces. Marcus made a distant wave to Oliver, who raised his eyebrows in acknowledgement. Then he caught Luisette's glance, and flashed a smile as he mouthed, *Bonne chance!*

Alexandra cast a sideways glance at Marcus, and exhaled audibly before noting, "I saw that, you know."

Marcus did his best impersonation of the French shrug-pursing of the lips gesture in response.

They made their way through a quiet pathway in the stately Jardin du Ranelagh, which abutted the museum.

"Well?" Marcus asked.

"Well, what?" Alexandra replied, nonchalantly.

"Come on. It's not every day my boss shows up unannounced at a social event I'm attending on the weekend. You must be practicing your Arthur Franz techniques."

"Please don't call me your boss."

Alexandra waited a few moments before continuing, "But yes, there are some things we need to discuss. And doing so in the office would not be appropriate. I overheard you trying to drum up attendance for the Ô Maison event with your new friends, all of the analysts and associates. So I figured I could find you there."

Marcus nodded, appreciating Alexandra's planning of the encounter.

"The chatter from the Russians has gone silent. When they learned about the SEC's investigation into Peppercorn, they seemed to have backed off. Hopefully that investigation didn't throw too much of a wrench in your negotiations with Gas Polskie. Obviously not, since you got the deal done. Congrats, by the way," Alexandra added as an afterthought.

"Thanks," Marcus responded dryly, then continued, "And yes, it was a little tough to explain away the launching of an SEC investigation during the middle of our negotiations with Gas Polskie. But ultimately, we convinced them that the SEC's claim was baseless. And we agreed to indemnify them completely if they suffer any losses because of that claim."

Franz and Alexandra had informed Marcus of the commencement of an SEC investigation into

Peppercorn's supposed manipulation of certain financial information in its buying and selling of stocks on both the Nasdaq and New York Stock Exchange. And, in not so many words, they also revealed that the investigation had been triggered by the Shareholder as a ruse to put some tension between the US government and Peppercorn, and hopefully put the Russians off the scent. Marcus was, of course, appreciative. But that investigation was now a perceived red flag regarding Peppercorn that Marcus had to deal with and explain away in business negotiations.

"Good," Alexandra concluded, as they exited the footpath onto the busy Chaussée de la Muette.

"We analyzed the picture you took of Roberto Broccatelli's business associate. His name is, in fact, Samih Salem. But he's a bit of a dangerous character, Marcus."

Marcus had to lean in close to hear her because of the noise of the passing traffic.

"He's Egyptian. His father was very close with Hosni Mubarak, and Mubarak sent the Salems all over the world as Egyptian dignitaries: Beijing, Oman, Venezuela, Canada, even. Samih Salem had a top-notch education and attended university at Cambridge. He lived in London for a few years working in finance, then moved back to Cairo to continue the family's work for the Mubarak regime. When that all ended with the Arab Spring, Salem fled the country and took up residence in Zürich."

Marcus recalled Salem's fine clothing, crisp English accent, and tony horn-rimmed glasses.

"What our intelligence unit has been able to gather is that Samih Salem is a very well-connected broker to some of the world's *personae non gratae*. He masquerades as a private banker, but the extent of his business dealings goes far beyond that. His friendship with Roberto Broccatelli is both telling and troubling."

The bony, dead-fish handshake from Roberto Broccatelli flashed in Marcus's memory, and a chill ran down his spine.

They arrived in front of Restaurant La Gare at the eastern end of the street.

"Oh, I had hoped this is where you were leading us," Marcus observed.

The converted old train station was Marcus's favorite restaurant in this part of Paris, and one of his favorites in the whole city. There was a classic, *Belle Époque* feel to the place. And while the downstairs dining room was the venue for Restaurant La Gare's formal lunch and dinner offerings, Marcus loved the airy, open layout of the more relaxed café on the ground floor. As they entered, he could smell the day's fresh croissants, piled high on a tray resting on a counter.

They were led to a seat on the back patio, which overlooked the path of the former train tracks, now overgrown by grass and shrubs, leading to the old station in the basement below. They were seated, and

Marcus looked across the table to find a focused and serious character to Alexandra's face. This jolted Marcus out of the lazy, dreamy effect that sitting in a café in the mid-afternoon had on him and reminded him of the serious turn that their conversation had taken.

"Listen," Alexandra instructed quietly, as she quickly scanned the room one more time, "People like Salem, and maybe even Roberto Broccatelli, are very dangerous individuals to get involved with."

A waiter appeared, made eyes and an inviting smile at Alexandra, completely ignored Marcus, and asked for their orders. Once he was safely out of hearing range, Alexandra continued.

"You remember the fatality that Franz told you about during your recruitment?"

It was a bit hazy, but something clicked in Marcus's mind as she mentioned it. He recalled walking down the dirt path on the backside of Montefollonico, Franz listing off all the things Marcus should consider in evaluating the job offer. And yes, almost glossed over by Franz, there had been a mention of his safety being in jeopardy, and a previous fatality.

Marcus nodded, indicating that he did remember that.

"Well, that happened when we were trying to do business with someone similar to Salem. This was a South Korea-North Korea exchange, so a different setting. And our operative was tucked into the ranks of a large, international law firm, so we were able to wipe the traces of our fingerprints from it. But this particular broker somehow learned that the operative was feeding us information, and he passed that along to the North Koreans."

Marcus sensed a vague recollection of a news story about some young, female American lawyer in the Seoul office of a law firm being lost for a few weeks, then found dead near the North Korean border. The gravity of it all rushed into his chest, and he had to fight off queasiness.

"Our little *rendezvous* with the Russians was a brush with danger but getting involved with someone like Salem could be real trouble. Be careful Marcus."

The waiter returned with Alexandra's *café au lait* and Marcus's espresso and croissant. The familiar smell of the strong coffee was a welcome, albeit momentary, distraction from the troubling revelation Alexandra had just shared.

"Where did you leave things with Mauro Broccatelli?" Alexandra asked.

"Our Peppercorn deal team is working on the investment case to present internally. Mauro and I have started negotiating a deal and certain big picture points, but he is now unavailable for the rest of the month."

Alexandra shot Marcus a quizzical look.

"He's visiting his various wineries to participate in the *vendange*," Marcus explained, referring to the annual process of removing the grapes from the vines, and then mashing them up into the grape juice that would eventually become wine.

"But," Marcus emphasized, "I have to go to London the first week of October to finish up the TeleCAR sales process. And while in London, Mauro has asked me to find time to visit the Broccagas Trading and Shipping office there to continue negotiations."

"Okay, good. You should be pretty safe in London," Alexandra noted.

Assuming the business portion of their conversation over, Marcus took a few bites of his croissant. He wiped off the bread flakes clinging to his two-day-old stubble, then downed the warm espresso.

"There's…something…else," Alexandra leaked out.

Marcus looked curiously at her over his coffee cup.

"Something you may need to ask Mauro Broccatelli for."

Marcus placed the cup on the small saucer in front of him, took a deep breath, and over the increasingly loud thump of his heart in his chest, replied, "Okay…"

"Marcus, it's a shame Franz can't be here for this part of the conversation, but he is tied up on other important business for the Shareholder, so he asked me to talk to you."

What the hell is she about to say? Marcus wondered.

"Do you have any idea how we found out about you? Why we decided to approach you to work with us?"

This was a rhetorical question of course, so Marcus remained silent.

"Graham Curry recommended you," Alexandra stated in a deadpan manner.

It was as if the floor had dropped out from under Marcus's feet. A sense of free-falling, utter lack of balance overtook his mind and body. He quite nearly fell out of his chair but managed to catch himself.

Alexandra just nodded slowly, glancing into Marcus's bewildered face and then around the room and back again.

Gears turned in Marcus's head. Portions of his conversation with Graham in Houston four years before replayed in his head.

"How…? When…? Huh?" This was as close to a question as Marcus was able to put together.

"It's a lot to take in, I know," Alexandra offered up, then continued, "Marcus, Graham has been working with us for almost ten years now. Not full-time, like you, but as an informant. He provides us with crucial information from time to time. His employer takes suggestions from us as to where Graham might be useful, geographically speaking, and then his employer looks the other way when Graham needs to interact with us."

Regaining his foundation slowly, Marcus thought back to all of the exotic international placements where Graham had worked: the Persian Gulf, Nigeria, Papua

New Guinea, and Colombia. It was genius, really. Even Marcus had never considered that Graham might be anything other than a petroleum engineer.

"Of course," Marcus uttered aloud.

"After we lost our last operative, we wanted to try something different. So we decided to look outside our normal avenues of recruitment. We were working with Graham at the time, we asked him if he had any suggestions. And he told us about you."

He thought back on all of those times that Marcus had told Graham about his aspirations to live and work abroad. How calmly Graham had absorbed Marcus's declarations. *Well, he was definitely listening*, Marcus thought to himself.

"Are we working with him now?" Marcus asked, seeking to advance the conversation.

"We were," Alexandra replied quickly, then paused before adding, "Until he disappeared in July."

Marcus blinked twice, before asking, "Disappeared?"

"Yes," Alexandra spoke matter-of-factly, "He was performing a service for us near Barranquilla, supplying some Venezuelan insurgents with much-needed fuel, when his fuel barge driver was found dead on the banks of the Magdalena River. There was no sign of Curry. But we believe him to be alive and being held in captivity by the Socialist regime in Venezuela."

Marcus decided to shake off his personal concerns over Graham's safety and approach the situation logically and analytically.

"But wouldn't that regime announce all of that publicly? You know, 'Evil Americans Intervene in South America Again!' and all that?"

"They would, unless they were acting on someone else's behalf," Alexandra's reply was direct. She was clearly in CIA-operative mode.

"And they are getting a boatload of money to deliver him to someone," Marcus resolved.

"Exactly. Which brings me to my initial point."

Marcus thought about the Broccatelli conversation and began to see pieces moving together as Alexandra continued explaining.

"We've been monitoring the illicit trade traffic as closely as possible, and we haven't heard anything about Curry. Curry previously did a job for us in Papua New Guinea, providing information about the Chinese presence there. We think it likely that the Chinese and Venezuelans are either haggling over a price to deliver Curry, how to get him to China, or both."

Marcus picked up the thread, "And if Broccagas Trading and Shipping is actually facilitating clandestine deals for the Venezuelans, the Iranians, the Chinese, the North Koreans…they could broker the trade for Curry."

"And," Alexandra raised her pointer finger straight up in the air, indicating the importance of what she was about to say, "They could deliver him."

"They could deliver him," Marcus repeated quietly, rocking back and forth, as he saw it all fit together. It was all so surreal, but so was everything else he had experienced over the past five years at Peppercorn. This had become his life.

"So you want me to ask Mauro Broccatelli to deliver Venezuelan hostage Graham Curry to Peppercorn Capital instead of the Chinese?" Marcus asked this ironically, suspecting there was a more nuanced strategy that Franz had already cooked up.

"No," Alexandra responded flatly. She took a long sip of her *café au lait*. "We want you to encourage Broccagas to deliver Curry to the Chinese," She paused, then a mischievous smile appeared on her face as she added, "And then we want you to steal him on the way."

CHAPTER 34

London, England.
Early October 2019.

IT HAD BEEN A FEW DIFFICULT DAYS OF negotiations, but by Wednesday of that first full week of October, Marcus and the Peppercorn team had managed to sign an agreement to sell TeleCAR to a Middle Eastern sovereign wealth fund keen on diversifying out of oil and gas and into other industries. *Thankfully, African telecom!* Marcus had repeated to himself many times throughout the negotiations.

The entire deal team had been camped out in Peppercorn's lawyers' offices in Spitalfields, and after a few days of haggling over the final purchase price, Peppercorn had managed to sell the business for a few million dollars more than they paid for it. Certainly not a win, but a potential catastrophe avoided, given how unsuccessful TeleCAR had been.

With the TeleCAR deal now done, Marcus had little time for rest. Instead, he sent a note to Mauro Broccatelli and Simon Walker-Kelly informing them that he was heading to the Broccagas office. Marcus had promised to begin the Broccagas Trading and Shipping negotiations straightaway once he was done with his other commitments.

Marcus, ever the enthusiast for public transportation and mixing with the people, fought off his innate urge to hop on the tube at Liverpool Street and ride it to Sloane Square. Maintaining his global dealmaker persona, he instead hailed a cab for the ride to West London.

"St Luke's Gardens, please," Marcus instructed as he entered the cab.

The ride west across Central London took about thirty minutes. Marcus had learned that Broccagas had two different offices here in London. One was a high profile, ultra-modern office with a massive trading floor, and was located in Knightsbridge, just across from Harrod's. This was the office where the majority of the Broccagas London personnel plied their trade on a daily basis.

The other office was smaller and much more discrete. It was located in Chelsea, a little bit off the King's Road and looking out onto St Luke's Gardens. This was where Mauro Broccatelli and a few other senior executives kept their offices. It was quiet, private, and separate from the hectic mess that running Broccagas from day-to-day had become. Yet, it was only a twenty-minute walk to the Knightsbridge office. So, close enough to make an appearance when needed.

This smaller, quieter office was also where Broccatelli preferred to host important meetings. It provided the advantage of not having everyone in the company see who was coming to visit.

Marcus's cab arrived at St Luke's Gardens, and as he exited, he eyed Simon WalkerKelly walking down St Luke's Street and heading his direction.

Marcus made eye contact, and, presuming that Walker-Kelly was walking over from the Knightsbridge office, asked, "No quiet senior executive office here in Chelsea for you?"

Walker-Kelly responded with a quick smile, then added, "A trader needs to be with other traders. But I've got a small office here too. Welcome, I'll show you in."

Marcus, who had already been given the go-ahead by the Peppercorn investment committee to make a suitable deal with Broccagas, was ready to get to work. There was a deal with the Devil to make, and a good friend's life to save.

The negotiations for a Peppercorn partnership with Broccagas Trading and Shipping moved at breakneck pace. Marcus had allowed the other members of the Peppercorn deal team and Peppercorn's outside lawyers to take the rest of that Wednesday off to recharge after signing the TeleCAR deal, but he had not afforded himself such a luxury. He spent all of that afternoon and most of the evening meeting with the Broccagas team advancing the commercial terms of the partnership.

***

WHEN THE REST of the Peppercorn team and legal counsel arrived at Broccagas's Chelsea office early on Thursday morning, there was much for them to catch up on. Marcus survived on catered pastries and sandwiches, and cup after cup of black coffee served up in ornate, decorated china that looked like Wedgewood teacups. *Not actual Wedgewood pottery, right?* Marcus wondered.

By early that Friday afternoon, the parties had just about papered up a deal that both groups were willing to accept. Peppercorn would acquire 49 percent of Broccagas Trading and Shipping for a healthy ten-figure sum, and then would be required to contribute additional funds over the next two years to purchase the remaining one percent to make the partnership a true fifty-fifty joint venture. This was the form of enterprise they wanted to create for a public listing on the London Stock Exchange.

Marcus and Broccatelli had agreed at the outset that they would not actually sign any of the documents that week. This had been a condition that Marcus put forward, but surprisingly Broccatelli had willingly agreed, almost seeming relieved by the ask.

"Once the paperwork is just about settled, let's find time for a little private chat." Broccatelli had stated.

With the documents just about ready to execute, Broccatelli thanked everyone for their hard work and explained that the signing would not occur until Monday. Everyone could return home and get some well-deserved rest.

Marcus saw his team off, and then intentionally lingered behind in the Broccagas office. Broccatelli made eye contact with Marcus, then nodded his head suggestively toward one of the meeting rooms. After about fifteen minutes, Broccatelli entered the room with a dark-brown leather work bag in hand and a sleek, stylish lightweight black jacket over his suit.

"How about a visit to the pub?" Broccatelli asked. Then, after glancing around quickly and noticing that there were still people within earshot, added, "To celebrate!"

That sounded just about right to Marcus on many fronts, so he quickly grabbed his things, put on his own jacket and followed Broccatelli out of the building.

The fickle early October English weather had turned in their favor, and what had been a drizzly Friday morning with a slight chill in the air had now turned into a clear, sunny, and pleasantly warm afternoon. The combination of a Friday afternoon and what could be one of the last warm and sunny days of the year had beckoned Londoners out of their offices and over to the pubs, with the outdoor seating options completely packed.

Broccatelli led Marcus about halfway down the block toward a building with blue window-awnings, wide-open glass doors and windows with white-painted wooden frames, and a pair of small, green trees sprouting from large, angular pots. The pub's name, *Builders Arms*, was emblazoned across the façade above the awnings. The outdoor tables were fully occupied with patrons with loosened ties, jackets removed, and pints of beer and glasses of white wine filled to the brim. Broccatelli cruised through the lively atmosphere outdoors and entered the pub.

Broccatelli nodded to the bartender, who quickly led them to a small rectangular wooden table in a back room, which, far from being dark and stuffy, was surprisingly bright and colorful. There was a skylight in the roof above, and the afternoon sunshine lit up the room to display the unlit old fireplace in the corner, the cozy, yet tasteful décor, and the two-toned off-white and French-blue walls.

The bartender scurried back to the bar but quickly returned with a bottle of red Burgundy and two wine glasses. Broccatelli deftly scrutinized the label on the bottle, then nodded appreciatively. A small taste was poured out, and Broccatelli did the honors. He found it satisfactory. The bartender poured a full glass.

Before the bartender could pour the second glass, Marcus broke in, "Actually, I'll take a pint of Fuller's, please."

The bartender stopped in a jerky motion, then gave Broccatelli a sideways glance. Broccatelli nodded curtly, and the bartender left the Burgundy bottle on the table and went to retrieve Marcus's beer. When he returned, Marcus raised his glass toward Broccatelli.

"Cheers, then. To *almost* having a deal signed up," Marcus stated.

There was no one else in the back room with them, but Broccatelli surveyed the room anyway. Given that they were speaking in Spanish, as was their custom when speaking privately, the risk of an intruder overhearing seemed low. But Broccatelli responded in a hushed tone, nonetheless.

"Hmm. Yes, almost indeed."

They each took sips of their drinks, and there was a pause between them. Broccatelli looked like he was trying to figure out how to phrase what he was about to say, then Marcus decided to jump in ahead of him.

"Mauro, there are two things that I need to discuss with you before we can—"

"Marcus, please," Broccatelli interjected. He lifted a hand up, as if to both stop Marcus and also apologize for interrupting. "Let me speak first."

Broccatelli took a long sip of his wine, closing his eyes as he quietly sloshed the dark liquid around his mouth before swallowing and breathing out deeply. Then he began speaking.

"As you know, Broccagas and all of its subsidiaries, including Broccagas Trading and Shipping, are owned jointly, 33.33 percent each, by my father Fernando, my brother Roberto—you met him at Le Clos Sainte-Magdeleine, of course—and me. Many of the important decisions above day-to-day operational matters can be made by a simple majority vote, so two out of the three of us. These would be things like selecting an accounting firm, selling assets under $100 million, et cetera."

Marcus nodded, he was familiar with this type of structure and had in fact drafted those provisions into private company governing documents himself many times before.

"But for the most important decisions, like selling half the company for example, the decision must be unanimous. My father, my brother and I must all approve."

Marcus wasn't surprised as this was also common.

"My family dynamic is…challenging." Broccatelli looked off into the distance and inhaled, then exhaled heavily.

Marcus took a sip of his beer and looked down at the table to give Broccatelli some space to unpack his thoughts.

"My father and I see eye-to-eye on pretty much everything. He will vote as I vote. My brother, on the other hand, is a very different story. He and my father have a very challenging relationship. And frankly, my relationship with Roberto is very difficult as well."

Marcus thought back to the icy handshake between the two Broccatelli brothers in Provence. This difficult relationship between the brothers wasn't that surprising, but Mauro admitting it was.

"In order for us to do our deal with your firm, Marcus, Roberto has to approve the deal. And you didn't exactly win him over when the two of you met."

Marcus thought back to his "strength with strength approach" with Roberto. *Maybe not the best idea after all*, he scolded himself.

"He has certain…reservations about you." Broccatelli looked a question at Marcus over the rim of his wine glass. Marcus shrugged this off as if he heard it all the time, then stared blankly back at Broccatelli.

"Roberto is not yet ready to give his consent for this transaction. It is going to take some time, and we are going to have to provide him with some…comfort, regarding his reservations."

Marcus nodded understandingly, took another sip of his beer and then narrowed his eyes at the table, as if concentrating hard on something.

"If you don't mind me asking, Mauro, why does Roberto care? Isn't the goal here for Peppercorn to provide some liquidity to the Broccatelli family, help stand the business up in advance of a public listing, and transition operational control over to Simon

Walker-Kelly and away from your family? I would think his only concern would be how much we are willing to pay for our 49 percent." Upon uttering this last thought, Marcus shot Broccatelli a look to convey that the price couldn't possibly be the issue. Peppercorn was overpaying and both Marcus and Broccatelli knew it.

Broccatelli closed his eyes and a near-painful look overtook his face.

"It's complicated, Marcus," He stated, almost whispering.

The bartender returned to their table and poured another two inches of the Burgundy into Broccatelli's wine glass, then laid a fresh beer down in front of Marcus. Marcus and Broccatelli both nodded their thanks and remained silent as the bartender distanced himself from the table.

Marcus thought about Broccatelli's last comment, and suddenly his mind began connecting dots that he should have seen earlier. A path forward from this impasse began to appear.

"Fair enough," Marcus concluded, then added, "Why don't we table that aspect of the deal for now, and perhaps I can share the two items I was hoping to discuss."

Broccatelli was slightly caught off guard, but he looked more relieved than anything. He gave a gentle nod, insisting that Marcus proceed.

"During our due diligence on…" Marcus coolly glanced from side to side, then in a quiet voice continued, "…*the target*, we noticed some…inaccuracies, or perhaps I should say, irregularities, in the target's balance sheet and cash flow."

Broccatelli looked up slowly into Marcus's eyes, his nostrils beginning to flare.

Marcus held up a calm hand, and clarified, "Good irregularities. In the target's favor."

Broccatelli looked back down at the table. His body was tense, and he looked uncomfortable.

"The thing is, Mauro, I," Marcus pointed at himself, "And not necessarily Peppercorn, need to know what is behind those irregularities before we can proceed with this transaction. If I know what they are, then I should be able to explain it away to our deal team and our committee."

Broccatelli took another sip of his wine and seemed to have regained some of his composure. He gave Marcus an intense and searching look, then asked, "You plan to return back to Paris this afternoon, right?"

"Yes," Marcus said slowly, looking back into Broccatelli's eyes. "On the Eurostar to Gare du Nord at 5:15."

Broccatelli nodded gently, then replied, "Why don't you change that to the 12:01 train tomorrow afternoon. There's a great run through Hyde Park I was hoping you could join me on early tomorrow morning. Someone else will be joining us as well."

Marcus indicated his assent.

"Good then," Broccatelli replied, picking up his bag and putting on his jacket. A certain cocksureness seemed reinstalled. "We'll meet you outside your hotel at seven a.m. It'll be about seven miles all in, so fuel up accordingly."

Marcus shared an ironic smile, then stated, "But I didn't tell you where my hotel is."

"You didn't have to," Broccatelli replied in stride, as he zipped his jacket up and nodded to the bartender. Then, as if in afterthought, he asked, "And Marcus, what was your second item to discuss?"

Marcus remained seated at the table, his nearly full beer sitting in front of him. He looked up at Broccatelli, and with the corners of his mouth curling up slightly, replied, "Seems like a good topic for tomorrow's chat."

CHAPTER 35

London, England.
Trafalgar Square.
Early October 2019.

T HE TRAFALGAR ST. JAMES HOTEL WAS NOT exactly a fit for Marcus's cover persona as a rising star in the European private equity world. The Savoy, the Berkeley, or the Dorchester all would have been more appropriate, as those hotels were well-renowned, lavish, and much more expensive. But Marcus had brought a large Peppercorn deal team over from Paris for the TeleCAR transaction and the Broccagas negotiations, so he wanted to be somewhat conscious of their lodging expenses. And he liked the Trafalgar St. James. The location was great for their purposes; right on Trafalgar Square, well-situated between the City, where the TeleCAR meetings had been held, and Chelsea, where Broccatelli's office was, and very close to St. James's Park, Green Park, and Hyde Park.

Marcus stood outside the hotel Saturday morning at a few minutes before seven. He stretched and loosened up while he awaited Broccatelli's arrival for their scheduled jog through Hyde Park. Marcus wore jogging shorts and a long sleeve shirt, as the finicky weather had turned back toward fall with a slight chill and a mild breeze in the air.

Marcus looked out onto Nelson's Column towering above the square, guarded by four bronze lions at each corner of the pedestal. The morning fog was lifting, and he could see across the square to the white and gray neoclassical façade of the National Gallery. He heard the humming of bicycle wheels coming his way, then saw two athletic-looking figures dismount their bikes and find a place to lock them up.

The first man was unmistakably Mauro Broccatelli: incredibly fit, short, black hair, decked out in high-tech spandex, and dismounting a designer around-the-town bike. The second man was sturdily built, rode an old-school steel Italian road bike that looked as though it had been purchased second- or even third-hand, was dressed in standard, nondescript running gear, and had short brown hair and a beard. It was Simon Walker-Kelly.

"Morning," Marcus announced with a smile, "Where did you two bike in from?"

Broccatelli replied with a pleasant yet cynical grin. This was somewhat of a rhetorical question, as Marcus knew that Broccatelli lived only a short distance away in a beautiful Regencystyle townhome in Belgravia. But Marcus did not know where Walker-Kelly lived.

"Wimbledon," Walker-Kelly replied quietly.

"Wow, that's quite the warmup." Marcus responded, genuinely impressed. Wimbledon to Trafalgar Square had to be close to a forty-five-minute ride, but then again Marcus recalled Walker-Kelly's cycling prowess from the ViaRhôna trip.

"Shall we?" Broccatelli asked, nodding his head toward the alleyway leading to the Mall and heading off in a jog.

Okay, jog and talk it will be then, Marcus concluded.

They made their way along the Mall, jogging along the unique red concrete of the road. The leaves on the trees in St. James's Park were just starting to show some yellow, and it was quiet save for a few fellow runners.

They found a steady, comfortable pace before Broccatelli began speaking.

"This morning's discussion is for your knowledge, Marcus, and yours alone. Not anyone else at Peppercorn. I understand your need to know about some of the...matters...you described. But I'm also going to hold you to your claim that you can, how'd you put it? Explain it away?"

As they veered to the right past Buckingham Palace and toward Wellington Arch, Marcus indicated his confirmation.

"Good," Broccatelli continued. "I've asked Simon to join us because my technical knowledge of the matters is limited, but not his."

Broccatelli took a deep breath, then looked thoughtfully ahead before continuing.

"The financial irregularities that your team so impressively discovered are the result of my brother's involvement in Broccagas Trading and Shipping's business. You see, my brother is a very ambitious man. Very ambitious, Marcus. And he uses our family's company to do certain...political favors...for people."

They were now in Hyde Park, heading north along one of the wide walking paths. There were few people in the park at this hour, so they were able to spread out and Broccatelli spoke louder. He also picked up the group's pace a bit.

"My father and I both have tried to prevent it from happening. But because of certain things that Roberto has done and information that people have about him and our family, we don't have many options." Broccatelli shook his head in clear disappointment.

"Marcus, the truth is that Roberto and his associate, Samih Salem, use our company to facilitate transactions that most international businesses are not allowed to do. Beyond that, I know very little. I've tried to bury my head in the sand like an ostrich."

Broccatelli spoke with remorse and candor. Either he was an excellent liar, or it truly was Roberto

Broccatelli that was driving Broccagas's illegal operations. *So Franz has been right all along*, Marcus thought, *but maybe not about all of the Broccatelli family.*

They had made their way to the western end of Kensington Gardens and were passing behind Kensington Palace. Broccatelli had halted his explanation.

"Okay, interesting," Marcus stated, breaking the silence. "But what, exactly, are these political favors and illegal transactions? On whose behalf are they carried out? Who are the counterparties?"

Broccatelli looked over at Walker-Kelly, then replied, "That's why I've invited Simon. Outside of Roberto and Salem, and maybe a few lower-level Broccagas Trading and Shipping operations personnel, he's the only one in the company that knows about it and how it works."

Walker-Kelly looked up hesitantly, starring into Broccatelli's eyes.

"Go ahead, Simon," Broccatelli responded. "I've ignored this for long enough. If we are going to get this company where it needs to be, then we need Peppercorn. And if we don't tell Marcus the truth, then we won't have them."

Walker-Kelly nodded reluctantly. "Okay," he replied quietly, then began his explanation.

"Our company produces, transports and refines oil and gas all over the world, right? Argentina, Colombia, Ecuador, Turkmenistan, Algeria, Libya…places like that. And our shipping business moves those products all over the world, mainly from places that produce oil and gas to places that don't produce it and badly need it. But we don't just ship our own product, of course, we use our shipping contracts to ship other people's products as well. Basic allocation of resources."

Marcus was following. There were only a handful of businesses in the oil and gas world that remained "fully integrated," meaning that they kept ownership of their oil and gas from extraction out of the ground all the way to the ultimate sale to an end user. Most other companies focused only on one particular aspect of the business, such as exploration and production, but once oil and gas was produced, they sold it to someone else to transport. Then that transporter moved the product to a refinery where a refining company would convert it from a raw product to a refined product such as gasoline.

"Now, because we handle so much product and move it over such long distances, we also trade around those products to try to make additional money. So if an opportunity to buy extra crude oil from Ecuador comes up, and the price is favorable, we buy it, even if we don't have a specific buyer lined up at that time. We are confident that we can find a market, and a favorable price, for that oil at some point down the road."

Marcus nodded his understanding, and chimed in. "Right, a physical trade. I imagine that you guys do lots of financial trades as well."

"Exactly," Walker-Kelly responded. "In addition to the physical trades, we do lots of swaps, shorts, hedges, those types of things. And the trading side of the business is extremely profitable for us."

Marcus peeked over at Broccatelli, who was concentrating very hard but had a somewhat lost look in his eye.

"Okay, but lots of people trade that way. Nothing illegal there." Marcus observed.

Walker-Kelly tilted his head and looked sideways at Marcus.

"Well, every once in a while, I receive an encrypted message from Salem informing me of a trade he wants Broccagas Trading and Shipping to execute. For example, to buy refined gasoline from Iran and deliver it to Venezuela. Or buy large quantities of Libyan crude oil and sell it to North Korea. Or even to just place a huge buy order on discounted Venezuelan crude oil and sell it on the open market."

"All of those trades are, technically speaking, what you would call 'illegal' given that they violate current sanctions. But they also happen to be wildly profitable because those counterparties are desperate to transact. Salem brokers the deal, and our company executes the logistics behind the trade."

"So where does Roberto come into all of this?" Marcus asked, genuinely perplexed.

"Good question," Walker-Kelly acknowledged. "Roberto gets requests from the Argentine government to make these deals happen to help these particular countries out. Then he talks to Salem, and Salem uses his vast network to connect the right people to come to terms for the deal."

"But what does the Argentine administration get out of it?" Marcus could surmise the answer to this one on his own, but he wanted to hear Walker-Kelly's response, and he didn't want to appear too much in-the-know already.

"Favors, influence, money, not being outed by some of the countries for past bad acts or collusion," Walker-Kelly responded flatly, as if the response was the most obvious thing in the world.

Marcus's mind traveled back to his conversation with Franz in Paris a few months back, outside the café on the Rue du Bac when Franz was discussing the Broccatelli family's potential involvement in nefarious activity on behalf of the Argentine government. *It's also quite possible they carried out the Nisman Affair*, Franz had said.

Of course, Marcus thought.

"So why Roberto? Why did the Argentine government choose him?"

Walker-Kelly cast a glance at Broccatelli, then down to the ground. Broccatelli had a pained look, and a dark shadow came over his face.

"That is not something I can share with you, Marcus," Broccatelli replied sternly. Then with a grave look on his face, he added, "But I can tell you that my father and I ask ourselves a similar version of that question every day."

Clearly there was a deep fracture between Roberto on the one hand, and Mauro and his father, on the other.

"Fair enough," Marcus responded quickly, raising his palms in the air to signal deference to Broccatelli's statement. "But back to the trades, how do you execute them? I mean, it's not like you can just pick up gasoline from the port at Bandar Abbas in Iran, then unload it all in Venezuela at Puerto Cabello. Aren't the same agencies that monitor everyone else monitoring yours?"

They were now entering the final stretch of the run, passing by Buckingham Palace again and running along the southern end of St. James's Park.

"It's a shell game," responded Walker-Kelly, with a hint of amusement in his eyes.

Marcus dipped his head and raised his eyebrows at Walker-Kelly, encouraging him to explain further.

"Are you familiar with Hurd's Bank?"

"No," Marcus responded truthfully.

"In the Mediterranean, just east of Malta, there is a shallow offshore bank. Large tanker ships can actually dock there, but there isn't any port. There's an informal ship-to-ship trading network that allows products to move from one large tanker to another. It's outside of Malta's territorial waters and not under their jurisdiction, nor anyone else's for that matter."

Marcus was fascinated by this and shocked that he had never come across it before. Given the look on Broccatelli's face, he clearly felt the same way.

Marcus began working out the sequence in his head. A few seconds later, he stated it out loud.

"So a tanker leaves Iran with a ship full of gasoline. It goes around the Gulf of Aden, into the Red Sea, through the Suez Canal and into the Mediterranean. It lands at this Hurd's Bank. Meanwhile, you guys have an empty ship coming back from say, China, a legitimate trading partner of yours. On that ship's way back home, it also stops at Hurd's Bank. A ship-to-ship transfer of gasoline for money, or something similar, occurs in territory that is essentially out of anyone's jurisdiction. Then your ship sails home…It's brilliant, really."

"Something like that," Walker-Kelly responded. "And if it's not Hurd's Bank, it's some other version of that type of deception in some other part of the world."

"But then, how do you deliver the gasoline to Venezuela?" Marcus asked, trying to figure out the last leg of the trade.

"That's a little more complicated, specifically for Venezuela," Walker-Kelly replied. "We deliver the gasoline to our port facility in Colombia, then have FARC dissidents or Venezuelan agents smuggle the gasoline across the Colombian border into Venezuela."

Marcus's heart began beating faster as he appreciated the Broccatellis' influence in Colombia and

Venezuela, thinking about how that could be useful for retrieving Graham Curry.

"So," Broccatelli said, "You still want to buy half of our company? Still think you can gloss over all of this for your Peppercorn colleagues?"

The run had reached its end, and they slowed to a walk on the sandy-colored gravel in front of Horse Guards Parade.

"Well, perhaps now I have some leverage over Roberto and can make him agree to our deal," Marcus replied with a smile.

"Ha, leverage. You mean blackmail," shot back Walker-Kelly.

"I'm kidding. Of course I would never let Roberto or Salem know that I'm privy to this information. But..." Marcus came to a full stop, looking directly into the eyes of Broccatelli, then Walker-Kelly's, "...I do want to see it."

"See what?" fired back Broccatelli, genuinely confused.

"Hurd's Bank. I want to see how it works."

Broccatelli and Walker-Kelly each rolled their eyes, then exhaled. The two men realized that Marcus was being serious, and that, if they wanted Peppercorn's investment, they would have to honor this request.

"Well I guess I should see it, too, then," Broccatelli finally replied.

The three men jogged back over to Broccatelli and Walker-Kelly's locked-up bikes.

Broccatelli began putting on his helmet, then stopped and looked at Marcus.

"What was the second thing? Yesterday, you said there was something else that you wanted. What is it?"

Light flooded into Marcus's eyes, and a broad smile spread across his face before he replied.

"Not some*thing* else...some*one*."

CHAPTER 36

Unknown Location. Unknown Time.

H E MADE ANOTHER MARK ON THE WALL IN A continued effort to count the number of days he had been in captivity, but it was of little use. His captors would search his quarters every so often and obliterate anything they could find that helped him know how long he had been there. His clothes, the military outfit that they forced upon him once he came to this camp here in the jungle, had grown ragged and loose around his emaciated frame. And his face, which he himself had not seen since his capture, was covered by an unkempt beard.

Graham Curry had been in captivity for nearly four months, but he had no idea where he was, how long he had been there, and how the hell he was going to get out.

That wasn't entirely true, though. Graham did not know his exact location, but he did know it was probably somewhere near Cúcuta, Colombia, but on the Venezuelan side of the border. The jungle around him was thick, and numerous mountains surrounded them. Many of his captors spoke Spanish with a notable Venezuelan accent, although some of them had more of a Colombian accent.

They had knocked him out with the butt of a gun to the head when the first trip down the river ended at some informal dock. Graham woke up here.

Every so often, they lined him up in front of a tree, with guns pointed to his head from all around, and made a video of him. They tried to make him identify himself, but he never did. The first few weeks they had beaten him for his insubordination, but after a while they sort of just left him alone.

His sleeping quarters were an old, worn-out shipping crate. Graham concluded that it wasn't too bad; at least this one didn't have the fresh blood of his former colleague, Juan, covering half the crate.

He had stopped trying to figure out why he was still alive, or why they had not taken him to Caracas and put him on display for all of the world to see. He had already spent weeks doing that and had nearly driven himself crazy with all the rabbit holes his mind went down.

Graham tried to eat as much of the bland, simple food that they fed him. And he tried to walk around the camp as much as his captors would let him. But he wasn't sure how much longer he could keep his spirits and his efforts up.

He recalled Edmond Dantès from Dumas's *The Count of Monte Cristo*, who after six years of being locked up in the Château d'If gave up all hope and tried to kill himself by starvation. Graham thought maybe that is what he should do. But out here, of course, there would be no Abbé Faria in the cell next door to come scratching through the walls to save him.

He reasoned that he wouldn't resort to those measures just yet—at least not tonight. He laid down in the makeshift pile of blankets that served as his bed and tried to get some sleep. Just as he was dozing off, he heard the noise of a construction vehicle's wheels coming his way. Then he heard a loud clang of metal on metal. And shortly after that, his shipping crate was lifted from the ground.

CHAPTER 37

Menaggio, Italy.
Early November 2019.

A BLACK MERCEDES-BENZ HAD BEEN WAITING for Marcus outside of the arrivals hall at Milan Malpensa Airport. A polite, unassuming driver in a black suit, white dress shirt, and solid black tie helped Marcus load his carry-on bag into the trunk of the car and began speeding them northeast toward Lago di Como. *This man looks like he's dressed for a funeral*, Marcus thought as he buckled himself into the back seat.

Marcus sat quietly for the first half hour of the ride, as they passed through the industrial corridor north of Milan. He thought back on what all had transpired over the last month, and whether this whole excursion was a good idea or not. Even Arthur Franz, who was typically quite the risk taker, had reservations. Franz had explained that this trip was perfectly ripe for a trap, but then again there was no other way to retrieve Graham Curry without involving the military. Franz did not have the authority to do that, so Marcus was their best option.

As they switched off the A9 to the SS340, the breathtaking panoramic scene of Lago di Como beneath the angled crags of tree-covered rock jutting high into the sky spread out before them. The autumn foliage was in full force as reds, oranges, and yellows mixed with green leaves. The backdrop surrounded colorful little clumps of villages sitting on the lakeshore and all of it reflected on itself off the calm, dark-blue water. Marcus, who had already been to Lago di Como a handful of times before, remained in awe looking out the window as they wound their way north along the two-lane road hugging the narrow banks of the lake.

They arrived at the small town of Menaggio on the western shore, just across from a peninsula jutting out into the middle of the lake where Bellagio was. The driver continued along past the center of the village and a few minutes later pulled into a gated driveway with a guard station out front. The driver rolled down his window and uttered something in rapid Italian to the guard, who opened the gates.

Red bricks laid along either side of the loose-gravel driveway, and it wound past curated but wild-looking plants mixed with tall, well-trimmed cypress trees, and in the general direction of the water. They turned the final corner and Marcus spotted the palazzo in front of them. It occupied an entire promontory over the water and was made of sandstone and light-brown stone, ornamented in the

Liberty style. There were white columns along the various balconies, and a central square-shaped tower rose up to what looked like an observation deck on top. As they pulled up to the front door, Marcus looked out towards the water and saw a decorative oval fountain and steps leading down to a large dock on the lake.

It was late afternoon by the time they arrived, and the sun was just dipping below the mountains rising behind the palazzo. An older Italian housekeeper greeted Marcus at the front door and informed him that *Signore Broccatelli* was staying in Milan with *Signorina Ravello* this evening and would not be arriving until the next morning. Marcus was shown to a large bedroom on the third floor with a stone balcony looking out onto the lake.

Marcus unpacked his suitcase and changed into a more casual outfit of colorful trousers and a navy knit blazer with a nautical sweater underneath. *I am in Lago di Como, after all*, he justified to himself.

He enjoyed dinner for one at a small osteria on the main square in Menaggio. The food was basic Italian cuisine, meaning it was excellent, and he treated himself to the better half of a nice bottle of Barolo and a small piece of tiramisu. He kept a watch out for anything curious or suspicious but saw nothing. After dinner, he returned to Broccatelli's near-empty palazzo and enjoyed a good night's sleep.

MARCUS ROSE EARLY the next morning and suited up in his running gear. He took a peek of the lake from his balcony and through the early morning mist rising from the water, he could make out two-story white ferryboats crisscrossing the lake, making their first runs between Menaggio, Varenna, and Bellagio. At this time of the morning, the lake was as smooth as glass, with tiny ripples extending from the back of the passing ferryboats.

Marcus jogged into the center of Menaggio, then pushed himself to scale the switchback roads heading up the mountain behind the town. He eventually found a beautiful golf club a good way up the road and headed for the clubhouse as Franz had instructed him.

Marcus spotted the contact standing on the clubhouse's balcony and saw her make the drop. He casually jogged over in that direction, trying to look as much like an interested tourist as possible. He retrieved the package, tucked it into the waistband of his jogging shorts beneath his shirt, then turned around and started back toward the palazzo. As he was descending into town, he noticed a helicopter flying over the lake and heading directly toward Menaggio. It soared above the town and began descending near the golf course that he had just left. He felt fairly confident he knew who was inside.

Marcus legged out a hard final push from the edge of Menaggio to the gates of the palazzo. He waved at the guard, who looked at him skeptically, but opened the gates, nonetheless. Marcus walked his way down the driveway and past the fountain, then to the dock. He stood at the edge of the dock and gripped the rail as he looked out over the iconic scene of the stunning alpine lake and the gigantic, jagged mountains all around it. He breathed in deeply as he thought about the plans for the day ahead.

This was it. He had faced challenging situations in his career with Peppercorn Capital before, but not like this. Today was going to be as close to the equivalent of running into a burning building as he would likely ever face. And it had a personal element to boot. The anxiety that mounted inside of him was not fear of the activity itself, but of having to wait any longer before it began.

He pulled one of his ankles back behind him to stretch, and then heard light steps over the loose gravel behind him. Marcus knew who it was, so he felt no need to interrupt his stretching routine.

"It's my favorite scene in the world," Mauro Broccatelli stated in his strong Argentine-accented Spanish. "There is a scale and gravity to the combination of the lake and the mountains that I haven't seen anywhere else. And then during the fall, when the leaves are changing like this, I feel like I could just look at this scene and then fade away forever and not be sad about it."

Marcus performed a few more stretches, continuing to face the lake with his back to Broccatelli.

"I can't argue with that," he stated, matter-of-factly. Then turned to greet his host.

Broccatelli stood in front of him, solid as stone. The dark-brown, almost-black eyes were full and alert. He was dressed fashionably in a textured and subtly patterned navy-blue sweater under a navy-blue bomber jacket. He wore snug black jeans and had on a pair of stylish black leather sneakers.

Marcus, in his long-sleeved running shirt and basic black running shorts, stared back at Broccatelli unfazed.

"Are you ready for today?" Broccatelli asked.

"Yes," Marcus responded quickly, then added, "Ready for it to be over." He flashed a smile and advanced toward Broccatelli with an extended hand.

They went over the details again and reassured each other that it was a good plan.

"Do you actually think this is going to work?" Broccatelli asked Marcus.

Marcus stepped back and looked out over the lake as he considered his response. Then he replied, "Yes, but probably not exactly as we've planned it."

They both nodded, as much to themselves as to each other. They stood there in silence for a few moments.

"What are you going to do?" Marcus asked Broccatelli. "You know, when you transition out of Broccagas. What do you see yourself doing?"

The question was a welcome break from the tension, and Marcus saw Broccatelli chuckle appreciatively.

"Ooh, good question," Broccatelli replied, then continued, "Well, believe it or not, I do actually want to buy a European football club, despite our previous failed efforts. So there's that."

Broccatelli breathed in and out, then stuck his hands into the pockets of his jacket before adding, "But what I really want to do, Marcus, is to focus on our wine business. Not just owning the wineries we have, but changing the focus to actual winemaking, as opposed to the more commercial approach. I'd like to acquire new vineyards in lesser-known wine-making regions and get fully steeped in the process of developing great wine estates."

This did not come as a shock to Marcus, as he recalled Broccatelli's level of engagement during their visit to the Musée du Vin in Châteauneuf-du-Pape.

Broccatelli continued, "I know a little bit about it, but there is so much more to learn. I know people like Caroline Dumont, but they already have their own business, their own estates. What I really need is a good partner, someone who knows the wine world inside and out but isn't going to also be a competitor."

Broccatelli sighed, then looked at Marcus wistfully. "I just haven't been able to find the right person."

Marcus nodded empathetically and controlled the bubbling excitement within him. Finally he replied,

"Well, Mauro, I think I've got just the person to introduce you to."

"You are just full of surprises, aren't you Marcus. I'm not sure exactly how I should interpret that," Broccatelli looked at him with a curious face, then shook his head a few times.

Before Marcus could venture a response, Broccatelli looked down at his watch. "You should run up and get ready. We leave in thirty minutes."

CHAPTER 38

Valetta, Malta.
Early November 2019.

T HE MORNING HAD BEEN QUITE THE EXERCISE IN
logistics for Marcus and Broccatelli. First, they
were driven from Broccatelli's palazzo up the mountain to a helicopter pad at Bene Lario, passing the golf
course Marcus had seen earlier that morning along
the way. Then they took Broccatelli's helicopter to a
private hanger at Milan Malpensa Airport. And from
there they boarded Broccatelli's private jet for the flight
to Malta International Airport.

Both Marcus and Broccatelli dozed off for much
of the flight but as they neared Malta, they roused
themselves and decided to go over the plan once again.

Broccatelli began the briefing. "As you know, your
gratuitous tip off to Simon Walker-Kelly, and then indirectly to my brother and Samih Salem, regarding an
opportunity to broker a high value...person of interest...exchange was successful. It seems to have been
enough to convince my brother to move forward with

our Peppercorn deal. I guess he likes that you seem to dabble in the gray side of the business world."

Marcus nodded once, looking solemn and focused.

"Now," Broccatelli continued, "Salem reached out to his contacts with the Chinese and the Venezuelans and offered to broker the exchange of this…friend… of yours. Apparently we are getting paid a fee of $20 million." Broccatelli raised his eyebrows at Marcus, who showed no response and continued listening.

"Salem coordinated the delivery with Walker-Kelly, and only Walker-Kelly. Remember that neither Roberto nor Salem has any clue that I know anything about this. They believe I am completely in the dark…which is where my brother always likes to keep me," Broccatelli added with ire in his eyes.

"Walker-Kelly has given us the details of the exchange. It will take place this evening on Hurd's Bank. The Chinese have a tanker coming to pick up Libyan crude oil but will stop at Hurd's Bank along the way. We have our own tanker bringing refined petrochemical products from Colombia to the Italians at the port in Cagliari, Sardinia. Ours is a fully-legitimate transaction, by the way," Broccatelli clarified.

Marcus smiled, then added, "Except for the person of interest, of course."

"Not after our operation," Broccatelli corrected with a pointed finger and veiled smile. He then continued the briefing.

"Our yacht, the one you rode on from Port-Saint-Louis-du-Rhône to Cassis, is docked at the port in Valetta here in Malta. The captain of the Broccagas Trading and Shipping vessel knows that we are coming, but not anyone else. And apparently only he and one other crew member are aware of your friend's presence on the boat. They are keeping him in a container."

Marcus grimaced at the thought of Graham Curry being stuck in a container, especially on the high seas. He couldn't begin to imagine what type of awful shape Graham must be in.

"So we will take our yacht to Hurd's Bank early this evening, board our vessel, find your friend, and get him out of there as quickly and quietly as possible. We take the yacht back to Valetta, head to the airport and take our plane to London overnight. When we touch down in the UK, he is all yours. I don't ever want to see him or hear about him again, okay?"

"Of course," Marcus stated quietly. Then he added, "And your captain of the Broccagas Trading and Shipping vessel, his plan is to deny any knowledge of the passenger?"

"That's right," Broccatelli confirmed. "As far as he knows, he is supposed to unload half of his refined products cargo to the Chinese. At least that's what he will tell them."

"And when your brother and Salem find out that there was no exchange, we let WalkerKelly take the brunt of their frustration?"

Broccatelli gently shrugged his shoulders. "That's all we can do," he replied. "WalkerKelly will pretend to be as mad as they are, and say he has no idea what happened. They aren't going to fire him, because they can't run around telling everyone in the company that Walker-Kelly failed to deliver an illegal hostage from the Venezuelans to the Chinese. And Salem's reputation in the shady business community in which he lives will be damaged, but what's that to us? The Venezuelans and the Chinese can't exactly report the incident to the authorities either."

"Well…" Marcus dragged out his response. "It's not perfect, but I guess it should work."

"If we are going to start making Broccagas Trading and Shaping a fully legitimate enterprise, we have to start somewhere. Getting back your friend is as good of an opportunity as any," Broccatelli stated with conviction.

"I guess you're right," Marcus said, nodding his head. But a curious feeling of uncertainty in his gut just wouldn't go away.

UPON LANDING, MARCUS and Broccatelli were driven to the port at Valetta. Broccatelli's massive yacht was easy to spot, and they made for that direction. They boarded the boat, which already had the engine running. Evening was beginning to fall, so they needed to move quickly.

Broccatelli led Marcus out to the front deck, and they found a good vantage point for the voyage out to Hurd's Bank.

"Marcus," Broccatelli stated suddenly, interrupting Marcus's observation of the surrounding banks of Valetta. Marcus looked over, and Broccatelli was holding a small black handgun. Marcus remained calm and put on a show of surprise.

"You know how to use one of these?" Broccatelli made to hand the gun over to Marcus, who instantly relaxed as he realized that Broccatelli was giving him the gun, not intending to use it on him.

Marcus handled the weapon, lifted it up and examined it. He nodded his head gently, and uttered calmly, "I do."

"Hmm...I figured you might," Broccatelli replied with a crooked grin. "I'm going to keep mine back here." Broccatelli produced a duplicate of the same gun, then slotted it in between his designer black jeans and his lower back. "I suggest you do the same."

Marcus slowly placed the gun Broccatelli gave him next to the gun he already had in the back of his waistband.

"You can probably tell, but it is loaded. And the safety is on. No reason we should need to use them tonight, but you never know."

Marcus nodded his understanding.

A few minutes later, Marcus looked out onto the eastern horizon and spotted a gathering of ten or so tanker ships evenly spaced out in a horizontal line. At first, Marcus thought they were just anchored at sea. But then, Marcus realized that this was the infamous Hurd's Bank. Those ships were effectively docked on a sandbar.

"That must be it," Broccatelli observed. "Come on, let's head over to the launch boat."

Marcus breathed deeply and tried to clear his mind for the task ahead. He followed Broccatelli to the launch boat, and after the yacht was a little closer to Hurd's Bank, a member of Broccatelli's crew helped them in. Broccatelli informed that crewmember that Broccatelli himself would drive, and that no further help was needed.

They sped away from the yacht and toward the darkening figures of ships before them. Marcus held tightly to the strap on the side of the launch boat, as the waves made for a rough ride and the cold, salty water splashed onto his face. They neared one of the boats, and saw a flashlight go on and off a few times from the deck.

"That's our captain," Broccatelli stated.

Broccatelli skillfully moored the launch boat to one side of the larger vessel, and then led Marcus up a boarding ladder to the main deck. The captain spotted them and came walking hastily over. He was a tall, thick, and well-appointed man wearing neat and tidy nautical clothing, but his face was worn from age and time on the water. He was flushed and had a look of urgency in his eyes.

"Mister Mauro Broccatelli, I presume?" The captain asked, extending his hand quickly. His English was good, but notably accented. Marcus guessed Greek, and likely ex-Hellenic Navy.

"Yes, that's right. And you are Captain Pallas?"

The captain nodded quickly, then excitedly added, "Sir, I just received a call from a helicopter heading this way, requesting permission to land. It's your brother and some other man. They want to…how did they say it…oversee the exchange of certain cargo this evening."

Broccatelli's face was frozen for a moment, as if turned to plaster. Then he turned to look at Marcus, and Marcus returned the same concerned look. Goosebumps overcame Marcus's body, and he felt his heart beating faster.

In the distance, they began to hear the faint hum of a helicopter blade. Marcus read the look that came over Broccatelli's face as the reality of the moment sprung them into action, and he barked, "Extraction, now!"

Captain Pallas stood at attention, then realizing what Marcus meant, led them at a run into the bowels of the ship.

CHAPTER 39

Hurd's Bank, Extraterritorial Waters in the Mediterranean Sea. Early November 2019.

B Y THE TIME CAPTAIN PALLAS LED THEM TO A rusty container on the complete opposite end of the ship, the sound of the approaching helicopter was loud enough to make it clear that it was about to land. Marcus and Broccatelli exchanged an intense look of urgency, then Marcus shook his head from side to side.

"There's not enough time. We need a new plan," Marcus screamed over the pounding sound of the helicopter blades.

Broccatelli nodded once, then yelled back, "Just get your friend out, I'll deal with Roberto and Salem." Then Broccatelli looked at Captain Pallas and made a strong gesture toward the container. "Open it up, then you need to come with me," he shouted to the captain.

Pallas unlocked the exterior of the container, then took off at a run after Broccatelli. Marcus eyed the open lock, then positioned himself in front of the heavy container door. He heaved the external bolt up and then over to the side, allowing the door to swing a few inches. Then he put all of his weight into pushing the door open.

The intensifying moonlight and a tepid light bulb from a central compartment of the ship shone upon the interior of the container. Marcus spotted a small metal table and two chairs, both empty. He stepped into the light and looked to the back of the container.

At the far end of the makeshift cell was a man, huddled up in a clump against the back wall. Marcus stepped closer, and then to the side so as not to block the light. The man's frame was almost skeletal. The face was gaunt and angular. A brownish-gray beard hung down to the middle of the man's chest. But this was Graham Curry, Marcus had no doubt about that.

Marcus was amazed at the change in Graham's physique, and how much he seemed to have aged. He heard the ascent and then subsequent distancing of the helicopter.

There will be time for all of that sentimental stuff later, Marcus quickly reminded himself. He rushed over to his old friend, who drew back at Marcus's advance.

"Graham, it's me. Come on, we don't have much time," Marcus said rapidly, reaching down to help Graham up.

A wild, incredulous look overtook Graham's face. "Marcus? Marcus Hugo...? Holy shit!"

A powerful sense of hope and excitement spread over Marcus, and he couldn't help himself from smiling. "Yes, it's me. Now get your ass up and move!"

Marcus bent down and tried to put one of Graham's arms over his shoulder to help him walk. But Marcus quickly realized that Graham's hands were cuffed together. He adjusted his grip and tried to grab Graham's outer hip and help steady him along.

They exited the container onto the ship's deck. It was slow going, but they made for the outer rail. Marcus turned them in the direction of the ladder that he and Broccatelli had scaled from the launch boat below. All of a sudden, he heard a loud scream.

"Marcus! Stop right there!"

Mauro Broccatelli screamed in Spanish in his recognizable Argentine accent. He turned to face Mauro while standing directly in front of Graham Curry, almost shielding him from sight. Trailing behind Mauro Broccatelli, huffing and puffing, were Roberto Broccatelli and Samih Salem. Roberto and Salem were both sweating through their dark business suits, collared shirts, and ties. They looked completely out of place, here on a giant tanker in the middle of the Mediterranean, and they both were clearly angry and confused.

Marcus tried to think quickly, but he had no idea what yarn Mauro Broccatelli had spun them, or even if he could still trust Mauro. Marcus stepped back and lifted the back of his shirt slightly to display to Graham the two handguns tucked into his waistband. Graham, who was hardly strong enough to walk, seemed to summon a reserve of strength as he realized the intensity of the situation. Marcus raised his hands into the air, and then felt Graham come closer and grasp one of the weapons. *I hope he can still fire a weapon with his hands cuffed together*, Marcus noted.

Mauro began walking toward Marcus, screaming at the top of his lungs. His accent had become so thick, and the background noise of the ocean around them so loud, that Marcus could only make out about half of what Mauro was saying. When Mauro had reached a distance halfway between Roberto and Salem, on one end, and Marcus and Graham, on the other end, he stopped.

There were a few moments of silence, then Roberto began his own screaming. The aspiring politician's polished veneer cracked, and Roberto Broccatelli's accented Spanish was as difficult for Marcus to comprehend as Mauro's had been. But there was one phrase that kept being repeated that Marcus understood perfectly: "CIA."

"Enough!" Mauro yelled, the tense situation clearly weighing on him. "Marcus," Mauro Broccatelli spoke slowly, loudly, and more clearly now. "Roberto and Salem tell me that your friend, Mr. Graham Curry, is wanted by the Chinese because he is a CIA informant. And he spied on the Chinese while working in Papua New Guinea, and apparently was also doing the CIA's bidding in Colombia by helping out Venezuelan rebels."

Marcus felt Graham slip one of the handguns out of his back waistband and heard a cocking noise.

Marcus didn't know anything else to say at this point, as they were caught red-handed. He remembered his training and tried to stall. *Stall for what?* Marcus thought. But then he recalled that time, whether it be in a field operation like this or in a financial model for an investment, was the greatest element of unpredictability.

"I told you, Mauro; he is my friend. That's why I want to rescue him."

Mauro Broccatelli scoffed and did so in a way that Marcus hadn't seen before. Then he replied, "That's exactly what I told them," Mauro gestured back toward Roberto and Salem, "And they said that must mean that you, Marcus, are also a CIA informant."

Marcus felt two pats on his right hip from Graham, and then prepared to make the maneuver over to his left when the time came. But for now, Marcus kept his hands held high. Mauro knew that Marcus was armed, and Marcus didn't want to give Mauro a reason to start shooting.

"Kill Hugo if you need to, but we need Curry for the prisoner exchange," Roberto instructed loudly, having regained his composure. He stood with his arms folded over his chest. Salem stood next to him in a similar pose, the two of them feeling as though they had regained the upper hand in the negotiation.

Marcus stared at Mauro Broccatelli, desperately searching for a sign of his intentions. He didn't want to kill Mauro, but they might not have any other options. Mauro stared back blankly, his dark-brown eyes cold as ice.

"On three," Graham whispered.

Mauro was watching closely and seemed to notice something change in Marcus's countenance. Mauro's eyes narrowed and the concentration on his face intensified.

"One…two…"

And in a flash, just as Marcus began to jump to his left, Mauro Broccatelli raised his weapon like a trained assassin and fired twice. Both bullets hit their targets dead on.

EPILOGUE

Paris, France. 7th Arrondissement. Saturday, November 23, 2019.

IT WAS A CHILLY MORNING IN CENTRAL PARIS. The temperature was in the mid-40s and rain clouds lingered above but refrained from pouring down on the city. The trees lining the Avenue de Ségur and the Avenue Duquesne clung to the last leaves of the season, all of them having changed colors from green to gold and now to auburn. The Parisian women walking the streets had swapped out their light jackets and flats for stylish full-length trench coats and stack-heeled boots.

Gaspard Breton cleaned off one of the outside tables and rearranged the bistro chairs to line up with all of the others. He performed a cursory glance down the Rue d'Estrées toward the corner of the Avenue de Breteuil. That was the direction from which the American usually came, but not this morning. Breton had not seen his usual patron for over three weeks, and he was surprised to not see him this morning. It was pretty much a given that the American would be at Breton's café on Saturday mornings.

Breton shook his head, then shrugged his shoulders. He strolled back over to the front of his café to seat a new arrival, a man in a dark topcoat and a cashmere flat cap. He seated the man in a back corner of the café as the man had requested and returned to the entrance. He instructed one of his waitstaff to attend to the newcomer, then buried his head in a folded copy of the morning's *Le Figaro*.

Breton dove into an article about the initial reviews of 2019's Beaujolais Nouveau, as he wanted to be knowledgeable about what critics were saying about the multiple cases of the seasonally popular wine that had just arrived at his café the week before. He heard footsteps approaching, but he felt no need to allow that to distract him from reading the article.

"Bonjour, Monsieur Breton," the source of the footsteps announced.

Breton kept his head down, but a smile crept over his face. The pronunciation of his last name, Breton, while not bad, was so obviously American that Breton immediately identified the speaker.

"Monsieur Hugo, bonjour!" Breton looked down at his watch, as if to signal that Marcus was arriving later than usual.

Marcus acknowledged the gesture, then, speaking in French, explained, "A little slow getting out of bed for my run this morning. The cold weather kept me under the covers for a few extra minutes."

"It's been a while, I thought perhaps you had left us." Breton looked up at Marcus with a smile.

Marcus chuckled at Breton's response.

"*Pas encore*," he replied.

BRETON LED MARCUS to his usual seat in the corner of the outdoor seating at the front of the café, then signaled at one of the waitstaff to bring Marcus's usual order over. Within minutes, a plate with two medium sized *brioche suisses* arrived, along with an espresso and a more traditional *caffè Americano*. Marcus nodded at the server, then breathed in deeply through his nose to take in the surroundings. He smelled the fresh pastries on the table, the powerful aroma of the coffee, and the burnt tobacco blowing his way from a few tables over. He felt the chill of the late-autumn morning and pulled up the collar on his dark-navy field jacket. He removed the crisp copy of the *Financial Times Weekend* from under his arm and settled back into his seat as he began to read.

It had been nearly a month since he had sat in this chair to partake in this Saturday morning ritual, and this time he appreciated it more than ever. His near-death experience on Hurd's Bank had weighed on him, and he was still recovering, both physically and mentally.

He downed his espresso and enjoyed a few bites of his brioche. He was patiently working through the headlines, reading the normal articles that would typically draw his interest, not wanting to skip ahead. And finally, after finishing his pastries and moving on to his *caffè Americano*, his eyes landed on the article that he had been waiting for.

Scion of Wealthy Argentine Family Dies in Yacht Explosion

By Conrad Samples and Lisa Yoshino

VALLETTA, MALTA—The remains of the body of the older of the two wealthy Broccatelli brothers, Roberto Broccatelli, was found near an exploded yacht just a few miles from the port at Valetta, the capital of Malta. The remains of another man, Samih Salem, an Egyptian national and resident of Zürich who was a private banker to some of the world's wealthiest individuals, was also found near the yacht explosion. The Maltese police, who claimed jurisdiction over the matter, were unable to confirm the causes of death. But numerous media outlets suggested it was from the same explosion that destroyed the yacht whose remains were found near the bodies in the Mediterranean Sea.

The Broccatelli family is widely considered to be the wealthiest family in Argentina, and are the founders and owners of Broccagas, the international oil and gas company. Roberto Cesare Martín Broccatelli-Müller was the oldest of two sons of Fernando Broccatelli, the current chairman of Broccagas. Roberto Broccatelli was involved in running the more sophisticated of the Broccatelli family's businesses, nearly all of them outside of oil and gas. He was also rumored to be preparing a run for public office in Argentina, and many saw him as a potential Peronist party presidential candidate.

Less is known about Samih Salem, although there is rampant suspicion that some of his banking clients had deep criminal ties. Mr. Salem previously worked under the Mubarak regime in Egypt, but since the Arab Spring uprising in 2011, he had been living and working in Zürich, Switzerland.

No members of the Broccatelli family could be reached for comment, and there has been no mention of a ceremony for the late Roberto Broccatelli.

The exploded yacht was considered a jewel in the Broccatelli family's collection of prized assets. It was rumored to be purchased by Fernando

Broccatelli for over $100 million, and then given as a gift to Roberto and his younger brother, Mauro. The cause of the yacht's explosion is unknown, although both Maltese police and Swiss insurance-related investigations are ongoing.

In what appears to be unrelated news, Broccagas Trading and Shipping, a division of the Broccagas family of companies, agreed to a joint venture with New York and Paris based Peppercorn Capital, a multi-strategy private equity firm, under which Broccagas Trading and Shipping sold 49 percent of the company to Peppercorn Capital. Additional details related to the transaction have not yet been released to the public.

Marcus finished his coffee and laid the newspaper down on the table. He dug his hands deep into his pocket, closed his eyes, and leaned back into his chair with his face raised up to the sky. He exhaled deeply as he thought about what had transpired that night on Hurd's Bank, and how close it had come to being him for whom the obituary was written.

"There's a lot that article doesn't say," a familiar voice observed from next to Marcus's table.

Marcus opened his eyes to see Arthur Franz, with a dark topcoat draped around his body and a warm-looking flat cap on his head, standing there.

Franz had an energetic look in his eyes, and he tilted his head toward the street and stated, "Let's talk a walk, shall we?"

FRANZ LED MARCUS past the front of the Église du Dome near Marcus's apartment, and then around the back of the Musée Rodin. They zigzagged their way through small, narrow backstreets until they landed onto the leafy Boulevard Saint-Germain. It was still relatively early in the day, so Saint-Germain was not overly busy, but provided enough background noise for Franz to begin his questioning.

"Well, first off let me say congratulations on a job well done. And I'm glad to see you in the flesh. I understand it was a...dicey situation."

"Thank you," Marcus replied appreciatively.

"I read the debriefing report that you gave to Alexandra," Franz patted the side of his top coat to indicate he had the only paper copy that existed with him. "But I wanted to hear it all from you."

Marcus nodded his head in assent, then replied, "Well, where should I begin?"

"Did you know that Mauro was going to side with you? That he would turn on his own brother like that?"

"No," Marcus replied quickly. "I knew there was bad blood there, and also bad blood between Roberto and his father, but I was fully expecting Mauro to fire on me, not Roberto and Salem. The truth is, I'm not even sure Mauro knew what he was going to do until the very last instant. There was something that Roberto did along that way that Mauro and his father never forgave him for. And in that moment, on the tanker in the middle of the Mediterranean, Mauro saw me, well, Peppercorn really, as a way out from the trap that Roberto led their family into."

"He said that? That Peppercorn was the way out of the trap?" Franz asked, trying to drill down on the exact details.

"No," Marcus clarified, then added, "But he didn't have to. There's no other reason that I'm still alive today."

"Hmm," Replied Franz, with a tilt of his head. "And so then…Mauro Broccatelli was willing to part with his prized yacht to clean it all up?"

"Well, he didn't have many options. It took Mauro a few minutes to recover from what he'd done, but the Chinese tanker was set to arrive within the hour for the prisoner exchange, so we had to act fast. The yacht idea actually came from the captain of the tanker, Captain Pallas."

Franz looked at him sideways, with a hint of curiosity. "Captain Pallas? That was the name of the tanker's captain?"

Marcus nodded, and Franz chuckled. "Fitting," he stated.

Marcus looked confused, and Franz waved it away with a hand gesture.

"So you exploded the yacht with Roberto and Salem inside. Then presumably took the launch boat back to the port at Valletta, destroyed all evidence of that boat, drove back to the airport in Malta, flew to London that night, and then Broccatelli erased all evidence of the flight. That about right?"

"More or less," Marcus replied back casually.

"And what about the prisoner exchange? How did you handle that?"

Marcus smiled, then responded, "Just as you drew it up, only easier with Roberto and Salem gone. Captain Pallas told the Chinese that he was told to unload refined products, and had never heard of a prisoner exchange, and certainly didn't have one on board. Then, with Salem out of the way, neither the Chinese nor the Venezuelans had any direct connection to Simon Walker-Kelly or Broccagas Trading and Shipping. When they eventually questioned Walker-Kelly, he said they had never picked up any cargo with a prisoner in it and asked them to provide the proof that their vessel had ever done so. Which, with it being an illegal prisoner exchange of a suspected American CIA informant, they of course didn't have proof. Salem and Roberto were gone, so the Chinese and Venezuelans couldn't get mad at them. And they had never dealt with Mauro Broccatelli, so they couldn't approach him either."

Franz had navigated them to the Left Bank of the Seine, and they crossed over the river on the Pont des Arts. The pedestrian bridge, often lively and full of picnickers, was nearly deserted at this hour, owing to the cold and potentially wet weather.

"And what did Mauro say about his father, Fernando?" Franz asked as they passed over the dark river below.

"You know, I asked him about that. But all he said was that Roberto and Fernando were so estranged, that Roberto's death would likely be a relief for their father. It was as if whatever Roberto had done, which had clearly created such a rift within the family, would suddenly go away upon Roberto's death."

Franz nodded, began to say something, but then closed his mouth and continued walking east along the quai on the Right Bank. Then he observed, "But it doesn't look like any of that prevented you from getting the Broccagas Trading and Shipping deal done, did it?"

Marcus breathed deeply and exhaled audibly, then replied, "No, quite the contrary actually. The way the Broccagas corporate documents were set up provided for an immediate transfer, pro rata, to any surviving members of Fernando, Roberto and Mauro, upon any of those individuals' deaths. So Fernando and Mauro immediately became fifty-fifty owners of all of the Broccagas company voting interests when Fernando died We had the written authority from Broccagas to do our deal within a week of Fernando's passing."

Franz had been listening intently but slowed his walk to a stop. They were standing on the gravel pathway abutting the Rue de l'Amiral de Coligny on the far eastern side of the Louvre. Franz turned to face the Louvre and looked upon its façade in awe.

Marcus turned to observe the façade as well and found himself curiously mesmerized. He had walked by this side of the Louvre's exterior many times, but never actually stopped and observed the Colonnade standing before him. It was indeed awe-inspiring and beautiful in a grand yet reserved way.

Marcus looked over at Franz again. He was staring admiringly at the façade.

"This is as beautiful a piece of architecture as you'll find anywhere in the world." Franz declared in an unemotional and confident way, "Look at the symmetry of the Corinthian columns and the arched windows below. The scale, and yet inviting nature of the central pavilion and its triangular pediment above. It is this Colonnade, built in the 1660s and 70s, with its combination of ambition, classical influence, and geometric order, that shaped the next two and a half centuries of French architecture. For me, this building forms the basis of French style."

With no further explanation, Franz continued walking away from the Seine and turned right down the Rue de Rivoli. They walked under the covered arched walkway for a while, and then onto the sidewalk along the busy street.

"So what will Broccagas Trading and Shipping do now when the Argentine government comes calling again for a favor?" Franz asked.

Marcus realized that this was akin to Socratic questioning, as Franz already knew the answer to his own question.

"Who are they going to ask?" Marcus humored him, "They only dealt with Roberto, and did so on a discreet basis. If they approach Mauro, he'll deny any knowledge of it, and he has no interest in continuing to do their bidding. And again, what will the Argentine government do? Tell the market that Broccagas Trading and Shipping has been carrying out illegal trading transactions to flout sanctions at the Argentine government's request?"

Franz nodded a few times, then stopped as he seemed to be pondering deeper.

Marcus continued, "Oh sure, they can make life hard for Mauro if he tries to return to Argentina, or they can try to nationalize the Broccagas assets. But the truth is that Mauro's life is here in Europe now; he has no interest in returning to Argentina. And Broccagas has diversified so much of its interests outside of Argentina, that a nationalization of their Argentine assets would have a very minimal effect on its business empire. And Mauro's father, Fernando, splits his time between Uruguay and Italy, and barely goes back to Argentina himself."

Franz could never have foreseen Roberto Broccatelli's death, and certainly not at the hand of his own brother in a clandestine fashion. But something in the look on Franz's face made Marcus feel like everything had played out just as he had somehow planned, or perhaps more accurately, hoped for, when he thought up the idea of Peppercorn getting involved with the Broccatelli family.

"And what about Graham? How is he doing?" It was Marcus's turn to ask a question.

"He's doing well, getting back on his feet," Franz nodded with assurance. "Once he got stateside, we set him up in a hospital in Houston. I believe he is already back at his home there and is going to return to work in his company's Houston office in a few weeks. The company prepared a report saying that Graham fell very ill while vacationing on the Magdalena River during his Colombian post, and that he had to stay in a hospital in Bucaramanga for a few months to be treated for a rare disease. As a result, he is leaving his post in Colombia and returning to Houston to focus on the company's US domestic operations."

Marcus smiled, then added, "For now."

"*Touché*," Franz replied with a slight nod of the head.

They had taken a left onto the Rue de Turenne, and now they turned right, and Franz led them into the stately Place des Voges. They walked up to one of the four fountains in the internal courtyard and stood looking into the basin with coins from all over the world splayed out on the bottom.

"So, job well done then, Marcus. Nice work." Franz turned to him directly and offered a formal handshake.

"Thank you. I take it this means that you won't be attending the wine tasting party at my apartment this afternoon, then?"

"Oh, I'd love to…but," Franz patted the side of his top coat where Marcus's handwritten report was stowed, "I've got to take the red-eye to Washington and give the Shareholder an update on the investment."

Marcus nodded understandingly. He was grateful that it was Franz, and not him, that had to make that trip.

"Safe travels," Marcus offered with a friendly smile.

Franz nodded his head, then turned to walk off in the direction of the uniform, red-brick and white-stone buildings surrounding the perfectly manicured courtyard. He stopped, then turned back in Marcus's direction.

"And Marcus?"

Marcus raised his eyebrows to signal his attention.

"I understand the Shareholder has a new investment they may want to pursue. And they'd like you to take the lead on looking into it."

***

THE GUESTS BEGAN arriving at Marcus's apartment at Place Vauban around five o'clock that afternoon. After leaving Franz in the Place des Voges earlier in the day, Marcus had hopped on the Metro at the Bastille station, changed over at Concorde, and then gotten off at École Militaire. From there he walked over to Rue Cler to visit a *boucherie* and *fromagerie* to buy meats and cheeses to satiate his guests during the wine tasting. It had taken all of Marcus's self-control not to entirely deplete his supply of *saucisson sec* and *fromage de brebis* prior to the first guest's arrival.

In addition to all of the hospitality that Mauro Broccatelli had shown his guests during their bike trip down the ViaRhôna, Broccatelli sent four cases of wine to each guest's home. There were two cases from Le Domaine Dumont, consisting of two bottles of each Domaine Dumont vintage of Hermitage going back for twelve years. And then there were two cases containing two bottles each of the vaunted 2016 vintage of Châteauneuf-du-Pape from twelve wineries in the region. Broccatelli was clearly following Caroline Dumont's offhand guidance about buying wine during their visit to her tasting room.

"Always buy two bottles! One to drink, and one to age," she had advised.

Marcus thought the best way to appreciate the generous gift from Broccatelli than to host his own wine tasting with friends. He planned to conduct a mini-horizontal tasting of six of the twelve 2016 Châteauneuf-du-Pape wines. Upon returning from his adventure off the Maltese coast in the Mediterranean, Marcus realized there was no better time than the present to enjoy the wine.

Olivier Lafont and Luisette Dussaix, whose last name Marcus had finally learned, were the first to arrive. Marcus had not asked them to work as part of the evening's events, but he did ask them for a little help in setting up the display to make the presentation at least look like a real wine tasting. Olivier looked chic as usual, in a very French combination of black-on-black. Luisette was wearing tight, dark jeans, and chocolate-colored calf-high leather boots. She unfastened the belt on her charcoal-colored wool trench coat, and Marcus helped her remove it and stowed it in his coat closet. She was wearing a ribbed red sweater that clung snugly to her full figure. Her long blond hair danced over her shoulders as she turned to face Marcus and offer greetings. She was more beautiful than Marcus had remembered.

"Thank you both for coming early and helping set up," Marcus said.

"Are you kidding me? This is the least I can do after you got me partnered up with Mauro Broccatelli to help him grow his wine empire," Olivier responded with enthusiasm. "I never thought you would actually mention my name to him, but I'm grateful you did. He and I are going to have a lot of fun working together. I just hope he actually shows up tonight."

It was true. In somewhat surprising fashion, Broccatelli had reached out very quickly after the events on Hurd's Bank to get the name of Marcus's suggestion for a partner to help grow his wine business. Marcus had made the introduction, and Broccatelli and Olivier had hit it off from the start. They were in the midst of formalizing their wine business partnership.

In short order, a number of other guests arrived. A few colleagues from Peppercorn came, as did a handful of Marcus's acquaintances in the Paris business community and a few of his friends from the local running club he was a member of.

Marcus was pleased when Nicholas Sewell, the English investment banker from the ViaRhôna trip, made good on his surprising acceptance of Marcus's invitation.

"I try to make it over to Paris every six weeks or so for work and to keep my French on par. And plus, there's an old girlfriend of mine that I'm due to check back in with," he had informed Marcus.

Nicholas looked the part of the posh Londoner, as he wore a fawn-colored mackintosh coat over a white button-down shirt, navy-blue blazer, and forest-green trousers. His "old girlfriend" accompanied him, and Marcus was quite certain he recognized her from advertisements of a very high-end French fashion line.

"She does a little modeling from time to time," Sewell had explained during their prior exchange. Marcus was very much looking forward to the wine oneupsmanship he imagined that Nicholas and Olivier would engage in during the evening's tasting.

One of the last guests to arrive was Alexandra Mouer. Bamba Diop arrived with her. This was the first time Marcus had seen them as a couple of sorts, although he had long suspected that was the case. He smiled and welcomed them both, genuinely happy to see them together.

Alexandra's eyes lingered on Marcus's for a half-second when he took her coat, but then she returned her attention to Bamba. Just then, Luisette walked over to them and introduced herself to Alexandra and Bamba. She looked at Marcus and said, "Marcus, aren't you going to show me the nice view from your balcony?"

Marcus shrugged his shoulders and responded, "*Mais…oui! Bien sûr.*" As he made to walk Luisette out to the balcony, he caught a sideways glance out of the corner of his eye aimed in his direction from Alexandra.

As they stepped out into the cold Paris night, Marcus removed his wool and cashmere blended blazer and pressed it over Luisette's shoulders. They stepped out to the edge of the balcony and looked out past the magnificent Église du Dôme before them and onto the illuminated lamps and the golden statues of the Pont Alexandre III over the Seine in the distance.

"I haven't seen you in a while," Luisette observed, speaking in French.

"I know," Marcus replied in a guilty tone, then added, "But I'd like to change that. I'd like to see much more of you."

The French translation of what Marcus was trying to say had much more of a sexual connotation than the same phrase in English. Luisette cocked her head in a questioning look, with a smile hiding beneath.

Marcus chuckled, then clarified, "I'd like to see you more often...that's what I meant."

Luisette laughed, then leaned over and kissed Marcus warmly on the cheek. She leaned into him and interlaced her arm in his.

"I'd like that too," she said quietly.

The moment was interrupted by Olivier calling out to Marcus from inside the apartment. "Marcus, someone's here with a package for you...and for me, too, apparently."

Marcus raised his eyebrows at Luisette, then returned inside and made his way to the front door. A deliveryman was carrying a bag in one hand, and a bucket of ice with a magnum bottle of champagne in the other.

"Marcus Hugo?" he asked.

"Yes, that's me."

The deliveryman handed over the ice bucket and champagne. Then he looked at Olivier.

"Olivier Lafont?"

Oliver nodded.

The man handed the seemingly heavy bag over to Olivier. Then he produced a letter and handed it to both Marcus and Olivier.

"*Compliments de Monsieur Mauro Broccatelli,*" The deliveryman said, then vanished before Marcus could give him a tip.

Marcus opened the letter and he and Olivier read it together.

Dear Marcus and Olivier,

Apologies for not being able to make it to this evening's tasting. I've had something come up in Milan related to business that I need to deal with this weekend. Hopefully these two gifts will more than make up for my absence.

Please consider this a token of my appreciation and excitement for the new partnerships we are embarking upon together: with Marcus in the trading and shipping world, and with Olivier in our new wine venture.

Abrazo grande,
Mauro

The magnum bottle of champagne was clearly one of the two gifts from Broccatelli. As to the other, Olivier was already extracting the heavy object from the bag before Marcus had finished reading. The wine bottle that Olivier now held before him looked vaguely familiar to Marcus, and a beaming smile overtook Olivier's face as he looked at the label. Olivier glanced over at Marcus, then rotated the bottle to show the label. He was holding a bottle of 1961 Domaine Dumont Hermitage La Chapelle.

ACKNOWLEDGMENTS

The Approach is the result of years of crafting the story, developing and drawing on the underlying experiences, and countless hours in the chair writing the book. But above all, it is the work of a team of people. First and foremost among those is my wife, Katie. This book would not exist without your love, encouragement, and you inspiring me to stick with it. Your and our travels and experiences were the source for so much of the scenery of this novel. Your love of culture, travel, and fun bleeds through these pages. Your editing, thematic, and storyline advice were invaluable as well. You are both my hero and the love of my life.

I'd also like to thank Olivia Hammerman for assistance with the cover and overall book design, and Cooper Lee Bombardier at Indigo: Editing, Design, and More for assistance with editing.

A special thanks to the following people: To Matt Herzog, an accomplished reader of spy novels and thrillers, an incredible travel companion, and a provider of sage advice in describing the involvement of Russian interlopers in *The Approach*. To Ky Cooksey for editorial advice and insight with respect to the gas and power markets. To Eliot Cotton for thoughts on the private equity industry and for other very helpful comments to the story.

To Bill and Linda Spencer, for your excitement in the development of the book, your interest in the story and the characters, and your contributions to the revision of the drafts. To David Mebane, Mike Franz, and the whole FTBT team. In addition to being great bosses and friends (and showing me that one can be both a boss and a friend), you gave me the opportunity to live and work in Paris. That has forever changed my life and who I am, and I am eternally grateful to you for that.

To my mother, Susan Lee. Thank you for always encouraging me to pursue my dreams.

To my father, Samuel Lee. Your development of a love of reading later in life has been so much fun to observe, and it has inspired me to make the effort to finish *The Approach*. Your editorial comments were very helpful, as was your encouragement all along the way.

And finally, to you, the Reader. I hope you have found *The Approach* entertaining, enlightening, and encouraging. May Marcus Hugo's career growth inspire you to go after your dreams, and may his adventures prompt you to get out there and see all the wonderful mysteries this world has to offer.

ABOUT THE AUTHOR

PARKER LEE is a lucky husband and a proud father of two young boys and a dog named Enzo. He is a transactional lawyer at a large, international law firm and now, an author. Prior to becoming a lawyer, he was a bike tour guide in Paris. He lives with his family in Rye, New York. Part of him will always be in Paris—or perhaps part of Paris will always be in him.

Made in the USA
Middletown, DE
09 December 2021